I0729408

MOON BEETLES

B. JOYCE

MOON BEETLES

Copyright © 2021 by B. Joyce

All rights reserved. No part of this book may be reproduced or used in any manner without the written permission of the copyright owner except for the use of quotations in a book review. For more information, contact b.joyce.author@gmail.com

This is a work of fiction. All names, characters, places, and incidents are either the product of the author's imagination or are used fictitiously. Resemblance to actual persons, living or dead, events, or locales is coincidental.

First paperback edition December 2021

Cover Design by B. Joyce

Interior Formatting by Evenstar Books
evenstarbooks.com

Edited by EditElle – Writing & Editing Services
editelle.com

Map and Graphic Design by B. Joyce

ISBN: 978-1-7779077-0-9
ISBN ebook: 978-1-7779077-1-6

Visit the author's website at
bjoyceauthor.carrd.co

For the ones with the sinking feeling.

MOON BEETLES SERIES

Book One: *Moon Beetles*
Book Two: *Soul Tether*
Book Three: *Mind Fracture*

Moon Beetles Companion Novel

Shadowless

Note: Shadowless can be read at any time. This novel takes place during the same time period as Moon Beetles. It is a stand-alone novel that provides more exploration of Illyson and the beloved characters within the Moon Beetles series.

CONTENT WARNING

This book contains instances of anxiety, depression, suicide, derealization, death of a loved one, violence and death, sexual assault, discrimination, self harm, drug use, blood, gun violence, and illness/vomiting. If these are sensitive topics for you, please only read if you are safe to do so.

THE PROVINCE OF EMBERSTEAD
Jiaan
Lorisal
Sii
Akinnera
Meris
Tien Bay
Tsuna
Vensya
Senn
Braya
KEY:
Ancestral Shrine
City
Capital

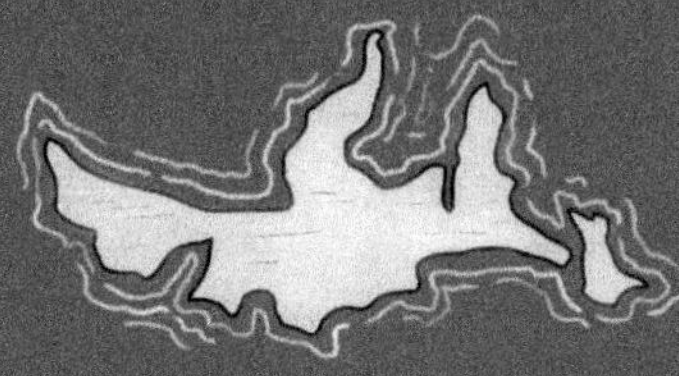
ILLYSON
Sea of the Lost
TORETH
ARIA
VALISOR
SARR
Lotis
Sea
EMBERSTEAD
EETH
YUGON
LAKAR
HALAAN
Atorian Ocean

ENERGY ALIGNMENT

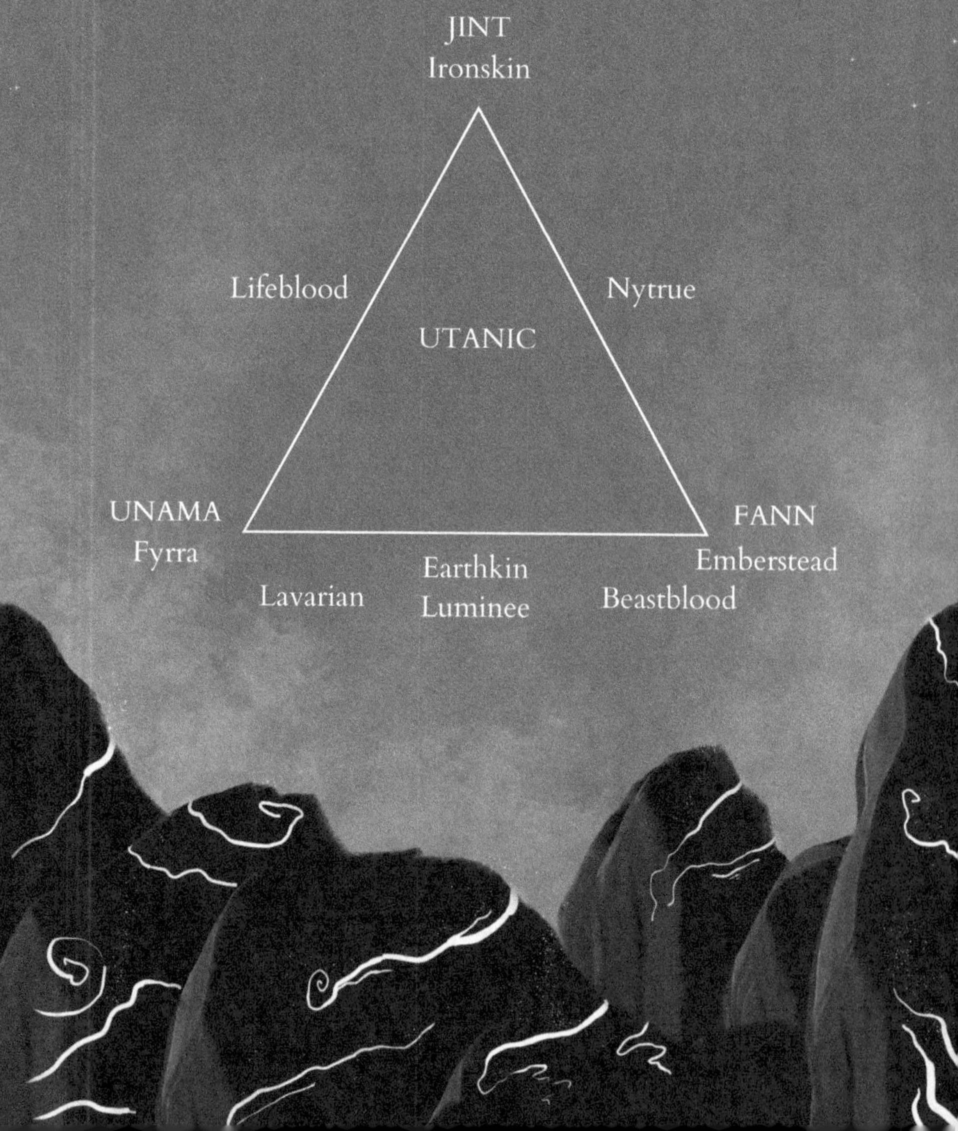

ANCESTRY

The Nine Hédin Lineages of Illyson,
Their Essence Affinities,
and First Known Ancestor

Ironskin: Body: Keena

Emberstead: Fire: Zenta

Nytrue: Water: Reel

Lifeblood: Air: Afa

Luminee: Light: Vin

Earthkin: Earth: Thesta

Lavarian: Weather: Seena

Fyrra: Vegetation: Holia

Beastblood: Animal: Fōsten

1

RIN

I PEEKED OVER THE EDGE OF THE COFFIN and wished it wasn't him. I wished it was a dream, something I just made up in my head. But when I saw his face, drained of colour, it was the most real moment in my life, and I didn't understand it at all.

Flowers surrounded him—tucked beside him, scattered on the floor—but no vibrant colours sparked my attention. No green hues to calm me or pink petals to soothe and brighten. Everything was grey, stinging and suffocating.

I had an urge to touch him, so I reached out, but only glided my finger across the glossy black casket. The word casket played through my head as I focused on the reflection of light off the gloss. I had just learned what it meant—another word for coffin my mother had said. Casket. Coffin. Dead.

Liam tugged at my skirt and my heart lurched, pushing a

slimy lump into my throat. His company was welcome, though, needed. I picked him up and held him close. His heart pounded against mine, his lungs heaved for breath. Wiggling in my arms, he turned to the casket, a whimper escaping his lips.

"Dad," he cried.

Casket.

"He's gone, Liam," I whispered, leaning my head on his shoulder.

He screamed louder and my father's few Guardian friends turned to see. Their pity swept through the room, jumping from face to face, drawing tight mouths and tears. It stung so deep I had to shut my eyes and squeeze Liam tighter. My knees shook, my stomach ached. I sank to the step below the casket. Liam weighed me down as I rocked him back and forth, saying to him over and over, "It's ok, I'm here. I won't leave you."

His breaths evened, and his screams quieted to whimpers. Shivers prickled my skin as his sweet, innocent noises raged through me. I locked my eyes on the stray petals on the floor; they blurred and twisted in front of me.

He was never coming back. My father was never coming back. Why'd he have to die?

I tightened my arms around Liam, as if holding him would keep me from falling apart.

Casket.

"Rinnaya," Mother said to me, stiff and vacant. "It's time to go."

I didn't move, just stared up at her tall, thin frame robed in a simple black dress. The ghostly complexion of her face made it as lifeless as my father's. With such dull grey eyes, I could never read her. They weren't a window to her soul; they were steel doors keeping everyone out. Her nose was too pointed and her chin too angular. Her mouth never hinted at a smile, and after this, I didn't think it ever would.

Behind the stone pillar of my mother, the Kingsman family approached. Mr. Kingsman, Father's partner, wore his Protector uniform. My eyes refused to see the blue of the fabric or the glint of his metals.

Mrs. Kingsman put her hand on Mother's shoulder. "Cassy, dear," she said.

Mother shrugged her comfort away.

I rubbed my face, trying to hide my tears like my mother did, but Johanna's green eyes saw me. They always saw right through me.

"You okay?" she mouthed to me.

The breath in my chest released. I shook my head, opening the floodgates. Johanna, my only friend, nodded. She didn't come over to me, just stood there with her own eyes glossing over, giving me a look that can only be held between twelve-year-old girls. The kind that doesn't need explanation, that isn't muddied by time or scars.

"Thank you for coming to honour Peter," Mother said, back turned to the Kingsmans. "But we should be going." She bent down to take Liam from me.

My tears burned like fire as he left my arms. The hurt swelled and pushed the tears out in waves. Sobs from deep inside shook my shoulders, and my lips quivered as I attempted to hold them back.

Mr. Kingsman put his arms around his family to steer them away. "We'll leave you be then. Carnity's blessings."

Once they were gone, Mother handed Liam to my older

brother, Stephen. I didn't even see him come over through all the tears.

"Crying's not going to bring him back, Rinnaya," Mother said.

Her cold words froze my cries. Her eyebrows squeezed together and angled themselves in such a frightening way that I couldn't tell if she was angry with me or sad. Murmurs from the funeral attendees spilled around us, but she kept her eyes on me, placing her hand on my shoulder. It was as icy as her tone.

"We will never all be together again, that's just the way it has to be. But remember what the ancient Ironskins used to say: Our skin as strong as iron, our blood stronger, our hearts stronger still." Her eyes glistened with tears, but instead of wiping them away, she let them fall and used her sleeve to clean my face. "You have to be strong now, Rinnaya. For your brothers."

I didn't understand why she said that to me. But she pulled me away from the steps before I could ask and led us out of the building without Father. None of us said anything as we made our way home. A few words were spoken at dinner, but we fell silent as we got ready for bed.

In the middle of the night, Mother came to my room. I kept my eyes closed so she would think I was asleep.

Stroking my cheek with her frigid finger, she said, "Be strong."

I should have opened them.

The next morning, my eyelids were heavy and ran across my eyes like sandpaper. Making my way from my room to the stairwell, somehow the air was smothering. It was eerie, weighing on me as I went down the stairs, getting heavier with each step. Stephen sat at the kitchen table, head in his hands. Dim morning light spilled through the windowpanes, casting unnatural stillness over the room. It was like it stole his awareness of the world around him. He didn't stir as I came up beside him.

A chill snaked down my spine.

Next to his elbow lay a single sheet of paper, my mother's writing on it. With a shaking hand, I reached for it. I read each dreadful word slowly so that maybe I would understand. The words sunk the chill to my bones. My hands went numb and . . . and . . .

Stephen sniffed. It rang through my head like a gong.

I blinked. Tears streamed down my face. My fingers tingled.

Why?

Reading it one more time, my heart pounded with every word. But even then, I couldn't grasp why it would be better to die than to keep living. I couldn't understand.

Why'd she leave us?

I want the memory out of my head. But the grey sticks to the back of my mind like soot on the walls of a hearth. It sends momentary paralysis down my arm, icing my blood, drying out my mouth. My fingers twitch in a silent nudge to breathe.

Leaves cover their names again, so I pick them away just like I've done on this day for five years. Once the graves are cleared, the familiar inscriptions stare at me. Peter Burgheim: Loving father, husband, and Protector of the great land of Illyson. Cassy Burgheim: Cherished mother and wife. May she rest in peace.

I trail my finger over the smooth stone of Mother's grave, lingering on her name, sliding into each indent of the inscription. A piece of dirt grinds between the stone and my skin in the space between words. The breeze prickles my arms and whips short strands of hair out of my braid, leaving them to dangle around my face.

A bush to my left rustles, prompting me to draw my eyes away from the graves. In the shadow of the leaves, a Rover sits on its hind legs. Its round eyes flash gold, snake-like tail swishing around him. It scratches its pointy ear, letting out a low warble.

Registration. I need to get going before I'm late. My stomach drops but I stand, and the Rover scampers away.

I swat dirt from the back of my pants and light a lantern by each headstone—two flames to guide and warm their spirits and keep them close. The flicker of light taunts me. They're gone, flicker, flicker, and you're still here, flicker, flicker. It pushes me away.

Weaving around the dead, I make my way to the gate under the trill of birds. At the gate, an orange flair-wing moth flutters in front of me. It stutters, wings faltering, and falls to the ground, stunned by the strong jint alignment of my Ironskin essence. The dumb things always get too close. I hold tight to the handle. Maybe I shouldn't come here anymore? I do the same thing every year, sit, say nothing, and leave. My chest tightens with a sharp pain. No, I couldn't stay away.

I push open the gate and jog down the narrow streets of Senn decorated for Registration. Strung between the dingy, stacked apartment buildings, folded paper flowers sway in the wind, and in every doorway there's a glowing lantern with a mountain and an ember lily on it.

An Emberstead family piles into a cruiser ahead of me, no doubt headed to the Registration Hall. Before getting in, the mother hands her daughter an ancestral good luck charm. The daughter, dressed in a sparkling red dress, her red hair held in place by beaded pins, holds the charm to her forehead, then to her chest, then links it to a chain around her wrist. Across the street, twin Lifeblood boys are surrounded by doting grandparents, beaming parents, aunts, uncles, and younger cousins. The boys, with dark hair slicked back and smiles spreading their golden cheeks, almost look like upstanding citizens instead of the self-entitled jackasses they are at school.

"Strength of the ancestors," they shout to the other side of the street. The greeting echoes from the Emberstead family, instead of the "fuck off" that would be fitting for any other day.

Out of the way of happy celebrators and back in my neighbourhood, I slow my pace so I don't wake the homeless man sleeping beside the dumpsters. Across from my building, a Luminee woman is hanging her lantern. She watches me with squinted eyes. Her skin is like a dirt path—dark and pitted—with the circular markings of a dual-power Luminee sage on her forehead.

"Run along, ghost girl," she says, still glaring.

Silver bells to ward off Wander Wraiths clang above her door as she slams it shut and wafts a cloud of incense over me. The floral musk clings to my clothes as I run to my apartment building. Outside, the walls are covered in graffiti. Inside, the plaster crumbles, covered by flyers for Ascension teams, restaurants, and Ease distributors. My fingers stick to the tacky banister as I grab it to propel myself up the steps two at a time.

Up one flight, an elderly man sits outside his door, running his wrinkled hands through his hair, still a touch red from his younger days.

"You shit son of a titpick . . . mother fucker . . ." his wife yells from inside.

The man smiles to himself as if her gravelly insults were soft kisses.

Up another flight lives a young man with his one-year-old daughter. The baby's scream penetrates the thin walls, but the man's voice washes over it to soothe his girl with an off-key melody. The next floor up, the sickly sweet smell of Ease prickles my nose, so I clear the landing as fast as I can and sprint the last flight of stairs to my apartment.

Oron stands outside my door, arms folded across his broad chest. He seems taller today in his clean suit, a drastic change from the grubby coveralls and sweaty face after long shifts at the core-energy plant. The work keeps him fit for his age, but his stomach is starting to slip over his belt. His skin has taken on a tinge of grey and crinkles around his eyes as he gives me a piercing stare, pulls his rough hands through his whitening hair, and sighs.

"Where the hell have you been?"

Avoiding his eyes, I fumble for my keys.

"Rin, as your legal guardian, it's my job to get you to the registrar on time but how'm I supposed to do that if I don't even know where you are half the goddamn time?" he asks, sticking his hands in his pockets. "You know I had to change shifts to take you to Registration."

I jam my key into the first lock. The key clunks off the metal hole already turned to the unlocked position. Swallowing hard and taking in a quick breath, I expel the air through my nose.

I shove the key into the lock and twist to lock it, twist again to unlock.

"I have to get you there before the afternoon time block. In what Illysonian city would registrar workers let an Ironskin register late, huh? Not this one," Oron mumbles behind me as I twist each lock back and forth.

"Why was my door unlocked?" I say once the ritual is complete.

"Rin—"

"I never leave it unlocked," I say with a tight jaw.

"I just talked to Liam." Oron rubs his hand over his face.

"He should've locked it again."

"I've been standing out here, he's fine."

I can't even look at him. Oron should have told Liam to lock the door. Rolling my eyes, I wave him off with a flick of my hand. "Whatever."

"Why do you do this to me? You know this day is important. Does Liam know what this day means?"

I press my lips together and my shoulders fall. This day affects Liam too. "Yes, he knows if my essence is above a level two, I'll have to train away from him for one year. And he knows I want to do Guardian work."

"Good. The importance of this day isn't lost in that thick head of yours, so why are you running around instead of being with him?"

"I had people to see, Oron," I say. I step into my apartment and slam the door in his face.

Of course I know the importance of Registration. Can he blame me for taking a little extra time to clear my head, to visit the people that should be with me on this day? I'll have to endure the names and the looks just because I'm an Ironskin. The registrar workers will be agitated just like at Stephen's Registration.

Stephen. Just couldn't make time in his busy Guardian schedule to come to his sister's Registration. Just far enough away to stay away. I shake my head. No more wasting time today. I just have to get this over with. Pushing aside all thoughts of Stephen and my parents, I find the pieces of a smile. Stay strong for Liam.

I take a deep breath of my apartment air, musty with notes of old wood, a little mould, and the coffee I put on to brew before I left. Liam sits at the table in the dim light of the kitchen eating breakfast. The wood slats of the floor creak under my feet as I move to kiss the top of his head and mess with his sandy blond hair.

"How'd you sleep, buddy?" I ask, filling a mug halfway with coffee. I take a pinch of ground cinnospice and sprinkle it on top.

"Pretty good. You gonna eat something?"

I shrug. "I'm not hungry."

Liar. My stomach churns. I take a sip of coffee. The warmth soothes the ache a bit, and the sharp taste is distracting.

"You've got five minutes, Rin," Oron shouts from the hall.

I jump. "Yeah, yeah," I shout back. I down the contents of my mug and rinse it out.

"He sounds pretty mad," Liam says.

"Mhm."

He snickers behind me. "You're tryin' to make him mad."

"Am not." I smile to myself, warm water spilling over my hands, Liam's knowing giggles lifting the smallest weight from my mind.

"Are too."

"Four minutes."

Four minutes. Plenty of time. I take some water to the herbs on my windowsill. A deep breath in and I get lost in the biting, earthy scent of cinnospice sprigs, the dewy freshness of scolya, and the lightness of the flowering whisper weed.

"Oron brought you something to wear to Registration. I put it on your bed," Liam says, sitting on his hands and swinging his legs under the table. I take his plate and put it in the sink. I'll wash it later. I'm wasting time again.

I move past the curtain that separates my bed from the rest of the one-room apartment. Lying on my quilt is a knee-length, navy-blue skirt and a white blouse. I run my fingers over the soft blue threads that weave intricate floral patterns through the skirt. It probably cost him more than he could afford, and today I've been selfish.

Oron was appointed as our soulkin father when I was three and has been around ever since. All I've given him is sass and trouble even though he's done more for us than anyone else. He's not around much, but he always manages to make an appearance when it counts. I'll apologize for stressing him out this morning, I will. It's less than he deserves, but it's all I can give.

Holding up the skirt in front of me, the waistband is a little wide and the white shirt might make me look paler than I already am. I put it on anyway. As I trade my old boots for my good ones, with laces that aren't frayed and black leather that isn't scuffed, the silk slip swishes around my legs. I pull my hair out of its braid to let it fall in mousy-blond waves around my shoulders.

"All right, Liam. You ready to go?" I say, walking out from behind the curtain.

Liam stays seated at the table. "But Stephen isn't here yet."

Weight piles into my stomach, weight that's been built up over five years. It unloads in his absence and returns in his presence—even just talking about Stephen makes it heavier. I take a long breath and pull at the hem of my shirt.

"I know."

A clang sounds from beyond the thin windowpane behind me, followed by shouts and the roar of a cruiser.

"Why isn't he here?" His words are soft, innocent against the backdrop of commotion. He stares at me with watery ocean eyes, eyelids squinting, head tilting.

I swallow the choke in my throat, and giving Liam a smile, I say, "I guess he just got tied up."

Liam hums a sombre note. It's like he sees past all Stephen's beastshit excuses and my phoney covers for him and just knows that Stephen should be here, no discussion. Liam's face drops into a frown. He slides out of his chair to catch me in a big hug. "Registration's gonna be ok, Rinnaya. I'll be with you," he says.

"Thanks, bud," I say, sinking into the hug.

I can't freeze now, so I pull away and make sure Liam's grey collared shirt is tucked in right and his belt buckle is straight and shoo us out the door.

Before locking up, I transfer the hug to Oron, and he engulfs me with strong arms and the minty musk of his soap.

"I'm sorry," I whisper. "Thank you for the new clothes."

"Of course, sweet girl. And I'm sorry too. You know I just worry about you."

At the end of our street we catch an airbus, and the congested space slaps me in the face with a wave of body odour. We find three seats together at the back just as the bus lifts off the ground. It lurches and wobbles at a standstill for a moment. With a crackling sound, an orange glow warms the street below the bus, and it glides forward.

Outside the smudgy windowpanes, the city passes in a blur of lifeless grey buildings and neon lights. My eyes only focus once we near the city centre. In the shadow of the looming excuses for adequate living stands an ancestral shrine—my favourite building. It is a tiered, three-storey building with vibrant red panelling and terracotta tiles lining a peaked roof. I've always wondered if the shrine looks just as nice on the inside, or if it's dusty from neglect and lack of devotion from the people of Senn.

We get off the airbus downtown, exchanging the sour air from inside for a gritty plume of exhaust. Flames burst from a trolly parked on the sidewalk as the vendor slaps greasy skewers of meat on the grill. We wait to cross the street while a wailing siren stings my ears. The prompt to cross registers in my brain seconds after the pedestrians begin to move. Liam pulls me along with the hoard just as a guy in a sleek silver cruiser honks at me.

The stream of pedestrians dissipates, leaving behind an unwanted sample whiff of every perfume on the market and every bodily function mixed in. I rub my arms, looking up at the Registration Hall. Straight and strong with no frills. The white stone is misted with grey at the base. A mysterious puddle leaks along the bottom of the steps and the tinted glass of the front doors is streaked with water marks.

"Damn place get's uglier every year." Oron puts a heavy hand to my shoulder and gives me a weak smile.

"What's that?" Liam says, pointing to the puddle.

Heart clamouring in my chest, I pull Liam up the steps. "It's piss, Liam. In we go," I say, and we duck inside as the ever-present clouds thunder overhead and raindrops darken the pavement.

Inside the large hall, kids line up in front of the nine Registration booths, one for each hédin essence lineage in Illyson. All my classmates are here, plus kids from other basic ed schools in the city, the majority of them filing into the sea of red-headed Emberstead. The Emberstead line trails from the booth all the way to the entryway, whereas the Ironskin line is empty and so is the line for Lavarians.

Oron nudges me in front of him and I lead the three of us to the Ironskin booth.

The Luminees and Lifebloods who know me give me blank stares. The Beastbloods and Nytrues continue to laugh and talk among each other. An Earthkin girl gives me a nod. The few Fyrra who line up beside the Ironskin booth smile sweetly, something I only expect from Fyrra. They're like a safe haven in this city, a garden of people with pink, green, and peach coloured hair, their dark skin tinted with purple. They may not associate with me, but they would never say anything rude.

I clench my teeth. I just have to get this test over with.

A female registrar worker waits inside. She appears to be Emberstead, with tan skin, sleek red hair, and pale-green eyes. She sits, perched on the edge of her seat, biting her nails, staring off into space. I clear my throat as I approach. The woman jumps then smooths her hair a few times.

"Name?" the woman asks, her voice tight.

"Rinnaya Burgheim."

Keys clatter as she enters my name into the Personal Automated Technology device.

"Legal guardian, state your name and relation to Rinnaya."

"Oron Kruger. Soulkin father."

She taps it into the PAT. "Witness, state your name and relation to Rinnaya."

"Liam Burgheim. Brother."

After entering Liam's name, she rises from her chair to mess with the settings on a metre in the centre of the booth. The metre is a glass column about three feet high with an inner tube containing the white glow of core energy. Along the outer glass are markings for the four enhancement levels. On top of the column is a metal hand plate, and beside that are three switches for the energy alignments—jint, unama, and fann. Even though the metres in each booth should already be calibrated to the specific energy alignment, the woman's fingers fumble over the jint switch.

"Rinnaya, step forward to the metre and I will explain the testing process," the worker says and folds her arms like she has a chill.

I step forward, crossing my arms to mimic her discomfort. Her jaw tenses and she drops her arms to her sides.

"At seventeen, your essence is fully mature," she says. "We test and register each Illysonian to promote safety, offer guidance, and provide proper training to develop their abilities. This metre measures the power of your essence, or your enhancement level. If your essence level is higher than two, you will be required to attend an Essence Academy of your choosing or apply for Guardian training."

Her words run together. Face tight, eyes darting, limbs held close and stiff, she recites each word in a shaky tone.

"Inside the metre is core energy drawn from the centre of the Karess. When core energy interacts with our blood, an aura is produced. The colour of the aura indicates the affinity of the person's essence. For example, the aura produced for an Emberstead is red because of the lineages' fire affinity, blue for a Nytrue water affinity, and so on. The aura produced is measured on the outside of the column and indicates your potential strength. Essence level one and two are most common."

Although the space is small, the woman starts to pace. I curl my fingers into the soft fabric of my skirt as her eyebrows furrow.

"For Ironskins, it's different because more than one aura colour can be produced. The physical body affinity of the Ironskin essence leads to multiple enhancement categories as well as the possibility for dual enhancement. If you are an Ironskin with only the basic impenetrable skin enhancement, then the aura will be white. If you just have a speed enhancement, it will be orange, and if you have a strength enhancement, it will be purple."

Please, just hurry up.

"If you have dual enhancements, then the aura will be black. The final difference with this test is that if you have impenetrable skin we cannot draw blood from your finger, so we have to take it from your weak spot. Will it be necessary to take from a weak spot?"

With hands clamped in front of her, she stops talking. My head spins from the information she's vomited. I didn't know about the colours. Father and Oron went into the booth with Stephen when he Registered. His aura must have been black for his strength and skin enhancement. But what about his death affinity? I clear my throat to ask.

"Or if your skin is unenhanced, we can use the hand plate," the woman says.

I roll my eyes, huffing at her interruption. At least if Liam doesn't end up developing impenetrable skin, his Registration will be short and sweet.

"Weak spot." My words exit my mouth abrupt and unfeeling; my heart skips a beat.

The woman motions for me to follow her behind a curtain to the right. I join her and she pulls the curtain closed. I give it another tug, just in case. The darkness of the small space presses on me. I stand still except for my hand wandering to my weak spot. Under the hem of my shirt, I follow the raised scar running across my lower back. Only Johanna has found out about my weak spot. She doesn't know about the scar though. Now this random Emberstead woman will know.

As the woman fiddles with something on a stand, I conjure up an image of a black aura. A cloud maybe? A shadow? Will it sparkle? I developed impenetrable skin at age five and punched my fist effortlessly through a wall when I was eight—an accident that landed me in my room to think about what I had done.

"Please indicate your weak spot and I'll take a small sample of blood," the worker says. Her squeaky voice shreds my nerves. She picks up a syringe.

I point to my lower back and turn around, lifting my shirt.

"Oh," she says under her breath as she takes in the scar on my skin.

I squeeze my eyes closed.

She pokes around, but her sweaty fingers stick the needle too high on my back and it snaps. The metal tip tinkles across the tile floor and under the curtain.

"Shit," she huffs and grabs another needle.

A breath builds pressure in my chest once she finally finds a place to stick the needle right below the scar. There's a pinch, a swell of heat, and her hot hands pull the needle out. I drop my shirt. Flinging the curtain aside, I rush back over to Liam. He wraps an arm around me and leans his head on my side.

The woman slips the syringe into a slot by the hand plate and flips the switch to release my blood into the core-energy tube. The drop slips through the glistening white energy, maintaining its shape until it settles at the bottom.

"It will take about a minute before the aura—"

A black shadow stirs at the bottom of the column.

"That was fast," she says.

An ebony cloud takes shape around my blood. Inky swirls churn through the core energy, licking the side of the column, rising to the first marker. A flash of blue light fills the booth. The woman jumps. A flash of red replaces it, and I draw a tight breath through my teeth.

"What do those flashes mean?" I ask.

"The flashes mean you possess both the life affinity and the death affinity. It's uh … very rare these days," she says, backing away from the metre, the blue and red flashes painting her skin in an energetic glow.

The colours move with a life of their own. They are two heartbeats pulsing, charged with power like lightning. In the red, I imagine Stephen's eyes, burning in the dark of his room the night he discovered his death affinity. And Mother. Her eyes would change to this electric blue. It hid her grey eyes, filling the room with cold light that touched something inside me with gripping ghost hands.

I have both spirit affinities?

A chill spills down the back of my neck, clashing with the heat in my lower back and the stinging needle prick. The aura from this one drop of blood emits energy into the booth. It sweeps through the stale air with gentle power, raising the hairs on my arms. I take a small breath. The air prickles my lungs.

The aura grows past the second marker. Oron crinkles his brow. Liam watches intently and tightens his arm around me. I rub my hand on his arm, his skin awakened with goosebumps under my touch.

The aura passes the third marker. The red and blue lights flash together, merging their hues. A burst of violet light emanates from the aura and the cloud boils past the fourth. The glass splits down the centre, and I throw both arms around Liam just as the hand plate explodes off the metre and the glass column shatters.

My blood aura billows away from the wreckage. It hangs in the corners of the booth as the core energy spills over the floor. Energy leaks away from my body, leaving me frozen with my pulse pounding through my neck, my arms stiff as sticks, and my lungs slow to expand. I can't take my eyes off the shards of glass piled around the base of the metre. The ceiling cracks, dropping bits of plaster among the glass. I clench my teeth.

This damn day can't get any worse.

The Emberstead woman's mouth hangs open as the core energy reacts with the air and turns into mist, seeps out, and pools around the curious seventeen-year-olds pressing in close to the booth.

"What the hell did she do?" A sandy-faced boy says, pushing his way through the crowd.

A Luminee girl with jet-black hair crosses her arms.

Squinting, I decipher a familiar face under all her makeup—Nala, captain of my school's Ascension team.

"She blew up the metre," she says. "Leave it to the cutch to screw things up."

Her words burn through my ears and spark fires in my cheeks.

Oron steps into the doorway, blocking their view. "I suggest you all get back to your lines," he says, his voice a powerful growl.

I squeeze Liam, my heart pounding and my hands slick with sweat.

The woman, now shaking, smooths her hair for the hundredth time and claps her hands together.

"Well," she says over the sound of parents urging their children not to get too close to me. "It looks like it will be imperative for you to attend an Essence Academy for training and to finish your academics." She moves back to the PAT and types something in.

"You will have three months before you need to register for an Essence Academy. The closest one is in Braya. If you wish to attend a Guardian Academy to become a Protector, Warrior, or Medic, you must take the entrance exam to make sure you are fit for training."

While she works, she takes one hand away from the PAT. My eyes are magnetized by her slender fingers as they hover over the desk. The trembling hand turns upside down and clamps around the underside of the desk. A small click sounds; it startles me as if it's inside my head.

"We usually dissuade students who have level two essence or lower from choosing a Guardian Academy, but we won't have to do that today, will we?" Her eyes lift from the screen and she attempts a smile. It comes across more as a toothy grimace.

As she finishes her speech, a Local Protector comes through the back side of the booth. A navy-blue uniform pulled tight over his muscled frame, a firestone rifle strapped to his hip. His Protector shield-badge catches the fluorescent lights, sending streaks through the hazy air. I blink a few times and turn back to Oron. His arms are crossed over his puffed-out chest, his feet spread so his wide frame blocks most of the doorway from prying eyes. His stony expression wavers with a part in his lips, as his eyes take in the extra body in the small space.

Liam squirms, but my arm is a vice around him. "Rinnaya, what's—"

"Shh, shh, just be quiet, buddy."

Pressure builds inside my head.

"What seems to be the problem?" the Protector asks. His head is round, hair shaved, and his neck is swallowed by his collar. He takes in the mound of glass and metal. A pool of core energy still seeps through the glass so it steams like a spikey pile of beastshit.

"This girl broke the metre, has body enhancements, and dual spirit affinities. I-I'm not sure what to put on her card," the woman says, her head whips back and forth between me and the Protector.

Ball-head Protector sighs. "It's just a level-four enhancement and under specifier you put dual spirit affinity. That's all." He shrugs.

"Oh." A smile flickers over the registrar worker's blanched face. "Right." She taps the information in without hesitation. "Is there anything else we need to do"—she clears her throat—"in this situation?"

"No, ma'am. The protocol is the same for all citizens Registering today." Ball-head addresses the woman but turns to me. Kindness fills his eyes with warmth and a solemn frown pulls shadows over his brown skin. "Just remember that you can only practice essence manipulation in your private home with a Registered adult with the same abilities. And the young boy cannot be present."

"But it's a dual spirit affinity Ironsk—"

"Anything else, ma'am?" The Protector straightens his coat. "I have other business to attend to."

The woman huffs, her face glistening with sweat. She flicks her hair over her shoulder and turns her back to the Protector. "No."

She presses a button on a machine beside her PAT. The machine chugs as it prints my Registration card. The tangy smell of ink slips into the booth, adding to the pressure in my head. My heart jitters, and for some reason, my eyes filter out the light in the booth, so the woman appears dark and vignetted. As soon as a slip of white card pokes out, the woman has her hand poised to grab it. With each chug, my chest tightens, my toes tense in my boots, ready to turn and leave.

The machine quiets, and the woman snatches the card and plops it in an envelope. "You must have this card with you at all times in case of emergencies. It also allows you to purchase any power-stone-related items. You're free to leave." She points me to the door with wide eyes. Her damn hands mark Carnity's blessing over her heart to cleanse her after being in such close contact with an Ironskin "infested" by a demon and a fallen angel, or so they say.

I grab the envelope and flee the booth. I push through the ogling crowd, avoiding eyes, ignoring the laughs, just trying to breathe the thick air around me.

"Rin . . . You broke the metre," Liam says once he's caught up to me at the entrance.

The little man better watch it. I know what I did, don't need him rubbing it in. I turn to face him, mind spinning, ready to snap, but his eyes shine at me, a smile spreading ear to ear. Oron smiles too.

"You broke the metre," Oron says and slaps me on the back. "You might be the strongest Ironskin in all of Illyson." He picks me up and twirls me around. Setting me down, he kisses me on the cheek. "Your parents would be so proud to see what a strong young lady you've become."

"Your aura was beautiful, Rinnaya," Liam adds.

I tilt my head to him, trying to get my face to smile. But there's a tingle in my finger, and eyes still staring at me, and flashing red and blue lights in my head. Beautiful? How is destruction beautiful? Those lights, that black aura, is that really me? How could I not be aware of that power inside me until now?

But it left so quickly and now my skin is dry and lifeless, my body void of energy.

Oron lets loose a hearty laugh that shakes me. Liam squeezes my hand, beaming.

Their celebration is interrupted by the clopping sound of heels hitting tile behind me. I turn to find the last person on the Karess I want to see today. Johanna stands a few feet away with her usual frown plastered on her ruddy, freckled face. She wears an outfit I've seen her mother wear before, but it hugs Johanna's muscular body. Her heels define her calves, making her just tall enough to look down on me.

"Congratulations, Rin, another thing to add to the list of things you've broken," she says.

"Johanna," I say through gritted teeth. "Happy belated birthday." The sarcasm oozes from my mouth.

My birthday was two days ago, Johanna's birthday two days before that. When we were little, we celebrated our birthdays together. Since our fathers were partners, it worked best to do one big celebration when they were both home. Doesn't make sense to have birthdays together now, when all we share these days is the bit of bile at the back of our throats every time we see each other.

"Cut the crap." She flicks her long, copper-red curls, and her perfectly groomed eyebrows draw together, deepening the ever-present furrow. Her green eyes flash. "You know, there are still only four enhancement levels. Just because you broke the metre doesn't mean you're not a level four. We're still even," she says, looking back at the Emberstead booth that she just came from.

"Whatever helps you sleep at night," I say.

Johanna scoffs. The sound churns inside me. It solidifies into a barrier between us and all the sounds in the room fade, letting her disgust linger on my ears. I swallow the sick taste on my tongue and turn my back to her.

I take a step to the doors, but a display to my left catches my eye. A banner printed in bold letter states: **Become a Guardian. Keep the people within our city walls safe as a Protector or defend the provincial borders as a Warrior.** Beside the banner stands a Warrior herself in a forest green uniform decorated with glittering gold and silver badges, a stack of applications in her hands.

"Go ahead, we'll wait for you here," Oron says.

I head to the table with Johanna's heels clipping behind me. She clears her throat as we both browse the pamphlets. "Looks like the Aria Academy is accepting out-of-province applicants." Her matter-of-fact tone comes out awkward, trying so hard to be civil.

"You should apply," I say.

"Or maybe you should. You go freeze in Aria, and I'll go to Akinnera." She sizes me up with a quick swipe of her eyes.

"Maybe you should apply for early admission, you know, beat me at somethin'. You'd love that."

Johanna clicks her tongue. "Still won't be rid of you fast enough."

Dropping her eyes to the bits of information at the booth, she adjusts the waist of her skirt and scratches her head. The smell of styling cream with an undertone of singed hair bites my nose as if it's the aroma of Johanna's disdain.

I glance at the Warrior still standing in serene quiet amid our squabble.

Opening a pamphlet, I scan the contents. Nothing I don't already know—four years in a Guardian program will train students in essence control and combat as well as finish up academic education to prepare for Protector and Warrior work.

"Johanna," Mrs. Kingsman's voice calls over the chatter in the hall. "We need to get home before your grandparents get there."

I steal a glance at Johanna. She runs her tongue over her teeth, still looking at a sticker with the Aria Academy crest on it.

"Johanna, now. I told Nima and Nipan to be at our place at

noon."

"Relax, Mom. We've got an hour." Johanna tosses the sticker back on the pile.

"You need to clean up your room before—oh, Rin."

"Hi, Mrs. Kingsman." I stuff the pamphlet in my skirt pocket.

Mrs. Kingsman folds her hands in front of her, glasses sliding down her nose. "I didn't see you there. It's been so long."

I press my lips together and nod. Johanna grabs her mother's arm and tries to pull her away.

"My, you look pretty today. I had to fight Johanna's hair for a whole hour to get the curl like this." She slips away from Johanna's pull to touch her daughter's hair, which is already starting to resist its hot-iron curl and revert to frizz. Mrs. Kingsman's hair holds its curl in soft, ruby-red ringlets. She glances back at me. "That blue suits you so well."

"Thanks," I say, fingering the lace. "It's just something from Oron."

Behind her mother, Johanna scrunches her nose at me and rolls her eyes.

"Johanna, don't roll your eyes," Mrs. Kingsman says with a stiff smile.

"Ugh, Mom, let's just go." She grabs an application from the silent Warrior woman.

"Now you're ready to leave, are you?" Pushing her horn-rimmed glasses back into place, Mrs. Kingsman sighs. "Strength of the ancestors, Rin."

"Strength of the ancestors," I repeat as the Kingsman women leave me.

Even with my heart thrumming in my chest and feet itching to move, I remain at the booth. I pull the pamphlet out of my pocket and my eyes are enchanted by the Akinnera Academy crest printed in silver at the top—a woman in armour, hands wrapped around a sword, standing in front of a tower with two beetles on either side of her.

"Akinnera is a good school."

I jolt at the Warrior's sudden remark.

"I went there myself." She hands me an application. Her face is golden brown and round, perfect like a doll, unbroken by a blush in her cheeks, or a smile, or a furrowed brow. No signs of life streak her skin, but the grey in her eyes pulls me with energy. A familiar silver-grey energy.

I take the application.

The Warrior nods, and a curly, blond hair slips out of her cap. She turns her energetic eyes back to scan the sea of seventeen-year-olds.

I rejoin Oron and Liam. We leave the Registration Hall, the sound of cracking glass in my ears and an application to become a Guardian in my hand. The smell of Johanna's hair is still stuck in my nose. It sifts through me to join a sinking feeling in my gut and stirs an image in my mind of when her hair wasn't so red.

My feet stepped out of the grocery store's abrasive light into heavy fog, in the direction of home. Not home.

It was a few weeks after we'd buried Mother. We were still living in the old house, but it wasn't home anymore. I needed to find us a new place.

I shifted my bags and urged my feet to move faster. Oron

was with Liam, but he'd be leaving for work soon. I should have bought food the day before. I moved a little faster. I needed to get to Liam.

Mist licked my face. Shivering, I wiped my cheek on my sleeve, but it was too damp to do much. My stomach growled.

Chicken, green rice, tomatoes. Tomorrow I could make a big soup to last us a few days. How do I make soup?

In my mind, I sifted through recipes I never learned and self-taught cooking techniques with eyes fixed on my boots, fingers going numb from the plastic bags.

A splash of freezing water hit my legs and I jerked my head up. My heart jolted in my chest as a boy my age skidded passed me on my right, a second passed on the left. They snickered and blocked my path. Another bashed me in the shoulder from behind. The blow shifted the leverage I had on my packages, and they flew from my arms. I tumbled after them, one knee making a soft landing on a cluster of pinichu berries I purchased and the other in a puddle. Grunting, I swiped the blood-red slime from my leg.

"Whoops." The boy laughed. "Ironskin down."

"Why you walkin' so slow, huh?" one of them jeered. "Thought Ironskins were supposed to be fast or somethin'."

I swallowed hard and took a breath. It went in shaky with a convulsion of shivers now that I was completely soaked.

One of the boys snatched a bag that hadn't busted open, the one bag with contents I wanted but didn't need—coffee and coloured pencils for Liam. A new vigour leaped into my heart, and I lunged after the boys. They scattered, but I zeroed in on the one who took my bag. I ran so fast that the city lights blurred around me. He sprinted across the street just before an airbus roared through the intersection to block my path. I skidded to a stop.

The bus passed, and the boy laughed at me, jogging backward and holding my bag in the air like a trophy.

He whirled back around but got close-lined by an Emberstead girl. The smack jumped across the road to my ears. Even from that distance, I could tell it was Johanna. She grabbed the bag from the boy. "Get out of here, you little dick," she said, shoving his shoulder, and he scampered away into an alley.

My stomach cinched and my face flooded with heat as Johanna sprinted toward me, bag in hand. I turned around and slapped my cold hands over my burning cheeks.

"Hey, don't you want your bag?" Johanna yelled at me as I walked back to my trampled produce.

I knelt and gathered the remains of my purchase as the rain started. A crowd gathered nearby to watch my scene.

"Where are these kids' parents?" a man said.

A woman scoffed. "Serves the little demon spawn right."

Their words pelted me, the rain drenched me, but I steeled myself to ward off their attacks.

"Rin," Johanna shouted. She stooped down in front of my mess and shoved the bag in my face.

"Yeah," I muttered, and grabbed it from her.

"Would it kill you to say thank you?"

Her hair, more orange than red, hung in heavy, rain-soaked kinks around her face. A crinkle formed between her brows as I frowned at her. She grabbed a pack of chicken that I hadn't shoved in a bag yet and put it in with the coffee and the pencils.

"I was handlin' it, Johanna," I said and stood up. Water squished in my boots.

"Clearly." She rolled her eyes.

I huffed and set my feet back on track.

"Hey, why are you being such a jerk to me all of a sudden?" she called after me.

I pulled up short. "Why are you always a jerk?" I turned my head to look at her.

The crease between her eyes deepened.

Johanna crossed her arms. "Never seemed to bother you before."

"It doesn't. So why can't I be the jerk sometimes?"

"Not to me. I'm your best friend. You don't get to do that." She took a step closer. "Come on, what's up your ass?"

"Nothin'." I shrugged my shoulders and my bags crinkled in my arms.

"You're pissy. That's not you."

"What do you think is going on, Johanna?" I snapped.

My body was so heavy, like I had rocks in my bones. As I clenched my fingers, stiff with cold, a raindrop slid down the bridge of my nose. I brushed it aside with the back of my numb hand and stalked back to her.

"My parents are gone, I haven't heard from my brother in weeks, and I'm broke."

Johanna just stared at me, dissecting me, before lifting her chin to look down her nose. "What does that have to do with us?"

My mind was blank, cold, like the rest of me. "I don't know."

"Beastshit. You and me, come on." She poked me in the shoulder.

A waft of spices prickled my nose as someone left the restaurant behind her and brought me back to reality. I had to get home to Liam. "Get off my back. I don't have time for this."

Before she had a chance to respond, Mrs. Kingsman caught up with us.

"Johanna," she screeched without pulling her echo away from her ear. Her straight, burgundy hair was pinned in a bun and rain speckled her horn-rimmed glasses. "Sorry, my daughter just ran off on me," she said into the echo. "Honestly, Johanna." She glared at her daughter. "I understand, we'll be there as soon as possible."

"It's urgent, Jannette, there's no time to waste," came a garbled voice through the device.

"Yes, yes. On our way." Mrs. Kingsman switched off the echo and grabbed Johanna by the arm. "For Zenta's sake, why'd you run off like that?"

Johanna bit her lip and squinted her eyes at me. "No reason," she said, yanking her arm away from her mother.

"Well, then let's go. You can talk to Rin at school," Mrs. Kingsman said. She glanced at me, trailed her eyes from my head to my toes, then snapped them shut and refocused on Johanna. "There's something urgent happening down at the Guardian station, something to do with your father."

They turned. They left.

My gaze clung to them for as long as it could—until the two fires turned the corner, until the sinking in my stomach left me dizzy. Stomach rumbling and eyes stinging from the rain, I started home again. No, not home, to Liam.

2

JOHANNA

I SHOULDN'T HAVE TALKED TO HER. Now her voice is in my head. The way she talks with that South-Senn accent—rounding her vowels, skimming over syllables, sharpening consonants— annoys the shit out of me.

Mom leads us to the exit. The sway of her hips is nauseating. With her natural hour-glass figure swinging back and forth and ringlets bouncing down her back, she catches the eye of one of the Warriors standing by the door. She pushes both doors out of the Registration Hall so they swing open around her like she's the Empress of Illyson.

I tromp behind her, groaning internally and externally at the show. My stomach tosses and a pinch in my temples pulls tight as we step outside. Maybe if we get home soon enough, we'll have a quick lunch with Nima and Nipan, and I'll get some time to myself, play some tech games. Maybe.

The damp, smoggy air sticks to my lungs. I yank the gold hoops from my ears and pull my curls into a floppy bun. Mom swishes her hand above her head. A flash of orange light spikes the ache in my head and bleaches my sight.

"Holy Zenta. A little warning?" I say, rubbing my eyes.

The light fades and an orange pentagonal plate of fire hovers over her head. Rain drizzles over the plate, sizzling as it hits and turns to steam above her head.

"You're not supposed to manipulate in public." I push past her and down the street to our cruiser.

"It's just a barrier, perfectly legal." She tsks behind me. "Oh, come on, I didn't do your hair just for you to scrunch it up again."

"It's going to get ruined by the rain anyway."

"Well make yourself a barrier."

"I can't make a barrier." My head pounds with each step. Our blue-grey cruiser sits like a lumpy beetle between newer models. Just half a block and I can take off these pinchy heels.

"What do you mean, you can't make a barrier? I showed you how weeks ago."

The pain in my head creeps from my temples to the back of my skull. My stomach shifts with sick like a fish is wiggling around inside. "We haven't really had time to work on it."

"Well, you just spend all your time away from me—"

"For the love of the All Creator and all the holy ancestors, can we just go home?" I slam my hands down on the hood of our cruiser, stomach lurching and head spinning.

"What is wrong with you?" Mom plants her hands on her hips, purse sliding from her shoulder down to her wrist so it twists around her leg.

I shut my eyes against the circular motion.

"No really, what is wrong with you? You're pale," she says, and puts a cool hand to my forehead.

"I don't know. I feel like I'm going to barf."

A speeder roars down the road, tire squealing at the intersection. A group of men across the street catcall Mom, which she returns with a flip of her pinky finger and not so much as a glance in their direction. "Think you can make it home?"

"Hopefully."

We get in the cruiser as the men laugh and whistle at us. I kick off the heels. Resting my elbow on the window so I can prop up my pounding head, I say, "You going to get mad at me for taking the shoes off too?"

Mom sighs and starts the cruiser. It chugs to life. The orange glow from the firestone core warms the wet pavement but sends spiky pains through my eyeballs, so I set my sights forward. Despite the sputtering sounds the cruiser makes and the annoying rattle from somewhere deep inside, Mom drives the cruiser like only an ex Local Protector can. She weaves through traffic without upsetting my stomach too much.

Tasteless buildings tower over the streets. They stack together like puzzle pieces that don't match in size or colour. Too many flashing signs vie for the attention of the disinterested residents. The city gets tighter every day—the smog thicker, the city walls taller, the patch of sky smaller.

I hold the Guardian application. The day I leave this place can't come soon enough.

Rin wants out too. We used to talk about being a two-woman, beast-slaying squad when we grew up. Now, the last thing I want is for that leech to follow me to Guardian training.

"You clearly saw her," I say before I can stop myself.

Drawing a breath, Mom flexes her manicured fingers, then clenches them back around the steering wheel. "What are you talking about?"

"Rin. You couldn't have missed her. Her boney ass was standing right there."

"Well, I was focused on you."

I jam my thumbs to my temples, making little circles to rub the pain away, but it just spreads throughout my scalp. "No, you weren't."

"I was—"

"Oh right, right. Focused on how long it took you to fix my hair, and how much of a hassle I am to you for not dressing like you. Not focused on the fact that I tested level four, and you said nothing about it."

"Johanna, we all knew you were going to test level four." Mom takes one hand off the steering wheel and starts holding up fingers. "I'm level four, your father was level four, Nima, Nipan—"

"Okay, I get it. I'm like everyone in the family."

"Hon." Mom tilts her head to me, a patronizing look in her eye.

A strike of pain stabs the back of my head. My mouth falls open. Clutching the window ledge and holding my stomach as it gurgles. "Mom, stop the cruiser."

"Wha"—she turns to me, her voice dropping—"Oh." The cruiser swerves to the side of the road. "All right, hon, out, out."

I scramble out of the cruiser in my bare feet and bolt into the alley. Bracing myself on a dingy brick wall, I wretch over a pile of sour garbage. Pale pinky-brown vomit with chunks of breakfast spatters the plastic bags. I groan, my legs giving way, and I crouch beside the sludge.

Mom trots up beside me, looking through her purse.

"Good time to reapply lipstick?" I say, clutching my head.

Her lips pull tight. She rolls her eyes at me—and she wonders where I get my attitude from. "No, I'm looking for a curestone." Shaking her head, she hands me a cool, cream-coloured curestone. "I just don't understand why you're sick. You haven't been working on Mind Fire without me, have you?"

"No." I press the stone to my head. Mist seeps from the stone, licking my skin, and the ache lessens. "Okay, maybe a bit yesterday."

"Well, that explains the headache." Mom crosses her arms and bends over to look me in the eye. Her nose crinkles as a waft of vomit is stirred up by a draft through the alley.

The curestone takes most of the pounding away and the pain only sticks in my temples. My stomach settles, but without the churning in my gut, my stomach drops. I don't think it was just from working on Mind Fire. I don't know how I know that, but I know.

A shiver crawls over my body. At the end of the alley, beside a dumpster, there's a flicker. It moves like wind come to life and sparkles like starlight. The light morphs into the face of a woman, and my body goes rigid. The hairs on the back of my neck stand on end. I stand up straight, just shy of headbutting Mom, still holding the curestone to my head. The face's eyes grow wide with bright, pupilless orbs, and her mouth gapes. She shimmers and disappears around the corner.

"Mom," I say, grabbing her by the arm and dragging her into the depths of the alley.

"What is it now? You're going to cut your feet, and I only have the one curestone," she says. Her voice hits a high-pitched note that sends my head reeling again.

I leap over a cardboard box, yanking Mom along with me. We skirt around broken glass, burnt-out firestone cores, and broken furniture. We clamber over a wooden pallet, and I stop short at the end, turning back and forth, searching for the glowing light. Mom rams into my back.

"Zenta help me. What are we doing?"

"I thought I saw . . ."

Rain pisses down on us. The stench of the burnt-out cores fills my nose, along with some fishy rot. I shiver again, but I can't find the light.

"I thought I saw a Wander Wraith." I drop my eyes to the wet pavement with fire burning in my cheeks. My feet sit in a puddle of water with a greasy rainbow waving back at me. As I press the curestone back to my forehead, Mom pats her soaking wet curls with a heavy sigh.

Pressing her eyes closed, she says, "Get a hold of yourself, Johanna."

My essence heats under my skin. "I saw what I saw."

Dad would have helped me look for the wraith. He would believe me.

"Wander Wraith or no Wander Wraith, we need to get home." Purse clutched in her fist, her face blooms red and she tromps back through the garbage. "Once your grandparents leave, you're going straight to bed."

Like I'm shut in a box, the air is stale as I follow her through the alley. My legs are stiff with fear that I've contracted some alley-to-foot disease. The stench of puke hugs my clothes. As I get into the cruiser and lean my head back on the headrest, my mouth is dry, a gritty taste on my tongue that I can't quite place.

3

RIN

"So you're going to go to a Guardian Academy, right, Rin?" Liam asks, sliding his hand into mine as the airbus wobbles to a halt at our stop.

Following my father's footsteps and making him proud are preferable thoughts to the awful explosion I caused at the Registration Hall. I'll fill out the application after lunch.

"What? You tryin' to get rid of me?" I say, and smile at his cute little dimples.

He scrunches his nose. "You know what I mean. So, are you going to be a Protector or a Warrior?" Straightening himself with the question, he steps off the airbus with mock sophistication.

Heat from the firestone core of the airbus wafts over my legs. Holding down my skirt, I take a moment, asking Oron what he thinks with my eyes. He sighs, crossing his arms over his broad chest.

"You've got the focus and stamina to get out there on the battlefield. Not so good at following orders, but I can see you being a Warrior, maybe even a Commander one day."

Commander? I can't see myself there. Then again, I can't see myself anywhere beyond the walls of Senn. The thought makes my head spin.

"I'll just fill out the application first."

"No harm in thinking big," Oron says.

I shrug, not willing to invite a conversation set so far in the future. "Exploding energy metres, grave site-seeing, and an absent brother are enough for me today." My comment suffocates the hot air from the bus with cold. "Being a Protector, I could request to be stationed here in Senn or one of the towns nearby," I say.

I imagine the disappointment on Oron's face, but don't look at him.

"Maybe I'll get into beast slaying, escort missions, or something with shorter assignments like that. I could just start as a Local Protector in Senn and work my way up."

That's always what I thought I would do; it's what my father did.

As we come up to our building, Liam runs ahead of me and Oron. He dodges puddles and scurries from overhang to overhang to avoid the drizzling rain. Oron and I climb the grungy stairs in silence. Once we catch up to Liam, I hand him my keys to unlock our apartment while I lean against the wall in the hallway.

"I'd like to have work where I could at least be home with Liam on weekends."

Oron gives me a look that I can't quite read. He lowers his eyebrows and draws them together but smiles underneath the shadow of his brows. "You do what you think is best, we'll be rooting for you. Won't we, Liam?"

"Yes, sir."

"Good man." Oron chuckles and starts up the next flight of stairs to his apartment. "You kids get changed into something more comfortable and come up for lunch when you're ready."

"How could I get more comfortable than this?" I say, turning toward my door so Oron can't see my smile.

"Mhm, I know you hate the skirt. Just change and come up when you're ready, sweet girl."

I don't hate it all that much.

Liam stays in his dress clothes and goes straight for his sketchbook and pencils. I close my curtain around my bed once again. Instead of changing, I sit and stare at the ground. Our apartment is quiet except for the muffled traffic and the occasional airbus backfire. The soft scrape of pencil on paper drifts around the curtain from Liam's side of the room. For a moment, I focus my ears on the scratch of his pencil and my eyes on a crack in the rough wood under my feet. I scrunch my boney toes. But the sound of the glass metre shattering plays over in my mind, attempting to push past the familiar ones of my apartment. The lace of my skirt starts to irritate my skin and the thick collar of the shirt tries to strangle me.

I pull the Registration outfit from my body and slip into my faded jeans and a black, knitted sweater. The sweater is soft and not as constricting as the shirt. There's a hole in the sleeve that's been there since it was worn by my mother. I stick my thumb through it and take Liam upstairs.

Oron's apartment is just big enough for his bed in one corner, a lounge chair in the other, and the dining table in the centre. A haze of onions, garlic, and salty terrin sauce consumes us as we enter. The aroma of a warm meal I didn't have to cook relaxes my shoulders, and my stomach growls.

Oron ushers us to the table with a grunt and thanks the ancestors for their protection, more out of habit than anything else. His salute to Carnity and Dien is cut short by his echo flashing on the kitchen counter. Oron sighs and pushes away from the table, not bothering to wrap up his thanks.

"Can I start, Oron?" Liam asks.

Good kid. Always polite.

"Yeah, yeah." Oron struggles to get the old lightstone to snap into the echo and receive his call. "Piece of shit," he mutters.

Liam takes a few eager bites. The terrin dribbles down his chin. Taking a bite from my own bowl, the thin, string-like noodles spread a layer of oil throughout my mouth and the flavours dance over my tongue, salty and tangy.

"Rin. It's Stephen." Oron holds the echo out to me.

My mind does a backflip. I had resigned to the idea that he wasn't going to be involved in this day—it was just going to be me, Liam, and Oron, like usual. Johanna was already more interaction than I wanted. My mental plan for the day has already been screwed up, so I drop my fork and grab the echo from Oron.

"Hello?" I say through a mouth full of iidai.

Oron rolls his eyes at me.

"Hey, Rin, sorry I haven't called in a while, work has been really busy lately."

"Mhm." Always busy.

"So," Stephen says.

His hesitation worries me. He only hesitates when he has something to say but doesn't know how I'll respond.

"I've been moved onto a new assignment and I'm really excited about it, which is why I haven't had much down time."

"Yeah, what is it?" I lean forward and prop my elbows on the table.

"I can't tell you much about it right now, but I'll be travelling out of province soon. I wanted to give you a heads-up in case I'm a bit late in wiring you the saphrite for the rent this month. It will get to you before you have to make the payment, though, so don't worry about that.

"Yeah, that's fine, I guess."

A new assignment is good. I'm curious to know more, but if he's not giving details, it's probably confidential, so I shouldn't pry.

"You're still helping Mrs. Khatari clean after school to keep a little extra cash on hand, right?"

"Right. Did her windows yesterday." I grit my teeth. Was that the same lie I used last time I talked to him? Five years of "cleaning for Mrs. Khatari" and neither Oron nor Stephen have found out that I've been fighting in shady Dawnranfet matches to make money.

"And how did Registration go?" Stephen asks, his voice getting tight, the cheerful attitude forced through the echo.

"Oh, was that today?" I wonder if he waited to ask until we had warmed up the conversation a bit.

"Hey, don't be like that. I told you, I've been busy."

"I know."

Liam and Oron look up at me as I stir my noodles with my

fork into one oily, stringy ball. Their eyebrows raise in unison, trying to tell me to lower the defensive tone in my voice. But I've been understanding for a long time now, and I just wish he would have been here like he said he would be.

Stephen sighs. "Did Oron and Liam do anything special for you?"

"Oron made iidai for lunch, so that's nice,"

"Good." Stephen hates iidai, doesn't like the texture of the noodles. "Good, I'm glad."

The lull in conversation lifts Oron and Liam's eyes to stare at me again. I don't know what to say to Stephen. I haven't known what to say for years now.

"Um, so . . ." The pressure builds in my chest and the small apartment is too cramped to hold the three of us with Stephen's intoxicating presence. "Lunch is getting cold, so I uh . . . I'm going to go."

"Wait, hold on. Tell me how it went."

"Fine, it was fine. You know, I walked in, got tested, and walked out."

Oron puts his fork down and leans back in his chair, shaking his head. Liam questions me with his innocent eyes.

"They didn't give you any trouble, did they?" Stephen asks.

If I grip the rectangular device any tighter, I'll crack the case. Words form and vanish in my mind. I shift in my seat, the chair creaks beneath me.

"Stephen," I say. The words stick at the back of my throat, swallowed in a whisper. "You should have been there."

A sigh sweeps through the echo. It stings my ear.

"It's complicated, Rin."

My sleeve finds its way into my hand and I squeeze. I roll

the wool between my fingertips. "No," I say. "No, it's not." The clock on Oron's wall that never registers a sound now ticks with a passion. "My essence is mature, and I should've had my family there to celebrate. You should've been at that test."

"What's there to celebrate, Rin? That test is arbitrary, totally inaccurate," Stephen says. "We're Ironskins, and you and I are enhanced throughout our whole bodies, every cell. Our blood is literally supercharged with energy, a high reading's inevitable." He scoffs. "That fucking test practically ensures every Ironskin goes to an Essence Academy."

The crackling glass and the dark, flashing aura sit behind my eyes. My head falls and I prop it on my hand. Liam's clear-blue eyes are on me. They dart all around me, a furrow on his brow, and his lips parted. The urgency in his stare sparks my nerves. That's a gaze for a catastrophe, not a dinner table.

Pushing away from the table, the chair scrapes against the wood far too loud for the small space, and I leave the apartment. The door slams, rattling the windowpanes.

"So what?" I say, kicking my toes at the wall. "I shouldn't have Registered? You know what would have happened. They would take Liam away from me." My words bounce around the dingy space, adding bitterness to the already gritty air.

"That's what I'm saying. The Registration process is disgusting. I don't want any part of it."

"But I had to, Stephen. I had to register, and I have to go to an academy because my essence level is through the fucking roof. I have to do all this so I don't lose Liam. Don't you get that? For Carnity's sake, if you don't care about me, at least do it for Liam."

"Something big is happening and—"

"What the hell do you mean by something big? You're not making any sense."

"I'm saying you need to give me a break and be patient with me. I'm working on something that will change the lives of all Ironskins. Soon we won't have to register and be separated from our families."

"Fuck this," I say under my breath and latch on to the last string of calm inside me. I wrap it around my words so I don't miss anything. "What about our family right now? I had to watch all my peers with their families at Registration. Moms, dads, grandparents. Is it so much to ask for my brother to be with me?"

"I just couldn't. This affects more than just you and Liam. Maybe look past yourself for once." Stephen's words are barbed wire—hard and unrelenting, pointed to rip and shred.

I swallow hard, but the tightness in my throat won't relax. It stifles my urge to scream at him, so I wait. Stephen huffs on the other end.

The electro zip signals the end of the echo and the glow by my ear fades. I keep the echo clutched in my fingers, pressing it to my ear. The quiet of the hall is dull, the walls far away from the deep pit that weighs in my stomach. Clinging to the pressure in my lungs as a sign of life in the wake of the conversational fire, I open Oron's door. I cross the room and sink into my chair.

"Rin," Liam says. "You okay?" He sits on his knees, one hand clamped around his fork.

I set the echo down on the table, swallow once more, and give Liam a smile.

"Yeah," I say. I squeeze his shoulder but grab my fork before he notices the tremble in my hand. I let the shake unravel the noodles before taking another bite.

"Did you tell Stephen your essence level?" Liam asks.

Noodles slip off the tines of my fork, frozen between my mouth and my bowl. "Uh . . . You still have that calculations sheet to do before school tomorrow, don't you, buddy?"

Liam looks down at his food, untouched since his first bites, and back at me. His cheeks pale, pulling down his face. His lower lip pouts. "Yeah," he says. "I don't want to do it."

"Well, we can do it together after lunch," I say.

"I have some time before I have to leave for work," Oron says, leaning forward to get his face in my field of view. "I can help him with it, sweet girl."

"No, no, it's fine. We can do it together." I shove a clump of noodles in my mouth and stand. My shoulders pull in, inching toward my ears. I drop my bowl into Oron's sink, still full of noodles. It clangs against a pot. "I don't have anything else to do today."

"Rin," Oron says, touching my arm.

I brush him off. "I'll help him, just need some air first." A prickle settles into the tips of my fingers. It creeps up my hands until they are icy and stiff. My breaths come faster as I lock my eyes on the door. My feet move and my hip slams into the chair, sending it clattering to the floor. I cringe, escaping through the door before Liam or Oron can say anything more. I sprint down the stairs, two at a time, moving faster as I near the bottom.

I burst through the front door of the building. Rain pelts my face. Sloshing through the puddle growing below the step, I run, and keep running until my lungs and my mind are full of the thick, smoggy air. I don't stop until the ice has melted in my fingers, and they pulse with life again.

After Father's funeral, we returned to the cold, empty pit of our house. I was sure we could all sense that this was no longer the house we knew, but none of us said anything about it. Stephen lit a fire. Mother made dinner. But the fire didn't make the house warm, and the food didn't make the pit smell like home.

We sat down to eat. I picked at my food, shifted my feet, and glanced over to the end of the table with the chair filled by the ghost of my father. Over and over again, my eyes were drawn to the haunted chair, hoping the ghost would never fade.

My mother didn't eat, she didn't move. She stared at the fire. The light and shadow fought for access to her pale skin. Darkness inched its way up her neck, deep inky shadows filled the bags under her eyes. Only her left cheek was washed in gold, but I don't think she could see the light the way I could—the way I could feel it.

I turned back to Father's chair and Stephen slammed his fist down on the table.

"Damn it, Rin," Stephen said, voice hammering through the silence. "Stop looking. He's not there and looking's not going to bring him back from the fucking dead."

I stared at him. His dark hair hung in short clumps around his head and his long face held weighted bags under grey eyes. He clenched his teeth. His chest heaved. I wished there was a way I could vault myself over the barrier thrown up between us and shatter the wall that hid the light from my mother's eyes.

Liam crawled into my lap and poked his finger at my chest.

"F-fuck you, Stephen," I said, ignoring the little hand at my heart. "I can look if I want to."

"Children," Mother said. Her voice shook. "Watch your language."

We all watched our mother's face morph from a blank white sheet to a horrifying display of anger and then back to the void. The firelight danced across her left cheek. On the other side, the magnetic depth of the shadow was mesmerizing. It pulled at me; I almost got lost in it.

"I thought I taught you better than that," she whispered, and turned her attention to her untouched food.

Liam poked me hard in the sternum. The pressure of his little finger digging into my skin struck a nerve.

"Liam, stop," I snapped, but he persisted.

His round, blue eyes locked onto mine and his eyebrows rose.

"What are you doing?" I asked, as a warm tear slipped down my cheek.

"It hurts," Liam said, then rubbed his hand over his own chest.

"Yeah." My breath caught in my throat. "It does hurt."

My eyes blurred, and hot tears spilled hotter. Stephen leaned his elbows on the table, covering his face with his hands. He dug his nails into his forehead. His whole body shook as he took in a deep breath. When he let the air go, he leaned back in his chair and a fresh wave of water sprung from my eyes.

"Liam, come," Mother said. "Let's get you into bed." She came around the table and knelt beside me. "For Carnity's sake, Rinnaya, stop crying." Taking her sleeve again, she wiped my face. "You're stronger than this."

She had to wipe multiple times, but soon all the tears were dried. She lifted Liam out of my lap. "Please do the dishes, children," she said as she turned her back to climb the stairs. I had to do what she said. I couldn't cry anymore.

4

ELIOTE

IT'S NOT UNCOMMON FOR HEDIN with powerful essence to struggle with the most basic manipulations. It is uncommon not to have any essence whatsoever. The test today confirms it; Vin did not bless me with light.

Mom gets out of the cruiser first. She slams the door shut and reopens it to retrieve the long train of her sash. Her aura sparkles a deep violet, billowing and churning as irritation gathers inside her.

"Those metres are nothing but junk," she says. Holding one hand dripping with gold jewellery to the sky, she tilts her head back and sighs. The sunlight moves over her brown skin in waves. The silver streams of essence within her calm as they drink in the light. She presses her hand to her chest and the essence in every channel of her body moves to her core.

Dad gets out of the cruiser and smooths his suit. Night-wing moths flutter out of the cruiser after him to rest on his shoulder. He steps to Mom, placing his hand on the small of her back, urging her forward, but she jerks away.

"Don't rush me, Byronn," Mom says, then she rushes herself up the black brick path to our home.

My dad's straight back twitches and the midnight cloud of his aura shudders.

I take the biggest breath I can manage with my lungs squished by the gold sash around my middle. Slipping the Guardian application out of my dress pocket, an application every one of my family members would make fun of, I step out of the cruiser.

"It's not like she's the one without essence," I say.

Dad turns on his heel to me, his brown eyes wavering but the rest of him still. "Being essenceless is nothing to joke about, Eliote." Turning away from me, he rubs the bridge of his nose.

Once my parents are inside, I raise my hand to the sky. The gold beads on my wrist click together. Even though it's already Setsonev, with fall fast approaching, the sun is hot and bites my skin as a warning not to stay too long. I shake my head.

I slip off my gold sandals at the end of a long train of my extended family's footwear collected along the walkway.

My fingers clench in the folds of my dress as I step through the wide arch into my home. Black slate tile cools my feet after walking across the sunbaked brick. A rush of voices grate my ears, but it's not a collective greeting to me, although it should be. Everyone ignores me—brown eyes catch mine and dart away. If I had essence, they would cheer, bowing to me for each mark on the metre my blood aura would have passed. They can't even bow once; a glance is even too risky.

The only one who takes the risk is my older brother. He stands with a cup of ale in hand, back to the plum-coloured wall. The firm line of his mouth pulls down. His aura swirls in a deep pool of magenta, bottom heavy, rich in pigment near his feet and hazy around his eyes. The ball of his throat bobs, and he takes a nervous sip from his cup because he's the only one who knows that description of his aura. He told me to keep it to myself.

I suck in another sluggish breath and straighten my shoulders. Brushing my lilac hair out of my way, I march to the kitchen. I'm going to tell someone today. I just have to figure out who. For now, they don't get to see me cower, they don't get to pass me over. Every one of these Luminee light suckers is going to see me today. I slap a smile on my face that will blind every one of them with radiance.

My mom and her mother stand side by side filling dumplings, my aunties bustle about in their purple, gold, and silver dresses swishing back and forth adding more movement to the storm of their auras tumbling over each other. I blink, trying to clear my sight as the smell of chive meatballs wafts over me.

My dad and his shadowy aura manoeuvres through the women over to my mom. He places his hand again on the small of her back as he sneaks a cookie sitting to cool by the window. Mom smacks his hand. "Hands that touch women not bonded to them are never clean. Wash, Byronn."

He leaves her in silence. Mom's aura solidifies into a violet ribbon that reaches for him, longing for his touch to spill light back into their relationship.

An ache wells in my chest, forcing my heart to beat in heavy thumps. My vision blurs. I blink a few times and steady my eyes on a platter of deep-fried cheese rolls. I grab the platter, urging my smile not to break.

"Eliote, you don't have to do that, here hand that to me," Dad says.

My grip tightens. "Oh, that's okay, Dad," I say in the sweetest, sunniest voice I can muster. "No one's here to celebrate me anyway." My voice cracks, letting the sweet glow fade.

Feet slapping against slate, gold beads bouncing on my chest, I storm out of the kitchen, ready to stuff cheese rolls into everyone's mouths, whether they like it or not.

"Hi, Uncle Sann," I say in a bursting voice that turns heads all over the room.

Uncle Sann glares down his nose at me. "Eliote, hello," he says, his moustache twitching.

"How's everything at your firm?"

"Fine." He eyes the cheese roll I stick on his plate with my bare hands.

"That's great." I smile so wide my eyes squint and my cheeks pinch into tight fleshy wads. "May Vin's light bless you with prosperity."

I move through the room overflowing with energy, handing out rolls until I have one left. I take it to the corner of the living room where the crowd of my relatives creates a wall around one fading aura of snow white. I haven't seen anyone talk to her all day. The beat of my heart slows as I squeeze through the wall and kneel before her. A smile unfolds through her crinkled, brown skin. She sits primly on the edge of a wooden chair, ankles locked together.

"Hi, Grandma, do you want a cheese roll?" I say in a quiet voice just for her to hear in the secluded corner.

"Oh," she whispers. Her glassy eyes disappear behind thin crescents of lashes as her smile widens. Instead of reaching for the roll, she wags her finger at me. "I have something for you, my light."

A chill sprinkles my skin with goose bumps. My eyes prickle as I bow my head, waiting for her to fish something from her deep dress pocket. Lifting my chin with a gnarled hand, the tears quiver but don't shake free. She holds a green lightstone out to me. Light reflects off the polished edges of the crystal. Cupping it for a moment in her hands, it glows soothing green light over the two of us.

"Green stones are rare. They represent balance." She fastens the stone around my neck with a simple piece of leather.

Grandma's worn this necklace as long as I can remember. It fits tight around my neck since she's such a tiny woman and I'm long and lanky. All of my cousins have been eyeing this stone, all secretly hoping they would get it. I thought it would go to Cassila, she's the real talent of the family.

The lightstone sparkles around my neck, warming my chest. Grandma cups my face in her hands and kisses my forehead.

"Thank you," I whisper, and kiss her leathery hand.

"Now off you go. You eat this one." She nudges the platter away from her, her aura shining like clear crystal.

My heart swells and the lightstone weighs on my neck. I walk straight through the room. Auras blister with envy, flaring with colour, and eyes pierce through me. I keep my course for the kitchen and stuff the last cheese roll into my mouth.

My aunties have dispersed with the rest of the food, leaving my mom alone in the kitchen. She turns as I set the platter down on the counter. Her eyes drop to my neck, a green glow glinting in her eyes. She gasps. "Did you—"

"No."

The wide saucers of her eyes shrink, and she shakes her head. "Thought she was waiting until Cassila's Registration."

The glow around my neck fades and the warm swell in my chest deflates with the rapid invasion of my heartbeat.

The enchanting rumble of my father's laugh spills into the kitchen. Mom glances behind her. Through the door, there's a straight sightline to her love. Dad takes a sip from his drink and his eyes shift to the kitchen. Mom's face sours. With a huff, she turns back to stacking dishes by the sink so we can wash them later.

"I know you still love him," I say.

"You know nothing of love, Eliote." Though her words are blunt, they sting like lemon juice in a cut.

"I can see it. Like really see it . . . in your aura." The words fluttered off my tongue so fast I'm not even sure if I said them clearly, or if I stuttered.

Mom plants a hand on her hip and rolls her eyes. "What in Vin's name are you talking about?"

"I-I can see auras, Mom." My face burns as I say it. Blood rushes through my head, I can barely think. "I've always been able to see them, but in the last year it's become stronger. I can see essence channels, too, and your spirit." My palms sweat damp patches into my dress. "I think your spirit is . . . it still loves dad. Maybe you can work—"

Mom smacks me across my face. My head whips to the side, and I stumble into the kitchen table with fire spreading over my cheek. The mix of a delayed shriek and a gasp bursts from my lungs.

"Those are not things for you to know," Mom says, the shake in her tone matches the shake in her hand still held in front of her. "You should only talk about things that Vin illuminates with light. My thoughts are not for you. Know your place." Her aura thickens and bubbles like a thick violet tar as her chest rises and falls.

Dad runs into the kitchen. "Silla, what happened?" His mouth hangs slack as his eyes dart between my hand on my face and his wife. A lock of purple hair falls into his face.

"I don't want to talk to either of you," Mom shouts.

Shock sends my father's eyes fluttering, his mouth sputtering.

Mom and I turn away from each other in unison and escape the kitchen through opposite doors.

Hot tears sting the welt.

I fit the part of good Luminee girl so well. I kept my hair long, never coloured, so it would always be purple. I studied law as an elective like my father and joined debate teams. My room is spotless, with jadenlily oil over a flame on my bedside table to fill the room with sweetness. Brass lanterns with intricate patterns hang from my ceiling, purple and gold bedding always washed and ironed every week. But none of this ever made my parents proud because they have to dim the lightstones in those lanterns for me every night.

The clamouring voices of my family swim into my room. My stomach churns, waiting for them all to leave, now eternally grateful for at least having that last roll.

Once the chaos has died down, I tie my hair in a tight bun on the top of my head and go back to the kitchen. A few of my aunties have stayed behind to clean up, my mom nowhere in sight.

"I'll finish them," I say.

They all continue cleaning and chatting with their backs turned.

"I said, I'll finish them," I shout.

They all jump, their aura prickling into jagged streams.

"Get out, I'll do it." I push my auntie out of the way and grab her apron as she fumbles to take it off.

I wash every pot, platter, crystal dessert plate, and silver fork. I wipe down all the counters and mop the floor. It's nearly ten o'clock. I've sweat salty stains into my dress and my hair is a mess.

As I put away the last of the dishes, I linger with a knife in my hand. The metal handle cools my skin. Moonlight streaks the silver blade. I spin the knife through my fingers, slash it through the air, and slam it down into a cutting board. The board cracks straight down the middle. The only time I have ever felt powerful was with a knife in my hand.

My fingers are wrinkled and sore, but I shove them in my pocket and pull out the Guardian application. In the light of the moon, I start filling it out.

Since I'm Luminee, I could apply to the school in Yugon but without enhancements there's no use getting special Luminee training. It would be farther away from my family though. Akinnera is only a few hours away from Tien Bay. To apply to an academy outside my province, I'd have to have exceptional entrance exam scores. So Akinnera it is then. I sign the application with an illegible signature.

In my bare feet I run out the door, down the black brick path, to the mailbox at the end of our road, all while clutching

Grandma's lightstone in my fist.

I pray to Vin, "Please give me the strength to do this." I drop the letter in the box.

5

RIN

IT'S BEEN A WEEK and I haven't filled in the application. I can't get my hands to write my name at the top. Each day my head is a little heavier, like a cloud is forming inside and I can't get it to dissipate. At school, the information I'm fed gets lost inside the cloud. At least at lunch hour my mind gets a rest.

"Rin."

My name splits the static in my mind.

"Rin."

"What?" I say, peeling my eyes away from my Guardian application.

Ace folds his arms on the table. "Think I lost you there for a second."

We sit outside the Senn public school at one of the tables in the courtyard. Our table. Ever since I broke his nose in athletics class five years ago, we've eaten lunch together at this table. Ace is across from me, a sandwich in front of him and fruit slices laid out in a glass container, packed lovingly by his mother. How she manages to take care of six kids is beyond me. Maybe it's because she got a good one like Ace who helps her out, no questions asked.

Pushing his black-rimmed glasses into place on his crooked nose, Ace sniffs and throws the hood of his sweater over his spikey, blue hair. "What's up?"

"Just thinking," I say.

"Have you eaten today?" Ace asks. His sweater has flowers on it, pink ones, which suit him. He's not the kind to adhere to one standard of masculinity. It makes him comfortable to be around.

"I have some dried spice-melon in my bag."

Ace tilts his head to the side and a frown shades his smooth brown skin. "The spiced-melon you've had in there for two weeks?"

"It's dried, it's fine." I pull my hair out of my face and knot it at the back of my head.

Chuckling, Ace hands me half a sandwich and slides my application in front of him. I bite into the sandwich as Ace takes my pen.

"What are you doing?" I say through a mouthful.

"You're going to eat that 'cause Nytrue never let anyone go hungry, and I'm going to fill this out for you. It's been a week since Registration, so you should've done it by now."

"Yeah, so shouldn't I do it myself?"

Ace shrugs. "I mean, I know most of the answers. I'll do that funny slanty thing you do with your letters so it looks like your writing. See?" He holds up the page with my name at the top. It's almost a perfect match for my writing. Except I didn't write it. My stomach drops.

Ace hunches over the paper, arms tucked into his sides as he fills in the information he knows. "Okay, Rinnaya Burgheim . . . Essence level four—"

"Shit, I never asked how your Registration went," I say, slapping my hand on my forehead.

With a groan and an exaggerated eye roll, Ace says, "I was thinking you forgot I was even enhanced."

"Stop, I feel bad." I give him a little kick under the table. "You were scheduled for the afternoon and I didn't get to see you that day. I've just been kind of out of it ever since."

"Yeah, yeah, make excuses." He chuckles. "No, I tested level four so I'm right up there with you."

"Of course you would test high. You're so good at everything."

Dipping his head to hide a grin, he taps the paper again. "How tall are you? Five foot seven?"

"Eight."

Behind Ace, Johanna pushes her way through a cluster of students. She tromps through the courtyard in a pair of black boots with thick soles. Plopping down at an empty table, she pulls out three containers from her bag. One looks like it holds fruit, the other vegetables, and the third maybe a keeta wrap. Johanna dips her head over her spread of healthy options and mumbles thanks to the ancestors. Raising her head, she glares at me, frizzy red ringlets bouncing around her face as she holds her pinky finger at me. I roll my eyes and turn back to Ace.

"I left the medical history and reason for applying for you to fill in." Ace slides the paper back to me and taps the pen on it. I take it and fold it over.

Out of the cover of the overhang is a puddle. A raindrop plips into the little pool, sending ripples through the water. Another drop, and another, and the water quivers like the earth is shaking and light moves along the surface. The soft plips form a song out of nothing and play no notes.

A hand waves in front of the singing mystery.

"Rin."

I turn to Ace. Eyes glued to me, sapphire-blue and piercing, he says. "Eat your sandwich, okay?"

I stuff the sandwich in my mouth. Letting it dangle, clamped in my teeth, I mumble, "I'm eating it."

Still with his eyes on me, he twists the silver stud in his earlobe. I drop my eyes to the application, my fingers starting to tingle. "Did you send in your application already?"

Looking past me and drumming his fingers on the table, Ace nods, a slow bob of his head over and over again. "I did. Took some convincing but I sent it in. Applied for Akinnera." He shrugs. "I'm going to do it. I think it will be good for me."

"What made you choose a Guardian Academy over Essence Academy and then advanced ed?"

His face lights up. "I thought about becoming a doctor like my dad, but I don't think that's really me. There's so much to learn out there, I could be happy anywhere. It's just hard to leave family."

I smile at him. His enthusiasm warms me a little. It will be strange heading away from Senn, away from our little table in the courtyard, but I guess he's right, there're things to learn.

"I need to do a few things before class," Ace says. You okay out here?"

"Yeah, I'll be fine. See you in class."

Ace smiles, dimpling his cheeks. He packs up and puts his foot on the bench to make sure his jeans are rolled up just right and his socks are straight. Each of his movements is precise. Purposeful.

My hands are heavy as I give each of my fingers a crack.

"Eat." He nods to the sandwich and turns away.

The chatter around me buzzes, drowning out the singing puddles. The five-minute bell chimes. I take a book out of my bag, the one I always bring with me, *Nolaria,* about a blind queen with both spirit affinities. My father gave it to me. I flip it open to store my application between the pages but stop to read the lines at the top of the page.

At night, her heartbeat woke her to a blood-red sight. At unprecedented hours of the day, her light enveloped her in blue. For weeks on end, all she saw was blue and red. Finally, once the deep troubles of her soul were on the surface, the lights shifted the dark world she had always known into shapes with meaning.

A pounding beat grips my heart as I read the words, but would it be enough to wake me?

I lift my head and no one is in the courtyard.

The soft song of water hitting water fills the air around me. I run my finger over the line of my application asking me why I want to be a Guardian. Me. Rinnaya Burgheim. I've always wanted it. Seeing Father filled with determination as he set out on missions always made me feel secure, even though he was leaving us. But is that it? Is that the only reason I want to become a Guardian?

I stare at the blank line. I want to fight . . . fight for . . .

others, my brother. I don't want . . .

I don't want to be here anymore.

Here. In this courtyard, this school.

What if I just didn't go back in?

My fingers, numb and shaking, button my jean jacket, stick my cap on my head, and sling my backpack onto my shoulders. And I'm running, straight out the school gate, half a sandwich stuffed in my pocket.

I run until I am downtown, my heart beating in a kinder fashion than when I was sitting stone still.

Should I even be out in public if I don't know when the affinities will show? Would they come out right here? In the middle of the city, under heavy clouds and gentle rain. Right here with gritty exhaust filling my lungs and someone's discarded underwear next to me on the curb. But Nolaria's heart woke her, and she was filled with light. All I'm filled with is tingling cold, fumes, and a heart that doesn't know the proper time to pick up.

My knuckles are white, the rest of my skin growing pink from cold. Heart beating, eyes open, and nothing. The small amount of light reaching this Carnity-forsaken city is muddied by my eyes like there's a dirty lens placed in front of them. And I can't breathe. At least not a full breath. Just small ones, quick and cold.

I shake my head. What is wrong with me? I should be in school, learning, getting good grades so I can be a good candidate for the Guardian program. Liam can't know I skipped. He can't know the things I do or the things I can't control, like crazy life and death affinities.

Grabbing the sandwich from my pocket, I chuck it on the ground by the dirty underwear. I pace back and forth, not knowing where to go. Stopping to stare at the store window, the words on the speckled glass register in my mind. **Powerstones, Potions, and Affinity Books.** Affinity books. That's what I need.

I grab the brass doorknob. I step through the door into a small shop with warped wooden slats creaking under my feet. The air in the room is weighty with the scent of powerstones and bushels of herbs hanging from the ceiling. In the centre of the room, stones of every colour are displayed on a table, sorted into roughly carved boxes with handwritten tags. Racks of jewellery line the cash desk in silver and gold, embedded with every kind of stone. Potions line the windows on glass shelves. The grey light from outside shines through them, morphing into blue, amber, and green glows like lights strung on a wire.

Making my way through the shop, my hands wander. My skin delights in the cold, smooth surface of a blue waterstone. The glow of a firestone the size of my palm radiates warmth over my reddened skin. The tips of creamy-white curestones the length and width of a finger shimmer in paper wrappings. I run my hand over them and the tips clack together.

At the back of the room, the wall is full of books. I rush over to them, careful not to hit any of the delicate items in the shop with my bag. The books are arranged by lineage affinity. Leather bindings spill the smell of knowledge into the earthy room. Tucked in the corner is a cubby just big enough for two Ironskin affinity books—one for physical affinity enhancements and one for spirit affinities.

Breath catches in my lungs as I pull the little black book from the shelf. Flaking gold Slyvic symbols mark the black leather with the life and death affinity. *Ee comtuyo en down comtuyo.* I crouch in the corner and spread the book open on my knees. The yellowed pages flutter under my hands, filled with all the symbols my mother taught me.

It's been a long time since I've studied Slyvic, so most of the book is a jumble of markings that I'll have to take time to decipher. But some words stand out. *Eeshna ownolada tens*—Angel Palm. *Deshna ownoloda tens*—Demon Palm. The ultimate abilities of the life and death affinities. Father told me about them when I was little. The same ache that filled me then seeps into my chest with each symbol. Air is trapped inside me, just like the meaning of these words. If I dig deep, maybe I can figure it out.

Minutes pass and the shop keeper tromps about the shop, cleaning, glancing at me, moving things around, glaring around corners.

Eeshna ownolada tens treyda ee tor pam keh odadown—Angel Palm sacrifices life for a person who is dead.

Is that really what it says? I run the words through my head, searching for other meanings, but I can't come up with anything and my armpits sweat and my face is hot. What about Demon Palm?

Deshna ownolada tens dentreyna ee—Demon Palm steals life.

Such simple phrases, but my head spins. I blink, trying to straighten out the symbols. Sacrificing and stealing life. How could I hold that kind of power inside me and not know about it? I snap the book closed with visions of my mother and brother flying through my head. Stephen is the only one who could help me understand this right now. But there's that weight in my stomach and the distance between us. He could have known that I might develop one of the affinities and still he didn't bother to show up, or even ask. It would be just more unwanted sickness in my gut to get his help. I'll have to figure out what the book says and that will be that.

I stand clutching the little book in both hands. On the glass shelf beside me is a silver bottle. A sleeping tonic. I take it and roll it over in my hand. For most, it provides some relief from insomnia, but for Ironskins it can be toxic, even deadly. But the little swirling letters don't describe its adverse effects. Drink this and I'd be dead like my mother. It would be easy, just drink and fall asleep.

My vision narrows on the bottle. The trinkets in the room fade into a sepia-toned wash around me and the only sound in the shop is the owner rummaging around in the back and my nails clicking against the glass as a tremble spreads through me.

"Find everything you needed?"

I jolt and drop the bottle. It clatters to the shelf, colliding with the other bottles, sending them rolling to the floor.

"Shit," I say under my breath. I turn to the shop owner, my eyes wide and body shaking. "I'm so sorry."

The burly man grumbles and crosses his arms above his belly. "I said, did you find everything you needed?"

"Yes." I nod and scurry to the checkout, flopping the book on the counter and holding out my Registration card to be scanned right away. The man swipes my card with hulking hands and plops the book into a paper sack.

I snatch my purchase and my card. With a final breath of the earthy shop, I barge out the door back into the grey drizzle.

Even though I don't make my way downtown much, I know where I am and there's only one place in this part of the city I want to go. I walk one block with the haze still around my eyes and chill in my bones. My feet tap on the sidewalk in a rhythmic beat, a calm sound to focus on, drowning out the noise of the traffic and the clutter of life and death symbols floating in my head.

I pull up to the gate of the ancestral shrine in the heart of Senn. The metal swings open with a groan. Pebbles crunch under my feet. The red panels are even more vibrant close up. Blue spiral patterns stream through the wood, and the tiles on the roof are blood red under the rain. Stubs of incense float in a puddle of water under a leak in the overhang. The puddle sings without melody. The building resembles those in the old Ironskin quarter. The quarter is gated off now, so people don't disrupt the "evil" energy left behind.

I want to go in. I want to see what's behind these doors.

Lifting my hand, I set it on the door handle.

There might be murals or memorabilia or books or something—something about Ironskin ancestry. Just something.

I press down on the handle. It doesn't budge. I press again and give it a jiggle. Trying the other side, a wave of cold washes down my neck, gripping my heart. I yank the handle and it tears away from the door.

The handle slips from my grasp. It hits the soggy wood with a thunk. Just like with Stephen and his barbed wire words, I'm locked out. But my feet can't run, they're stuck. The air around me is dead, the weight of my bag on my shoulders fades to nothing, and my body is a shell that holds nothing but the stagnant Senn air. I don't know where to go and I don't know why it's so hard to know the reason I want to be a Guardian or if I even do.

The rain sounds soaked into the top floor of our old house—just the sounds and none of the cold, at least when Father was home. I always thought it sounded like someone tapping their knuckles on the slanted roof.

I was eight years old. My teeth were brushed, I had my nightshirt on, and I slipped under my green, flowered quilt to wait for Father to come and say goodnight. Laying back on the pillow, I watched the rain splash on the window above my bed. On a clear night, the stars and the moon spilled light into the room, but that night I needed the little light on my night table. It had a round, fabric cover with flower cut-outs. It painted the pattern into the shadows of the room.

The rain-knuckles tapped the glass and my parents' voices joined in. In panicked bursts, Mother spoke words I couldn't make out. Father's low baritone carried into my room in incoherent murmurs. My stomach churned into knots. I clenched the quilt under my chin as I studied one of the gold flowers on the wall.

Mother's voice calmed. Father muttered a few more words to her and left with the sound of a kiss slipping through the night. He appeared from the shadows of the hall and said, "Ready for bed, Rinny?" He smiled at me and the bags under his eyes creased.

I nodded as he knelt by my bed, resting his calloused hand on my shoulder.

"How long will you be gone this time?" I asked.

"Well"—his head tilted to me, but his eyes looked away—"if all goes as planned, it should only be a week."

A flower glowed on his stubbly cheek. I pulled my hand from my covers and ran it over his scratchy skin. He cupped his hand around mine.

"Why did you become a Guardian?"

The tired shadows lifted from his eyes so they sparkled with their usual polished-silver colour. His lips parted in a smile. "Come with me."

Pulling the quilt away, he took my hand.

I shivered as we went downstairs, but he brought me into the light of the fire. We crouched down together, the fire warming my bare arms, and he pulled a book from the shelf. Wiping the dust off the cover with his sleeve, he said, "This is why."

I crawled into his lap to look at the book with him. "Who's Nolaria?" I asked as I ran my hand over the smooth gold letters of her name adorning the faded green cover.

"She was an ancient Ironskin queen."

My father flipped to a page in the centre of the book. On it, a woman stared back at me. She wore a crown of gold placed between black horns growing from her temples. Her eyes were clouded and blue, covered by a veil. Her long hair was snow white, her skin fair.

"Nolaria was born into royalty," Father said, and I leaned my head back against his chest. "But even with all the luxury around her, she was treated poorly because she was blind. Around this time, the life and death affinities were starting to appear. You remember what those are, Rinny?" I nodded, and he smiled down at me. "Well, at age seventeen, Nolaria manifested both affinities. She was forced to hide them from the public because they were viewed as a curse on the Ironskin nation."

The floorboards in my parents' room creaked above us. "A

curse?" I asked.

"No one knew how to control them, and many people got hurt and died. The ultimate abilities of these affinities played with life and death with a simple touch."

The words he spoke came into the amber-lit space with dry clarity. I lay my hands open over Nolaria's face, the knot in my stomach clenched tight. I never met my grandparents, or my mother's sister, or any other Ironskins except for Oron. How could our hands do so much?

"People were scared. Before, Ironskins had enhancements that gave our physical bodies strength, so they thought demons and fallen angels had possessed Ironskins and corrupted us." Father tapped his fingers on my palms, his voice hushed as the boards creaked again. Thunder rumbled outside. My father cleared his throat. "Nolaria's royal advisers thought it best to eliminate the affinities. But the only way for the affinities to go away was a ritual that required the blood of a dual affinity individual. The ritual would kill anyone with the affinities."

"The Death Ritual, like what happened in the Fourth Great War?" I asked.

"Exactly. And Nolaria went into her rule knowing she would have to sacrifice herself and her people to remove the affinities." Taking my hands and setting them on his knees, Father turned to the back of the book to a page more crinkled and stained than the rest. "She sought the council of an unenhanced woman named Renya, who could see the hearts and intentions of the people she met."

Pointing to the words for me to follow along, he read, "Renya said to Nolaria, 'Our skin is as strong as iron. The blood that flows through each of us unites us. Our hearts are stronger than any demon or angel. Do not give into the fear that surrounds you, Nolaria. You are not the demon. It is a powerful beast, but you are its master. You are not an angel. The angel is a manifestation of the goodness inside you. These affinities are gifts, not curses.'"

The fire crackled in the silence that fell over us. My father's chest lifted and fell.

"Nolaria took Renya's wisdom into her heart and was able to engage both affinities permanently, gaining her sight back through the life affinity and solid horns on her head through the death affinity. Her advisers were terrified of her. She told them there may be a time when we must take the fall for our strengths, but we who possess these blinding powers will not make that decision. Someone with clearer eyes will be appointed to keep the Death Ritual and advise on its proper use."

"Nolaria made Renya the first Keeper of the Death Ritual and set four guards to protect her. Nolaria and the Keeper taught the Ironskins with the life and death affinities how to gain control over their gifts. They taught kindness and hédin uniqueness as core values to guide her people to peace with themselves and the other lineages.

"But centuries after Nolaria's reign, her teachings were lost, the peace was lost, and fear grew. A feud began between the Ironskins and the Embersteads, both wanting power over the land. Our people used the life and death affinities in cruel ways. This led to the Fourth Great War where the Embersteads stole the Death Ritual to wipe out any Ironskin with death or life affinity.

"After the war, the Nine Lineage Summit for Union made changes to the Guardian system to be more inclusive and peace-focused by adding the role of Protectors. This is what Nolaria hoped for—all the lineages joining in community to make their lives among each other. It wasn't the way she wanted it to come, with so much loss. I joined the Guardians because even though our Ironskin Lineage was devastated, and we are treated badly, I can still protect the unity that has been started. I, like Nolaria, can look into the eyes of the people that mistreat me and be kind."

Father slid the book into my hands. "This book is yours now." He planted a kiss on my head. "You don't have to be a Guardian like me, but I hope Nolaria's story stays in your heart like it did for me."

My eyelids drooped as I wrapped my arms tight around the book. The warmth of the fire, my father's arms around me, and the knowledge of his good heart sunk inside me, but it didn't shift the dread I had of him leaving. It didn't bring me closer to my ancestors because all I had now were more questions.

Carrying me back up the stairs, Father hummed a melody I didn't recognize, and I clung to the book, my head on his shoulder. I drew in a breath. His shirt smelled of something musty, something I had never smelled on him before, something he picked up on a mission he'd returned from just that day. He lay me in bed, and I kept my eyes open enough to look into his eyes that had taken on the tired dullness again. They were strange. He was strange.

After tucking the covers under my chin, he stayed on his knees by my bed. Looking off into the shadows, he said, "Rinny, we must remember that our people did wrong in the past. We also cannot forget that it was wrong for the Emberstead to use the ritual. It's important that I am a Guardian because it allows me to bridge gaps between people by protecting and serving them. Does that make sense?"

I nodded, settling into the warmth of my bed.

"I do my job to protect all of us. And I want you to know that I'll always come back. I never choose to stay away. I choose to come back," he said, and he turned out the light.

6

J O H A N N A

I WOKE UP THIS MORNING WITH ONE THOUGHT. Something bad happened last night. But what? It's just a feeling, stupid. Maybe it was in a dream and it's just dampening my mood. But it stayed at the back of my mind. So, I came down to the garage to train.

The music blares, my muscles ache, and I've worked up a good sweat after an hour of training.

Something's wrong.

Despite burning lungs, I push hard to get just a few more reps in. I pound my fists into the bag as hard as I can, focusing to get my form right, pushing the thought from my mind.

The door to the garage swings open.

"Johanna," Mom screams over the music. She turns the volume down. "Honestly. This music's going to repel your father's spirit." Shaking her head, she turns back to the nook just inside the house. She adjusts the position of the ruby-red firestone next to Dad's ashes and caresses the frame of his picture.

A drop of sweat trickles down my neck, making me itch just like her comment about Dad.

"I can't drive you to school today, so get going. And for Zenta's sake, breathe while you hit that thing."

Her voice hits a shrill note above the noise that stings my ears. Out of the corner of my eye, I catch her frown. It digs in my gut as she crosses her arms.

"Johanna, now." She throws her hands in the air. "Honestly, the essence inside you must be cold," she mutters as she leaves.

The door slams behind her. I train every day. And each weekend since Registration, we've worked on Mind Fire together—no more barfing fiascos. She could at least be proud of my dedication, just once.

My fists drop and I turn off the music. Bent over my knees, panting and shaking, I get a moment of peace. Even with the core-energy hub in the corner humming in rhythmic tones, the quiet is intense. It washes over me, relaxing my mind—it's the best feeling in the world. Sometimes a fight's the only way to get some peace.

Sitting down between Mom's rusty blue cruiser and Dad's old speeder, my heart rate slows. Sweat cools on my back. Without much thought, my hands slide the broken speeder parts we never got to replace back under the sheet.

Mom yells from the kitchen. "You're not a Warrior yet, princess. Get to school."

"I'm *going*," I yell back.

I storm up to my room, legs burning with each step. I pull clean clothes over my sweaty body, stuff my feet into the chunkiest boots I own, and throw on Dad's old Protector jacket adorned with a pin that says "I hate everyone" on the front pocket. Just offensive enough. I think Dad would have liked it.

Grabbing my backpack, I hide my acceptance letter to the Akinnera Academy for Guardian Training in the safety of the front pocket where Mom can't find it. She'll get too excited and won't stop talking about it, or she'll bust my butt, making me train harder. Throwing the bag over my shoulder, I make to leave but turn right back around. She'll be pissed if I don't clean up. So, I make my bed, fold the blush-pink throw blanket at the end, straighten my Ascension trophies on my desk, and make sure my tech games are put away. Hopefully that will satisfy her.

I run back downstairs. In the kitchen, Mom pours herself a cup of coffee. Ready for work in her smart, black pantsuit, her hair is pulled back tight, and her eyeliner is just right. I tromp through the kitchen to the coatrack and she turns. I avoid her eyes as I put on my puffy coat. Expecting some weight from my port-gamer, I jam my hand in the pocket only to grab a half eaten weckler-nut Muncho Bar.

"Mom, have you seen my port-gamer? I thought I left it in here."

Moving into the living room with her close behind me, I turn over the couch cushions and check behind the quilted, red pillow on the chair, the only piece of decoration in the room.

"Johanna, you don't need that thing at school."

"It's not like I use it in class."

She turns away from me, sipping her coffee. "I don't want to get into this right now. You need to focus on your studies, not your tech games."

It takes every lick of energy to keep my shit together. I bite the inside of my cheek and let out a heavy sigh before grabbing the doorknob.

"Johanna, lunch," Mom says, holding a brown paper sack out to me. I snatch it with a roll of my eyes.

Her manicured fingers catch the sleeve of my coat before I can slip out the door. "I love you, princess," she says, and pats my cheek. I head out the door, but as I walk away, she adds, "Do something with your hair before you get to school, would you?"

I wave a hand in the freezing air to let her know I heard her without looking back.

Something bad happened.

I guess the adrenaline has worn off and it's back to this nonsense in my head. Entertaining the ridiculous thought, I pull out my echo to check the news. Scrolling through articles, there was a cruiser chase on the east side, no one was hurt, but nothing seems out of the ordinary, for Senn at least.

My foot skids over a patch of ice. "Shit." I flail my arms and catch myself on a lamp post, just shy of landing on my ass.

Hands still clenched around the pole, I catch my reflection in a store window. I sigh, fogging the air. My baby hairs spray out around my head like kinky, red sunbeams. I pull out the elastic and shake my hair. Now I look like a beast with a hangover, but I don't have time to fuss with it.

I get to the school yard and pass a group of girls from my Ascension team. They stare at me, the same way they've looked at me since first-year ed—like they're better than me. But they're not, just prettier. One of them flicks a cigarette butt in the snow in front of me. "Hey, Kingsman," she says. "You hear about the cutch and Tōmas?"

Rin and Tōmas? What would she be doing with that asshole?

A rumour probably, just leave it alone. But what if something bad happened to Rin? Jaw canted, I turn on my heel.

"Heard they did it at some party last night. Whole school's talkin' about it."

"Yeah? What party, Nala?" I ask.

Nala kicks the snow at me. "Don't know."

"So, you weren't invited?" I smirk. "Looks like Rin's becoming more popular than you."

The other girls cackle.

Nala scowls, tongue in cheek. "Yeah? Pretty impressive how the cutch can get dick and you can't, eh, Kingsman?"

Rolling my eyes, I turn away. Soon I'll be rid of them. Soon I'll be in Akinnera where I can start over, start something new and meaningful and not full of shit like their stupid, toxic gossip. Rin and Tōmas. It's ridiculous but specific, and Tōmas is way too popular to just let anyone say anything about him. What kind of shit did Rin get her dumb ass into this time?

At the door, a Local Protector checks my bag for firestone rifles, knives, Ease, and any other drugs. All the LP finds is my acceptance letter.

"AAGT. Congratulations," he says. "Good school."

I grit my teeth as the prick handles the letter—my ticket out of this rotten place. Away from my mom, away from him and the teachers who don't give a damn, away from the jerks and the bitches with their silky hair and makeup-plastered faces.

I grab the letter, pushing past him.

Cheap perfume, body odour, and the distinctive musk of water-damaged walls smothers me—a hostile scent to carry the rumours. It churns in my stomach. If only I could use that as an excuse not to come—allergic to school and all hédin in Illyson.

The bell rings just as I get to class. I barge through the door and let it slam behind me.

"Johanna." My teacher raises his eyebrows, glaring at me over the rim of his glasses. "Take a seat so we can begin."

There's only one seat available in the very back by Rin. She's like a ghost sitting behind our warmer-skinned classmates. If she was a few shades darker and her shoulders weren't so wide and boney, if she had some resemblance of a woman's figure—a cup size bigger maybe—she might be considered a catch and that rumour might actually make sense. Ignoring the disease of whispers spreading through the class, she hides her small nose in a book, her lips pressed and mousy-blond hair hanging around her narrow face for extra shelter.

"Don't get too close, Johanna, the slut might steal your soul," a kid to my left snickers as I sit beside Rin.

It's been months since Registration and these jokers are still going on about Rin's life and death affinity. It started as a rumour, but Rin confirmed it herself to try and shut them up. A lot of good that did.

"Mind your own damn business," I say.

Rin's weepy, grey eyes glance up at me. She flips a page of the book. As much as I try to resist it, I get a foul urge to talk to her. I need to know which school she got accepted to. A pain at the back of my head tells me I already know where she'll end up.

The teacher starts the lesson. My knee jiggles under the desk.

"Rin," I whisper.

Her head twitches in my direction.

"Did you get in?" I ask.

"'Course I did, the physical exam was a breeze," she mutters. "You?" She pushes her hair behind her ear and the ice in her eyes shifts to examine me.

"Please, like I'd let you get out and leave me in this dump. Which academy?" I write the title of the lesson in my notebook.

Her lips tighten into a thin line.

"Rin?"

She taps her fingers on her desk, flips another page of her book and mumbles, "Akinnera."

"Damn it, Rin," I say through my teeth. "I told you to go freeze in fucking Aria."

"Why wouldn't I go to the academy in our province? It's the closest to Liam."

My head buzzes, trying to find something to prod her with, to avoid the fact that I knew she wouldn't go far from Liam. I should have packed my bags with snow boots and sweaters and set my sights for Aria the moment I found out about their open admission. My grades are good enough and my entrance exam scores were top notch. Aria would have taken me. I don't know why I didn't apply, but I couldn't shake the feeling that Akinnera is where I'm supposed to be.

"And you're just leaving Liam by himself? Some sister you are," I say.

"I'm not leavin' him alone. I'm leavin' him with Oron." She raises her voice a little. The teacher glances in our direction.

"He's probably better off with Oron anyway."

"What'd you say?"

"The kid needs an adult, not a screwed-up teenager taking care of him."

"Screwed-up teenager? You're one to talk." Her South-Senn accent thickens, each word a sharpened version of itself. Mom brutally trained my tongue against this "lazy way of speaking."

"Come again?" I push back and get out of my seat. Stop, Johanna, you don't need to pick this fight today. Ugh, but she drives me crazy.

"Maybe if you had some proper parenting, you'd know when to mind your own business," Rin says, rising from her chair.

"Ladies, please, this is not the place," our teacher says.

"Yeah, Johanna. This isn't the p—"

I draw my arm back and throw my fist at her dainty face. She slams into the wall behind her.

What the hell am I doing?

The class jeers and the teacher yells for everyone to settle down.

"That all you got?" Rin leaps over her desk.

I sprint to the door and into the hallway. I ready myself. The second she rounds the corner, I swing my leg, but she ducks right under it. As I regain my footing, Rin launches toward me. Both her feet leave the ground to collide with my stomach. The air jets from my lungs and I'm sent tumbling all the way to the other end of the hall. I roll and get back on my feet.

"Bitch," I yell. My fists burst into flame, but before I can launch a fireball at her, my hand is frozen and falls heavy by my side.

Back at the other end, Rin stands with her arms crossed and her feet encased in ice. Rin's Nytrue friend, Ace, stands at the ready between me and Rin. His frosted hand outstretched in case I try something.

Our teacher comes out into the hall, his face red and his eyes furious. "All of you. Principal's office. Now."

The three of us sit side by side in the principal's office waiting for our parents to arrive. My shoulders ache from hitting the ground. The skin of my stomach pinches where Rin's feet dug into me. I pull up my shirt to inspect the bruise already forming over my abs. Ace glances at me, then rolls his eyes, looking away.

I thought that maybe, if I got away from Senn, I would find some peace in myself. If I had some time apart from Mom, our relationship would be better. Maybe if I got away from Rin, we could start over the next time I saw her. I could be my own person for a while, have my space.

Ace huffs and leans forward, resting his elbows on his knees. "You guys are going to kill each other before you even get to the academy," he says.

"Look, why don't you just stay out of it next time," I say.

"No. I'm sick of seeing you beat on my friend like she's a punching bag."

"I can take care of myself, Ace," Rin mumbles on the other side of him. "Don't worry about it."

I glance back at Ace. His eyebrows furrow above his glasses. "Whatever." He sighs and leans back in his seat. "I just don't want to peel you off the ground the next time Johanna takes a stab at your weak spot, like that time in athletics class."

I grip the arms of my chair, picking the wood with my nail. Ace jiggles his knee. I swear if Mom doesn't get here in the next five minutes, I'm just walking out. Never coming back here. Never.

Ace's knee stops jiggling, and he slaps his palms on his legs. "So, is it true? Did you sleep with Tōmas Leeman?"

I peer around Ace. Rin looks straight ahead with dead eyes, lips slightly parted, hands limp on her lap, like his question didn't even reach her ears. The clock ticks. She swallows. Her dark eyebrows draw together. "So what if I did?"

The emptiness in her tone drills into me. An inexplicable ache grows in my gut. I just know she didn't. They're making fun of her again. For the hundredth, thousandth time. For no good reason.

"They shouldn't be talking about it either way," Ace says.

A shiver jerks through me. All the fire that burned in Rin before our fight has fizzled out somehow. Somewhere between now and then the flame just vanished and nothing touches her. Was it the comment about Tōmas? Something bad really did happen.

It's her problem. Whatever is going on, she'll deal with it. If I'm going to keep my admission to Akinnera, I can't let this happen again. Just stay away from Rin and I'll be fine. Her eyes never see me anyway, so I'll keep my eyes down too. I just don't understand why I knew.

7

RIN

Spring crept up on me too fast. It sets in to warm the air, to melt away the frozen winter, but it can't melt the last four months. Like shadows hanging over me, they crawl on my skin with blurry images that I can barely remember, and some I refuse to think of. They clutch my heart in a grip of dread and regret. It's like I have been dreaming the whole time. Each day dragged on, and still, spring caught me off guard.

I can't lose this day like the rest.

Tomorrow I'll leave for the academy and Liam will stay behind. So, I take his hand. I squeeze it, memorizing the way each finger lines up between mine. I blink a few times, focusing on the world around me. Liam holds a smile on his face as his attention is caught between looking ahead to dodge people coming toward us and watching out for puddles. The sun has set, prompting the neon signs to flicker to life one by one as we walk to the grocery store to stock the icer with food for when Oron isn't able to cook for them.

I have to leave these months here, right here, right on this curb, like they didn't happen.

Liam tells me about his day at school. Each event from the time he got up this morning to this very moment is accounted for. The smallest detail becomes an epic adventure, and I stash his little stories in my heart like they are precious gems.

Thunder rolls overhead. It starts to rain as if the ancestors are crying for the people who live in this awful place. I stop to pull up Liam's hood. He grabs mine and has to jump a little to flip it over my head.

Liam presses closer to me. The tale-telling smile is gone, replaced by a flicker of neon green on his nose.

"I'm fine, Liam," I say, wrapping my arm around his shoulders.

Lifting his chin to look at me, his blue eyes are wide, and rain speckles his face—I tug his blue hood forward. He keeps watch of me for a few strides until his brow crinkles and he squints his eyes. "No, you're not. Tell me." He pokes me in the ribs.

I don't have the heart to spill all my worries on him. He doesn't need to know that I'm scared out of my mind and so nervous I could throw up. It's already unfair of me to leave him, even if it's law. He shouldn't have to be alone. For Carnity's sake, he shouldn't have to worry about having groceries in the house. He needs someone to wake him up for school and make him breakfast. He needs me to kiss him on the head and make him feel loved. But jobs are scarce here. I'll never find anyone to take a chance on me with only an Essence Academy diploma, and advanced ed is too expensive—what would I even study? Joining the Guardian forces is the only way for me to finish my education and save up some money. It's what I've always wanted, I just wish I could be excited about it.

The only thing I can say is, "I love you. You know that right?"

Liam smiles and sighs like it's foolish of me to think I could hide my feelings from him. I must have some sort of tell he can pick up on. I try so hard to keep my face neutral or smile to reassure him that everything is fine, but maybe he can feel the tension in my back with his arm around me, or he sees my posture change.

"I'm gonna be okay," he says, nodding. "Ya know why? Because I *do* know you love me."

Whatever he picks up on, I can't hide it, and his quick attempt to exterminate my fears soothes the ache in my stomach. We split apart for just a second to manoeuvre around a puddle, but we stick right back together.

"I'll be fine with Oron. I like being with him. Besides, you can't stay here," he says.

"What d'you mean?"

"You're too big for this place." He spreads his arms wide and jumps out in front of us. With his arms flailing, he becomes the one people have to watch out for. I pull him back to me before he hurts someone.

"Too big, huh?" I say through a laugh that slips off my lips and relieves tension from my chest.

"You can barely sit still through meals. You always wander to the window like you're looking for something. I know you're worried about me, but it's kinda stupid to keep a bird in a cage.

You gotta fly." He flaps his elbows. "You gotta go."

"Thanks, bud." I give him a quick squeeze. "How'd you get so smart?"

He shrugs his shoulders and gives me a goofy grin. The grin and his flappy arms reassure me he's not going to lose his joyful spirit easily. He's still just a kid.

Liam shoots out ahead of me again to swish his hands in a wide motion to make the automatic doors to the grocery store slide open. My feet slow with the rain weighing on me. He should be the one to see the world. Delight in simple things like automatic doors is the kind of spirit you want to explore new places, not the spirit to be stuck in this city that is better suited to be Dien's shit hole than home.

Someone shoves me from behind and I stumble through the doors to catch up to Liam who has already grabbed himself a shopping cart. An electro bell sounds. White light assaults my eyes. Chatter and beeping from a checkout counter swim around my ears.

"So, what're we buyin'?" I say, setting my hands on Liam's shoulders.

He steers me through the aisle stocked with snacks. Crouching down to examine packages of cookies, he flips his hood back leaving a trail of water droplets on the ground, and murky water pools under his feet.

"Rinnaya, grab a bag of fire-pepper crunchies," he says as he debates between two varieties of sweets.

The crackle of the packaging in Liam's hands pricks my ears over the drone of blips and conversation around me. "You don't like fire-pepper crunchies."

"Yeah, but you do. You should have some for your trip

tomorrow."

My heart picks up a thudding beat that radiates through my body, and all the tension I lost on the way over seeps back in. "Right," I say with a sharp breath. I turn on my heel, backtracking down the aisle to the crunchie section.

The shiny orange plastic bag sits on the shelf with numerous other bags of all different colours. I grab the bag of crunchies, and it squeaks between my fingers. Chills snake down my spine, one after another. My eyes narrow on the awful orange, the rest of the colours blurring around it. A song plays in my head, upbeat with a steady base, and pushes away all other sounds. The song that played the night I lost my taste for fire-pepper crunchies. And in this moment, that night doesn't seem so dreamlike.

I'm right there in the dingy wreck room, music pounding, dim light surrounding me turning everything red and shadows more intense. Crunchie dust covers my fingers, cold fills my lungs.

Shit. I can't think about this. I have to let it go.

I shake my head and turn back to Liam. But Liam isn't examining cookies, and the cart is gone.

"Liam?"

Still clutching the bag, I hurry down the aisle and into the next, but he isn't there either, only packages of noodles. I grab a few and go to the next row. A cruiser roars outside, tires squeal to a halt. Beyond the shelves stocked with bottled sauces and oils, three men in black leather stomp into the store, each with a firestone rifle. My heart skips a beat.

A trail of watery footprints turns into the next aisle. I scurry along the trail. Liam holds open the door of an icer, perusing the options. I grab him by the coat and slap my hand over his mouth.

As I pull him out of the long corridor of frozen foods to duck behind the safety of the shelves, he squawks behind my fingers.

My pulse pounds in my ears.

Liam presses into me. "What's happening?"

"Shh, don't talk."

There's a click—a firestone locking into place. Holy Carnity, they're going to shoot. A zapping sound stings the air as a rifle charges. Ice plunges through my veins. Screams erupt from the front of the store, tearing my eardrums.

A blast explodes from the front, glass shatters, footsteps pound the grungy tiles.

"Get back," a man yells.

My fingers clench Liam's coat, stitches at the seams bust under my nails.

What is happening? Are they coming down the aisles?

Pulling Liam away from the sightline, I peek around the corner. The blue of a Nytrue man's hair assaults my vision. The leather of his jacket scrunches together as he holds a smoking rifle to the cashier's head. The cashier cringes, tears running down his blanched face. Two shoppers huddle on the floor with quivering lips, eyes entranced, unblinking, fixed on the rifle.

"Give me the money. Give me the fuckin' money," the gunman yells, spit flying.

The cashier quivers, Liam's body is rigid in my grasp, my breaths quick and aching. The rifle smoke twists down the aisle and fills my nose with an acrid stench. My stomach clenches.

The cashier opens his mouth. A whimper escapes. A bullet blasts from the rifle.

Crimson blood ejects from the cashier's head. His eyes roll back into the abyss of his own skull.

"Hells of Dien," a woman screeches. A splatter of blood strikes her clothes.

Vomit creeps up my throat as the cashier's limp body doubles over and thuds on the dirty floor. I whip my head back behind the shelf. Liam's tears stream down my fingers, still clamped around his mouth. He shakes in my grasp, and I press my lips to the top of his head as the till is cracked open and other shoppers whimper.

A shadow spills over me and Liam. Metal presses against my back, digging into my weak spot. Hot breath slithers over my ear. "It would be a shame for our operation to go down just because some bitch snitched to the LPs." The voice growls and his putrid breath suffocates me with tobacco and rot.

My mind is a void, thoughts nonexistent. All I know is the unrelenting pressure of the rifle against my most vulnerable skin and the prickle of tears in my eyes for my most valuable gift in my arms.

The rifle clicks.

My eyelids fall, trapping the tears.

Every inch of fabric is like sandpaper on my skin, the ground is solid beneath my feet. Blood rushes through me. I am more aware of every muscle tensing at the ready than I have been in my entire life. The cool of ice and static fills my body. My eyes fly open, bursting with light.

The world is bleached in blue. My heart thumps. Hostile energy crackles through every cell in my body, gripping my muscles. It thrashes through me, bursting to life, and solidifies into brilliant wings. As the rifle cracks, the wings bash into the vile man behind me, absorbing the blow.

My wings move without command. They demolish

everything in their path. The lights above spark and go dark, but my vision locks onto every detail of my surroundings.

"Rin," Liam cries, but his voice is drowned by the thrum of energy.

Muscles trembling, I try to get my body and the energy to connect with my mind, but they are on different planes of existence. Every effort works against me. A cry escapes my lips, ripping into the vivid new world. Every part of me is buried under the unyielding, selfish energy syphoning my essence into colossal wings.

Rifle shots blast down the aisle. The ground rumbles, glass shatters, and dust fills my lungs as my wings barge through the surroundings to encircle me and Liam. Bullets ricochet off the featherlike shards of energy.

The pressure of this otherworldly essence pulses on us and Liam's body goes limp. A streak of red slips from his nose. Horror crashes in my heart and I scream for this insatiable ghost to release its grip on me. I plunge to my knees, wrapping my body around Liam to protect him from my monstrous wings. My life affinity.

Ripples of energy wash over Liam's face, and a small red slit appears on his forehead. Tears burn in my eyes as I press my trembling hands over his face.

"Keena." The desperate cry for my ancestor's help is swallowed in sobs.

I cradle Liam on my lap, his head on my shoulder, my fingers gripped in his hair.

I exhale.

My wings fracture. Shards of light stream toward me like sharpened daggers that fade to nothing back at my core.

The piercing blue light remains in my eyes, it illuminates every hair on Liam's head, reveals every movement of his chest as he breathes, but leaves the blood on his face an angry ruby red.

Heavy tread approaches, debris crunches. The ghost compels my body. I drop Liam, I'm on my feet and my hands snatch the rifle from the criminal.

The rifle goes off, blasting a hole at my feet.

I swing the butt at his face. It smacks his jaw. His body twists and collides with the ground.

The man who shot the cashier leaps over a fallen shelf, rifle trained on my face. The firestone zaps and sparks explode from the barrel. The bullet slams into my shoulder.

"Die, you fucking cutch," he screams, face twisting with disgust to bare his teeth and narrow his eyes.

With two strides, I close the gap between us. I suck in a breath through gritted teeth and slam my fist to his face. His mug contorts, whipping to the side as he tumbles back, unconscious.

My arms fall limp at my sides. The light is gone, shunting me back to reality with muted colours, destruction surrounding me, and four unconscious bodies, including my brother. I turn to Liam, breaths heavy, knees weak, eyes clouding. I blink to clear them.

I scoop Liam into my trembling arms. He needs help. But the hospital is too far. Ace's dad is a doctor, and they don't live too far away. Maybe he can help, he has to.

I stumble through the wreckage into the pouring rain. A cruiser splashes water from a puddle over my legs, shocking my system. LP sirens wailing in the distance spur me into a sprint before I'm slapped with more than a fine for public essence manipulation.

A block away from the scene, my heart still pounding, I take a deep breath to calm myself. But the darkness of the street swims around me, the cashier's blood with it. It weighs on me and stirs in my gut.

What if I could have helped that man?

My stomach spasms. I slap my hand over my mouth to stifle a gag. Bracing myself with a lamppost, I wait for the waves of nausea to pass. The heavy thud of the dead man pricks my mind. His eyes. Screaming. Was that me or the other woman?

What if I had done something the instant I saw the three men come in? Liam might not have gotten hurt. That man might not have died.

I turn onto Ace's street and sprint as fast as I can, bracing Liam close against my chest.

I have to get to the academy, and I can't come back until I can control this power. Liam can't be around me.

Every light in Ace's house is on. I stumble up the porch steps into the buttercup-yellow glow spilling from the window in the door. My hair is soaked, and strands stick to my cheeks.

Liam stirs in my arms.

"It's okay, buddy. We're going to get you some help."

He moans into my shoulder.

"I know, I know, I'm so sorry." I kiss the scrape on his forehead. "I'm so sorry."

Switching him into one arm, I press the doorbell. It rings into the cold. No one comes. I press it again and again so the rings collide. "It's okay, buddy."

I peer through the window. Ace trots down the steps. Unable to wait any longer for him to open the door, I grab the handle and barge into his home.

"Is your dad here?" I ask as Liam's hand squeezes my arm.

"Yeah, yeah everyone's home. What's going on? What happened to Liam?"

"I . . . I need your dad to look at him." My head spins, trying to find the words to describe what happened. "There uh . . . there was a robbery, we got caught . . ." A blip of energy courses through my body and I press my eyes shut, swallowing hard to push it away.

The sound of footsteps on the stairs fills my ears. Glasses clink in the kitchen.

"I um, the uh . . . wings. And there were men with firestone rifles. They shot at us, so I wrapped them around me . . ."

"Rin, slow down, take a breath." Ace sets a hand on my shoulder, and I open my eyes. His other hand sits on Liam's head.

I stare at Ace's eyes, wide with worry. His hair is pushed up on one side and he wears a baggy sweater and sweatpants. He's trying to relax and get ready to leave for the academy tomorrow. I'm messing everything up.

Ace's dad makes it to the last step. "What's going on?"

I step around Ace. "Mr. Dalaan, can you help Liam? He got knocked out by my . . . my uh . . ."

"Your life affinity?" Ace asks behind me.

"Yes." Tension clenches my spine. My heart just keeps drumming and drumming, and I can't make it stop no matter how many breaths I take.

Mr. Dalaan's heavy eyebrows pull together. Pushing up his sleeves, he says, "It's going to be all right. Let's take him into my study. May I?" He reaches to take Liam from me. I search his eyes with my jaw clenched and arms shaky with coursing blood. His eyes are much darker than Ace's, midnight blue with flecks of gold. They hold my gaze steadily.

I nod, expelling a breath caught in my throat, and transfer Liam into Mr. Dalaan's arms.

"Rinnaya," Liam says in a small voice like he's just woken up from a nap—the worst nap in the entire history of naps.

I open my mouth to speak but no words come out. What can I say that I haven't already said?

"Liam, we're just going to do a few tests in my office, okay?" Mr. Dalaan says, taking Liam through his office doors. The room is lit by a lightstone lamp, creating a warm glow that spills over a leather couch and shelves full of books and pictures of every member of the Dalaan family.

"My head hurts," Liam says.

Mr. Dalaan sets Liam down on the couch and kneels beside him. "I'm sure it does. Your sister is a very strong young lady." He turns to face me. A smile tugs on his lips. He nods. "I don't think we need to worry too much, but we'll check everything out."

From the kitchen, Ace's mom appears, a glass of red wine in her hand and her light-blue hair tied in a messy bun on the top of her head. "Honey, just come and warm up, okay?"

I clasp my hands around the collar of my coat, still watching Mr. Dalaan shine a light in Liam's eyes. A drop of water skitters down my neck. From one of the rooms upstairs, a baby cries. The pitiful sound triggers my memory with the noise that escaped my lungs as I tried to control the energy ripping from my body. I did scream, and I hate it.

"Ace, would you get Krish?" Mrs. Dalaan says.

"Yeah," Ace says, his voice quiet.

Mrs. Dalaan shrugs as Ace climbs the stairs. "He's the only

one who can get Krish to sleep these days." She sets her wine down on top of a cubby full of shoes. "Let's get that wet coat off and go sit down in the living room."

"I'd rather just stay . . ." I point to the office.

"Girl, you are dripping all over my clean floor and if I have to clean up after another hédin today, so help me I will flood the place." The few wrinkles around her eyes deepen, but she smiles and waves her hand in a playful flourish.

She takes my coat to hang it over one of her daughters' tiny pink rain jackets as I remove my shoes. With both her hands on my shoulders, she steers me into her living room. The overhead lights are off, leaving the many candles scattered throughout the room to supply the light. Heat envelopes me. Blue and white tapestries hang on the walls and a cream-coloured rug fills the entire floor. Mrs. Dalaan's oldest son lies on the couch in the glow of his echo.

"Arav, up." She slaps his feet. "Go check on the twins please."

Arav's eyes flutter away from the screen, and he hoists himself off the couch.

"Sit, hon."

I do as she says, taking a seat at the edge of the couch. The candle on the table next to me crackles, flickering light over the armrest, and a woodsy smell lingers in the air around me mixed with its heat. I breathe it in with hope that it will calm my senses, but each flash of light sends tension into my fingers, and I dig them hard into my knees. Ace hasn't come back down, and Mr. Dalaan's deep voice murmurs softly to Liam.

"Liam is going to be fine, Rin." Mrs. Dalaan crouches in front of me.

She holds her cardigan closed with one hand and rests the

other on my knee. I tuck my knees together and her hand falls away.

"It's common for essence bursts to knock people out. He'll be ready to go in no time." The candlelight is warm on her light-brown skin and a smile brightens her face even more. Every word she speaks is trusting, in herself, her past experiences, in her husband maybe. They fill me with calm that is heavy and uncomfortable as it washes over my tight muscles, melting my grip on my knees with its unprecedented gentleness.

I turn away from her, back to the hall. Ace comes down the stairs with his baby brother nestled on his shoulder. Mrs. Dalaan pats my knee and leaves the room. Ace stands in the middle of the carpet, swaying and patting Krish on the back.

"What happened?" he asks.

I stare at my socked feet, toes scrunching into the creamy carpet. "I guess"—my voice cracks and I clear my throat—"the life affinity just decided to come out and I couldn't control it."

"Are you okay? Like do you feel sick or anything?" Ace asks. His voice is hushed, and he tilts his head away from Krish's ear.

"I'm fine," I say.

Shadows dance with the light at Ace's feet as he sways back and forth. He's quiet for a while. Liam's voice slips in from the other room as he answers questions. Taking a long breath, Ace steps closer to me.

"Are you ready to go to the academy?"

"Yes," I say right away. "I have to. I have to learn how to control this."

Ace sighs. "Mom." He hands Krish off to Mrs. Dalaan. Sitting down next to me he says, "I'm not talking about tonight." The muscles in his neck twitch as he swallows. "I'm talking about two months ago."

The song starts its loop in my head again, echoing through all my dreamy memories. "I'm fine."

"Rin, come on." He leans his elbows on his knees.

"I told you I didn't want to talk about that night."

"It plays over in my head every day. I could have lost y—"

"I have to let it go." I stand, wrapping my arms around myself, and pace. "I have to. Somehow, I have to be over it or else . . ." I shake my head. "I just have to be."

"Maybe I'm not over it."

It's as if every candle in the room dims. My vision narrows in on one spot of the carpet. A slow breath parts my lips and static fills my head. Nothing from that night should have happened. I should have stayed in my apartment. Ace shouldn't have those memories torturing his mind.

I pull my cloudy eyes away from their anchor on the ground. Ace runs both hands over his face. My stomach drops.

"Whatever happened in these last months has to stay here," I say. "I . . . all I want is for this place to be safe, safe for Liam. I want this city, this place I grew up, to be a place where people can go to the grocery store and buy cookies in peace."

Ace lowers his hands so they just cover his mouth while he listens to me rant.

"I want people to be able to walk into an ancestral shrine and find the answers they're looking for. And I can't do that until I have a Guardian badge and control over my own essence."

My throat constricts, bringing my string of incoherent rambles to a crashing halt. I hold myself as still as possible. In the hall, Mr. Dalaan helps Liam put his coat back on. Liam has a smile on his face. I can't let the prickle of tears in my eyes undo me again. I have to find the pieces of a smile for him. Just a little smile for Liam.

"Okay," Ace says. He's up and he wraps his arms around me even though mine are still tight around my middle. His lemongrass scent fills my lungs. "Then that's what you'll do, and I'll be there with you."

I want to grab onto his words and feel his hug sink into me, but something inside resists. I stay stone still until he lets go. Giving him a quick nod, I pull my frown into a smile without meeting his eyes.

Liam rushes in, and I stretch my smile even wider as he catches me in a hug. "He says I'm going to be just fine, and he gave me some candy," Liam says.

"I'm so glad you're okay. I'm sorry this happened, buddy."

"Rin," Ace says. "We'll be driving to the academy tomorrow, why don't you just ride with us?"

I grab my coat from the crowded rack. "I already have a ticket for the train. But thanks. We should go. So sorry for bothering you guys tonight."

Mrs. Dalaan waves me off. "Don't even worry about it. Wish you would come by more often."

Pressing my lips together, my heartbeat taps through my body. Each Dalaan looks at me with a kind gaze. Arav smiles at me from the top of the stairs with the twin girls with matching blue braids holding onto his legs. From one of the rooms looking over the banister upstairs, Ace's younger brother Anik appears and gives a small wave. Ace nods to me, his sapphire eyes enforcing his promise to be there with me.

"See you at the academy, Ace," I say, and take Liam by the hand. He squeezes back as we step into the cold together.

I never choose to stay away. I choose to come back.

Even though I'm leaving for the academy this morning, and I'll be leaving many more times, I'm not choosing to stay away from Liam.

Oron, Liam, and I wait for the train to Akinnera. No one goes in and out of Senn on a regular basis, so the station is quiet. Oron stands to my right, carrying my suitcase. Liam stands to my left, holding a package of food for my trip. The fire-pepper crunchies didn't make it in.

My heart aches as I study Liam. He wears a dark-blue flannel with one side of the collar stuck up higher than the other. It's always like that, no matter how many times I tuck it down.

I'll see him in Jodvan. Ten months, Mar to Jodvan. Holy Dien, that's a long time. But we'll write letters then be together for two months after the school year. It's going to be okay.

Oron looks at his pocket-watch for the fifth time. "Train's late," he says, and stuffs the watch back in his pocket.

I take their hands. Oron's is rough and so big that mine is completely lost in his. On the other side, Liam's small hand grips mine, reassuring me, baffling me with his calm after last night.

Even with their comforting hold and the rare glimpse of the sun in the sky, the events of last night sting. The train whistles outside the city gate, but it morphs into rifle shots in my head. Splatters of blood strike my mind's eye. The blood was so red, the faces of the robbers appalled, the shoppers scared witless.

I shake my head. "So." I push the word out before the images sink further into the present. "I made an appointment for Liam to see the doctor next month. Last time we saw him, Liam's cells were clear of essence, no accumulation or degeneration, no essence at all. The doctor doesn't think Liam will develop any essence even though he still has time, but he wants to keep monitoring it."

Oron nods. "Rin," he says.

The blood is still in sight, the tang of metal at the back of my throat. Just keep talking. "I'll take him again in the spring when I'm—"

"Rin, I—"

"I also made a list of street names for drugs that have been going around schools lately. I left it on the kitchen table, so you know what they are. There's some saphrite in an envelope just for emergencies—"

"Rin." Oron sets his massive hands on my shoulders.

"What?" My eyes are glued to my shoes.

"You don't have to worry. Things are going to be fine. Tell her, Liam."

Liam shrugs. "I don't want to do drugs anyway."

I'm missing something, I must be. There's something I've forgotten to do. I pat my pockets, but I never carry anything in my pockets. "You'll go everywhere with Liam, right? And if you can't you'll arrange for the Dalaan's to pick him up?"

"Yes, sweet girl." Oron chuckles and the train rolls into the station. I latch onto Liam, giving him a big hug. His hair is soft against my cheek, and his arms are tight around me as a gaping hole stretches in my gut.

"Love you, Rinnaya."

"I love you too."

I love him with every one of my essence-filled cells. I just need him to know that. Carnity, let him know that.

"We're behind you all the way, sweet girl. You're doing the right thing," Oron says, and kisses me on the cheek.

I push all my thoughts aside just so I can climb the stairs at the very back of the train. Liam rubs his eyes and Oron sets a hand on his shoulder. The doors close to block them from my sight.

It's going to be ok. He's got Oron. But the rip in my gut expands and my hands go numb.

The train pulls away from the station.

Once it's clear of the city gates, the train picks up speed and moves swiftly through the countryside. Out the back window, Senn shrinks and the mountains behind it fade to nothing.

You're doing the right thing. Oron's words help to move me away from the window to find a seat.

All I've ever known is Senn. I've never left, no one really does, so even the fields outside the city are fascinating. We pass through the flatlands and leave the sleepy towns behind, the patchwork of fields rolling into green hills. Trees dot the horizon here and there—a patch of crimson sorrow-blossom trees, a row of monstrous, leaning, weckler woods. They multiply and tangle into dense forest overgrown with dainty gold energy suckles and tall grass among the weaving roots.

Glowing specks float away from the stream of core energy emanating from boulders on the forest floor. The specks hover through the trees until they react with the air and dissipate, blanketing the wood with a thin fog.

Among the specks, there's something else. Little beetles. They flit from boulder to boulder, delicate wings shining with the same light as the core energy—like life-affinity wings.

I draw a deep breath of train-car air heavy with leftover cigarette smoke. Over the empty, brown-cushioned seats around me, I paint a picture of what I must have looked like. A girl, a boy, a red hood, a blue hood, all wrapped up in that greedy, blue energy. I let go of the breath and my body relaxes into the lumpy cushions.

At least now I've felt it. One affinity has shown itself. But how could an affinity named with life be so ghoulish? And how much more of a fiend will the death affinity be? The life affinity made me fast and my eyes saw so much more than they usually do. In the affinity book, it said the death affinity should be similar, just red and hellish.

Something in the forest shakes the earth and rattles the windowpanes. The forest unravels into a clearing to expose a beast moving along the edge of a pond. The beast is at least two stories tall, with a wide, muscular torso. It stands upright on sturdy hind legs and his bowed front limbs dangle in front of him with sharp claws. In the darkness of the forest, its eyes shine like the bits of core energy and illuminate the charcoal fur of its bull-like face. Ebony horns adorn its head, twisting into spires climbing to the sky. With great precision, it thrusts its arm into the pool, pulls out a fish, and tears it apart with razor-sharp teeth before the fish has time to even wiggle once.

"Are you all right, miss?" comes a voice from the end of the car.

I turn as a Protector makes his way to my aisle.

"Oh, yeah, yeah, I'm fine. I was just wondering about that beast, you know, if it's dangerous?" The moment I say it, I can guess what he's going to say. Of course it's dangerous.

"Sure, no doubt about that. He won't bother us if we don't disturb him, though. If anything happens, we know how to deal with him." He taps a gloved finger over his gold Protector shield-badge.

"What kind of beast is it?" I ask.

"That's an Ancient Jhogran. He's been in these parts for centuries, I'm told." He nods to me and keeps walking, reassuring the few passengers in the next car that he's there to protect them and that there's nothing to worry about.

I've never seen anything like this before. Rovers get through the walls of Senn all the time, giving the LPs a lot of trouble, but I've never seen an Ancient. A smile creeps across my face and I bite my lip.

By midday the scenery changes to mountains. Tunnels steal away my entertainment, so I take the opportunity to eat my lunch. As I finish, I lean my head back. Closing my eyes, I try to clear my head of thoughts by focusing on the rhythmic chug of the engine. But my thoughts only get louder.

It was only a few months ago when a boy came to sit by me at lunch on a day Ace was out sick; a Lifeblood boy—Tōmas. I always thought he was handsome with dark hair cropped short to his head, golden-brown skin, and a smile that made me weak in the knees. His deep-brown eyes looked like they held secrets, but I didn't know what kind. I should have known something was up when he came to sit by me, but I was blinded by his kindness and thrown off by the attention.

He told me he knew I was doing Dawnranfet. It didn't seem like he would be the kind to sell me out, just wanted to see what it was all about. Who was I to tell him not to get involved when I already was? So, I met him outside the bar that hid the illegal goings-on of Dawnranfet.

It was 9:00 p.m. The wooden crate beneath me pressed cold into my bones and the sign above me pulsed neon flashes around the periphery of my hood. Even streams of icy air passed in and out of my body, escaping my hooded face in billows of fog, absorbing the flashes, distorting my gaze fixed on my shoes.

I should leave. I shouldn't be meeting him here. That was the only thing in my head. The rest was noise—the roar of a speeder, a clatter of laughter from the bar, pounding electropulse from every joint on the street.

"Well, we better get inside, don't wanna get caught by a Wander Wraith in dis chill." Tōmas' slick voice drew my attention away from the ground.

"'Bout time, Tōmas," I said. He just stood there, smiling. "Was starting to think you were backin' out on me."

"Nah, come on, I wouldn't do that."

But would he?

I popped my knuckles on one hand and looked him over. His black jacket had a fur on the hood, it was clean, too clean, not really fit for Dawnranfet. The sign cast ruby light over his skin so he glowed red like a demon. His smile was angelic.

"So, we doin' dis or what?"

"You can't tell anyone, remember? 'Cause if you do, it's both our asses on the line."

A smooth chuckle slipped off his breath. "Relax, it's just for fun."

I rolled my eyes and made for the door. I rapped my knuckles four times, waited a beat, then knocked again.

We entered stale air and stale glares from other contestants— the ones who could see my face at least. My winning streak didn't sit well with them. I led Tōmas through the crowd as if something else was controlling my body; I had been there too many times to pay much attention to the things around me anymore, but Tōmas was fascinated. He moved with the electropulse while the beats just bounced around me. The stench of spilled ale didn't seem to bother him. It always made my stomach turn.

We chatted while I waited for a match. I can't remember anything he said to me, let alone anything I said in return. Somehow, I made an impression on him. He laughed at least once. I'm not sure if I was trying to be funny. I just wanted to get in the ring.

After a match, the announcer's voice broke the cheer of the crowd. "Next up, Jin and Eshra Axton," he said over the ampliphone.

"Strength of da ancestors, *Jin*," Tōmas said, smirking at my alias.

My head buzzed, my heart pounded, my body itched to get in the ring. I don't think I said thank you, just handed Tōmas my jacket to hold while I fought.

With my head uncovered, I took the glares through a sea of boos, passed a group of Lifeblood healers, and approached the gate to the ring. Through the metal links, I locked eyes with my opponent. She was at least a foot taller than me, muscular, with sky-blue hair weaved into tiny braids all tied in a knot behind her head. A jagged white scar marked her bronze skin by her left eye.

She looks like she can pack a punch. Good.

The metal bar blocking my entry to the ring slid out of the way. A siren blared; the door flung open. My eyes locked on a beam over the ring. I could swing and hit her. I sprinted in, full speed.

She'll get there first.

Her long, tree-trunk legs propelled her to the beam. Just as she snatched the beam, I directed all my force to my legs. I shot toward her as she swung at me. Our bodies collided.

"Ugh," Eshra gasped. Her fingers slipped. We crashed to the ground. The crowd howled.

The sounds reverberated through my skull and merged with my energy, awakening my arms. I slammed my fist in Eshra's face. My knuckles clipped her bones. Blood spilled from her nose.

Hit me, Eshra. Hit me.

The thought raged in my mind, relentless, longing.

Eshra thrashed, throwing her fists wildly. I pressed my weight on her and bobbed my head to avoid her strikes even though the voice urged me to take it. Finally, one stuck. It was dull, like a lump of clay hitting my jaw.

Not hard enough. Try again.

I struck her face three more times, my knuckles picked up more of her hot, sticky blood with each strike. Her essence seeped through broken skin in silver wisps.

She threw her elbow at my temple. My head snapped to the side, my vision spun. For a moment, all the energy, all the buzzing in my head, stopped, replaced by one thought. *Knock me out.*

Eshra grunted and pushed me into the fence. She leaped off the ground and started throwing punches again. My body moved, it swung its fists, it dodged kicks while my mind screamed. The rest of me was ice, crawling with the terror of my thoughts. Why was I thinking like that?

Come on. Knock me out. Find my weak spot.

But I kept fighting.

"Damn it, cutch," Eshra snarled.

She threw a punch. I blocked it, grabbed her shoulders, and rammed my knee into her stomach. She gasped as my fist smashed her chin in an uppercut. I front kicked and she stumbled back. Leaping after her, I slammed my bloody fist into her face one last time.

I stared at Eshra lying flat on her back. Red fist prints painted her face. All the energy drained out of me. The announcer's voice was fuzzy as he proclaimed me the winner. The stands erupted with insults, even though half of them probably won a bet on me. The blood on my hands made me itch.

I collected my winnings and a towel to wipe my hands and went back to Tōmas in a daze.

What is wrong with me?

"That was amazing," he said. "Never seen anyone fight like that before. You're a cool girl, you know that, Rin?" He handed me my coat. I took it, eyes on the ground.

"Thanks," I said, with a stupid shyness in my voice.

Maybe I should just leave.

But Tōmas led me over to the wall, where it was less crowded. Even though we had lots of space, he stood close to me, his shoulder rubbing mine, his body turned half to me and half to the ring.

"So how come you don't talk to me at school?" he asked, lowering his voice.

I shrugged. "I don't really talk to anyone."

He moved his head closer to mine. The scent of pine wafted from his neck, with a touch of Ease, but maybe it was from someone else, not Tōmas. The scents pushed back the aggressive thoughts in my head.

"Well, maybe we should change that."

He brought his hand to my jaw. My heart pounded, maybe because of the fight, mostly nerves. He drew his finger in a gentle arc from my chin, up my jaw, and to my ear, tucking my hair back. The touch lingered on my skin like a fresh breeze, relief from the stuffy arena.

Touch me again.

There it was. Different, but with striking similarity.

"Think you'll fight another match?" he asked.

I couldn't answer because his hands moved to my waist, stealing all logical thoughts away. He pulled me one step closer.

We could have stayed like that all night. Close together. Just talking. Just together.

The sounds around me faded to a dull drone. Tōmas toyed with the hem of my shirt, and I stared at the dimples in his cheek. For a few seconds, it was quiet. Warmth spread across my waist where his hand rested. My fingers itched to touch his, to feel his skin with my skin.

His fingers wrapped around mine, he smiled, and tugged me away from the wall. "This way," he said, and led me to a hall where there was no one to disturb us. He pressed me against the wall, his hands slipped past the hem of my shirt and found themselves exploring my back. A thrill tore through me. I flinched, but he pressed his body around me.

"Relax." His lips were by my ear, hot breaths on my neck.

His fingers explored my skin, his lips trailed my neck, breathing me in. I took a long breath, and his lips collided with mine, soft, like they were melting into me. My eyelids closed. His lips parted and I let go of my breath. I slid my hands up his chest, around his neck, his body warm against me. Being so close to him filled something inside me, so I was a little more hédin.

He kissed me again, harder, like he was missing something and needed to find it before it was too late. I let my lips be soft, to enjoy being touched. His tongue grazed the corner of my mouth. He kissed me over and over again, each kiss rougher than the last.

Too fast.

But maybe not.

Yes. Too fast.

Before I knew it, one wandering hand felt down my backside, then another groped my breast, wet lips on my collar bone.

"Stop," I whispered.

He plunged his hand down the front of my pants. Heat thrummed through me and a sickness raged in my stomach. He found what he was looking for, but it was too much for me. My heart screamed. I didn't know what to do. *No one ever told me what to do!*

My arms went stiff, then my legs. The blood left my fingers, leaving me numb and lifeless as he felt me.

It wasn't what I wanted.

"I said stop." I grabbed his hand before he could go any farther.

"It's ok, just relax."

"Stop telling me to relax," I said and shoved him off.

His eyes flashed, revealing all the secrets he had been keeping. They told me I had fallen for his kindness, for his tricks. I made it easy for him to get his hands on me.

He yanked me back to him, his hands found their way back under my shirt. The touch was dirty as it moved up from my waist, along my spine, and under my bra strap.

"I don't want this." I put up my hands, trying to get some space, but Tōmas slammed both his hands against the wall by my head, caging me in.

"You think I give a damn about what you want, cutch?" His dark eyes squinted, and a smile snaked over his lips that were, just a minute ago, soft and sweet against my mouth. He scoffed. "You're nothing to me. Just a bit of fun. You should consider yourself lucky to get with me."

"Let me go," I yelled and pushed him off. He stumbled across the hall and smacked his head against the cement wall. Tōmas lunged forward and grabbed my wrist. I slapped him, drawing blood to his perfect face with a smack.

"Bitch," he yelled. Anything that was once beautiful about him was now ugly—his brown eyes dirty, his lips venomous. "I'll tell the whole school about this. I'll tell them you're a dirty whore."

"You can say whatever you want, but you will never touch me again." The words spilled out of my mouth, leaving me breathless.

I ran. As I pushed through the crowd, someone's shoulder bumped me, hands brushed mine, legs and arms tangled around me, eyes stared me down.

I burst through the club doors and sprinted up the stairs into the rain and the glow of the streetlights. The door slammed behind me and I ran as fast as I could.

How could I ever hold Liam with these arms again? These stupid, dirty arms that were touched by a terrible boy. How could I show my face in school the next day, my face, the one he stroked? Oron would not approve. Ace wouldn't respect me if he knew what I was doing in the middle of the night. Tōmas just wanted me to get him into Dawnranfet, he wanted me to give him pleasure, he didn't care about me.

I reached my building, soaked, panting, and numb, but couldn't go in. I crouched on the front step. I pressed my fingernails into the skin of my forehead, wishing the pressure would wipe away the night. It was a mistake to go. A stupid, stupid mistake.

All I wanted was to disappear. I'm not good enough to take care of Liam. I'm not a role model. I shouldn't be here.

I don't want to be here.

My legs went limp, and I sunk to the steps. Leaning my head back, breath left my lungs. Far past the cold grey buildings, past the intrusive lights, the clouds cleared a path to the stars. Their emerald glow stole my attention in the pitch black of the night—I don't know for how long. They seemed so much closer than anything else around me.

After an hour, or minutes, or maybe just seconds, I stood. My body was stiff, and my eyes were blurry, but not enough to miss the letter poking out of my mailbox.

I took the letter. The silver Akinnera seal caught the dim light and glittered around the clean, white envelope. I ripped it open, fingers trembling. As the paper soaked up the rain and started to go limp, I read: **Congratulations, Rinnaya Burgheim. You have been accepted to the Akinnera Academy for Guardian Training.**

The words sunk through me. They were hot gold spreading over my smutty, violent thoughts. They fell heavy in my gut. Words like honour, respect, and selflessness jumped out at me from the page. They described the Guardian experience, not the experience I just had—the experience I've had every night I've gone to Dawnranfet and beat people up for money.

I swallowed hard. I didn't deserve those words.

8

LANCE

I DIDN'T KNOW MY PAST COULD GET STUCK IN MY SKIN. Just right there, going everywhere I go. And when I think about it, my skin starts to itch. As I throw my bags into the back seat of my cruiser, ready to head off for my second year at the academy, I can't get rid of the itch.

Mom, Dad, and Chiara stand like the most comforting, supportive wall in front of the steps to our house. Chiara bounces on her toes, arms stretched out for a hug. I wipe my sweaty hands on my pants and exhale. As I wrap my arms around my little sister, Dad sets his hand on my shoulder, and Mom rubs my arm. I have to make them proud this year.

My mom and dad didn't get to tell their friends about their son's selfless decision to defend Illyson as a Guardian. Instead, they had to admit that their son had an uncontrolled essence pulse that killed a girl, and he chose Guardian work over years of community service. I didn't think I could trust myself without the school structure.

The itch runs over my arms. I let go of Chiara.

"We love you, Lance," Mom says, her voice choked.

Dad smiles wide, his massive black wings spread out behind Mom and Chiara. "We do, son."

I try my best to keep my wings relaxed. Chiara always says she knows when I'm stressed by how close my wings get to my ears. So, I give them a quick shake before bowing my head to my family.

I get into my cruiser wings first, one of the great challenges of being Lavarian. I'd just fly if Jiaan was closer to Akinnera, but with all my bags that's more stress than I need right now. The cruiser is musty, and the seats have cracks in the leather. My stomach flip-flops. Dad drove me to the academy last year, so this is the first time I've driven my cruiser in over a year. Under the musk, Khalie's perfume lingers, and the smell of Ease seeps from the leather. *Maybe this is a bad idea.*

I look over my shoulder. Chiara and Dad are already heading back inside, but Mom waves at me with one hand over her heart. I flash her a smile, waving back at her. Fanning myself with my shirt, I turn back to the steering wheel. Just getting into the cruiser has got me sweating—can't wait to see what the first day of training does to me. I'm going to be rank.

I stick my keys in the ignition but stop as my eyes veer over to the glove compartment. I pop it open, heart pounding. Next to a crumpled receipt is a pack of cigarettes. In the rearview mirror, I catch Mom's reflection. She leans to the side, looking through the back window. Her eyebrows are pinched, and she holds her arms tight around her middle. I slam the compartment shut. Waving again, I start the cruiser.

After a month of being home, where the only smells are Chiara's fruity lip balm and the occasional lingering scent of tore fish, I'd almost forgotten the smell of the dormitory. This side of the academy building is newer than the other. The staircase has some kind of finish on it that smells oddly like olives, and the mixing colognes and general body odour already spill in from each floor. I don't hate it; it takes a bit of itch away from my skin and brings a smile to my face as I drop off my bags in my room.

The good thing about being a second year is that I didn't have to pack up all my things, so I only have my clothes to unpack. Second good thing is that sometimes your roommate drops out of the program, leaving you with a room to yourself. The quiet is nice.

"Lancy boy!"

I jump and the underwear I was just about to put away tumbles out of my hands.

"Damn it, Mycul." My hand grips my chest over my pounding heart.

I turn, and my face heats as I'm greeted by not just Mycul, but also Aris and Litha.

Litha smiles at me with a glint in her eye. I haven't talked to her in so long. I avoided her last year because I didn't want to be involved with anything from my basic ed days, especially not someone who was at half the parties I went to. She chuckles, glancing between my fire-hot face and what I dropped.

"Not the first time you've dropped your pants in public,"

she says.

Okay, I can die now.

Mycul bursts out laughing and Litha laughs too, nudging him with her shoulder and leaning into him.

"Hey, buddy," Aris says as he scrambles over to help me pick up my underwear. His floppy brown curls bounce over his forehead and a smile stretches his face wide enough to squint his eyes. "How was break?"

"It was pretty good, spent a lot of time with my sister."

"That's great. Wish I had sib—"

"Dudes, I was just happy not to have Professor Lotera barking at me, you know what I mean?" Mycul says, flopping down on my bed. He props himself on his elbows with his knees spread wide.

"I kind of like Lotera," Aris says, sitting down on the very edge of the bed, giving Mycul practically the entire bed to himself.

Aris is literally the sweetest. The other two are like sour apple tarts—I kind of want more but the sourness is such a headache.

"You would." Mycul scoffs.

My essence jolts from my wrists to my fingertips with a crackle of electricity. I clench my fists, subduing the essence flow. Mycul's got to stop cutting Aris down like that.

I finish unpacking my things to try to calm my essence. Starting off the year with essence surges like this isn't a good sign. I take a deep breath as I turn back to the group. Shoving Mycul over, I sit between the only two friends I made last year.

Litha sits at my desk chair, lighting a cigarette. The crackle of my essence creeps up my arms. It heats my chest, and my lungs take rapid breaths.

"Litha, you can't do that in here." My voice cracks. I dip my head and clear my throat as Litha's purple eyes send piercing jolts through my gut.

"Honestly, who's gonna catch me? It's orientation, all the staff are busy."

"I'm just asking you to stop, Litha," I say, staring at my lap.

"Then make me."

My lap is now occupied with Litha's thighs. She leans into me, chest first, and breathes a stream of smoke in my face. My head swims as my eyes land on her lips, inhaling the smoke that used to live inside my lungs day and night. Heart pounding, I want to close my eyes, but instead, I catch Litha's gaze. Her pupils dilate and a blush fills her brown cheeks. She raises an eyebrow at me, daring me to take another whiff of smoke, maybe a kiss. We've done it before.

Mycul snickers. "What ya gonna do, Lance?"

I could lean into her, but I've known her long enough to know it's not really what she wants. She's always done things like this for attention, and it always works. She craves it.

Litha's gaze wavers and her seductive smile crinkles downward.

She deserves the attention, just not from jerks, and not from me—she deserves someone who wants her. She deserves better than me or Mycul and the trail of guys she's been with. Come to think of it, the only one she deserves in the group is Aris, but she's never so much as looks at him. Which means Aris doesn't deserve someone like her.

I can't make my family proud if I keep falling into the same patterns. Leaning into Litha would only fill the edge of the gaping hole in my chest, and in hers. When our lips would part, we'd be hollow again.

I pick Litha up in both arms and set her back down on the bed between Mycul and Aris. The blush spreads down her neck. My stomach plummets at the dejection in her eyes. Patting her on the knee, I say, "Just . . . don't burn the place down. I'll be back. Left something in my cruiser."

I hate the way Litha just stares at me, all dazed, taken aback. Her longing for me is so mixed up in the show.

I bolt out of my room and down the stairs.

The cigarettes in my glove compartment weasel their way into my mind. *They might be the only things that will calm me down right now.*

No, for Seena's sake. I'm going in circles. I've been clean for a year, and the minute I get back here, I'm losing it.

I stop running. The Akinnera sun blares overhead. New students and old swarm like flies all around me in the courtyard at the main entrance to the academy. I spin in a circle to go back the way I came, but the crowd has already closed behind me.

My arms hang limp at my sides. I take a breath and let my wings and my head drop back. I stare up at the windows with Legendary Guardians staring back at me from the stained glass. The whole world is proud of these people. I can't even make my parents proud, not like this.

9

RIN

"HEY, YOU GETTING OFF?"

I open my eyes. In my groggy state, I can't tell if I'm looking at an angel or a beauty model. Her skin is flawless—a sun-kissed complexion—with a sprinkle of freckles across her nose. Her eyes are like emeralds. She leans over to shake me awake and her silky blond hair, with the slightest tinge of red, slips forward, cascading over her shoulders. She looks like she could be in an advertisement for pinichu berry cider. All she needs is a sun hat and a bottle of the sparkling cider in her hand.

I look out the window. The train has stopped at the Akinnera station. My pulse quickens, tingling in my fingers. I'm here.

"You're going to the Guardian Academy, right?" the girl asks.

"Yeah. How did you know?"

"I asked the ticket inspector if he knew where you were headed so I could wake you. I'm going to the academy too," she says, as I lift my suitcase off the overhead rack.

"Thanks. You really saved me there."

Her pink lips part in a smile, revealing two rows of perfect white teeth. She nods then swings her bag over her shoulder. As she steps off the train her hair swishes all the way down to her knees. I'd be a tangled mess if I had a head of hair like that, but there're no knots at all. I run my hand through my own hair, yanking through tangles.

The girl turns around to wait for me. She's thin, with broad shoulders, toned arms, and long, strong legs. A tattoo of a tiger on her shoulder peeks from under the sleeve of her orange t-shirt.

I hop off the train and spot a sign for the academy in silver lettering. Silver like the seal on my letter. Nausea bubbles in my gut.

The girl heads in the direction of the sign. "My name's Adrianne, by the way," she calls back to me, her voice muffled by the commotion of the station.

Through the doors of the station, there are whitewashed buildings with wide windows to let in the sunshine. They're as clean as if they were built yesterday, placed alongside each other with care. Trees with pink blossoms are everywhere and spread a sweet aroma through the station. As we exit, I squint at the blue canvas of sky dotted with airships of all different colours like a flock of exotic birds.

People file in and out of the station, but none of them look hungover or Eased. Peddlers sell their goods on the street, some children play with a dog on the sidewalk, and a small circle of ladies chat over coffee. Everyone smiles. A man even gives me a "good day."

Adrianne looks back at me.

"Oh, uh, Rinnaya. My name is Rinnaya, but I prefer Rin."

"Rin it is then. Nice to meet you." She smiles again. "We have to walk about ten minutes to get to the academy. This way."

Adrianne leads us up a cobblestone street. As we walk, she pulls a pack of gum from her pocket. "Want a piece?" she asks. "It's cinnospice."

I take one. "Thanks."

She keeps quiet as we walk. Out of the corner of my eye, I catch her sniff and rub her nose. She sees me looking and shakes off my gaze with a scratch of her head. It would probably be better to talk to her than stare at her. Not yet though.

There's a knot in my throat. So, I take long breaths, and unravel the gum. I chew and the cinnospice bites my tongue just as the sun prickles my skin. The motion of my jaw loosens the knot a bit.

"What year will this be for you?" I ask.

"I'm a fourth-year. You excited for your first?"

"Yeah, I guess so."

She studies me for a second. "Don't really know what to expect, huh?"

"Kind of." I examine the stream of people headed up the hill. They all look about my age so they must be academy students. Smiles and energy radiate from them. "Everyone looks so excited."

"Yeah, it's fucking annoying," she says, straight faced. "You've always got the excited ones, then there are the ones who are scared out of their minds. Then some that just don't give a shit." She shrugs. "I'm not gonna lie, for the first week or so it's kind of a mess. But you'll get into a rhythm and things get better." As she talks, her hand wanders to her side to scratch under her bra strap.

"Good to know."

"Mind if I ask your lineage?" Adrianne asks as we follow the curve the cobblestone road.

"Ironskin."

"Really?" she says. "I had you down as a Beastblood. Hard to tell lineages these days, hey? I've never met an Ironskin before."

I let her comment slide and keep my eyes on the road.

Adrianne nudges me with her elbow. "I'm a halfie," she says with a light laugh.

That's almost as frowned upon as being an Ironskin. Since the lineages have only started to integrate in the last few decades, people like Adrianne who come from blended families have a bit of trouble fitting in. Halfies don't have a pure essence and the life and death affinities give Ironskins a supernatural essence—two things people don't really like.

"Do you—"

"Yup, got both essence affinities. Beastblood and Emberstead."

She blinks, almost a flinch, as if her eyelids pass over a scar that still pains her. But she walks tall with her shoulders back and her face is relaxed, fixed in a soft smile. She's probably been envied or made fun of for her whole life, just like me. She winks at me and yanks up her shirt sleeve to display the tiger in all its glory. Its eyes follow me—Adrianne's second soul. Even after minutes of knowing her, it feels right. Her playful smile and confidence match the ferocious animal. Adrianne chuckles.

But she holds her arms close to her body—with not so

much of a swing of her arm as we walk. Every so often, I catch a glimpse of her left forearm. Two long lines run along the lighter skin. A similar jagged line marks my back. A prickle sings across my vulnerable skin and I have to fight to keep my hand away.

My body tenses as we join a noisy crowd in front of the academy and my feet stop moving.

"New students have to go sign in over there at that table. They'll tell you what to do. It was nice to meet you, Rin," Adrianne says, her voice like warm honey.

"Thank you," I say with a weak smile.

"No problem. See ya around." She waves goodbye with her sleeve still rolled up, brandishing her soul. Even though she stands at least half a head above most of the crowd, it swallows her, leaving me alone at the edge of the mob. I hope I'll see her again.

The sun beats on my shoulders as I gawk at the building in front of me, unwilling to move into the crowd just yet. All the images of the academy I've seen in pamphlets, the way my father and brother described it, the way I imagined it, fade away. The main building gawks back with pristine white bricks constructing its face. It could almost be a cathedral for the All Creator with its green dome roof, skylights, and towers on either side of the main building, white marble pillars at the entrance.

The windows above the pillars are stained glass, showing images of Protectors and Warriors. I've known those faces laid in the glass since I was too little to talk. The centre image is the very first Protector to receive the shield-badge, Loria. Her eyes, cut from clear-blue crystal, catch the sunlight and flash a question. Do you deserve my badge? But I hear the thump of the cashier's body hitting the floor and Eshra's bloodied face stares back at me. The venom from Tōmas' lips spills into my blood, making me shiver. I can't answer Loria, so I peel my eyes away from her.

To the left, the land drops off a cliff to the sea. In the distance, a city sits in the clouds, built on a boulder that hovers high above the water. Core energy streams like wind around the crumbling base of the boulder. A breeze wafts a taste of salt over my lips. I breathe it all in, allowing the fresh Akinnera air to push every bit of Senn from my lungs.

Heart pounding and palms sweaty, I press into the crowd. Someone backs up and I sidestep around them, leading me into a cluster of chatting girls. One squeals and I jump like an idiot. Two guys charge at each other. I get out of the way before I get sandwiched. They collide and clap each other on the back.

Almost to the Registration table, a black Lavarian wing slices through the bodies to swat me in the face. I stumble and crash into the group of people behind me. They shove me off as I try to blow the tickle of feathers from my mouth. I grunt, rubbing my mouth with the back of my hand.

The culprit of my uncomfortable, feather-to-mouth experience turns around to assess the damage. His face flushes as he turns. He reaches for my arm but pulls back and rubs his neck.

"Sorry, are you all right?" he asks. Several students squeeze behind him, pushing him forward a step.

"I'm fine," I say, straightening my shirt with a huff.

"Crowds can be tricky for me, you know?" He shrugs his shoulders and his sleek ebony wings twitch behind him.

My mouth should be moving. I want to say "right," or "same here," but I can't because my arms are like lead weights. He's two feet away and two feet too close, but I can't get my feet to move.

I tilt my head back to get a better look at his face. Jet-black hair flops over his brown eyes. He has a flat nose, and his skin is light, sandy brown with a brightness to it, as if the sun is coming from inside him. A shy smile flexes his strong jaw. My heart flutters so fast it might jump out of my mouth, and I hate myself for it. I can no longer trust the pounding organ in my chest. Pretty boys have too many secrets.

I break eye contact.

"First year here? Don't think I've seen you around," he says.

"Yes." My voice breaks and I cringe. "I just need to check in."

I try out a smile of my own, but it feels stupid on my face. Heat spreads through my cheeks.

"Oh, right, of course. Can I help you with your suitcase?"

"No." The smile cracks, but I add a quick thank-you before walking away.

Glancing behind me, he gives me a small wave and dips his head. I snap my head back to face my destination just as the fires in my cheeks flare up again.

At the check-in, I'm given a stack of papers that I probably won't read except for my schedule. I'm also given my uniform, which I'm told is only worn on special occasions, including orientation after dinner.

Juggling my belongings, I head up the steps to the main building. Voices echo through the lobby, bouncing off the walls and high ceiling. Underneath my feet is soft, red carpet that marks a path through the white marble floor that reflects my face. A chandelier of glass and iron hangs above me, tinkling from a draft. There's a chemical bite in the air, but it's overthrown by the smell of meat roasting somewhere in this massive building.

Holding my suitcase close, I stay in the middle of the carpet path so I don't hit anything, smudge something, or break something. My dusty old boots shouldn't even be touching this carpet.

Some girls come in after me and gravitate over to the left side of the lobby, so I follow, keeping my distance. We come to a winding staircase at the end of the hall to the girls' dormitory. Up two flights of stairs, I find my room at the end of a luggage-strewn hall.

My whole apartment could fit in this room. It's furnished in tasteful hardwood furniture, and the scent of a citric wood polish tickles my nose. A Luminee family gathers on the left side, their hair all different shades of purple and their skin warm, ash brown. An older woman stands with her hands on her hips, crabbing at the man.

The younger girl, my roommate I assume, sits cross-legged on the bed, ignoring her parents' squabble. Silky violet hair, a few shades lighter than her parents', frames her square jaw and sharp cheekbones. Her eyelids and lips are darkened by an elegant plaster of black makeup. Two silver studs pierce her eyebrow, and she twists one of the metal rings in her ears with black painted fingernails.

Looking up at me as I cross to the other bed and put my things down, she tracks my every movement until I make eye contact with her. Her brown eyes are enchanting. A strange tension forms between us as she squints and tilts her head.

A tingle shoots down my back. What if we don't get along? She probably hates Ironskins, and she'll snub me like everyone else. I can deal with her if she's the type to just ignore me, but what if she decides to make my life miserable? And why won't she stop looking at me? Stop it.

The woman follows the girl's line of sight. She sighs and says, "Well, don't be rude, Eliote, introduce yourself."

Eliote swings her legs off the bed, marches over to me with long strides, and stops about an arm's length away. She's a few inches taller than me. With her head high she says, "Eliote Nohar of the Luminee." She holds out her right hand and clasps her left around her right elbow—a formal Luminee greeting to symbolize that she will not use her shadow state, that she is fully present.

The Luminee enhancements have always dazzled my imagination. Since their lineage has a light essence affinity, their essence connects with the power of the sun and moon, allowing their bodies to take the form of shadows or move at the speed of light. They can even manipulate light and shadow to create powerful blasts.

I return Eliote's greeting by taking her hand with my right and setting my left on my right shoulder in the fashion of the Ironskins, indicating that I am withholding my strength for an equal encounter. My father and Mr. Kingsman were the only people I've ever seen use the handshakes.

"Rin Burgheim, of the Ironskins," I say. Just as Ironskin leaves my mouth, the judgement in Mrs. Nohar's eyes leaves her daughter and falls on me. She clicks her tongue.

Eliote lets go of my hand at the sound. Her face is expressionless until I catch her eyes and hold the stare. A sly grin spreads her charcoal lips, her eyes sparkle and dance.

"Eliote, come," her mother says.

Turning on her heel, Eliote heads out the door. Her last

words to me are, "See you around, Bird Brain."

The name is so random I almost laugh as her mother storms after her. I don't know where she could have gotten it from.

Mr. Nohar lets out a long sigh as he stays behind. "She means well," he says.

He straightens the collar of his blazer. Three night-wing moths flutter out from under the coat tails. Rolling up the cuff of his sleeve and muttering to himself, he reveals a lunar sage tattoo on his wrist, explaining the moths fluttering around him, attracted to his powerful essence. He follows his family with a slight nod to me.

Even though we barely spoke to each other, I think I already know Eliote has good intentions. Still, from the hall, Eliote's mother's worries drift back to me.

"Do you want us to put in a request for a different roommate?" she says. "It's not too late, we can go do that right—"

"Mom, no, of course not. Why would you even say that?" Eliote's voice trumps her mother's in sweetness and sincerity. It calms the jitters in my fingers enough for me to open my suitcase to unpack.

I take out the first piece of clothing I had on top to protect the picture frames underneath. The shirt was one of my father's, an old green flannel. It hasn't had a wash since he died. It smells like him when he was at home, like wood shavings, fresh baked bread—I don't want to lose that. I stuff my nose into it and breathe its musk, then place it in the closet across from Eliote's expensive clothes. The rest of my clothes were my mother's—simple button-up shirts, soft long sleeves, t-shirts with no graphics, and pants which have all acquired holes in the knees or have lost their colour. The last thing I place in the closet is my Ease Beetles t–shirt, the only thing I've ever bought just because I wanted it.

The clothes did a good job of keeping my picture frames from cracking. One frame holds a picture of my mother and father, another a picture of Oron, and then one of me and both my brothers. They watch me unpack, but I can't bring myself to look back at them, especially my mother. I couldn't read her eyes when she was alive, and I can't read them now. I set them on the desk closest to my bed along with the spirit affinity book and *Nolaria* in all her tattered green leather glory.

Then there's the box, the last thing in the suitcase, the thing I can't bear to part with but wish I didn't have at all. I urge myself not to open it. Not now.

Maybe it is the citric tinge in the air, reminding me of Mother's excessively clean house, that prompts me to open the latch. It clicks and my fingers flip the lid. I stare at its contents: my father's Guardian badge, my parents' wedding rings, an old pocketknife from Stephen, and my mother's suicide note.

Fingering the folded page that has been crumpled and unravelled so many times, I get an urge to burn it. The words are already burned into my memory, so why not? If I burn it, maybe the words won't be needles in my heart, maybe they'll fade.

I am sorry, children.

Oh, Carnity, don't let the words come.

I can't take this life any longer. I'm not strong enough. I love you three with all my heart, but every day my heart gets weaker, every day it becomes more unbearable to breathe, and now without your father, I can't even take a single breath.

My throat constricts.

I am weak. Your father was always the strong one. You are better off without me. Be strong because I couldn't be. Please find the joy that

I cannot. I am so sorry.

Every nerve in my body fires, and I slam the lid closed, locking the memories inside. I put the heels of my hands to my eyes, pressing in the cool dark, pushing out the images of her scribbles. The pulse in my wrists taps my eyelids. And the beat, that dreadful party song, fills my head, my body losing all sense of contact with the bed so I'm falling. Falling so deep and so fast into the dark behind my eyes.

Breathe.

I draw breath inside me and push back against the dark.

I can't stay like this. I have to be uniformed and down for dinner at six and the opening ceremony at seven. I've got to get up.

I pull my hands away from my eyes, change, forcing breath in and out of my body with constant reminders, and look in the mirror by my desk. The uniform fits well except for the waist of the pants. I slip on a belt. It rumples the clean lines of the pants but thankfully the hem of the yellow blazer covers it.

With secure pants and an established breathing pattern, I peek my head into the hall. The other girls are walking down to supper, all in different coloured uniforms. Falling into the crowd, the crisp clothes feel awkward against my skin, but everyone is wearing them, and we look like Guardians. I smile to myself, straightening my shoulders.

As we shuffle down the stairs, my eyes are drawn to a picture on the wall. The picture is the youngest version of my father that I have ever seen, and I am only able to recognize him by his sunken, grey eyes casting a gentle gaze toward nothing at all. I can almost sense his strong arms around me. A terrible ache sweeps over me as I turn away.

An elbow jabs me in the ribs, shoving me off my step, and my feet skid over the next two. I snatch the railing to avoid landing on my back. My hand shoots to my weak spot out of instinct.

"Watch it, why don't you," I snap in a tone dripping with far too much Senn to be acceptable here.

"Stay out of my way," my assailant says.

Holy Carnity, it's her already. Not even a full day at the academy and our paths have already crossed.

Johanna looks down at me from her superior perch on the steps. She wears her uniform, but the yellow blazer is a comical combination with her hair.

I snort a laugh. "You look like the mascot for Garver's Good Grill."

"Shut up, Rin." She huffs and yanks a hair elastic from her wrist. She ties her mass of curls into a ponytail so the red is only touching the bright yellow at her back. "You're one to talk," she mutters as she passes me. "That colour washes you right out."

She turns away with that remark. My dumb mouth can't form any words. I grip the railing harder, trying to calm my mental hissy fit before I say something stupid.

Johanna disappears, leaving me alone in this over polished stairwell, just a ghost girl in a yellow blazer that was starting to make her feel worthwhile.

In the dining hall, the clamour of students makes me dizzy. I grab food as fast as possible and leave the line to find a seat in the corner where it's not as loud.

Even though the selection of food I can choose from is

extensive, I just nibble on some bread with butter and down a few pieces of fruit. I can't bring myself to eat more than Liam would be eating tonight, at least not yet, and the tornado of frustration whirling around my head isn't helping the food go down. I've got to walk. I leave my plate with the dish crew and make my way to the arena through quiet halls.

Johanna could've just told me to get out of her way like a normal person, but that psycho had to shove her elbow in my gut. Sometimes it feels like she's in my head, like she knows where I am, and then shows up.

A chill runs down my spine.

Mind Fire.

Is she already using it just to mess with me? She's probably been training like a maniac over the break to get it ready to show off. Instead of just pelting me with fireballs and using fire armour to block my attempts to smash her nose in, she's added mental abilities to her arsenal. Now she can fling me around with her mind. Lucky me.

My brooding is interrupted by someone calling after me.

"Hey, wait up."

The Lavarian boy I ran into earlier jogs down the hall wearing a green, second-year blazer. It seems he has an obscure ability to make any article of clothing look good, even a tacky green blazer.

"Not a big eater?" he asks, smiling.

That smile switches my brain from thinking about the new ways Johanna can beat me to a pulp, to frozen dummy mode. My stomach churns.

"You could say that," I say.

"Mind if I sit with you at the ceremony?"

"Uh, well . . ."

Before I can answer, he puts his right hand toward me and places his left hand behind his back, the Lavarian formal handshake.

"I'm Lance."

I put a sweaty hand forward to take his the Ironskin fashion. "Rin."

A few students pass our silent standstill. I wait for him to flinch now that he knows he's holding hands with an Ironskin, but he continues to hold on with a grip that is warm, welcoming, and at the same time, insanely uncomfortable. My fingers tingle wrapped in his, my arm tenses, and my shoulders go stiff.

"So, Rin, let's sit together." He drops my hand and starts toward the door, wings fluttering behind him. He stops in the doorway to see if I'm following, hands in his pockets. But my feet aren't willing to follow yet. They know better, now.

"Do I have a choice?" I ask.

"Always," he says.

Heat floods my face, taking hold of the tension in my shoulders and melting it away.

Sliding my hands into my pockets just like Lance, I walk past him. "Just checking. Sure, you can sit with me."

Lance falls into step next to me. I like that he doesn't talk just yet; it gives me time to collect my thoughts and get myself under control. But I get lost in the quiet, the cool wind, the faint crash of the waves beyond the cliffs. Lance looks at me. I think he just asked me a question.

"What?"

"I asked you where you're from," he says.

"Oh, Senn. It's just a small city."

He's probably never heard of it. No one's heard of it.

"It's in the east, right?"

Never mind, he knows it. Of course he does. I mean, why wouldn't he be good looking and knowledgeable?

I think I missed another question and give him a stupid look.

"Why did you choose to come to the academy?" he asks again.

"Oh." I pop my knuckles while I think. "It's closest, I guess."

"Yeah, but I mean, why a Guardian Academy?"

"What else was I going to do?" I shrug. "There aren't very many opportunities for someone like me in Senn."

The smile breaks away from his lips. His eyebrows furrow and his soft eyes question me. But I don't want to bore him with my problems.

"What about you?" I ask.

He clears his throat and shifts his eyes forward. "To right some wrongs, I guess." He shakes his head. "Do some good, protect people. That sort of thing. I don't know, it feels kind of fake when I say it out loud."

But his words drip with sincerity, not fake at all. Maybe I'm the fake one here.

I chew the inside of my cheek. He probably thinks I'm strange. Fake and strange. I can't even reply to his questions without taking a year to give an answer. My cheeks are getting warmer, and I have an urge to turn the other way and run. Run and keep running. But seeing as that direction would land me in the ocean, I decide against it. Not a great time to test my luck with swimming.

"Welcome to the arena, your new home. I swear, you will hate this place once you're done first year," Lance says, and speeds up a little, opening the arena door for me. His long arms stretch the fabric of his blazer. It creases, accentuating his deltoid.

I've never had anyone open the door for me. It's nice but also weird. I can open my own damn door. But he's being nice. It's a nice thing to do. Say thank you.

"Thanks," I say as I slip through.

"Sorry for bumping into you earlier," he says behind me.

"You already said that."

He smiles and laughs, a soft regretful laugh. "I know. I just don't like to see anyone get hurt."

The last bit of phantom weight collecting in my arms dissipates. I lift my chin a tad and catch his eyes—watchful, deep-brown eyes. Maybe this pretty boy will stay true to his word.

We go up a flight of stairs and through a pair of doors opening to the bleachers that wrap around the arena. It's a huge, oval-shaped space—four of those Ancient beasts I saw on the way could lie toe to toe. The ceiling is high, with a skylight letting in the sunshine. We take a seat a few rows up from the railing. Lance and I sit quietly for a while, just watching the commotion around us as the seats fill up.

It's nice to have someone to sit with, but every girl who passes takes a second look at Lance. They smile, giggle, or do some sort of flirty, hair-flippy thing. A girl sitting two rows in front of us looks back at him to check him out. She cranes her neck to see when she thinks he's not looking and snaps it back. She looks again. I grit my teeth and stuff my hands under my thighs to keep from squirming. She turns once more but Lance sees. She doesn't turn away this time. Instead, she smiles and her face flushes red.

Looking right at her, I raise an eyebrow. Her smile falls and her eyes narrow into an expression I know too well because it's the one that's permanently plastered on Johanna's face. I'm just in her way.

Lance leans to me and says, "You're pretty nervous, aren't you?"

Who is this guy? Can he see right through me?

"How can you tell?" I scoff.

"Well, for one thing, you keep cracking your knuckles."

I clasp my hands together in my lap, not sure when they slipped from under my legs. "Oh, sorry." I breathe a laugh. "Didn't even notice."

"That's okay. I mean, everyone's nervous, right?" He tilts his head to me.

Instead of spouting empty words, I just let his hang in the air. He's right, I guess. Who knows, maybe he's just as nervous as I am.

A few minutes pass and an Earthkin woman in a fitted, black suit walks to a podium in the middle of the arena. Her skin is a dark brown and her chestnut hair is thick and curly. She carries herself with grace toward the ampliphone, waiting for everyone to quiet before she speaks.

"Welcome." Her voice is deep and echoes over the hush. "My name is Evelyn Findel, and I am the headmaster. This is going to be an excellent year at the Akinnera Academy for Guardian Training." She adjusts her spectacles on her elegant nose. "To protect the lives and well-being of the citizens of our homes, we will strive for nothing less than excellence."

I risk a look at Lance. I don't know what it is about him, but he's intriguing. Maybe it's because he's a Lavarian. Their weather manipulation abilities are fascinating, and there aren't any of them in Senn. Their wings make quite a statement, to say the least. I can't keep myself from sneaking a peek at the tufts of silky, black feathers sprouting from Lance's back.

Or maybe it's . . . He looks back at me. Great. I'm just staring at him. It's rude, but I can't stop. Just look away. Before I do, he smiles. Yes, that's it. He smiles like he's trying to say something to me without words. I can't figure it out though. I'm not familiar with the language of smiles.

10

LANCE

MAYBE I DON'T HATE THE ARENA as much as I thought I did. It's different this year. Brighter. Breathable, even through the stale sweat. Maybe it's because last year a Monitor was at my side—at orientation, every training session, and at the graduation ceremony. She watched my every move and checked my essence pressure daily. I hated her, not the arena. No, I hated myself because she was chained to me like shackles.

I chose someone to sit with this year. I keep getting caught up with the same kind of people. Choosing someone to get to know, avoiding the flow of the crowd? That's different. How can I be sure I chose someone who's not going to bring me back down?

Even if I hadn't heard Evelyn's speech before, I still wouldn't be able to concentrate because Rin can't sit still. Every time she fidgets in her seat or toys with her hair, she wafts her smell of coffee and cinnospice over me. It's all I can think about and it's terrifying.

Something about the way her eyes refuse to smile along with her mouth is just like coffee. Every energizing sip brings a wash of bitterness. It hits something inside me, something that I didn't want to touch just yet. I wanted to hide out for a while longer.

Evelyn closes the orientation with an encouraging word that might have been motivating if I'd listened. Rin stands and yanks her pants back into place. I press my lips together, trying not to laugh at her.

"You gettin' up?" she asks, eyeing me with a steely gaze down her nose.

Her eyebrows, dark and thick, contrast the rest of her light features with the perfect dose of daunting shadows. Just terrifying enough for me to stick around and get to know her, someone new.

"Yeah." I run my palms over my knees. "Headmaster Findel's voice is just so soothing. I almost fell asleep."

"Well, I have to admit I wasn't listenin' much." Her voice clips from word to word, fast and sharp, with a slight rasp.

I stand and we shuffle into the crowd filing out of the arena. A cool breeze cuts through the mass of students from the open doors.

"You know anyone else here?" I ask.

"Yeah, actually two people from my basic ed class. Johanna and my friend Ace." Rin scans the crowd. "Keep an eye out for Ace. Tall Nytrue guy." She raises her hand above her head. "Pierced ears, glasses."

"What about Johanna?"

Rin's lips press together. Taking an elastic from her wrist, she ties her hair up in a bun on top of her head. "Ever come across a hungry Rover? All ornery and snippy? That's Johanna. She'll avoid me if we find her."

I laugh and the tiniest smile tweaks the corners of her mouth.

The setting sun paints the wispy clouds peach, and the sky darkens to a pastel purple. The last rays of sun wash golden light over the academy grounds and glows over Rin's skin as she searches for Ace.

"Oh hey, there he is," she says.

"Where?" Maybe I would see where she's pointing if I wasn't staring at her.

"There, by the second pillar under the stained-glass Loria."

Despite her short answer about becoming a Guardian—*because what else am I going to do*—the fact that she knows the first Protector is impressive. It's that duality about her again, one foot in and one foot out. Guardian work is what she wants, or is it? It's exactly how I feel about being a Guardian.

Under the giant Loria is a tall Nytrue guy waving at us. Rin weaves through the crowd, but does she want me to follow? Is it time for me to buzz off? She said I could sit with her, but maybe that's all she meant and it's time to leave, let her do her own thing. I follow, rubbing the back of my neck as we meet up with Ace at the edge of the crowd.

"I took the train and I still beat you. How is that possible?" Rin says.

"What can I say, I like to take my time." Ace wraps his arm around Rin's neck and pulls her in.

"You missed the whole orientation." She pushes his arm

away.

"Who are you, my mother?"

"Just sayin'."

"What makes you such a cynic?"

"I blame the second-hand smoke from below my apartment. It's all gone to my head."

"Yeah, that wasn't healthy." Ace laughs.

The angle of Rin's eyebrows softens. Her shoulders drop, and she leans to the side so she's not so stacked and rigid, ready to run as soon as I do something stupid.

Ace glances at me with sharp eyes. He runs a hand through his spikey blue hair and shoots a quizzical side eye back to Rin. Raising his fist to his mouth, he clears his throat, nodding to me.

A blush slips onto Rin's pale cheeks. My stomach twists and a smile creeps to my face.

"Oh," Rin says, scratching a spot on her head buried under her pile of hair. "Ace, this is Lance. He's a second-year student."

"Good to meet you," I say, greeting him with the smile I meant for Rin, and offer a handshake. Ace takes my hand with a firm grip but doesn't offer the formal Nytrue greeting in return.

"Glad to see Rin's meeting people." Ace nudges Rin but directs his comment to me.

"It was kind of an unfortunate meeting," I say.

The kindness in Ace's eye wavers with a twitch. He takes a step closer to Rin. My mind flips through all the possibilities of the statement I just made. Knowing Rin is Ironskin, there's bound to be negative possibilities I overlooked. With the swirl of thoughts, heat rises up my neck and I run my hand through my hair. I glance at Rin, then back to Ace, then to the ground, and back to Rin again. My mouth goes dry, longing for a hit of

Ease or a cigarette.

"What? She didn't hit you, did she?" Ace says, nudging Rin's shoulder.

"I did not hit him, Ace." She rolls her eyes, cheeks flushing even more, and her shoulders scrunch under her blazer.

"Seriously though, take notes from my nose, Lance. It used to be straight before I met her."

Slapping her hand over her face, Rin sighs. "Ace, come on."

"Oh, I think there's a story here," I say, shoving my hands in my pockets to keep them from running over my neck or hair for the hundredth time.

Ace claps his hands together. "Oh, there's a story."

"Not that much of a story," Rin mutters.

"So," Ace says. "I had just moved to Senn, okay? Hated it. Had no friends. I literally ate by myself in the bathroom because this idiot, Deren, had it out for me for some reason. Then one day we were working on an Ascension unit in athletics class. I'm not a big sports guy. I liked the martial arts units, but throwing balls around isn't really to my liking."

"Oh my gosh, Ace, get on with it," Rin says.

Ace waves his hands in front of him in apology. "Sorry, sorry. So, we're pairing off to practice pitching. Everyone partnered up until there was only me and Rin left. Rin grabs a ball and tosses it around a bit. Then she says, 'I won't hurt you, if that's what you're worried about.'"

Rin groans and steps behind Ace. Ace grabs her arm and pulls her back out into the open.

"And this little angel right here, despite holding back all her strength, left me with a bruised hand and hit me right in the nose with an Ascension ball. Blood everywhere."

"Oh god, those things hurt like hell, and a public-school ball? Nasty." I let my head fall back as I laugh.

"Okay but the best part was she didn't even apologize, didn't need to, I knew she was sorry, so sorry she couldn't speak. She insisted on going with me to the hospital, even went in with me to see the doctor. Stayed with me until I was all patched up, stuck with me ever since."

Again, Ace slings his arm around Rin. But Rin holds her arms tight around her middle, one hand rubbing her temple.

"Thank you, Ace, for tellin' him how I broke your nose. Love that," she says.

Ace shrugs. "I just like that you made sure I was okay."

I love the story. They seem to really care for each other. Even as they tease each other, they turn it around to make the other feel welcome. Each of Rin's movements is genuine, or at least I hope they are. She just reacts to everything in a way that seems unpracticed. And Ace holds himself with easy confidence. Their company lets me breathe. My mind isn't racing to figure out what to say next.

But the sun has hid beyond the horizon, switching out the pastel sky for the green glow of the stars. Rin wraps her arms tighter around herself and shivers.

"Oh damn, you're cold." My hand reaches to touch her arm and the second it touches her sleeve, I regret the choice. She flinches.

"We should get inside. You guys want to get coffee or tea?"

"I think I might just head to my room," Rin says. "I'm pretty tired after the train and last night I didn't sleep much."

Ace presses his lips together and cocks his head to the side. "You feeling okay after last night?"

Rin nods a few times, eyes locked on the ground. She raises her gaze a bit but doesn't look at Ace. "Yeah, I'm fine. Thanks for sitting with me, Lance."

"Of course," I say.

Her grey eyes flick a glance at me. There's just enough light to see the pink of her cheeks as she tucks a stray hair behind her ear and leaves us behind.

"I think I should head in too," Ace says.

"What floor are you on?"

"Third."

"Oh, so am I. I'll walk with you."

As we head inside, Ace clears his throat. "Tell me, Lance, where's the best place to study around here?"

His eyes are critical, his mouth still smiling, and there's a tease in his tone. He's testing me, isn't he? Seeing if I'm okay for his friend to hang around. Well, Ace, I don't know.

"The library's no good," I say, taking the stairs. "Everyone goes there, which turns the place into more of a rec room than a library. If you really want to get out of your room to study, take advantage of the nice weather and study in the courtyard or on the roof."

Ace nods along. I guess it was a satisfying answer.

At the top of the stairs, we turn onto the third floor, and I stop at my room. Ace stops too.

"So," he says. "Rin's pretty cute, isn't she?"

My eyes go wide and my mouth cracks into a cringing smile at his bluntness. No need to hide his interrogation I guess, and in that case, I shouldn't try to hide anything either. I drop my eyes to my feet and just say it. "Definitely."

Eyes glued to anything but Ace, my heart pounds in my

ears, making me squirm. My shirt sticks to my pits. The thoughts in my head go fuzzy, longing for a sweet breath of Ease to calm my nerves. I swallow hard as my essence gives my hand a jolt.

"Hey," Ace says.

My head snaps up.

"Rin is very important to me."

Quiet slithers around us, broken only as a guy down the hall turns music on.

"Yeah, I can see that," I say, lowering my voice.

Ace straightens up and crosses his arms. "If you plan on spending any time with her, you better treat her like she's the goddamn Empress of Illyson." He pokes me in the shoulder. "And I wasn't kidding about the nose stuff, if you hurt her, it'll be her who kills you."

"Wouldn't have it any other way."

"Huh?" Ace eyes me good.

"Wha . . . I just mean . . ." I scratch my head. "Its not like . . . Look, I don't want to hurt her."

That's the last thing I want. The tightening in my stomach makes me wonder if it would be better to just stay away, see how this year goes with only having monthly Monitor check ups, see how my essence control does with more intense training. But I'm still curious about her and her coffee scent.

"She's different," I say, my wings shrugging behind me.

"Damn right she's different. And she's Ironskin, so if you have any problem—"

"I don't. I don't have any problem with that." I look him right in his sapphire eyes. His jaw tenses and his ears stick out.

"Okay then." He pauses and takes a good, long look at my door. "I know where you sleep."

11

JOHANNA

Heat fills my eyes, it burns.

I think I might just head to my room.

Who the hell is talking so damn loud?

I'm exhausted.

The words sizzle through my mind—from one side to the other. I turn in circles. Every voice buzzes together but the voice in my head is distinct, and it calls over the crowd with a familiar pitch. It grates on my nerves. The heat from the exhausted voice tinges my stomach with a sick ache. I have to get away from it. Escaping the courtyard into the main building, I climb the stairs to my room. I haven't met my roommate yet, so the stranger invading my space must be her. She stands with her back to me as she hangs her uniform in the closet. Dark-brown curls cascade down her back with just as much volume as my own, but with more definition and elegance.

Her hair bounces as she turns to me. Her brown eyes are doe-like. She has full lips and a flowering pattern of creamy vitiligo crawling through the dark-brown skin of her right cheek.

"Hi," she says. "I'm so glad I caught you." Her voice is soft and smooth. She crosses the room to me in a few quick steps.

"Caught me?" I say, standing stiff in the doorway.

"Well, yeah, I was going to head out with some friends to this party we heard about. I wanted to meet you first. I'm Sasha." She offers me her hand.

I shake her hand with a quick jerk. "Johanna."

"Pretty name," she says as her whole body shakes from my greeting. Four gold rings glint in her ear.

Dropping her hand, I take off my blazer. "You're a fourth-level healer. That's impressive."

"Oh, don't be too impressed. I'm only essence level two, can't create a lick of wind but I've always been able to heal."

The sweet tone of her voice is nauseating. I busy myself removing my awful uniform. Sasha gasps and she turns her back.

"Would you like to come with us to the party? It's not against the rules, I checked. As long as we stay in the city and are back by eleven, we can do whatever we like."

I'LL SEE HIM IN JODVAN.

That fucking burning voice is too close for comfort. It

must be someone on this floor. I'm not too keen on listening to her exhausted thoughts all night, so maybe a party outside the academy wouldn't be a bad idea.

"Sure."

"Great. I'll just wait outside."

I change as fast as I can to avoid being caught in this room with the sizzle in my brain for longer than I have too. As I dress, my mom's voice glosses over the phantom in my head. *Johanna, you're here to become a Warrior, there's no need for parties. Johanna, where on the Karess did you get that sweater?*

The sweater in question is blue with black sleeves and cropped short to reveal my stomach. Staring at the mirror, the girl caught in the glass is unfamiliar. It might be good to go to a party and see who I am away from Mom and Rin and Senn.

I catch up with Sasha and her friends and follow them through the city as lampposts come on one by one. The residents of the whitewashed buildings turn out their lights or sit in the cool air on porches lit by candles. The sky is bigger here than in Senn. A few more stars make it into view. There's more room to breathe.

We take a few turns, and the streets get tighter, a little dirtier, until we come to a descending staircase with a sign for an underground train. The sign has a red X over it. The girls take the stairs into the dark tunnel. I stay at the top.

"Are you sure this is the place?"

None of them answer. They're too caught up in laughter. One of them is swaying her hips around to music I can't hear yet.

The hum of a cruiser thrums through the night. Pebbles crunch under my shoes as I continue down the stairs. Even though the sizzle in my brain has stopped, there's something not right about this place. Not in a bad way, there's just an extra dose of energy that pulses over the music vibrating through the tile walls. It's strong, like it's been around a long time. The energy flows through the tunnel with graceful whispers. It prickles my skin, keeping my mind sharp.

At the bottom of the steps, I let the drone of music lead me over a long walkway above rusted train tracks. If I didn't know better, I would say this tunnel connects Akinnera to Senn. Wafts of cigarette smoke and sour ale fill the air. Graffiti marks the white tiles. The alleyway near my house where I took my colossal vomit smells just like this and the energy was there too. A Wander Wraith—the spirit of a dead woman with unfinished business. Only women with Mind Fire are able to see Wander Wraiths and Mom said she saw the Wander Wraith there too when she walked past it one night.

Now, in this grungy tunnel, the shadows are awake with an inaudible voice. There must be a Wander Wraith down here too.

I find the party at the end of the tunnel. Sasha has been swallowed into a group standing at the end of a drink table, and by the looks of it, has already forgotten I tagged along. An old neon sign blinks over the dancing crowd in green. This track may not be in use but somewhere under Akinnera there must be others. The whole tunnel shudders but the party still rages.

Taking an ale for myself, I fit the party going vibe, but I don't have a circle. Sasha's circle is tight, filled with girls that look just as sweet and innocent as she does. There's a circle of guys that look like they're in a deep conversation about something that would be duller than whatever gossip Sasha's group has concocted. A cloud of twisting grey smoke hangs above a couple relaxing on a ratty leather couch. But in the centre of the platform, everyone moves. Not together, not apart. They just choose their own moves to the same music.

The song changes. The beat picks up and a clear melody sung by a woman with the richest voice I've ever heard fills my ears. She sings like an old soul trapped in a young body, forced to conform to today's standards of music. Adding a dark undertone to the upbeat song, she sings with the voice of a Wander Wraith. Drawn by her ancient tone, I enter the crowd.

My body moves side to side as I migrate into the very centre. I hold my arms out from my body as the beat flows through me and soon I've created enough space to dance undisturbed. My eyes fall closed, arms floating up to the ceiling, the ale still unopened.

No one knows me in this moment. Not even me. I am clean. Undiscovered. Every movement of my body is a new experience. I've never danced before. I've never been away from home or cut off from people I know. Right here I'm just Johanna.

Curls fall over my face. My body finds a rhythm for every limb, easy and specific. The music flows through me like honey.

But the music changes again to an electropulse song with an abrasive beat and no vocals. Hands back at my sides and body still swaying, I break the cap off my ale to take a sip.

The energy of the tunnel pulls at my consciousness. It urges me to search. I scan the faces around me, but none of them whisper. I follow the pull to the edge of the dancing crowd, to the edge of the platform.

Out of the neon glow of the party, is a silver figure. My attention narrows on the pure energy and the music dims to the back of my mind. A soul without a body, without distinct lineage features. She could be anything, but she is a woman. Her eyes are round, without depth or focus.

Her call starts as an echo inside me, but catches up with itself and says, "You are Soul Tethered."

The beat of my heart fills my ears, pounding in my chest. My fingers tingle as if the blood in my vessels is frozen. I take a short breath that sticks in my throat.

The Wander Wraith clenches her ethereal hands into fists. "Be careful. You are Soul Tethered."

The silver soul sharpens with a flash of light. The light vanishes, leaving behind nothing but the white tile of the train tunnel. My mouth is dry, and the acrid taste of ash coats my tongue. The rhythm of my heart won't slow. It's as if I have two hearts and they trade thumps back and forth to pump blood into separate bodies.

I force my eyes closed. A shiver shakes through me, and I wrap my arms around myself, the ale tucked in the crock of my arm.

Be careful?

I'm Soul Tethered?

It was a warning. The most fucked up, vague warning I've ever heard. Watch out, Johanna, there's a train coming down the tracks, better step back so your head doesn't get ripped off. That's a warning.

So maybe it was a joke. Wander Wraiths have been known for playing tricks on people, invading people's bodies in the winter just to feel warm, or going around causing trouble for no apparent reason.

A few more clambering beats pulse ice-blood through me. With a steady breath, they calm. Heat returns to my hands. The music infests the quiet.

It wasn't a joke. I know it. That damn wraith warned me that my soul is fucking tethered to something. I'm not just Johanna.

Tension seizes my shoulders and the space between my brows. So much for a moment of calm. I chuck my ale into the tunnel, right where the Wander Wraith stood. The bottle smashes, the glass bursting apart like the spread of light from the wraith.

12

LANCE

Just as I sit down with a book for the rest of the night, Mycul and Aris barge into my room.

"You'll be reading texts nonstop for the rest of the year, Lancy boy," Mycul says. "Ditch the book and come out with us." He snatches the book from me.

"Out where?" I ask.

"The orientation day party," Aris says.

"The what?"

"Oh, that's right, we didn't rescue you from your isolation until almost halfway through the year." Mycul presses his palms together and draws them to his mouth. "Listen here, my man. Every year there's a party on orientation day, different location every year, usually some creepy, long-forgotten dugout somewhere in the city. Tonight, we're partying in an abandoned, underground train station." He raises his eyebrows.

He's certainly dressed for a party with his button-up shirt left open to show off the physique he's acquired from last year's training. But he still hasn't managed to rid his face of acne. The guy's like a mythical creature—half legendary Warrior, half naïve little boy.

"I don't know, guys, might just stay in tonight."

"See, that's the thing I don't get," Aris says. He wags a finger at me, curls bouncing. "I was talking to Litha, and she said that you were at every party in basic ed."

I cringe, running my hand over my face. "Yeah, but that was basic ed, this is Guardian training."

"And in Guardian training, we learn never to leave a comrade behind," Mycul says.

I glare at him. Comrade. That's what we are, I can't deny it. They were there for me last year, picked me up out of a pretty lonely place. It might be okay to go to a party again.

Aris purses his lips and nods his head. "He's got you there."

The closet is thrown open and I'm tossed a jacket and my hat. I'm dragged by the arms out of my room until I'm fully committed to walking on my own to the party. Every step closer brings a familiar jolt of energy. The anticipation swims in my head just like it used to. It was like I needed it back then, but now I'm not so sure.

A blurry image tugs at me—laughter echoes, pain stabs me between the eyes, there's something sticky on my hands. I walked home with someone else's shoes on my feet, or at least, the direction of home. I don't think I made it inside, just passed out on the steps.

At the top of a staircase downtown, I freeze. "Uh, guys, I

don't know about this."

Mycul throws his head back. "Come on, man, you're killing me."

"What is it, Lance, you afraid to get crazy again?" Aris says.

"For Seena's sake, you shouldn't listen to Litha so much."

Aris shrugs, his face turning bright red. "She's not that bad."

At least Litha can't tell them everything about my party days. No one knows everything, and I'd like to keep it that way.

"There's nothing wrong with having some fun." Mycul nudges me down the stairs.

It's an opportunity to hang out with my buddies, that's all I'm going for. Just some bonding time before everything gets busy with training and academics.

With each step I give myself a reminder.

If I'm offered an ale, I say no.

If I'm offered Ease, I say no.

If I'm offered a cigarette, still no.

I square my shoulders. Music pumps through the tunnel, the walls shuddering with the beat, or is that an underground train? Neon flashes around me and we're sucked up into the crowd. Mycul and Aris grab ales. The lids pop off. The glass clinks. I follow behind them, trying to relax and not let my wings press into someone's personal space.

We break through the stuffy centre to a ring of couches. Mycul flops into one of the leather chairs with stuffing squirting out of the arm. He downs a gulp of ale. Aris and I take a seat on the couch across from Litha and some other guy who lights a cigarette for her. He has a stocky build with hair buzzed to his scalp. A mystic beast *Vishal* marks his tan forehead.

Litha's eyes are closed as she takes a long drag. Smoke

twists around her, veiling her sandy skin, but she opens her eyes and smiles at me. "I knew you'd find your way to one of these Guardian parties eventually." With one hand holding the cigarette by her lips, her other arm drapes over the back of the couch.

I glance at Aris as the Beastblood dude wraps his arm around Litha. Aris' eyebrows pinch and the smile on his face wavers. Shaking his head, he turns to me. "Gotta have some fun while we can, hey, Lance?" he says, slapping my knee.

"I guess. I hear third year's the toughest, so might as well get the partying out of my system for—"

"I don't know, Lance," Litha says. "I think it's deep in your blood."

"So, what's the latest, guys—what's the news for the new year?" Mycul says, his shirt now flung open, revealing his entire torso.

"I heard there's an Ironskin at the school this year," Litha's mystery man says.

My ears perk up and my eyes tear away from an ominous green stain on the ground. "Yeah, actually I—"

"Oh god, really?" Mycul rolls his head back.

The words that were about to come out of my mouth pile on my tongue. Heat rises up my neck. Drumming my fingers on my knees, I try again. "I actually m—"

"Last time there was an Ironskin at the school, he trashed one of the practice rooms with the death affinity. It was pretty messed up," Litha's man says.

"Wait, what year is the Ironskin in?" Aris asks.

"First year, dumbass." Mycul's eyes narrow and he shakes his head.

Aris' shoulders slump forward. "No, I mean, like, don't we get transfers sometimes?"

"Doesn't matter, man. All that matters is staying away from them. They're so unpredictable."

Come on, Lance, just say it. I met her today and she's really nice. She's really nice. Just say it.

A plume of smoke envelopes my face as Litha leans forward. "In other news, Lance's got his eye on a pretty first-year girl."

"Really, Lance?" Aris says with a smile and nudges me in the ribs. "What's her—"

"You holding out on us buddy?" Mycul says.

"What is she, Beastblood? She looks like she might be avian beast affinity." Litha's face twists into a wry smile and she raises an eyebrow.

Mycul laughs.

She's Ironskin, actually. And she's really nice.

"What does that mean?" Aris asks. "Do avian girls have a specific look?"

Everyone laughs.

"You don't know about avian girls?" Mycul says.

There's something Aris and I have both missed, but the others bust their guts without explanation.

Every inch of my skin crawls. My head spins and my knee bounces of its own accord. The air is full of smoke. My fingers twitch.

On the table sits the pack of cigarettes. I drop my eyes to the green stain, hands braced together, elbows on my knees, even though they jiggle up and down.

"Aris, you're such an idiot," someone says.

And now I remember why I drank in the first place. The

scene is always the same. No one cares, they just want their own voice to be heard. For a second, they're interested, but then they move on. Moving from high to high, from gossip to gossip, and if you don't keep up, you're discarded. I could never keep up, so it was easier to be seen when I was the loudest drunk in the room.

"He's not an idiot," I say.

No one hears me—the cloud of smoke is too thick and the music too loud.

A girl in the centre of the dancing crowd sways to the music with her arms above her head and an unopened ale in her hand. Her eyes close. She pays no attention to anyone else in the room. I wish I had that kind of control.

My fingers twitch. They snatch the pack of cigarettes from the table. A lighter finds its way into my hand. A spark ignites, bright, enchanting as it catches the rod between my fingers and a trail of smoke streams to the tunnel ceiling.

I inhale.

The rich smoke is heavy in my lungs, warm in my mouth. I stare at my hands. My fingers no longer twitch; my knees are still. I take another breath.

I can't trust myself.

After a year of being clean, I still can't even stand up to everything I hated back then. Mycul and Aris really have been there for me. I don't know what it would say to them if I just up and left. But it's not good for me to be here.

My teeth clench. I urge myself to let go of the cigarette, but I finish it instead.

The least I can do is leave. The least I can do is step away from this familiar environment that I keep falling into.

I stand. My wings flex and I flick the butt to the floor, stamping it out with my toe.

"Later, guys."

No one responds.

I swallow and plunge my hands into my pockets. As I leave the party, a sickening void sinks into my stomach.

13

ELIOTE

They'll never let you in, Eliote. My parents' voices swim through my head. *You better not embarrass the family name here,* they said before they left yesterday. But they're wrong. People without enhancements can be Guardians. I've honed my own set of skills and they're going to see them today; I can be an asset without sparkling essence.

As I push their negativity out of mind, I push myself away from the mattress and rub the sleep from my eyes. Rin still sleeps across the room, sheets pulled up under her chin. Turning onto her side, the shift stirs her aura. Yesterday it took my breath away, today it draws me in. I squint to get a better look.

Her essence is still. It fills every cell of her body, glimmering like crystals, instead of swirling through essence channels like every other hédin. Her spirit is pure white and shines like a star.

Her aura doesn't stretch out around her, it stays tight. Ethereal and storm-like, it thunders, projecting from her core only to be pulled back in. Red and blue streams flow violently, protecting her soul.

A glob of energy breaks away from the blue stream. It flutters with the wings of a bird. The bird soars around Rin's brilliant centre. Up and around and straight through. It splashes back into the blue stream, inspiring a twin red bird to spring forth.

I cup my hands in my lap. No light spills from me. There are no swirls of energy, no sparkling essence, just dull flesh. I am a dud lightstone that casts a shadow for other Luminee to shadow phase through.

I check the time. 8:45.

I'm an idiot. Class starts in fifteen minutes.

Pushing my blanket aside, I throw myself off the bed and sprint to the closet.

"Get up, Bird Brain," I yell and grab something to wear from my closet.

Rin just groans and rolls over.

"Not today, chicky." I grab the boot sitting by her bed and chuck it at her just as she pulls the sheets over her head.

"Hey." She yanks the sheets back down and she reappears dazed with her hair falling over her face.

"We slept in. We're going to be late for combat training."

As I hop up and down to get my leggings on, Rin drags herself out of bed. I open Rin's side of the closet and grab just about the only things that are suitable for combat training; a pair of sweats and the yellow Akinnera t-shirt. I throw the clothes at her and while she changes, I pull my hair back into a ponytail, which will be the only primping I'm allowed today.

"Thanks for getting me up," Rin says. "I can't believe I slept in."

"Yeah, yeah. Hurry up or else you won't get anything to eat until lunch," I say and head out the door.

Rin runs to catch up with me.

"If my parents find out that I slept in on the first day of school, they'll kill me."

I huff as we enter the dining hall. The kitchen staff is already taking away breakfast, so we grab whatever we can get our hands on. We got ready so fast that there's still a few minutes to eat, so we take a seat. Rin prioritizes a cup of cold coffee over food, and she even takes the time to sprinkle cinnospice in it.

"We're supposed to meet in one of the smaller training rooms in the arena," I say between bites.

She nods. "Right. So . . . I didn't see you at orientation," she says.

I look up from my plate and glare at her. "Less chit-chat, more eating," I say and look back down.

"I mean, it's not like it's a big deal, you just kind of disappeared."

With a sigh I tell her, "If you must know, I went to dinner with my parents." They prayed that Vin would bless me with his light for over an hour. "Besides, I didn't want to go to a stupid orientation."

"But it was mandatory."

"What, are you going to tell on me?"

"'Course not." She downs the last of her coffee, avoiding eye contact. "I've got your back."

I focus on her aura again. All the power that people fear about the Ironskins is condensed into little birds fluttering around her.

The potential to give and take life is right at her fingertips. But I check on her spirit, burning pure in her core. The red and blue swirls and feathered animations guard it more closely now that she's awake.

She nods and says, "I mean it." Tapping her fork on her plate, she tilts her head. "Why are you looking at me like that?"

I run my tongue over my teeth, my cheeks heating. *I can see lineage essence and a person's spirit. When they interact, they create an aura. From the aura, I can feel emotions. Just by looking at a person's essence, I can feel wants and desires.* Even if I tried to explain, my mother's hand has already slapped the words out of my mouth.

"You done with that?" I take her plate before she can answer and put it with the others.

We get to the arena only a few minutes late. We scurry past the other first-year students in the arena and find a small group in the training room. There are only about fifteen or sixteen other students gathered around one instructor. Most students don't notice but one spots us and Rin waves to him. He waves back, tapping his wrist. Rin rolls her eyes at him.

From a distance, he's not much to look at. He's a lanky Nytrue with rich-brown skin and vibrant blue hair. His ears stick out, but they are pierced with little silver studs—a feature I'm always drawn to. Through the glare on his square-rimmed glasses, I catch his crystal blue eyes and he smiles. Even when I squint to peek into his aura, he doesn't look away. His aura spreads out around him, a calm, clear pool pouring out from the gentle spring of his soul. Still. It tugs at me.

"A friend of yours?" I whisper to Rin.

She nods. "Yeah, that's Ace."

Ace's aura stretches out to her. Rin's storm calms a little but doesn't return the gesture as we fall in with the group beside him to listen to the tall, muscular instructor at the front.

"Welcome to your first day of combat training," the instructor says. "My name is Marcus. I'm an Emberstead-Earthkin with fire affinity, a recent AAGT graduate, and I'm here with you for a specific purpose." He stands with his hands behind his back and his chin raised so he looks down his nose. The warm red glow of his aura fills the open space around him, deepening his dark-brown skin and accentuating his hair's copper tone.

"You all have been put in this group because you have demonstrated knowledge of hand-to-hand combat or weapons training during your entrance exam. Because of that, we're looking at putting together an advanced team."

My heart jumps. Did I hear that right? Not only did I make it into the academy, but I'm better than all those students outside in the arena. While all the other Luminee children were learning how to teleport through the shadows, I taught myself how to throw knives and practiced the Luminee martial art of Shodahet. This group right here is the first sign of pay off.

Marcus paces before us. The steps with his right leg are cut short with a limp and he forces the flow of his essence into it. He can't be much older than us because his essence hasn't been tamed by age. His aura is disciplined into calm, red rings, but a wild burgundy cyclone stirs at his core.

Running a hand over the stubble on his chin, he says. "Being in this group doesn't give you the right to think more highly of yourself, and if I don't think you make the cut, I'm sending you back to the regular first-year class tomorrow. Now, in order to see how good you kids really are, you will showcase your skills to the class in one-on-one duels. That way I can also assess what damage has been done in your training and whip you guys into true Guardian shape." He motions for us to follow him and arrange ourselves around a square mapped out on the floor about ten feet by ten feet.

"Hussle up. Toes on the line, back straight. You should not be touching anyone," he says and points to the two guys closest to him. "I want you two in the ring first. Fight when ready."

The guys circle around each other and take a few tentative jabs in turn. The shorter one has better form but the taller has more strength and reach. Marcus gives a few pointers and urges them to fight harder to land a blow. The fight picks up and they get some shots in, but the match is decided as the taller boy executes a powerful, yet awkward, roundhouse kick to the other boy's side. Marcus calls the match, and the boys leave the square, the one who got hit clutches his side.

Marcus calls Rin into the ring and puts her with the tallest guy in the group.

"All right, Bird Brain, let's see what you can do."

Rin's face flushes, she smiles but shakes her head at me as she steps into the square. Shaking out her hands she takes a stance I've never seen before, standing straight with her knees only slightly bent. Fists up, she bounces back and forth on the balls of her feet. The guy struts into the square.

"My name's Roth," he says through a crooked smile.

"Rin."

"Where you from Rin?"

Rin scoffs. "Doesn't matter. Let's fight."

"Eager for a loss, that's fine by me. Let's get this over with."

Roth sets up his guard. A smile crosses his lips that's infected by a cruel sickness in his soul. "I'm not going easy on you."

They start off the same way the other two did but once they've circled around a few times Roth throws a punch, quick, right to her nose. Rin ducks and sidesteps. Roth swings his other arm, but Rin throws up her arm to block. Their bones collide with a snap. Roth punches over and over again, pressing Rin to the edge of the court as she avoids his fists. Rin's essence is calm and steady. Her face relaxed, eyes fixed on Roth's every move.

I glance at Marcus. He sighs and rubs the bridge of his nose.

"Hit him, Rin," I say.

Roth swings, his fist collides with Rin's cheek. Rin's head snaps to the side and she takes a few steps back. She blocks a kick and adjusts her footing.

"Yeah, hit me, Rin," Roth sneers.

Good light of Vin, he's a real jerk.

Rin cracks her knuckles on one fist. Her eyebrows draw together and her essence pulses. Like lightning, her fist flies to his face, smacking him in the cheek. Jab, cross, front kick. She lands every hit. Roth stumbles back with a grunt. I can already see a little bruising where she decked him on the cheek. Rin bridges the gap between them and with a swing of her leg she lands a crescent kick to his head. Roth hits the ground.

But Marcus doesn't call the match and Roth isn't about to give up.

He pushes himself off the ground, coming back swinging his fists in wide desperate arcs. Rin ducks and blocks, throwing her weight around the square.

Roth pants. A bead of sweat slips down his cheek. Rin takes a step back, calculating her next move, taking long, even breaths.

She bounces back and forth.

Heaving a breath and a grunt, Roth moves in. His arm extends, and Rin shifts to the right, avoiding the blow. I focus my sight on Rin's essence just as every cell in her body lights up, fortifying with energy. She thrusts her fist into his stomach. Roth flies back, the other students jump out of the way. He hits the ground far outside the square and tumbles clear across the room.

My jaw drops.

The other students gasp and laugh, all but Ace. He watches with his arms crossed, cringing at the sight of Roth crumpled on the ground, but he smiles as Rin puts up her guard again, ready for round two. Roth hasn't found his feet though. He groans, turns to the side, and heaves his breakfast onto the floor. Rin rushes over to him.

"Roth, I'm so sorry. I tried to hold back," she says, putting a hand on his shoulder. He brushes her hand aside and pushes himself slowly off the ground, grunting.

"You," Marcus says to one of the guys. "Take him to the infirmary and find me a mop. You." He points at Rin. "You get the first spot on the team."

The other students snicker. "Dirty Ironskin," one of them mutters as Rin makes her way back to the group.

"Hope they find someway to expel her," says a girl to my left.

Rin's eyes swipe to the girl—I think someone called her Jaya. Their eyes lock and Jaya flicks her pinky finger at Rin.

"Cutch," she says, sneering. The Ironskin slur burns my ears. Rin fixes her eyes on the ground as she steps into line next to me, leaving the other students to mock her without a fight.

"Not great at making friends, huh?" I say to Rin.

"Excuse me?" she says.

"I get winning the match, but taking his dignity like that? Ruthless." I hold up my hand to her. "Nice work."

Rin stares at my hand like it's a piece of rotten meat.

"You're supposed to hit it, dummy," I say.

"Hey, that's fun." She smiles at my gesture of congratulations and slaps my hand. Setting her hands back on her hips as she gets in line, she adds, "I don't usually get congratulated after a fight."

"Luminee girl," Marcus says, looking down at a clipboard. "Eliote. Stop gabbing and get in the square, you're up."

You're up. The phrase runs in a loop through my head, stalling my feet. I clamp my hand around Grandma's lightstone. I still try to get it to light sometimes, with no success. But even a regular stone can be a weapon if you chuck it hard enough.

I step into the square and Marcus pairs me with Jaya.

I've watched the lights dance in other people for so long. For once I'm in the centre, not picked last, not just watching. I've trained hard to get here and I'm taking a spot on this team.

I lock my eyes on Jaya, but we don't exchange pleasantries like Rin and Roth. Right away, I get into the waning crescent fight stance, with my right leg bent low to the ground under me and my left stretched out straight in front. Palms open, my left arm mirrors my left leg and I raise my right arm high above my head to complete the crescent. Jaya takes a simpler stance— left leg forward bent at a ninety-degree angle, right leg straight back, fists clenched in front of her.

"Begin," Marcus commands.

Lunging forward, I drop my right arm behind me, and in a wide arc, I swing it as fast as I can to slam my wrist up to Jaya's chin. Her head snaps back and I swing my arm back down on her shoulder. She winces. I grab her arm and yank her down. She tumbles over my leg but catches herself to transition into a roll. On her feet again, she throws a punch. I twist to the right to avoid her fist. She punches again, and I spin to the left. Anticipating the movement, she catches me in the gut with a front kick. My breath escapes me, but I only have to shuffle back a step to recover.

She's not strong, neither am I, but I can work around that. I let her throw another punch and this time catch her fist with one hand and jar her elbow with a quick jab to the joint.

She screeches.

I swing myself under her arm. With my momentum and her arm twisting under my control, I flip her head over heels. She flops face first on the ground.

"That's a match. Eliote, stay after class," Marcus says.

Staring down at Jaya, Marcus' words run through me, pulsing with my heavy breaths and my pounding heart. I bite my lip, trying not to smile too much.

Rin holds her hand up. I slap it.

After a few more fights, the last two students take the court—a massive Earthkin guy and an Emberstead girl. The girl's aura rages scarlet red around her blush-pink soul. Her aura thrashes out around her, but before it can reach anyone, it's suppressed by a spiralling green haze.

Rin shifts her weight next to me, and her aura shifts too, pulling away from the Emberstead girl's powerful, suffocating presence.

The habit of watching others is hard to break. My little moment on the court has come and gone. Just a flicker in the dark compared to all of them. I close my eyes to clear it all from my sight and open them again, bringing back the smile I tried to hide.

14

JOHANNA

FACE BURNING AND fists CLENCHED, I ready myself in the centre of the group. Rin stands across the square from me. The Luminee girl, Eliote, stands right next to her even though Marcus told us no one should be in range to touch. Eliote whispers something to Rin. They both laugh and my eye twitches.

A hot pain shoots through my head. I suck in a breath and press my lips together. My body tenses. I must look constipated, but at least the pain subsides. I exhale an audible breath, dropping my eyes to the floor.

In this moment, there are no Wander Wraiths, there are no voices in my head, and winning definitely doesn't mean I'll be on the same team as Rin, even though it does. Right now, all I have to do is my best—and I can't let her beat me.

I shake my head and focus my attention on my opponent,

nothing else. He has dark skin and long locs tied behind his head. He holds his massive arms out, palms open and stance wide.

I mirror his form. My mom is a strike-first kind of girl, so that's my plan. Strike first, hard, and precise.

"Begin," Marcus says.

I punch at the guy's face. He deflects, grabbing my arm to pull me in and over his bent leg. My body flings itself over his leg. I crumple into myself, tucking my chin to hit the ground with momentum and kick back at him. My foot slams into his chest. He lurches away. Swinging my legs under me, I push toward him with sharp strikes. He blocks each one. Pain stings through my arms and my breaths come quick and full.

Our fight takes us all around the square. He comes at me with a series of spinning crescent kicks, his legs whip around him like a hammer. I duck and counter.

The spinning kicks aren't working for him, so he changes his tactics. He draws back his fist for a powerful strike, engaging his whole body with the movement. I leap at him to deflect his fist in the air with one leg and hammer the other into his chest. He falls back, but springs to his feet in one swift motion. His fist flies to my face again. I bend backward to avoid it and swing my leg behind me to twist to the right.

"Time," Marcus says. "Both of you stay."

Fire burns in my chest. I grit my teeth and punch my last strike at the air. "Damn it," I say under my breath.

"What, you don't want to be on a special team?" the guy says.

Special team with Rin? No, thank you.

"Just not a fan of a tie," I mutter and turn away from him. "You fight like my mom."

He chuckles behind me. "Well, if she's the one who taught you, I'll take that as a compliment."

"Wise ass."

"It's Jeff-Ray, actually. You're Johanna, right?" His voice is low and quiet behind me.

I turn to face him again. He towers over me. A small smile crosses his face, shy, unnerving in its kindness.

I keep my mouth shut and fix him with a stare that I hope will discourage him from asking any more questions. He motions for me to join the small group left in the training room as Marcus dismisses the rest.

Setting my jaw, I force my legs to move to the group, avoiding Rin's eyes. Standing this close to her makes my insides squirm like they're going to spill out of my mouth. I scooch into the group by Ace—the one person I'm surprised to see here.

The boy Ace fought walks up to us. "Hey guys, I'm Niko." He puts out a hand.

"Yeah," Ace says, rubbing his jaw with one hand and shaking Niko's with the other. "Your fist met my face earlier."

"Ah, yeah. No hard feelings, right?"

"'Course not. But I still don't know why I'm in this group." Ace glances at me.

"Don't look at me, ice boy. I'd send you back to basics. What you did out there was crap."

Ace turns to me, eyes crinkled, head pushed forward. "You've been next to me for what, two seconds, and you've already got shit to say?"

Pleased with myself, I let the cruelty of my statement seep into my smile.

"Wasn't that bad," Niko says with a nervous laugh.

Niko is half the size of Jeff-Ray, and Beastblood by the looks of it, with tan skin and short, dusty-blond hair that stands up a bit in the front. He seems friendly enough, but he also seems like an arrogant little dick standing there with his arms crossed and a mischievous grin on his face. His dark eyebrows raise a little when he laughs.

"I guess that junior training program paid off, hey, Jeff?" he says, and nudges Jeff-Ray with his elbow.

"Junior training program?" Ace asks. "What's that?"

"Some cities that aren't shit-holes have programs for basic ed kids who want to prepare early for Guardian training," I say. "Waste of money though. I got here on my own."

"Well, some of us aren't possessed by some unnatural desire to be the best," Ace says.

"Aw." I touch my heart. "Ace, that's so sweet of you to say."

He rolls his eyes at me. "I think it sounds like a cool idea," he says, adjusting his glasses.

Marcus clears his throat as he approaches the group. Sliding his hands into his pockets, he leans to one side, looking us over.

"Every year we have registrar workers and entrance examiners notify us of students who might surpass their first-year peers," he says. "This year, you and the other students here today were flagged for your talents, you six in particular. Headmaster Findel had me assess whether I thought you would make the cut for an accelerated training program."

"What about this one?" I ask, slapping Ace on the back.

"Well, some of you are here for your combat skills, others for essence control, some of you for both. With what you showed me today, I think you guys will work well together."

Work well together? Yeah, right. If he wants us to be all

nice and chummy, then he's mistaken. But if he just wants us to kick some butt together, then yeah, we could do that.

"Since all of you have unique skill sets, we'll focus a lot on teamwork to blend your strengths."

Niko, standing next to me, shoots up his hand. Marcus raises his eyebrows at his enthusiasm. I change my mind, Niko's just annoying.

"Yeah? Question?" Marcus asks.

"Are we still going to be in first-year classes?"

"Academic classes, yes, but we'll train you in hand-to-hand combat and weapons at the second-year level. Which means we'll be able to condense your years at the academy down to three, with a few more academic classes in your final year than normal. Any other questions?"

Only three years at the academy does sound appealing, so maybe this team isn't a complete nightmare.

Niko's hand flies up and almost smacks me in the face. I glare at him and try to resist the urge to wring his neck or fry him. I lean away, imagining puppies and rainbows, anything to take my mind off hédin arson.

"What about today, do we go to our scheduled weapons class now?"

"Yes, today you will follow the schedule that you have been given. Tomorrow you'll meet back here." Marcus looks down at his watch. "Looks like you have about five minutes to get to your next class so—"

Niko puts his hand up for the third time. "Are you going to be instructing us?"

My hair shifts with the wind stirred up from the swing of his arm. Some less than constructive criticism is about to fly out of my mouth if this little shit doesn't quit throwing his hands in the air. I bite my tongue.

"Would you cut it out with the hand?" Marcus says, then sighs. "I have been selected to teach you essence control so that the first-year instructor can continue with regular lessons. Now get out of here and get to class. The weapons-training room is in the main building." He motions with his hand to shoo us out.

Everyone follows Niko out of the training room like a band of baby Rovers. I stay put. *You are Soul Tethered.* The words stick in my mind. The Wander Wraith might as well have taken up residence inside me. Her ashy aftertaste fills my mouth.

I clear my throat. "Marcus, I have a question," I say.

Marcus turns to me. He rubs his chin and his eyes are wide. "Yeah? Sorry, I didn't realize you stuck around. What's up?"

"Well, I had sort of a weird encounter last night."

Shifting his legs, Marcus' brow furrows as he waits.

"They . . . well she said something about a Soul Tether. I was just wondering if it was like an essence thing, maybe?"

"Soul Tether? I can't say I've ever heard of it before. I'm pretty familiar with Emberstead techniques, ancient and contemporary, so I doubt it's Emberstead related."

I nod but the movement of my head insights a pain between my eyes. It slices around the crown of my head. My eyes are still glued to Marcus. A silent scream parts my lips as my jaw drops.

"I can ask around for you, if you want." Marcus tilts his head. "Are you okay?"

The pain slithers down my back and dumps into my stomach. "No worries," I say with acid rising up my esophagus. "It's probably nothing. She was drunk. See you tomorrow."

I sprint from the training room and through the arena.

Outside, the sun stabs my eyes. Sizzling fills my ears, along with a jumble of distorted sounds. They could be words or music, but it all just aches through me. What happened to that distinct voice?

A trash can sits by the door. I grab hold of it with both hands, dunk my face inside, and barf up my breakfast.

"Johanna." A clatter of footsteps approach. "You okay?"

Someone's hand is on my shoulder. I shove it off and wipe my mouth with the back of my hand. The fiery pain sears a loop around my brain, spiking in severity at my temples. The loop hits the spot between my eyes and subsides. My stomach is at rest. Everything is fine. The only things on fire are my cheeks.

I turn, eyes on the ground, and hand at my temple to ward off another round of absurdity. There are five pairs of feet around me. Ace, Niko, Jeff-Ray, Eliote, and Rin.

Ace's hand is hovering by my arm.

"Put your fucking hand down. I'm fine."

Bitterness lingers at the back of my throat. I try to swallow it and adjust my shirt but stop with my hands clenching the hem. Rin stares at me. She wraps one arm around her waist, the other holds her shoulder. Her mouth hangs open.

"Rin, shut your damn mouth."

I shove her to the side and start toward the main building. The group follows, silent. I stop and they pile into me.

"Would someone else go first? I don't know where I'm going."

This is ridiculous. What the hell is wrong with me?

15

RIN

Johanna's cheeks are bright pink, her forehead and neck pale. She doesn't get sick much, and when she does, she toughs it out. Except a few months ago. She had the same two-tone colouring as today and kept touching her temples. The next day, she wasn't at school. Her absence made everything strange, like the furniture in the classrooms was out of place and people's faces were covered with masks.

A knot ties in my stomach and from there, everything inside me tightens. I had no expectations for the day and yet I rushed through breakfast, fought for a spot on the team, and now I rush to the next class. Johanna being sick is just as unexpected as everything else.

But I need to keep moving. I can't worry about her and learn to swing a sword at the same time. Besides, she wouldn't give a damn if it was the other way around.

In the training room, the rest of the students we beat out of the advanced team are already grabbing practice weapons. Our instructor is an older Lifeblood woman who looks like she could kill a beast with her pinky finger. She has dark hair with silver strands pulled back from her wrinkled face in a tight bun. Wiry muscles bulge under her dark, leathery skin as she hands me a sword.

"My name is Livia Lotera. You will address me as Master Lotera," she says to the class.

She has us move apart to create enough space to swing the swords around a couple times and get a feel for their motion.

"In this time slot, you will learn the basics of weapons handling and practice essence control. After this session, every other day I will work on weapons with the advanced team and the regular stream students will work on essence. In weapons training, we will focus on *seya le kaset lon Illyson,* way of the Illyson long sword."

Even though her Slyvic is awful, the words are calming. Slyvic was used before people were enhanced. Ironskins kept using it as our official language even after the lineage split. Some words remain in use within the public like the ever-so-lovely cutch—dirty—and words used for martial arts practice, but my people are the only ones to use it in conversation.

"You will soon notice that it is much easier to learn the basics of weapons and essence incorporation from the start rather than integrating them later. Today we will start with a basic strike and essence incorporation." She marches to the front of the room and raises her own sword. "Dominant hand nearest the blade."

I adjust my grip around the smooth leather straps, then

loosen it again to let the metal weigh on my hands. Ahead of me, Eliote steps and swings her sword in one graceful motion. She swings again like she's dancing with a metallic partner. I try to match her grace, but my arms swing too fast in an awkward arc against the air. I take a breath and try to control my spastic movements.

"One foot of space between your feet. Left foot forward, right foot back. This is your *set fassoa,* your stance."

Master Lotera demonstrates the set fassoa at the front holding her sword at shoulder height on her right side. Right side. I hold mine on my left, and with my left foot forward, I'm off balance. I switch the sword to my right, switch my hands to match Lotera. My body squirms with my dominant left hand on the bottom. I switch everything so I have my left hand on top, right foot forward, left back.

Lotera strikes. I try to mirror her from the left side. I swing. It feels wrong. Must have missed something when I was changing hands. "One fluid motion," Lotera says, demonstrating again.

Maybe I should just do it right-handed for now. I switch and swing again. Ew. I let the sword drop to my side and shake out my arms. It didn't feel right, but I did exactly what she did.

"Find a partner and practice this simple strike against each other to become familiar with the feeling of the clashing swords."

Ace comes straight to me. He's just a beginner like me, but somehow he picks up the steps easily. Even though I'm terrible at this, he's patient and shows me the steps once again.

"How are you doing?" he asks.

"What do you mean? Can't you see I suck?" I blow a stray hair out of my face and try to straighten myself out.

"I mean, how are you doing being away from home?"

"I've been trying not to think about it. Yesterday was weird." I lower my sword. "I miss Liam."

"I bet. And to top it off, looks like we'll be spending some quality time with Johanna."

He nods in Johanna's direction. She's working with Jeff-Ray. The normal ruddy red colouring of her face has returned, as if she hadn't just barfed her guts out minutes ago. With her colour evened out, my muscles uncoil. She's her usual self again with a crinkle between her brows, already figuring out the new moves. Looks like I'm the only one who can't grasp the concept of a fluid motion.

Ace and I clash swords a few times as Master Lotera inspects each group. She paces toward us, hands behind her back, and my armpits start to sweat. I focus on my footwork, my arm swing, my grip. Our swords collide. With a spark and an ear-piercing crack, the top of Ace's sword snaps off and crashes to the floor.

Ace's jaw drops and his eyes go round. Taking one hand off his sword, he shakes it out, then the other.

"Sorry," I say through a grimace.

Lotera tsks. "Don't channel your essence into the sword until I have instructed you."

"Oh, no, I'm not—"

"You first years are always so eager to get to the flashy essence strike, but without proper instruction it's dangerous."

"Sorry, Master Lotera. I guess I just swung too hard."

"Swung too hard?" Raising a brow, she eyes me up and down.

"Ironskin."

"Ironskin, ah." She frowns and steps back. "Well, find your partner another sword and come back. Ironskins can't channel essence the way other lineages can. You'll have to practice your steps on your own while I instruct the others in essence channelling."

"Yes, Master Lotera."

Lotera marches back to the front. She instructs us to form lines in front of the targets along one of the walls.

I head to the rack of practice swords with tension creeping into my shoulders.

"There's got to be some way for you to do an essence strike," Ace says.

"Take my sword. You're supposed to be getting in line." I hand him my sword and grab a new one for myself.

Ace gives me a questioning look, but I nudge him into line.

Lotera takes her set fassoa. "In your entrance exam, you should have demonstrated basic control over your essence in the form of an essence strike, transformation, or strength restraint and release. Now, just as with a normal weaponless essence strike, we draw our essence from feet to hands, allowing the flow to generate energy, feeling the power surge through our bodies. The faster your heart rate, the faster your essence can be released."

Everyone seems to know what she's talking about. They nod and practice shifting their weight, opening and closing their palms a few times. But I've never felt a flow; it's more of a conscious effort to "restrain and release" my strength. When Master Lotera came to watch us, my concentration was all over the place—on her, my steps, the blade—I couldn't focus.

"Use the set fassoa to balance your energy, your step to mobilize it, and thrust your arms forward to channel it to your hands, directing it through your sword," Lotera says. She inhales, steps, strikes. A stream of air billows down her blade and blasts her target. The target slams against the floor and flips upright again. "This technique is effective for beast slaying, or to keep distance between you and your opponent." She sheathes her sword.

The other students gasp and whisper to each other.

"If you're a Beastblood, take this opportunity to transform before, during, or after your basic strike. Take turns targeting and return to the back of the line."

I take a few steps away from the group to practice my sword swing and footsteps. I must look silly swinging my sword solo, but for some reason, Eliote does the same, except she's lovely, brandishing her weapon with poise.

Step, thrust arms out, and swing. It's simple, but doing it right-handed makes my movements sloppy.

I lower my sword for a moment to watch my classmates. Most of them struggle to get any kind of essence strike to flow from their hands down their swords. Johanna lets loose a stream of flames that explode around the hilt and spews smoke in her face. She grunts, wiping a furious hand over her face.

Ace takes his turn, setting his feet in a perfect set fassoa. He takes more time than the other students to calm himself, drawing long breaths, and focusing his eyes on the target. He steps and slashes. A flash of silver light blinks from his hands. Frost spreads across the blade. At the tip, a sparkling icy stream speeds to the centre of the target. The target wobbles.

I drop my sword and clap as Ace leaves his place at the front of the line.

"I think I know why you made it on the advanced team," I say.

Eliote also claps, nodding with approval.

"It's nothing," Ace says and lowers his head humbly to hide the smile on his blushing face.

For a moment, the room moves around me. Apart from the other students at the back of the room, my feet stay planted, my sword lies on the ground. A rush of breath fills me, and time catches up with me. My body tingles with my heartbeat slipping into my consciousness. I've jumped from moment to moment without thinking in the last few days. It's like my body is registering the change—the difference in how the school runs, the cleanliness, the attitude in the air. It's so different from Senn, and something lingers around me, removing me from everyone else.

It was my second visit to the principal's office that year—the first was for skipping class to buy an expensive book.

Mrs. Kingsman stood, smoothed her skirt, and turned on her heals to the door. "Johanna, suspension is the last thing we need right now. Get your things and let's go," she said, leaving us in her wake with a billowy cloud of perfume.

Johanna stomped off after her.

Mr. Dalaan set a hand on Ace's shoulder to steer him out of the room. Ace looked over his shoulder with a parting smile that didn't reach his eyes. He was only given detention for essence manipulation.

Oron was silent with his arms crossed over his belly, eyes lowered. He had his work coveralls on. The metallic scent of the core-energy plant wafted through the small office, fighting Mrs.

Kingsman's floral musk. He tipped his head to the door. I pushed away from my chair with lead in my legs, and space in my head filled with buzzing.

Once outside the office, Oron set his hands on his hips, regarding me with disappointment that sent an extra crackle through the buzz in my head. "Are you Dien's child or did your parents not teach you right?"

I swallowed a slimy lump in my throat and turned my back to him.

"Skipping class, now this? You can't keep pulling shit."

I hadn't even made it to second bell before Tōmas' sweaty hands crawled out of last night's frolicking to mar my name. Skipping class, fighting, that wasn't the half of it, and Oron drenched me in judgement. If only he could pick a stance. One second, he's angry with me, the next he buys me lovely outfits for Registration. I never expected him to brush off my behaviour, but it was too hard to be pulled back and forth all the time when I messed up.

"Damned hells, Rin. Get your books. I'll wait for you outside." His heavy tread faded down the hall.

I kept my eyes on the ground as I went to my locker. The floors became a little more familiar, a little greyer, the blue of my locker less sky-like and a little more drunk man's glazed eyeballs. My feet were less sturdy on the ground.

The murmur of my teacher's lesson that I had been shut out of hit my ears in dreamy tones. My mind took hold of it as a sadistic punishment and my hands busied with my combination lock. The extent of my attention didn't include footsteps.

At the back of my neck, hot breath slithered over my skin. It sunk invisible needles into my legs, pinning me in place. A hand stuck to the locker next to mine, barricading me, and another felt down my side.

"Can't hit me here, Rin." The fiend's voice swallowed me. "Not unless you want a longer suspension."

A quick jab to his gut would do the trick to get his slimy hand off my hip. But my arm wouldn't move. My eyes were fixed on my lock. *Is this the way it's going to be for the rest of the year?*

My mouth was the only thing that would move. "Get your hand off me."

He tugged at my hip, spinning me to face him, and planted his hand on the other side of my head. The phantom needles spiralled down my arms, numbing every bit of muscle. Tōmas dipped his head so I was staring at the inky puddle of bruise on his cheek.

"Better?" he said.

Heart in my throat and a pulse behind my eyeballs, every part of me wanted to disappear—his eyes were as invasive as his hands. I had to figure out how to get away from him without losing too much dignity. Class was about to end, the hall would crawl with students, they would see me caged by this popular boy and think even less of me.

"You make me sick, but I don't mind sticking around to ruin your day," Tōmas said.

I urged my hand to move. My finger gave in to my command with a jolting twitch, like a nerve impulse breaking rigour mortis as my dead arms regained life.

Tōmas lowered his lips to my ears. My stomach twisted with the tingle on my lips that remembered how soft his were on mine.

"One day you'll go through the fire," he said.

Whatever he meant by that cryptic phrase, I didn't care to find out. I whipped around, my head knocking him in the nose. I yanked the cheap metal, and the lock busted right off the locker. Spinning back around, Tōmas' pretty face scrunched into a shape just short of a snarl, and I grabbed his belt buckle. Tugging him to me so that his hips were almost flush with mine, I jammed the lock down his pants.

He jumped away from me, jittering his legs to get the lock to come out of the bottom of his pants. I took the opportunity to get my books from my locker while Tōmas uttered curses under his breath.

"*Fenlech calaikah*," he said.

The lock clattered to the floor.

Was that Firtōn? Why would his Lifeblood ass be using an Emberstead language? All the more reason to get away from the creep.

With a ringing in my ears and breaths like razor blades, I rushed down the hall and burst through the doors.

"Let's go," I said. The rushed words left me breathless again.

Oron tromped beside me, hands in his pockets, giving me sidelong glances every few feet. I knew there were daggers in those eyes, but I didn't care. I knew traffic roared around us, all I heard was ringing. I knew my nose should've registered the stench of the trash bins we passed, but all I knew was the sting of bile on my tongue and all I could do was swallow it down and keep moving.

The next day, Eliote and I are up and out of bed early enough to sit down, eat a full meal, and have a warm coffee. We even get down to the arena before everyone else. As we wait for the others, Eliote stretches. Even though my strength enhancement makes it so I could never tear a muscle, I stretch too. I just have to keep up and expect what Adrianne told me to expect—a mess. That means anything from Johanna barfing her guts out to a Rover sprouting rainbow wings.

"Why didn't you go through the essence strike lines yesterday?" I ask Eliote as I bend to touch my toes.

Eliote tilts her head to the side and her silky purple hair swishes. A half smile presses her black lips into a thin line and dimples one cheek. Dark eyeshadow shimmers as she blinks. "You're pretty curious for someone who doesn't talk much."

I shrug and strain my reach, only grazing my ankles with my fingertips.

"I don't have Luminee enhancements," she says.

"Not even lightstone manipulation?" I say, eyeing the massive green lightstone hanging from her neck.

"Nothing. On Registration Day my blood went into the metre, and nothing happened. I already knew I was unenhanced. I had tried shadow phasing hundreds of times, but my mom made us wait half an hour in the Registration booth to see. All we had to show for it was a dozen angry Luminee, and you don't want to see a Luminee angry." She wags a warning finger at me. "But I have this ability to see a person's aura."

I straighten up and rearrange my sweatshirt which has inched its way up my torso while I reached for my toes without success. "Like, you can see my spirit and stuff?"

"Spirit, aura, essence, emotions. All of it."

"So . . . what do you see in my essence . . . aura?"

She's quiet for a while, looking at the ground with her hands on her hips.

I can't imagine what she must see. It can't be good, not with the life and death affinities in me. Her silence makes me squirmy, so I stretch my arm for something to do.

"There's a crazy darkness around you. A tremendous goodness too. The power of your essence is totally out of control, but in a way, it's still controlled, or maybe *controllable* is the right word. It's terrifying but I kind of like it." She winks at me then starts to jog in place, shaking out her arms.

Terrifying, crazy darkness. Sounds lovely. I shake my head.

"You don't really seem surprised," Eliote says.

"I guess because I'm not. There's this woman in ancient Ironskin history named Renya. They say she could see the hearts and intentions of the people she met."

Eliote stops moving all except her moth-like eyelashes fluttering as she looks at me. "I didn't know there were other people like me."

The rest of the team trickles in and before long our instructors show up, Headmaster Evelyn Findel among them. To her right is a tall, middle-aged man with dark hair, greying in patches at his temples, and a pasty complexion, who peers at us over the rim of his glasses. On Evelyn's right is a younger woman with shoulder-length, frizzy, blond hair.

Following behind them is Marcus along with the girl I met coming off the train—Adrianne. Her eyes are focused, sombre almost, but as she looks up and I catch her eyes, her seriousness vanishes. She smiles at me so wide her eyes squint. I can't help but smile back at her and wave.

Evelyn sets her box down and beckons us with open arms. "Gather around, students," she says drawing us in with her magnetic presence. Folding her hands gracefully in front of her, metal bracelets click together around her wrists. "I have many things to get to today, but first I wanted to congratulate you all. We are impressed by your skills and pleased to have you train at an advanced level." She nods and steps to the side. "These are your instructors. Professor Hans Griven," she says motioning to the tall, pasty man.

"I am looking forward to seeing what you all can do," he says.

"Brand Highcaller, a graduate of the academy and an esteemed Warrior Commander who volunteered to oversee your training," Evelyn says, and the young woman with the blond hair steps forward. Her face is like a doll with wide expressionless eyes, and her golden-brown skin is flawless except for the cluster of freckles on her left cheek. The doll resemblance ends with the tired bags under her glassy, grey eyes.

Evelyn and professor Griven wear the navy-blue academy uniforms like the rest of the staff, but Brand's is forest green, decorated with badges. She leaves the blazer open and the button at the top of her blouse undone. She remains silent, a small smile on her face. I get a chill of familiarity from her. She's not just familiar, the chill is familiar. I got the same feeling when I picked up my Guardian application on Registration Day.

She was there.

Her hands are the ones that handed me the application that got me here. But how could one encounter create such a sense of comfort in me when her demeanour is so cold?

"Of course, Marcus Ericsson."

Marcus raises a hand to us.

"Finally, Adrianne McCarthy is in the Medic program and will be training you in defensive procedures as a part of her fourth-year, public-aid requirement."

Adrianne steps forward. "I'm really excited to work with you guys," she says with a quick nod. She steps back and grabs a chunk of her long hair, smoothing the ends between her fingers.

"All right, I'll leave you to it, Brand." Evelyn makes a swift turn on her high heels. She hands over her mystery box to Brand and clip-clops her way out of the training room.

Brand opens the box, revealing communication devices that can be worn around the head. She clicks a small switch on the side before handing it to Niko.

"Your task today is simple—get to the top of Moon Hill in one hour." She hands a device to each of us. "These coms allow us to see and hear what you do while you are in the field. They will relay your perceptions to be displayed on this PAT, so that Marcus, Hans, and Adrianne can observe from here." She pulls a new model PAT out of the box. It's a thin, sleek, silvery screen. "They will monitor your heart rate and breathing so we can be aware of your fitness levels."

I take a device from her as a chill runs down my spine. Her voice lingers in my ears, blunt and monotone. My fingers clench the flimsy device and my stomach flip-flops.

"Are you all right?" Brand asks me, raising an eyebrow.

"Uh—" I shut my mouth and nod. Why does she make me feel so weird?

Brand moves on to hand a com to Eliote. I struggle to get the headpiece to sit right, but I can't seem to get the hang of it. Johanna snatches it out of my hands. With a roll of her judgemental eyes, she flips the device over and sets it right on my head.

"You're a useless idiot, you know that?" she mutters.

"Says the girl who exploded her own flames in her face yesterday," I say.

Johanna lifts her chin and glares down her nose.

Brand turns back to us. "Are we done here, ladies?" Her pointed words freeze any desire to continue the spat with Johanna.

"We're good," I say.

"What's her deal?" Eliote asks shrugging a shoulder to Johanna.

"That's just Johanna being Johanna," I whisper to Eliote.

Brand presses a button on the PAT and a metal door at the back of the room opens with a mechanical whirr. We are at the base of Moon Hill and the city wall gate is open wide. The hill is covered in lush foliage with bright-pink, flowering trees dotting the sea of green. From the door, a path stretches up the hill into the core-energy mist swirling through the trees.

"There is an airbus at the top of the hill. It will wait only for one hour, so you'd better hurry," Brand says. "This is a simple exercise in speed and stamina. But remember, Illyson is a wild place. That's why we're all here, isn't it? You have five minutes before I start the timer. I suggest you converse with each other." Giving us a slight nod, she steps back to the other instructors.

"Okay, team," Niko pipes up. He opens his arms wide like Evelyn did, but we stay where we are. He tries again, flapping his arms like a bird. I move in and the other do as well until we're in a tight huddle.

"We're going to have to book it up that mountain, so we

really need to watch out for each other," Niko says. "What's everyone thinking? Shoot out some tips." He claps his hands together.

"We need a working formation," Ace says.

"Rin's slow so she can take up the rear," Johanna says. "Want to take the lead on this, Niko? Call shots? Seems you like the attention."

Niko's eyes narrow at Johanna, but he moves on and beckons for everyone's participation.

"Shouldn't we know each other's abilities, essence levels maybe?" Jeff-Ray asks.

"Sure," Eliote says looking down at her nails. "That's easy. I don't have any."

The rest of the team nod their heads, taking in this new information.

"Okay, well, I'm a level three, with basic earth manipulation and all that, and I'm working on gravity manipulation," Jeff says, clasping his hands in front of him.

One by one, everyone says their essence level and abilities. Niko is a level three with a bear beast form. Ace explains that he's a level four and mainly uses ice. Once Johanna's done listing her many fascinations with fire manipulation, armour, weapon creation, and moving objects with Mind Fire, the team turns to me.

I drop my eyes to the floor, fiddling with the collar of my sweater. "Essence level four, strength enhancement and impenetrable skin."

As I raise my eyes, Ace looks at me expectantly. Johanna's eyebrows spring up, and she scoffs to the side. Can they blame me for omitting the spirit affinities? It's not really an ability if I can't use it yet.

"I got it." Niko breaks the circle and starts moving us around into the formation he's mapped out in his head.

He pulls Ace in front of Eliote and places Johanna and Jeff on either side of her. I fall back behind Eliote and Niko steps in front of Ace.

"I'll be the first look out, Ace, you're the second—you see anything you crush it with an icicle to the head. Johanna and Jeff-Ray you fall in with power shots; fireballs, boulders, the works." They all nod as Niko dishes out his instructions. "Eliote, you help anyone who's struggling and Rin, keep an eye out for a kill shot. Everyone good with that?" Niko looks back at us for our input. No one says anything but Jeff-Ray.

"Yeah, one thing. I think we're gonna need to get Rin new shoes after this."

Everyone's gaze shifts to my beat-up brown boots. The threads holding them together are fraying, but they're all I have. Everyone else has special shoes for easy running. Johanna wears a pair of bright yellow ones that match her yellow shirt. Taking in everyone's nice, athletic clothes, heat spreads through my face.

"All right, we'll work on that," Niko says. He turns to Brand. "We're ready, Commander Highcaller," he says, pumping his fist in the air.

The corner of Brand's mouth twitches. She clears her throat. "You can call me Brand."

Niko's fist pump brings a smile to my face. Adrenaline rushes through my body. I tap my fingers together and explore the fine ridges of the tips. Every ridge registers a little bump. I am ready for this.

"Begin." Brand's command is like a rifle shot in my ears,

redirecting my energy to my feet. We shoot out the doors and into the sunlight.

16

JOHANNA

Wᴇ ʙʀᴇᴀᴋ ꜰʀᴏᴍ ᴛʜᴇ ᴛʀᴀɪɴɪɴɢ ʀᴏᴏᴍ. As I settle into a brisk jog, the sun beats down on me. I welcome the heat with deep breaths of the fresh Akinnera air. It feels right to be here. But Niko sings some sort of Beastblood drinking song up front. The sun will perk me up just fine, don't need a song to do that. I could strangle that kid.

"Hey, Niko," Jeff says.

"What's up, my man?"

"I was just thinking you should leave the tunes alone for a while."

So maybe some of us on this team have their heads on right.

"Doesn't bother me," Eliote says.

What's with this girl? Is she going to protect everyone from any minor stab? It's good to have your differences and not agree all the time. Because differences aren't what keep people apart.

When we were little, Rin and I were friends. We were different, but we were friends. We pushed each other—that's what made us good for each other. But as we grew up, I've found who she really is. I don't need someone who can't handle me, someone who can't be there for me.

I focus on the path, my yellow shoes peeking in and out of my sight line. Bright yellow to match my sunny personality. I concentrate on my breathing the way Mom nags me to. Even though I'm a whole province away, that woman is in my head.

She's a whole province away. I'm outside the city walls. This isn't the time to be thinking about anything other than getting to the top of Moon Hill.

Back in the moment, I catch Jeff-Ray looking my way. He smiles. I refuse to return the friendly gesture, instead I let my death stare do the talking. I'm not happy, so why waste my strength to force a smile? Although, I did speak with him this morning and I could actually bear him, unlike all the other sweet, perky, first-year students who make me want to jump off a cliff. The conversation with Jeff wasn't forced; it was easy, real.

Jeff checks over his shoulder. I check too. Rin lags behind the group a few paces. A stab in my gut tells me to switch up the formation. If Rin gets attacked from the back, she could be out like a light, and I'm the only one who knows that might kill her. Her weak spot is more vulnerable than any part of me. It makes me feel like I'm responsible for her—for this little blond puppy who keeps following me around.

"Ace, take my place," Jeff says. "I'm going to fall back with Rin, so someone's got her back, ya know?"

Okay, enough, she's fine. I need to focus on this task.

I scan the forest. The tall trees make our path a nice, cool temperature for running. The core-energy mist prickles my skin. Now that Niko's stopped singing, the sounds of the life around me fill my ears. Birds sing while the leaves rustle, and the wind whistles. The crunch of gravel under our feet is rhythmic.

But there's something else—a twig snaps, a low snort, a growl.

I even my breaths.

Thundering footsteps break the quiet.

A beast leaps from the undergrowth ahead, a blur of shadows and fur and glinting teeth.

Rin shoots out to my right. She jumps, plants both feet on the side of a tree, pushes away from the trunk at full force, and collides with the horrific beast. She grasps the creature's sharp teeth with her bare hands. Even with an arm's length between us, the beast's breath is hot on my face, and I am frozen.

Its body tenses under mangy patches of fur. Amber eyes glint, intent to kill. Its bottom jaw juts forward and steam spews from its deep pitted nostrils. All four paws dig into the dirt as it struggles against Rin.

A bright flash of light bathes both Rin and the beast in blue.

Rin grunts and rips her hands free from the fangs. She grabs the beast by the horns and hurls the creature into a massive tree. The wood splinters, and the beast, timber, and branches crumble to the forest floor with a deafening crash.

I gasp. "Holy shit."

For a moment, I catch Rin's gaze. I know the colour of her eyes all too well, but they aren't their normal sickly grey. An intense electric blue fills her eye sockets. As she blinks, the blue fades, and her irises return.

"Holy Zenta," I whisper as chills crawl across my body from head to toe. It's like Rin wasn't even in her body, like something else infested it. Without the light, she looks at me. The grey is soft. She is soft. Her hands are loose at her sides and her shoulders are low as if her fingers are weighted. Nothing steals her stare away from me. She sees me.

"Rin, get back in position. They're behind us," Niko yells.

I whirl around. The ground rumbles under my feet. Jeff's whole body tenses, and the ground comes to life. Dirt, roots, and rocks assemble into a wall, blocking off the beasts. But a beast smashes through it, lunging at Jeff.

Jeff grunts and he falls back. My hands shoot out, a pulse of heat spreads over my body, and a smouldering wave of flames streams from my palms. The flames smother the beast, throwing it back. The beast hits the ground, howling and writhing.

My heart pounds. A pack of the beasts come for us from every direction, kicking up dust. They snarl gutturally, saliva dripping from their mouths.

I draw out the thrumming energy of my essence. Dark-red flames surround my arms and head, flickering and steaming until they settle into a warm glow of translucent red plates.

A beast leaps out from behind a boulder, I lunge forward and catch it in the jaw with a fiery fist, sending a wave of flames around its body, singeing its fur. It pounces at me, but I dash to the side. Jeff hurls a rock at its face. It smacks the beast in the jaw. With a screech, the beast recoils. I slam my flaming foot to the side of its face. With a crack of bone, he goes down.

I turn to my teammates. Ace fashions a sword out of ice and hurls it toward Eliote. She catches it, swings it around her, and slashes at a beast's throat. Blood splatters across the path. The beast's gold essence snakes into the air from the gash.

More come from the left. Niko stands right in their paths. With a flash of brilliant, white light, Niko transforms into his Beastblood form—an enormous, white bear with gold armour and red eyes. He charges toward the beasts, slashing his paws, knocking beasts down left and right.

Three beasts head straight for me, a perfect opportunity to use Mind Fire.

"Rin." I spit her name out like it's poison. She takes another beast down behind me with some help from Jeff. "I'm going to line them up."

My breath catches in my lungs and fire burns through my veins. I imagine the essence inside me and the life inside the beasts. Their growls churn through my mind. Energy flows through me.

I exhale.

Sparks burst from my eyes, and they stream toward the beasts. A glowing red haze engulfs the beasts connecting my mind to theirs. My nerves sync with the beasts' systems in aching spasms. I fight to keep my shaking muscles from crumpling to the ground. "Now."

Rin sprints toward them, leaps, and slams her foot into the first beast who collides with his friends. Ace lets loose a razor-sharp icicle, skewering their skulls together.

The team forms up—fingers frosty, ice-swords in hand, fists clenched, armour in place, earth spheres circling at the ready. But no more beasts come. The forest regains the sweet song of breezes and birds, and the sweat cools on my brow.

The corpses of the feral beasts lie in bloody heaps all around us. I unclench my fists and my armour dissipates into smoke. My essence still surges through my body. My arms shake, my legs quiver. I hunch over and grasp my knees to keep myself steady.

"Shit," I mutter.

I've never killed anything before. Never taken a life. Never fought to save my life. A breath of wind spreads the stench of hot, metallic blood across my face, and I shudder.

Niko's back in hédin form and rests his hands on his head while he catches his breath. Eliote's breath is shaky, her face pale. She clasps her hand over her mouth. Bolting to the side of the path she doubles over, a jet stream of puke spews from her mouth. Ace moves over to her and pulls her hair out of the line of fire. He speaks to her softly, reassuring her that she can do this.

I glance at Rin. Hairs have slipped out of her ponytail and fall in a mess around her face. She just stands there with arms at her sides and head bent, staring at her shoes which are completely ruined.

"What the hell, Rin?" Niko says. He marches over to Rin. Her head snaps up.

"What?" she says.

Niko glares at her. "Jeff almost got clobbered because of you."

Rin shakes her head. "Sorry," she mutters.

"We had a formation for a reason, Rin," Jeff says.

Rin's lips part. She looks from Jeff to Niko and back to Jeff. Just for a second her eyes meet mine.

JOHANNA WOULD HAVE BEEN DEAD IF I HADN'T DONE SOMETHING.

My stomach clenches. There's no heat left in my body, only

that thought, *her* thought. Even though Rin avoids my eyes I stare straight at her. That was her thought. It swirls around my head with a sizzling echo, hot and biting, with a slight distortion in tone.

I just read her thoughts.

I WAS TRYING TO PROTECT HER.

The searing heat of her thoughts drops to a bitter cold as the sizzling distortion fades. Now each word is clear with Rin's voice and tone. They blow through my mind like a snowstorm.

"And what the hell was that? That glowing energy shit you just pulled?" Niko shouts pointing a finger at Rin.

"It's the life affinity. It just happened. I didn't mean to." Her shoulders pull up and she drops her eyes to the ground.

Niko's brow furrows as he grits his teeth. "You mean you can't even control that power? What the fuck? And you didn't think to tell us about it?"

"Niko come on," I say. "Don't be a dick about it."

"Let it go," Jeff says. He lays a hand on Niko's shoulder, but Niko shrugs it off.

"I can't believe this. Eliote told us about her lack of enhancements, ever think maybe that was a good time to let us in on your little secret too, huh? Damn cutch," Niko yells.

"Niko." Ace grabs Niko by the shoulder, shaking him with his grip. "Get your shit together. You're way out of line." His blue eyes shoot daggers at Niko.

Eliote heaves another round of vomit, and it splatters into the bushes.

A shadow streams over us and a torrent of wind blasts from

above. Hot breath slithers over my forehead. My heart jumps into my throat. A flying beast with waxy black wings, skeletal body, and gaping mouth full of jagged teeth hovers above us. A screech rips from its throat.

A zap sounds through the trees and a powerful crack sends a bullet whizzing through the air. It strikes right through the beast's eye and ejects out its skull with a splatter of black blood. The impact flings the beast into the trees, and it crashes to the ground.

Brand drops down from the trees behind us with a firestone sniper rifle braced against her shoulder. Her appearance summons a spell of silence on all of us. She looks us over with a hand on her hip.

Kicking one of the beasts on the ground she says, "These are unstable Nodaha Downfōsts. You can tell instability by the amber colour of the eyes and essence. And this," she nudges the winged beast with the butt of her rifle, "a Noltwyn Alzuke. You're lucky it wasn't an essence syphoner. You'd have been drained in seconds at this range."

Brand weaves between us, sunlight speckling her in gold. Stopping right in front of me, the smell of rifle metal and acrid stench of drained firestones envelopes me. Her eyes are unblinking, her face slack.

"This is the real world," she says. "There are no walls to protect you. There are no Local Protectors, no professors. Whatever grievances you have against each other, the battlefield is not the place to bring them up. You fight with each other and for each other, always." Moving to look each of us in the eye, her heavy tread accentuates every word. "You fight for your home and for your family, and if you let your squabbles get the best of you, you don't get to go home." Brand pops the used firestone out of her rifle and loads a new one.

I nod, swallowing down the grim reality.

Evelyn gave a similar speech, but it wasn't so plain, so tangible. With the stench of the blood, a smoking rifle, and my aching body, Brand's candour is welcome. This is real, and unfortunately, I have a few squabbles to settle.

17

RIN

We ride the airbus back to the academy in silence. Niko was right. I should have stayed in position. Someone could have gotten hurt. I had to protect Johanna, though. It was a pure gut feeling like having a firestone rifle to my weak spot. But where were my wings? Why didn't they come out to bash every beast that came my way?

Brand leads us into the training room. As her combat boots hit the floor, the sound isn't right. There should be a tap, but it gets absorbed by the give in whatever the floor is made of. It bounces and doesn't sit well with me. The air is stale but humid, cold but sweaty. Water rushes through pipes overhead. One of the lights near the door sways from the wind, making the light around me shift.

"I want Adrianne to do an essence pressure test on each of

you before we get started on anything else," Brand says as she sets her rifle down.

There is static in my brain from being attacked by the life affinity and my arms are jittery. I hold them tight around my middle as we line up for Adrianne. These random life-affinity popups can't keep happening. Not telling Stephen about the affinities was a mistake. I need someone to teach me how to control it.

"An attack like that, paired with rapid utilization of essence, can lead to poor essence regeneration, causing health problems down the road. Especially for cellular essence."

Brand's silver eyes dart to me. Shivers parade down my shaky arms. Is it possible that Brand is Ironskin? Those eyes. That familiarity. I just have to find a way to ask her.

Adrianne has tested Jeff-Ray, Johanna, and Niko and everything seems fine. A frown pulls at her face as she reads the little round device attached to a cuff wrapped around Ace's arm.

"Ace, when was the last time you had your essence pressure checked?" she asks.

Ace smiles and says, "Last month. It's low, isn't it?"

"Surprisingly low."

"My dad, he's a doctor, says there's nothing wrong, just naturally low."

"All right, but we'll keep an eye on it throughout the year because we don't want it depleting. Your monitor showed a pretty big flow spike during the exercise."

"Which means?"

"When you have low essence pressure, a flow velocity spike can be jarring to your system and can damage your essence channels. With some more physical training you should be able to balance the two."

Ace's eyes squint a little. He takes the information with a nod and moves out of the way so Adrianne can test me.

I push up my sleeve, offering my arm to Adrianne. Her pink lips smile at me and her hair swishes behind her with the same wind that stirs the lights. She wears a windbreaker zipped right to her neck, maybe to ward off the sweaty chill. But I remember the longs scars on her arms as she tugs the sleeves down.

Ripping the cuff open, she wraps it around my arm, her fingers clammy on my skin. She places the sleek, oval-shaped monitor in the palm of her hand. After a few seconds it blips, vibrates, and a reading for blood pressure appears on the screen, but essence pressure just shows three red dots.

My chest tightens with a long breath. I catch Adrianne's eyes. She blinks and bites her lip.

"These monitors are shit at detecting cellular essence," she says.

She leaves the cuff on a few more seconds, watching the little dots skitter across the screen.

"I'll have to do it manually." Adrianne rips off the cuff.

"Oh," I say, pulling my sleeve back down.

Dropping her eyes, Adrianne says, "It's a little unpleasant." She crouches down to look in her med-kit. One of her hands wanders under her jacket to scratch her back while she searches through bandages, pain tonics, curestones, and gloves until she pulls out a scalpel.

My stomach turns itself over. I run my hand over my weak spot. The tips of my fingers find the bump of flesh.

Adrianne keeps her eyes to herself. A slight tremor shakes her hand, and a glint of light hops off the blade of the silver knife.

"I have to make an incision on my thumb so that when I press it to your arm the essence in your skin will pulse through my thumb as it interacts with my blood."

I can't take my eyes off the scalpel. "You have to hurt yourself to test my essence pressure?"

Soft green eyes find their way to mine. "It's fucked up. But most of the time when I don't have a cuff, people are more horrified that I have to bleed on them than me cutting my thumb to do it."

The muscles in my jaw draw tight as Adrianne brings the knife to her thumb.

"My gosh, stop looking at me like that." She chuckles and nudges me with her foot. "I'm not sacrificing my first-born child for you."

Adrianne makes the cut quick. A line of red seeps over the pad of her thumb, silver essence licks the air around us. She presses the cut to my forearm, not on any particular artery, but on the muscle where the skin is soft. A bit of blood pools between my skin and hers.

I clear my throat. "So, after three years of being here, is this year exciting or are you ready to get out of here?"

Her mouth twitches, but the tilt of her head hides her eyes. "Four years actually."

"I thought you said you were a fourth-year."

"I did. I just had to do first year twice." Adrianne bends down to grab a pack of wipes from her bag. She rips it open, wipes my arm clean of blood, and presses her thumb to my other arm. "But to answer your question, I'm still happy to be here. I think I took the amount of time I needed."

I wonder why she had to do first year again. I don't know

if I should ask her though. In our quiet, I concentrate on the pressure of her thumb on my arm. A small tingle shoots back and forth where the cut touches me. That must be her essence flow.

"You didn't mean to engage the life affinity, did you?" she asks.

I shake my head.

"Unexpected essence bursts can interfere with the electrical conduction of the heart, so I'm going to check your heart sounds when we're done with this."

I can't believe how thorough she is, especially when this process is so uncomfortable for both of us. I expect her to rip her thumb away from me any second, but she keeps it on my arm just as long as she kept it clamped on the other one, unwavering in her hold.

"What does it feel like?" I ask.

Adrianne cocks her head to the side. "Prickly," she says. "Gritty?" A giggle escapes her and I smile. "Alive. Healthy. I gauge the pressure by how far I can feel it through my body. It should reach the same place for every part of your skin I test. I can feel the prickle all the way to my toes on both sides."

Once she's finished with this crazy process, she wipes her blood away and presses a curestone to her cut. A small burst of mist escapes from the stone, leaving the creamy-white colour a touch duller. Her thumb comes away pink with no evidence of harm, not even a scar.

She presses a stethoscope to my chest. "Okay, you're fine and healthy. Better get over to the others."

"Good. Thank you." I resituate my sweater sleeves and give my arms a shake. They're a little less stiff. It's strange to come away from a fight cleaner than going in, to have someone's blood on my skin and have it wiped away with careful hands.

But the eyes are the same. I'm watched closer than anyone. At Dawnranfet, everyone watched me as I moved through the crowd, making sure I didn't do anything but win some money. Here I took longer than anyone to be tested and they watch me take my space at the end of the line smelling of disinfectant.

I rub the spots on my arms where Adrianne tested me.

"Hans, please explain the drill," Brand says as she picks up a clipboard and a pen, a little less menacing equipment than a few minutes ago, but I'm sure they will be used in a tactical way. She dons round spectacles from her pocket. A sharp-shooting sniper and yet she needs reading glasses?

"Each of you will take turns striking the bag," Hans says. "First time through, just a fist strike. Second time you'll execute a knockout blow." His manner of speaking commands attention with a bitter edge. He stands with his hands by his sides and his feet hip distance apart as he explains the drill. "The idea here is to conserve your strength with the first strike and maximize your strength with the second. Both are needed in combat. This punching bag is embedded with a star crystal that will absorb the blow. The crystal is connected to a metre that will measure the energy expelled from your strikes."

"Thank you, Hans," Brand says as she takes notes. "Niko, would you start, please?"

Niko takes his place in front of the bag.

As each of my teammates takes their turn, they approach the exercise with different martial arts disciplines, although there's something similar about them. Something about the way Niko's fist contacts the bag with such an odd snap back. It's not quite ready to strike again, and it's not in a good position to counter.

Jeff-Ray holds his eyes on the spot where he intends to plant his fist. Eliote is too poised. Practiced. They've all practiced. I have, too, on Eshra's face. Blood streaks my vision and I shudder. The punching bag is just as red.

Hans watches with his glasses on the tip of his nose. He mutters something to himself and records readings.

I step over to Brand, who watches from behind the line.

"Brand," I say, my voice smaller than I intended.

She raises her eyes from her clipboard.

"Is Professor Griven Emberstead?"

"I believe he is." She tucks a curl behind her ear, and I crumple sweaty fists inside my sleeves.

Brand holds her shoulders back without being too stiff. One glance of her eye is scolding and cloudy, and I want to duck my head or put my shoulders back just like hers. Instead, I just sweat.

Swallowing hard, I ask, "Are you Ironskin?"

Her stare lingers and I might as well be melting. I've been asked that question hundreds of times, but the last time I did it myself, I wasn't even in basic ed.

"An Ironskin hasn't been a paid instructor at a Guardian institute since before the Fourth Great War."

Is that a yes or a no? Shit. Maybe she's Beastblood or a halfie and is offended that I would suggest she looks Ironskin.

"Not much need for instruction for pure jint alignment now is there?" she adds.

Heat creeps into my face. Yeah, employment based on essence alignment is really fair. I bite the inside of my cheek, fists still clenched. My eyebrows scrunch together. "You're a volunteer though."

The pen in her hand stops moving. The skin of her perfectly

bronze cheek wrinkles with a smile to her notes. She steps away from me. "Ace, I'm assuming you picked up Dawntimdato from basic ed athletics class?"

"Yeah, pretty much," Ace says.

"I'd like you to go back to your Nytrue roots and learn Noladakatz. It's better for low essence pressure and reduces the chance of flow spikes." Brand paces around the group. "You should all be familiar with multiple techniques, which is why I will teach lessons on each throughout the year. Eliote, I'd like you to incorporate some Fōsttimdato moves into your arsenal to replace Shodahet strikes. Adrianne is one of the best Fōsttimdato fighters I've ever seen. The discipline is good for maximizing strength without essence. Pay close attention in her classes as well. Rin, you're up."

I step up to the bag with sticky arm pits and try to stay light on my feet—slight bend at the knees, feet shoulder width apart, right foot forward, elbows tucked. I'm itching to strike the bag but I lower my fists. Turning back to Brand I ask, "Can I actually hit it without . . ." I make a motion with my hands depicting an explosion.

A sound escapes her that I swear is a laugh, but she hides it with a clear of her throat. "Go for it."

Back in my stance, I smack my fist into the bag. The bag swings high, whipping the air, and hammers back toward me. I stop it with open palms.

"Good," Brand says. "Now let's—"

"You can't be serious, Miss Highcaller," Hans says. He pushes up his glasses with one finger and raises an eyebrow.

"What's the problem?"

"The girl hit without the least bit of control, relying entirely on her strength enhancement. This is exactly why she has no control over the life affinity."

I force breath into my lungs as the rest of my body refuses to move. I'm afraid if I open my mouth the only thing that would come out would be some foul expletive dug up from the gutter of my mind. I keep my mouth shut.

"If the key to manipulation is essence flow, then for cellular essence mental and physical awareness of oneself is the key to engaging the spirit affinities," Hans says.

Despite his condescending tone, it makes sense. It's probably why I didn't know about the affinities in the first place. I always seem to lose myself.

Hans peers down his nose, taking me in. "Not to mention her stance was terrible."

Marcus leans into Hans. "Maybe we should have her do some extra training every month to ensure she has good control over it," Marcus says under his breath. With a hand to his chin, Hans nods.

Brand lowers her clip board and comes over to me, her boots making the weird tap on the bouncy floor. "Rin, show me your set fassoa."

I exhale and take my stance.

Clicking her tongue, Brand says, "You're right, Hans, there is something wrong with her stance." The sarcasm drips off her tone, her face unchanging. She places her hand under my elbow and lifts it, so my fist comes just a breath closer to my jaw. "There. Students, this is a perfect Telando set fassoa. *Heerenada, Rin. Yet tuyonna shietz.*"

Brand's Slyvic words slip into the humid air, chilling the nervous sweat on my body. It's still not a firm conformation that she's Ironskin because Master Lotera spoke to us in Slyvic too. For whatever reason, Brand doesn't want people to know she's Ironskin. The knowledge tears inside me, dropping weight on my shoulders, and a heavy frown on my face. All I can do is hope she might help me.

After morning combat classes, Eliote and I head back to our room to change before lunch.

"I'm heading down," Eliote says, shaking her hair out of its ponytail. She hikes up a pair of black pants that hug her long legs and adjusts a low-cut tank top.

"Hold on a sec," I say. "You okay?"

Eliote hides herself under heavy eyelashes, looking anywhere but my eyes. She toys with the bottle of perfume she sprayed earlier that has spread through our room—a sweet, earthy aroma that makes me think of stargazing in a field even though I've never been stargazing in a field.

"Yeah," she says, setting the bottle down with determination. "I'll be okay. I've just never felt . . . a life die before." Her fists clench.

For a second, I can't breathe, as if her long fingers are clenched around my throat. My heart takes on a slow, heavy beat.

Crying's not going to bring him back, Rinnaya.

Every day my heart gets weaker, every day it becomes more and more unbearable to breathe.

Eliote dissects me with her piercing, brown eyes. I grab my sandals from the closet to escape them.

"That must feel awful," I say, sitting down on my bed.

She comes to sit by me, close enough that the bed dips in and slides us together.

"It really does." She rubs her hands on her knees, gaze fixed on the door.

I sit with one shoe on, the other in my lap, wishing I had some words to say to her—a word, any word.

"Energy just escaped all around us, with nowhere to go. I felt it. Like it was ripping out of me." She clutches the lightstone around her neck. With a blink, she snaps out of her daze. "Your parents. They've moved on to be with the ancestors?" She claps her hand on my knee and squeezes.

The snap of her hand stirs memories of my parents. My mother panicking in the dead of night from a past I didn't know about, maybe a future she dreaded. She shrieked and my father soothed her with the same words every time—*It's okay. I'm here, Cassy.* The silhouette of my father walking away in the early morning light to a mission that would be his last. My mother kissing him hard before he left like she always did.

"Uh—" Can she see these memories too? Feel them? I swallow, shake my head, and find a smile. "Yeah. They're dead."

"I'm sorry," she says in the same tone I heard her use with her mother, sweet and sincere. Too sincere.

I squirm as much as the crowded space will let me.

"Are you okay?" she asks.

"Oh yeah, I'm used to them being gone."

"No, I mean about today. The life affinity is pretty intense." She pokes my knee.

"Yeah, fine." I shrug.

Eliote raises an eyebrow and smiles her half smile. "Mhm." She keeps staring at me like she's waiting for me to say something more, but I don't know what she wants me to say. "That's fine. You don't have to talk. I'm going down to eat. You coming?"

"I'll be down in a bit. Go on without me."

Eliote pats me on the knee again, then readjusts her pant legs before leaving the room.

I slip my other sandal on, still engulfed in Eliote's starry scent. Voices in the hall fade.

Rubbing my fingers together in small circles, round and round, feeling the tiny ridges of my skin, the silence sinks in. The events of the last few days weigh on me. Faces of the people I've met fill the space of my mind in hazy flashes. The beasts. I had no problem killing them—I didn't even think about it. All I wanted was to protect Johanna. I press my nails into my skin. Why did I want to? The life affinity hooked its icy claws into that need to protect and took over everything. I was out of control and in complete control at the same time, just like Eliote described my essence.

Somehow, despite its weight, all of it is distant, like I wasn't a part of it at all. Adrianne said she has been here for the right amount of time. I'm not sure if I've made it here yet. I must be somewhere outside the Akinnera gates, still on the train and looking at a towering Jhogran through a windowpane—not fighting beasts. All I've felt in the last few days is hot and sweaty. I'm dreaming. It's all a sweaty nightmare, too real and not real enough. The edge of my vision is blurry, and my hands are miles away.

But I know I'm not dreaming.

It's happening again. I don't want to end this year with faded memories.

I jump up. I swing my arms, I blink and breathe and clap

my hands, anything to bring the life back to my body. Moving to the window, I stick my head out to suck in a huge breath of salt and sea and wind and trees. It washes me. I cling to every touch of air on my skin, the light of the sun bleaching my eyes. My heart is alive. Inside the window frame, some of the paint is chipping. I pick at it with my nails. Tiny flakes of white break off to reveal rough, brown wood underneath. I need every touch, every white flake, and every tiny cracking sound they make as they break off because I can't fall into the place where my memories hide.

I'm okay. I'm here, at the Akinnera Academy.

But how could I be okay? I don't remember what that feels like for things to be good. Inside, I'm heavy, like there's a stone sinking in my stomach. It gets heavier the more I think about it.

But I'm here and I need to be here so I can get back to Liam, so he can be safe. I push my feet to the door, into the hall, and down the stairs.

18

LANCE

This month they've sent me a new Monitor, Officer Merez—a huge Fyrra with light-plum skin, white hair cropped short to his head, and tattoos covering the parts of his neck and hands that aren't concealed by his Protector's uniform. He meets me in my room smelling of herbs and carrying a bulky med-kit.

Merez takes out the standard document my old Monitor would check through each day. "No alcohol?" he asks in a thick Fyrra accent.

"No," I say, and Merez makes a check on the document.

"Caffeine?"

"Only easy-caff."

"Any smoke inhalation of any kind? Cigarettes, Ease?"

After the accident, there were weeks when my Monitor would mark big red X's over each of the boxes Merez marked with a check today. But soon the checks were more frequent. It's been a year since I've had an X. I swallow hard, running a hand over my chin. "I had a cigarette two days ago. Just one though, that's it."

Merez narrows his eyes at me, humming a quiet note of acknowledgement. He grabs an essence pressure cuff from his bag, slaps it around my arm and pulls it tight, pinching my skin.

"Any problems with essence control since then?"

I shrug. "I only use it in training, but yeah, no problems."

"Pressure is elevated. I'll give you an enhanced scolya root tonic to bring it down," Merez says, and marks down the pressure and his prescription on the checklist. "They said you were having nightmares."

"Not so much anymore." I rub the reddened skin on my arm.

"Not staying up late, are you?"

"Eight hours of sleep a night."

"Good." He hands me a small glass bottle of green scolya root tonic. The smooth glass is familiar to my fingers. "Next month we do the psych evaluation."

Clenching the tonic in my fist, I nod.

"Drink that and then eat a balanced meal." Officer Merez grunts. He slides on a pair of sunglasses—the ancestor charms around his wrist clink together. Grabbing his med-kit, he nods and leaves. I stay seated on my bed once the door slams behind him.

Even after a year and a half of Monitor visits, they're still what makes my skin itch the most. I run my hands over my knees. At least my old Monitor smiled and asked me about my day. *Eat a balanced meal.* This guy's concerned about my health, so I guess he's on track.

I roll the bottle between my fingers. The liquid sloshes around, creating little bubbles, making the sludge extra appetizing.

I pop off the cap, tilt my head back, and down the contents in one gulp. It coats my tongue with a gritty, bitter film. As the sweet aftertaste kicks in, the first time I downed the shot hits my mind. My hands shook like crazy as my essence surged through my body, dysregulated by a swirling mind, heavy with self-prescribed, non-medical medications.

The bottle is empty, so I'm starting over. Again.

Compelled to follow my Monitor's orders, I grab the book on my nightstand and leave my room. The book—a story about Dar Mornson, a lover, a fighter—has a sun-faded cover and fraying edges, cracked spine, creased pages. It's taken on a dusty iidai-esk smell. I stuff it in my back pocket and trot down the stairs.

Maybe I'll see Rin in the dining hall. My stomach clenches, my heart pounds. I should see her because we all have lunch at the same time, but she'll probably be sitting with other people, like yesterday. Should I have said hi yesterday? She might think I lost interest by now. Obviously, I haven't. Is she interested?

The second I enter the dining hall, I search the tables for her pretty blond hair but don't see her. Crossing the hall, I check again, might have missed her. Still no sight of her.

I take a plate at the food line, piling on keeta greens with lemon dressing, a piece of fried tore fish, roasted potatoes with gravy, and a beef fen wrap. I'd say that's balanced enough.

Reaching for an apple, I scan my fellow students for the third pathetic time. Rin is at the end of the line wearing jeans rolled up at the ankles and an Ease Beetles t-shirt. Her hair falls in shiny waves around her shoulders. The apple thunks to my plate, splatting gravy on my shirt. "Damn it," I say under my breath.

Rin stares into the crowd, her eyes intense as hell. She bites her lip, then stalks over to an empty table.

I grab cutlery and a couple napkins to scrub away as much gravy splatter as possible. Fork grasped in one hand, balanced meal in the other, I take a breath and flick my wings. I start my feet moving toward Rin's table.

Next month we do the psych evaluation.

Three steps in and I lose my nerve. The itch fills my body. I have to be evaluated, monitored each month, there's no way pursuing a girl will go any better than last time. But the voice printed on the pages of the book stuffed in my pocket tells me to go for it. Dar always went for it, even if he knew things could go wrong.

I can't deny the connection I felt with Rin on orientation day. It was like we were on the same page, and I want to find out what that page is.

Still clenching my fork like a maniac, I slide my plate onto Rin's table and sit right across from her. "Hey."

She looks up. Her eyes, terrifying storms of cool grey, fill me with a surprising calm and paralyze my tongue. So, I smile. *Please say something.*

Rin stabs her fork into a piece of meat. "What is this?" she asks and shoves the meat in my face.

"Looks like kechling."

Rin frowns.

"Kechlings are birds that are only found in this area. I honestly don't know why we eat them. The poor things are going to go extinct," I say, trailing off. I shouldn't babble.

Rin eyes the little chunk of meat for a few seconds, but nevertheless moves it to her mouth. "It's weird," she says, chewing. "I've never had it before."

"Clearly." The word stumbles out of my mouth, muddled by a chuckle. I slap the stupid grin back on my face because my brain-tongue connection seems to be malfunctioning.

Rin smiles back and laughs for the first time since I've met her. A nice laugh, soft and unexplored, like it's new to her, not just me. I want to bottle the sound to keep it safe and untainted.

"So, how have your first days at the academy been?" I ask.

Taking another bite of kechling, Rin cringes and washes it down with a sip of water. "Well, I'm on an advanced team." She sets her cup down, shrugs. I follow her gaze to a rowdy table to our left. "I killed a beast for the first time today. Johanna, who hates my guts, is on my team and I don't really feel like bein' near her right now, so here I am with you."

"That them over there?" I motion to the table just as a scrawny Beastblood jumps out of his seat. He flaps his arms. The whole table bursts into laughter and an Earthkin guy pulls flappy-boy back down to his seat before he can dump his plate on himself.

"Yeah, that's them," Rin says. She scrapes the leftover kechling to the side of her plate.

"Congrats on the advanced team thing. I don't think the school has put one of those together in years."

"Thanks."

I take a few bites from my plate and she from hers. Her hand shakes a bit as she brings the fork to her mouth, kind of how Khali would shake when she was Eased. Rin's not Eased, I know that. Still, my stomach clenches and my brain gets fuzzy. *Damn it*. Essence pulses to my fingertips. With a breath, I force it to calm down. I guess the tonic hasn't done the trick just yet.

I push my gaze up from her fork to her eyes, fingers still thrumming with energy.

"You okay?" she asks.

"Yeah, it's just loud in here."

"It is."

I take a bite of tore fish.

Rin props herself on one elbow and picks out another piece of kechling that was hiding under a keeta leaf. As we sit in silence, her hands steady, and her face relaxes into a smile—when she's not stuffing it with keeta. A strand of hair falls into her face. I get an urge to tuck it behind her ear, but thankfully she does it before I can embarrass myself. Embracing the silence and her terrifying calm, my wings unfold a bit.

"My mom works in an essence testing development lab," I say after a bite of potato.

Rin raises her eyes to me. She has both hands wrapped around a fen wrap and takes an enormous mouthful. She chews a few times. "That's cool." A smile threatens to let the wad of fen wrap tumble out of her mouth, and she brings her hand up to hide her mouth.

"Yeah." Where am I going with this? "She says that in about a year or two we might move away from needles and core-energy tubes for Registration."

"Wait really? The Registration process was honestly kind of embarrassing for me."

"Well yeah, that's what my mom says. They want to make the test less invasive for Ironskins with weak spots and people with needle phobias like me."

Still holding the wrap in one hand, Rin stares at me. "Lance, that's so cool. How are they going to change the test?"

The way she says my name sends a flutter through my chest. "I think they're making it electro-tech based."

"Damn," she says under her breath and looks off to the side. "I wish that was already a thing."

The buzz of the dining hall fills my ears as Rin goes silent. Her eyelids fall halfway, her stare unwavering and cloudy, like something I said took her to another place. I hope it's not a bad place.

Once we're both done eating, I stack her plate with mine.

"Do you want to meet me this evening? We could study or train if you want." My heart pounds. Is this evening too soon? Maybe I should have said tomorrow.

"Oh," she says.

Shit, what does that mean?

"Yeah, sure."

Oh, thank Seena.

"I'd like that," she adds.

"Good. I'll meet you in the centre courtyard, say around seven?" I pick up our plates, trying to keep from shaking so our forks don't slip off the plates.

Rin nods. "See ya then," she says and heads out of the dining hall.

This is good. Maybe things will be better this time.

I drop the plates off at the kitchen with a smile on my face. It feels good to smile about someone again.

$$19$$

RIN

I PRESS MY HAND TO MY CHEST. Rapid beats of my heart tap against my palm like a marching band under my skin. My head swims, all stupid and giddy. I feel stupid all the time, but never giddy. And despite my sloshy brain and restless, pounding heart, there's a lightness in my feet. I might float away.

Once through the dining hall doors, I jog down the hall to anchor my feet to the ground. At the end, familiar voices drift around the corner, stifling my giddiness.

"I'm impressed to see you've obtained such a prestigious position so early on in your career." The condescending quality marks it as professor Griven.

"Thank you. I appreciate that," a male voice says, boyish but articulate and smooth. Stephen?

My legs stiffen as I turn the corner. Stephen stands with

Griven outside the history classroom, just a few metres away—the closest he's been in a year. He looks over his shoulder and smiles at me. His thundercloud eyes remain disengaged, unreadable, and the most familiar thing about him. I return the smile, tension in my jaw.

"Hey, kid," he says.

Shuffling my feet, I cross my arms. My eyes don't know where to look. "What are you doing here?"

"I came to see how you're doing. I just ran into professor Griven, and he tells me that you're on an advanced team. That's great."

My cheeks grow hot. When was the last time I received a compliment from him? Stephen's smile widens to show his perfect teeth and a small glint in his eye. Is he actually proud of me?

Professor Griven takes a step closer to us. "Yes," he says. "I was telling Stephen that your life affinity manifested this morning. We're concerned about your ability to control it."

"Oh, I see." I glance at Stephen. He keeps his eyes on Griven, blank faced, no telling how he feels now that he knows about my affinities. But his uncharacteristic eye twinkle fades.

"As Marcus suggested, Commander Highcaller and I would like to work on it with you individually on Freeday evenings," Griven says, straightening his posture.

"Right, uh, okay," I say.

Brand will be there, that's good. It's a step in the right direction.

Griven nods. "Stephen, good to see you again."

They shake hands and Griven makes his way into the classroom.

"He's a good teacher," Stephen says. "He helped me control the death affinity while I was in school."

"I have history with him in a few minutes, actually. Can I catch up with you later?"

Stephen's eyes dart from me to the students filing into class. He rubs the back of his neck. "No. I can't stay. But I need to talk to you. Let's go to the courtyard." He takes me by the arm, half dragging, half leading me outside.

In the courtyard, Stephen lets go of me and strides ahead to a bench by the trickling marble fountain in the centre. A cool breeze rustles through patches of dainty, white whisper weeds along the edge of the path. Jaden lilies sway back and forth, flourishing their silky green petals. A sorrow-blossom tree in the corner of the yard drapes its tendrils studded with blood-red blossoms over the flower beds. The afternoon sun filters through the blossoms to create a shady patchwork over the cobblestone path. Behind me, the door clicks, shutting out the noise in the academy halls.

A bell sounds for the start of afternoon classes. Great, I'll be late to another class.

Stephen leads us around the fountain and speaks low enough for the trickling water to cover any words that might make their way to a passerby. "Griven will understand. It's not every day that your brother shows up," Stephen says.

No kidding.

Stop it.

Now is not the time to get defensive. I kicked myself in the teeth by not letting him know about my affinities. I shut him out. I don't want to fight. Just hear him out.

Keeping my face neutral, I ask, "What did you wanna talk

to me about?"

An airship crosses the sky, casting a shadow over the blooming courtyard. Stephen stands a few metres away from me with his hands in his pockets, back turned to me. The muscles of his neck tense.

"When I called you on Registration Day, I told you I was working on something new," he says.

My body roots itself to the ground. If I move, my mouth might move, it might say something that would make him walk away. I need to listen to what he has to say because I never got the answers the first time.

His head turns at my silence. "It wasn't a Guardian assignment. I'm working with an Ironskin organization." His face is grave and his stare unwavering. "Ironskins have been trampled on for far too long and we're going to change that."

My scalp prickles. The stiffness in my legs seizes my whole body, freezing my heart and lungs, my eyes on his eyes.

"We need to change things, or everything will stay the same." He takes a step toward me. "I want you to join us."

The sound of crashing waves spills over the walls of the garden. Stephen looks down at me. His mouth is drawn in a tight line. There is an inky darkness to the skin under his eyes. He's not so tall or distant with his vulnerabilities so visible to me. The roar of the waves could be the roar of his mind. But I'm not sure what he wants from me, what he wants me to join.

"But things are changing—"

"No, Rin—"

"Slowly." I take a quick breath. "They're changing slowly. Someone just told be about new tech for Registration, making it more accurate for Ironskin essence."

"It's just a theory. They don't have funding for it, and they won't get it." Stephen shrugs, his hands deep in his pockets. "Can't you see? They always make us do extra training because of our spirit affinities." Urgency spikes the volume of his voice, and the fountain no longer trickles over it but under, the rush of water annoying at the back of my head. "They're still scared of us."

"Not everyone."

"Yeah, because the rest think they own us."

I try to swallow but the lump in my throat is tight.

Move along ghost girl.

Maybe loosen up a bit and someone would like ya.

Cutch.

Bitch.

My mind clogs with the memories. I shake my head. "I'm making some friends here."

"They're all pretending." Stephen spits his words at me. "They don't want you to know that they're scared so they can get the upper hand, just like they did to me." He turns away, one hand on his forehead, the other on his hip. Whirling back around, the death affinity paints the corners of his eyes ruby red. "They only want us when it's convenient for them."

I drop my eyes to the ground as Tōmas' phantom hands grab my waist and pull me in like a toy. The fountain behind me is a cold wall. Tōmas cages my mind with his hands on both sides. I slump to the bench, heart pounding.

Stephen puts his hand on my shoulder. "We almost have everything we need to make our people great again. It's only a matter of time."

"What do you mean you almost have everything?" I ask,

shrugging away the warmth of his hand.

"We need an Ironskin with both spirit affinities. I know you have both. Oron told me."

My face flares with heat and Stephen no longer looks at me.

"Why? I don't even know how to control them."

"Rin, if you come with me, we can have the lives we've always wanted. Geret can teach you more about the affinities than anyone at this school can. You can use the affinities for the good of all Ironskins."

I put up my hands so he doesn't say another word. I try to keep my voice as even as possible, but it quivers. "Why do you need me?"

"To bring Ironskins back from the dead."

My heart pounds deep and heavy. I stand, shaking my numb hands. I pace to the far end of the courtyard, the sound of the crashing waves beyond the wall swells around me. The cobblestones bend the thin leather of my sandals, squishing my toes. Stephen sighs behind me, and it's like a tornado in my mind.

I throw up my hands and let them slap down to my legs. "How?"

"The Emberstead used the Death Ritual to wipe out all the Ironskins with life and death affinities in the Fourth Great War. We can reverse it with the Revival Ritual. We have the stones." The words roll off his tongue.

A rock is caught between the stone path and his foot. It crunches under his weight. His hands are at his sides and his chin level with the ground. The dark bags under his eyes are lighter now that he's got to his point.

"The Revival Ritual?" A gasp escapes me with a pinch in my chest. "But the last known Revival stones were destroyed."

"But they weren't, and we have them. The ritual will bring back all Ironskins who died because of the Death Ritual and every Ironskin who has died from Angel Palm or Demon Palm since then. With our numbers increased, we'll be able to have our voices heard."

This can't be happening. He can't be serious. My pounding heart nudges out the pinch and builds an ache in my chest. "I can't do that." I push past Stephen, back toward the school. "I can't . . . I can't . . . No. It's too much."

I just got here. Finally, I got to a Guardian Academy. Out of Senn and ready to do something that matters.

"Stephen," I say, stopping in the middle of the path. A few steps ahead is the door. I can go through and continue my training. A few steps behind is my brother. I've wanted to be this close to him for so long, but I can't seem to close the gap. I hang my head. "You don't know what I had to go through to get here, what I've faced alone. This is a good place for me."

"I thought so too, but I've made no difference as a Protector and look where it ended Dad. He's dead. Our mom is dead. They put all this work into life, and they ended up in the ground. I tried it their way." Stephen's voice softens, thick with conviction. "This is a new way."

"But how can you ask me to play with death like that?"

"The Embersteads stole so many of our people's lives. Now we have a chance to build up our people, people who lost their lives can finish them. We can give our people a chance to see their culture."

"I want that. But won't bringing so many powerful Ironskins back to this world be a threat? Won't the rest of Illyson be afraid? What if . . . what if it starts a war? You said it yourself, they're scared of us."

Stephen falls silent as if to cast a spell over the garden, dimming the bright green lilies, clouding the sky with thunder from the ominous grey of his eyes. The truth is unspoken, it lingers between us, charging the air.

"Then we fight," he says.

His voice has lost all the innocent boyish quality. It unleashes the charge from the air and my hands twitch with a jolt of adrenaline. Part of me latches on to the idea, the part that holds every insult thrown at me and all Stephen's accounts of his classmates who made his life a living hell. People stare at my family with disdain from that place inside me. Maybe things aren't changing, maybe they all just pretend.

The energy is fickle. It fades fast like the high of Ease. I'm left with the faded colours around me to weigh on my eyelids.

"No." I clench my fists and squeeze my eyes shut.

He makes it sound so simple, so rational and inevitable. But to bring people back to life, and risk the chance of violence that would threaten the safety of Liam and Oron, Johanna and her mom, and the people I've met here that have been kind to me? There is so much unknown hanging on the ritual. It all makes my stomach sick. I'm not the one he's looking for.

"I'm going to become a Protector," I say, but my words are so soft they barely reach my ears.

With shaking knees, I turn to the door.

"Please, just let me take you to the Revival and hear what Geret has to say. All we would need from you is a bit of blood for the ritual and you could leave." Stephen says, trying to pull me back, but I keep moving to the door. "Geret wants what's best for the Ironskins. He wants to give people their lives back. He wants us all together."

Together. My insides churn, and the ache in my chest turns to ice. I kick a stone into the flower bed. "We already could have been together, Stephen." The gentlest hush of wind licks my nose and becomes a wall between us.

"This is bigger than just us."

The ice spreads through me, matching the dim world around me with sluggish thought. I shrug—the only movement I can afford. "I'm not sure about that. I'm not going with you."

"Fine," Stephen snaps. His eyes cloud with a deep darkness. I see Liam in him and my father, my mother in that dark, everything we've ever been through. Is that enough to wage another Great War?

"We'll look for someone else with both affinities. If we don't find one, I'll come back before the Two Moons Festival." He clenches his fists. "Just think about it. All we need is you and three Revival stones, and we can give all those Ironskins their lives back. Our lives back." He yanks open the door to the hall and leaves me in the courtyard.

As I let go of my breath, the ache in my chest drops to my stomach. It sinks lower and lower. Just sinking and going nowhere. I have to move or else I might burrow into the ground and never come out.

I pace back to the fountain. The clear water in the pool captures my reflection. But the shower of water from the spout disrupts the image. My face is unrecognizable, even though I know it's me. I dip my hand in the water. I know it's real, I know it's cool, but I don't know why I can't feel it.

Liam slept with his face to the wall, his knees curled to his stomach. Quiet breaths hushed the annoying, leaky faucet. Stephen's suitcase lay open in the middle of the floor. He was in Senn for the winter break, first time since the funerals. His attendance at the funerals was an exception to the mandatory one year of essence training—an exception, a duty to family. This visit was just a hassle.

Stephen was out. Walking maybe, getting a coffee, taking a run or whatever the hell he had been doing the last few days of his stay. I crept around the suitcase, careful not to make too much noise while I straightened the pillows on the couch where Stephen had been crashing. I gathered the dirty dishes he left out and washed them so they wouldn't add to the stink of the apartment that now had two boys living in it instead of one little one. I closed the suitcase and shoved it between the couch and my dresser.

His backpack was under the couch. With a huff, I grabbed it to set on top of the suitcase. A book tumbled out of the open bag. I cringed, peeking at Liam. He would be cranky if he didn't get his nap, and I wasn't in the mood to deal with that.

The book was thick. Black leather with a cracked spine. Pages dog-eared, marked, and ripped. Breath caught inside me and my thoughts scrambled. It sat like a living being on the rough wood floor. It whispered a dark note inside me. A book of forbidden essence manipulations and stone-energy conducting techniques.

I snatched it from the ground as if it would run away. A piece of the leather spine crumbled in my hand. I rounded the couch with the book clutched in both hands. My eyes were on the door and Liam at the same time, my heart in my throat and copper on my tongue.

Stephen should not have this book and I should not read it.

He could walk in at any moment, but if I put the book away, I wouldn't get any answers. There would be no conversation about the book. I'd sooner eat rancid Rover meat than bring something like this up with him.

I opened the book to a page marked with a piece of paper near the back. Skin crawling, I took in dark images of monsters and Slyvic markings. Along the margin, Stephen had written, "primitive cloning using Revival stones to offset Angel Palm death."

Cloning of what?

The hand-drawn images of contorted figures with gawking eyes and emaciated bodies couldn't be hédin. A cold rush down my spine told me it wasn't beast either. The renderings loomed in front of me. I couldn't get my hands to close the book. Each second passed, bringing my attention closer to the monster and less to the rest of the apartment clouding at the corner of my vision.

A hand snatched the book away from me. With a start, I jerked my head up and a string of nausea coiled in my stomach. Stephen's eyes were lightning, and the rest of him was swallowed in shadows of my dim apartment.

"What is that?" I asked, my voice choked by the chill the images set in my bones.

"What are you doing going through my stuff?"

I dug my fingers into my knees. "I was moving your stuff out of the way."

Stephen scoffed, shaking his head. He manoeuvred around the couch to grab his backpack. "You shouldn't be looking at this."

"Neither should you. Why would you bring that in here?" I lowered my voice to a near hiss.

"Just mind your own business."

Stephen shoved the book in his bag and zipped it shut. Pulling a hand through his floppy dark hair, he sighed, his eyes squeezing shut.

"Is there something I should know about?" I asked. I twisted on the couch so I sat on my knees to face him.

"No, this doesn't concern you."

"Is everything okay at school? You haven't told me anything."

"There's nothing to talk about, Rin. It's the same thing as always. And you wouldn't understand." He shook his head. Throat bobbing, he turned away from me, hands moving to his suitcase.

The beat of my heart spiked.

"What do you mean I wouldn't understand—"

"You wouldn't. You're only twelve and you don't know what it's like to have a death affinity. To be thought of as a demon."

Those things in that book were demons, not Stephen. Demons cause pain. Stephen has felt too much pain to be anything other than hédin. I know he only lashes out when he is in pain. So why did he have the book? Why was he interested in cloning that was supposed to produce those things?

"Just tell me then." I looked straight into his electric-grey eyes. But he hid from me as he pulled the suitcase from the nook

I'd just shoved it in.

"No, I'm done talking," he said. "This was a mistake. I shouldn't have come. I'm going to a hotel."

It couldn't be happening. He just got there. For months I hadn't heard from him, and after three days he was done with me.

Liam was sitting up. His cheeks were flushed from sleep and his eyes wide, glassy with tears. "Stephen?"

Silence swept over us. Stephen took a shuddering breath then two long strides over to Liam. Cupping his hand around the back of Liam's head, Stephen bent down and planted a kiss on his forehead. "I'll come visit. I promise."

"You don't have to leave," Liam said. His eyes wavered back and forth between me and Stephen. I clutched the front of my shirt like I was holding my heart trying to keep it from breaking down.

Stephen turned, opened the door, and pulled it closed behind him.

I leaped, catching the door just before it closed and ran after him. His long legs took him down the stairs too fast.

"Wait, I'm sorry. Please don't leave," I said as I tried to keep up, my voice reverberating through the hall.

"If you're so horrified that I'm looking into the full extent of Ironskin abilities then I have to leave, you don't want me here."

"I want you to talk to me."

"I can't do this." He burst through the doors into the blustery winter air.

"Please don't leave, I can't . . . I . . . I can't. Please don't leave—"

"Why?"

I couldn't find any reason for him to stay so I just started talking to stall him. "If you just stay a little while longer maybe . . ."

A grey and white cat darted in front of me. My body went stiff as a memory threatened to surface from the back of my mind. I refused to let it in. The refusal stuck my feet to the ground, but I floated outside my body because it was safer to be separate from my brain for a moment so that dark night didn't seep into the present, the night where my skin broke by my own hand, and a damn cat had everything and nothing to do with it. My vision dimmed to a dull grey-brown.

"What's wrong with you? What are you doing?" He took a step back to me, his eyes trained on me. For one brief moment his face softened, his eyebrows relaxed, his lips parted to let out a breath that swirled in the air. But he shook his head. "You're exactly like Mom. I hated when she would do that. This is too much."

I let him leave as my hand went straight to the scar on my weak spot. He doesn't know and will never know why because I will never tell him. He doesn't get to know about the things I've suffered alone. Not when he keeps leaving. But if Stephen's pain made him hédin, what was I? I didn't want to share my pain with him, and I didn't want to feel it. I was something else. No wonder he wanted nothing to do with me.

For the rest of the day, I try to push the visit out of my mind— all his visits. I focus as best I can in my academic classes and put on a sweater. The weight of the fabric on my shoulders and the friction on my skin soothes the ache inside me. By the time seven o'clock comes around, the ice in my chest has melted.

It's just past seven and Lance sits on a bench by the fountain as I come to the courtyard door. His wings hook over the bench and criss-cross behind him, the tips just skimming the ground. Leaning forward, he flips a page of his novel, tilting his head to see the underside of the page before it's fully flipped. The message on the page furrows his brow. He bites his lip. The garden around him sways in the wind like it did when I was here earlier, each flower moving in its own patterned dance. Lance flips another page.

They're all pretending. Just like Tōmas. My feet stay frozen, and I crack my knuckles. *They're all pretending.* But Lance looks up from his book and waves to me. He smiles just enough for me to push Stephen out of my head. A cool breeze kisses my cheeks as I walk to meet Lance with my hands in my pockets.

"Take a seat," he says, closing his novel.

I sit down beside him, stiff legged, knees together, and hands clenched in my lap. Am I sitting too close or too far away? I cross my legs. This doesn't feel right. I bring one leg up onto the bench so I can turn and face him. Better.

"Did your day wind down any after lunch?" Lance asks.

Blood and Revival stones. My brother wants me to revive a whole nation. I can't tell him that. I can't tell anyone that.

"My older brother stopped by. I haven't seen him in a while."

Lance cocks his head to the side and asks, "Was it a good visit?"

"No, not really," I say, forcing a laugh.

"Family is tough."

"What's your family like?" I lean a little closer to him. What's behind that smile?

"Patient, I guess. Got a mom, dad, and a younger sister. They've put up with a lot, but they never let me down. Even when I mess up, ya know?"

He tells me about his sister, how beautiful and sweet she is. About how his mother is an engineer and his father is an advanced ed professor. "They live in Jiaan, so not too far from here. I get to see them a lot throughout the year. What about your family?"

I rub a finger along the rough wood of the bench. "My little brother, Liam, is all I have right now. Stephen, my older brother, he's just not around." I dig my nail into the wood. "Ever."

Lance nods slowly as I talk, eyes glued to me. I squirm and look back down at the bench. "Parents?" he asks.

"Dead."

Wow. Okay, normal people don't tell strangers about their dead parents like that.

"I mean, they're with the ancestors. But I have a soulkin father."

Lance's gaze softens and his eyebrows pinch together. "Sorry to hear that," he says.

"Liam's great, though. He's an artist and more popular than I've ever been or ever will be." My voice trails off. "Probably because he doesn't have any enhancements."

"It would be fun to meet him."

I snort. "You've barely met me."

Lance's face flushes red and he looks away. The second he does, I want him to look back. The night air is colder without his stare.

"Yeah, that's true," he says, rubbing the back of his neck

while a shy smile plays at his lips.

How can I make this awkwardness go away? "Lance, are you any good with weapons?"

"I'd say I'm pretty good. Why? You need help?" He looks back at me and the tension in my shoulders loosens.

"I'd say I'm pretty bad, actually, so yes."

He laughs. "The weapons-training room is always open. Want to go now?"

"Okay, yeah, let's go."

I'm about to get up but Lance's eyes widen. "Woah, don't move," he whispers.

I freeze. "What?"

Lance points to my shoulder, smiling ear to ear.

I glance to the side. On my shoulder sits a little beetle, the size of a saphrite coin. Its delicate wings twitch, flashing a pale white glow over me and illuminating the beetle's iridescent body. It crawls down my arm leaving behind a glimmering trail of light.

"What is it?" I ask.

"It's a moon beetle."

"Are moon beetles rare like kechling?" I ask with a small laugh.

"No, these pesky little things are everywhere in these parts, something about the salt in the air. But they don't like hédin essence, except for Ironskins."

"Why?"

"They really like core energy—that's why they glow. The theory is that Ironskin essence and core energy have the same alignment. You'll learn about the three alignments in elements class. There's jint, fann, and unama, which means—"

"Sustain, destroy, and give," I say. The moon beetle crawls into the palm of my hand. I hold it up so we both can look at it.

"Yeah." Lance's deep-brown eyes sparkle in the light of the beetle. "You know ancient Slyvic?"

"Mhm. My mother taught me."

Lance smiles. "Core energy is pure jint and Ironskin essence is the closest hédin essence to pure jint. That's why this little guy likes you."

"What happens if you get close to it?" I ask.

Lance lifts a finger up to the beetle, slowly getting closer. The beetle's wings flash and it crawls backward onto my wrist. Just a little closer, Lance's finger brushes my palm, sending tingles up my arm. The beetle flies off with a pulse of light and a flash of shiny green and purple.

Just as the one beetle leaves, three more land on my arm. I gasp at the enchanting glow surrounding me. "What the hell?"

Lance laughs. "Maybe we should get inside before they swarm you." With one quick flap of his wings, he launches himself halfway back to the academy. "Coming?"

He motions for me to follow but I just stare at him. How could this guy who holds the door for me, takes my dishes, offers to train with me, and has a soft spot for little glowing beetles be pretending?

I shake my arms and the shiny insects flutter away in spiralling paths to the starry sky.

In the weapons room, a group of students lower their swords and turn their heads as we barge through the doors. A Luminee girl with long, dark-purple hair tied back in a braid looks me over, hand on her hip. A sickening smile crosses her misty brown complexion.

She nudges her friend. "Ironskin," she says, and the other three give me stares that make me itch.

I smile and wave to them. Maybe it will make them look away. But they wave back and return mocking smiles.

Lance picks up a sword from the rack along the wall. He gives it a few swings while I peruse a glass cabinet displaying the real deal.

Whispers drift over to me.

"No way, you think that's her?"

"I heard she's on some special advanced team."

"Probably just to get her out of here as fast as possible."

"Look at her, she's as pale as a fucking Wander Wraith."

They snicker.

"Let's just go. Don't want to get the blame if she destroys something."

Their footsteps echo in my ears and pound on my heart. The door slams.

I shouldn't pay attention to them. I'm here to train. Comments like that never got to me in Senn, so I just need to let them go.

I stare into the cabinet, grabbing the sight before me, giving it all my attention. My eyes focus on the largest weapon in the case. The inscription on the plaque below it says: **Ancient Ironskin Two-handed Sword**. The blade is as wide as both my hands set side by side, engraved with ancient Slyvic markings down the centre—*Otan sho com tuyo com slyv, otan kin tuyonne, otan caat tuyonne tiho*. Red-leather straps wrap around a thick, gold handle. Small gems lay in the gold, swirling delicate patterns all around the hilt. It must be as tall as I am and probably weighs more than me too.

Lance comes up behind me. He puts his hand on my shoulder and I jump a little.

"You're probably having trouble with weapons because you need one that's made for you. Like that one."

It's like the sword is calling me, taunting me to break through the glass and give it a whirl around the room.

"Too bad you're stuck with this dinky little guy." He holds up the sword I broke in weapons training yesterday. "Is this your handy work?" he asks with a wry smile.

I laugh and he presents me with another one, fully intact. I snatch it from him.

The floor in this room doesn't bounce. Thank Carnity. I slip my sandals off and plant my bare feet on solid wood.

Lance gets me to show him what I remember from class. After I show him, he goes through the steps again. He stands right beside me, doing each move with me, right-handed and left so I can be comfortable with both. After a while, he switches to face me and we mirror each other, going through each step, then on to attacking and blocking.

"Try to keep your hands a little more flexible," Lance says.

"Flexible?"

"Yeah. What you can do when you're striking is keep your top two fingers loose so there's more room for the sword to move. Keeping your hands loose allows you to manipulate the movement of your blade more freely."

I twiddle my fingers around the handle a few times to loosen up. "I guess that makes sense."

Lance lowers his sword. "Unclench your jaw." Playfulness

smiles from his eyes.

"Oh." I dip my head and resituate my body into a more relaxed stance.

A few swings with this new grip helps my movements become fluid, and less like a child waving around a stick.

Lance swings his sword. He comes at me fast, striking high, then low, then high again. I block all his strikes with swift movements, letting my hands be loose and ready. Lance's strikes keep coming. I lean into the rhythm of my muscles, back and forth between blocking and striking.

My vision clouds with hazy electric blue. Energy rages through me like another soul awakening inside. It palpitates across my skin, takes control of my body, pushing my mind's grip on my movements aside.

"Faster," Lance says.

My sword is a breath in my hand, a brilliant torch illuminated by my vivid vision. I swing it at Lance. Three slashes, and he blocks them all. He attacks again. A clang explodes from the clash of metal and his weapon flies off to the side, clattering across the floor. The electric haze drifts away, the pulsing energy in my skin subsides, and my mind locks back into place.

Without the life-affinity ghost swarming in my blood, my arms fall to my sides, the metal between my fingers is ten times heavier, my grip tighter. I gasp for air and press my shaking hand to my heaving chest.

"That was incredible," Lance says. I lift my eyes to meet his. His mouth hangs open, eyes wide. He jumps in place, then shuffles over to grab his sword. "Let's go again."

How can he be so calm and sweet after seeing the life-affinity ghost attack him like that? My body jolts with blue flashes, my blood churns inside me. I rip my eyes away from him. I swallow back the attempt of the life affinity to infest my body again.

"Whoa, Rin. Are you okay?" He bridges the gap between us, laying his hands gently on my shoulders, lowering his head to look me in the eye.

The warmth of his hands, his closeness, suffocates me. I put up my hands and take a step back.

"Sorry." Lance pulls back. "I shouldn't have pushed you like that."

"It's not your fault. I just don't know how to control it yet."

"I know what that's like."

I latch onto his words, their genuine tone, and the silence he leaves behind. I drink it in, focus on it so I can get the affinity out of my head. The life affinity, a thief that has stolen all my energy. It amplified everything I had, and now I'm left with nothing but heavy hands. I put my sword back in its place and head toward the door without saying anything more to Lance.

"Rin," Lance calls after me. I force my eyes to meet his. "I can tell you've got a lot on your mind. I'm not going to pry, but do one thing for me?" His lovely wings droop behind him and he wrings his hands.

"What?"

"Meet me back here tomorrow, same time."

I smile and nod. "Yeah, I can do that."

20

JOHANNA

"All right, team, listen up," Marcus says as we file in for morning training. The summer months have brought on a nasty heat that fills the room, drenching the air with humidity to mix with stale body odour that never seems to leave.

Zenta, please let us be doing something interesting today.

Most of our combat training has focused on broadening our techniques with different martial arts styles and incorporating them with more advanced steps. I like a new combination to kick ass just as much as the next guy, but it's getting stale.

"What do you have for us today, boss?" Niko asks, bouncing on the balls of his feet next to me.

"Well, since Hans is teaching a segment in first-year combat class, and Adrianne is at the Guardian clinic, you're stuck with Brand and me. We still feel like you guys could work on your teamwork skills," Markus says, crossing his arms.

"All right," Jeff-Ray says. He claps his hands together and rubs them. They make a sifting noise that grates on my nerves.

"Excited, are we?" Raising an eyebrow at him, I scoff.

He stares back, eyes calm. That shy smile of his spreads his lips, and in a cool tone, he says, "Got something against teamwork?"

No, not really. I'm curious about what might happen. We haven't done a teamwork exercise since the beginning of the year. In that exercise, it was like Rin saw me for the first time in a long time. As much as I wanted to get away from her, in that moment, something was reset. If teamwork is what it takes to get that again, it might be worth a try.

Rin stands with Eliote at the other end of our semi-circle around Marcus and Brand. She stares at the ground. I take a slow breath, focusing on only her. My mind heats as I try to make a connection to her mind, but the cool sensation of her thoughts is absent. I only get static.

"I haven't seen her bite yet." Jeff-Ray nudges me with his elbow.

I lean away from his nudge. "*Yet*," I say, crossing my arms.

"Brand's going to take the lead on this one." Marcus nods to Brand.

I straighten my posture as Brand steps forward, hands behind her back. She's swapped the tailored Warrior uniform she usually wears for a camouflage print t-shirt, dark jeans, and combat boots. A silver chain with two circular pendants lays over the collar of her shirt.

"The focus of today is teamwork, and we'll work in a few elements essential for Guardian work." Brand's voice bounces around the training room. It's commanding even though she hardly raises her voice. Each word reaches me driven with purpose—much easier on the ears than Mom's screaming. Wish she could learn to project like this. Brand's words make me stand on my toes, ready to tap into her Warrior mindset.

"First, Guardian equipment." She moves to the side of the room, and we follow her to a row of bags lined up along the wall.

"Essential pieces of equipment for any Guardian, whether you choose to be a Warrior or Protector, are your kit"—she motions to the bags—"and your weapon."

Behind Brand is an extensive arsenal of knives, swords, axes, and hammers. There are even shields and a bunch of stuff I don't recognize. A firestone rifle that looks like the kind my father preferred is propped up against the wall. He said he liked the range. As a Protector, he knew he would have to kill, but he thought a bullet wound was more respectful than maiming with a blade, opening large wounds that spilled so much needless blood. I lift my eyes to the lights, away from the weapon, so I can concentrate on what Brand is saying.

"To carry a weapon is your choice, but all Guardians are issued a standard combat knife. Please take one and attach it to your person. Then select another weapon to carry with you today."

We each take a knife. The blade is secured in a leg holster. I fasten it on my leg. Looks like my sweatpants were a good idea today. They give enough bulk to keep the knife in place.

Eliote struggles to get the straps tight enough to keep the knife from sliding down her silky leggings. I thought she would have learned to dress for combat by now, but she still goes way over the top, piling on makeup and twisting her hair into perfect little buns to crown her head. Today she wears a tight, black top that exposes her navel and matches her leggings, Tether brand high-top runners, and that chunky green lightstone around her neck.

"Each kit I have here is packed for a specific Guardian job," Brand continues. "Two are basic packs, one Warrior and one Protector, which are essentially the same." She moves along the row of kits and points to each one. "Then we have tech, beast tracker, and environmental patrol kits. Finally, your med-kit, which is the heaviest by far." It doesn't look too heavy the way she picks it up with one hand. Her bicep bulges and her veins distend, but the rest of her body is relaxed. "Who would like to volunteer to take this sucker?"

Eliote shoots her hand up. Maybe she's totally insane. That kit is massive, and all Eliote has is skinny arms and spider legs. Brand tosses her the kit. It thuds against her chest as she catches it. She's going to weigh us down today if she takes that thing.

"I can pull my own weight, Johanna," Eliote snaps. Her eyes find me with a quick turn of her head.

"I didn't say anything."

"Your aura says it all." Eliote's eyes narrow on me, like they've done a thousand times now, rummaging around my crappy aura, seeing things she has no right to see. She throws the heavy bag on her back and snaps the buckles to secure it around her waist.

"Mind your own damn business," I mutter.

My face burns. For Zenta's sake, I'm just as bad. Moments ago, I tried to do the same thing to Rin.

Brand clears her throat, glancing at us with warning eyes.

"The rest of you can grab a bag as well," she says. "The point here is that not every member of a squad is going to carry an equal load. Each Guardian chooses their own burden, and they work together despite their differences."

We all grab a kit. I peek inside and find some essential items—blanket, sleeping mat, compact food bars, and then four tech devices. The devices are all slim, none larger than a book, and two of them can fit in the palm of my hand, making the kit a manageable weight. I swing it onto my back and buckle up.

"So, what are we doing?" Niko asks.

"Today you will carry Marcus to the library."

I laugh.

"Wait, what?" Marcus says. His eyebrows shoot up and his arms fall to his sides. "We didn't discuss this, Brand."

Brand paces around the group, face neutral, her gaze on the floor, her hands behind her back. Even though we all giggle like children, she continues her instructions. "Today, you are my squad. I am your Commander, Ace is your captain, and Marcus is a civilian you are assigned to protect because he has sensitive information from neighbouring provinces. You were ambushed, and Marcus was injured, impairing his sight." She stops pacing by Marcus and pulls a piece of fabric from her back pocket. "Please put this over your eyes."

Marcus grabs the fabric from her, his brow furrowed. He sighs and cinches the band around his head. Hands on his hips, he huffs. "This is ridiculous."

A smile appears on Brand's face, but the curl of her lips is gone in a second. "Ace, let your team know how you would like them to proceed back to base, a.k.a the library. Every team member must be touching Marcus at all times. If someone lets go, you're all running sprints."

"This is becoming more and more uncomfortable every second, you know that right?" Marcus says.

"Lie down, you're injured," Brand says.

Ace rubs his chin as a reluctant, blindfolded Marcus lies down on the floor.

I groan. This is going to take forever. Ace is whip smart but way too careful. I tap my foot, making sure he can hear the slap of my shoe on the floor.

While we wait, I grab the firestone rifle from the weapons table. There are no stones in it. The metal is cool and weighty in my hands. At Emberstead funerals, it's customary for the family to lay the fallen Guardian's weapon in their hands so it's with them as they are cremated. A Protector presented my father's rifle to me as I stood at the coffin's edge with Mom. We both were stone still. Neither of us shed a tear in that moment—they were all gone. I held the rifle with sweaty hands, my heart pounded in aching beats. After minutes of waiting for me to put the rifle to rest where it was meant to be, the Protector came back. He tried to take it and do it himself, but I screamed at the top of my lungs. I wrapped my body around it. My feet left the ground as the Protector tried to pry it from my hands.

Mom let me scream. Her eyes still had fire and her posture remained strong. In a steady voice filled with the darkness of the nine hells, she turned to the Protector and said, "Let go of the rifle, it belongs to my daughter now."

In a few years, I'll use that rifle just as he had to keep this land safe.

My hands are sweaty now. As the others come forward to grab a weapon, I wipe my hands on my pants. The rifle has a strap, so I sling it across my body. It sways at my side; the strap digs into my neck. I readjust the knife on my legs and synch the kit strap around my middle a little tighter. As Rin picks up a short sword, her eyes wander over to me. I trace their movement as they flit from the firestone rifle to the sweat marks on my pants and to my eyes before returning to the ground. I'm not sure if she knows why I took the rifle. She didn't see me scream and defy cultural practices, but she knows Dad used a rifle. I wipe the sweat from my upper lip.

"I think Jeff and I will carry most of Marcus' weight," Ace says.

"You mean my butt." Marcus raises his hands with another exasperated sigh and lets them flop back to the ground.

"But isn't Rin our strongest member?" Eliote asks.

Ace shrugs. "I just didn't think Rin would want to carry Marcus' butt."

"I didn't sign up for *anyone* touching my butt," Marcus says.

"Don't worry, buddy, we'll just cradle you gently like a baby." Ace glances at Jeff and they both chuckle. "So, Jeff-Ray and I will take the middle, Rin and Johanna take his shoulders, Eliote and Niko take his legs."

The team gathers around Marcus in their assigned positions.

Every inch of my skin is sweaty, and my cheeks burn. I glance at Rin. She's staring at me, through me. I run my tongue over my teeth. "So, maybe we should link our forearms." I step over to Marcus.

Rin follows me without acknowledging my suggestion. She squats down on one side of Marcus, and I squat down on the other. We slip our arms under him. A drop of sweat skitters down the dark skin of Marcus' bicep and onto me. My arm brushes against Jeff's, our skin sticks together. A shiver of repulsion jerks through my body. I find Rin's arms; they're cool and dry. I grit my teeth, willing my face not to be beet red. It's so hot it could sizzle, but Rin is ice. Her small hands grip my forearms with steady pressure. Mousy-blond hairs dangle around her face and her steel-grey eyes focus on Marcus.

"We'll lift on three," Ace says.

I'm still waiting for Brand's affirmation, but sometime between now and her last instruction, she's left the training room.

"All right, ready?" Ace asks. "One."

I adjust my grip, pushing down the fire inside me to be cool like Rin. If we can do this exercise together, then maybe things will be different. Maybe I won't want to punch her in the face. *Don't even think about it. You can do this. Just be calm.*

"Two."

Jeff's arm flexes against mine.

"Any day now, Ace." I roll my eyes.

"Three."

We lift Marcus off the floor. I sidestep and crash into Jeff. He steps on my foot.

"Watch it, asshole," I say through my teeth.

"Move to the door to the arena, guys," Ace says.

"Could have said that sooner," Jeff mumbles.

Ace stays calm. "Sorry, it's shorter to go through the arena than around."

Our weapons clank together, and my pack keeps getting caught on Jeff's. With every other step, Rin pulls away from me. "Rin, maybe if we just sidestep it would be better. You keep pulling away from me when you cross your feet." My voice stays even and low. Pressing my lips together, I brace myself for her response.

Rin is quiet. Her grip on my arms twitches.

"Yeah, guys, just shuffle," Ace says.

A few more steps and Rin settles into a sidestep that matches mine. Of course, all it took was Ace to convince her that I know what I'm talking about. I take a slow breath, keeping the stream of air in and out of my body as steady as possible, avoiding any sharp gasps that could turn into pointed words.

"You can let me carry more of his weight, Rin." The sweetness in my tone is odd. I'm not sure where it came from—some dusty corner inside me. It draws Rin's eyes to me. Her eyebrows furrow.

"It's fine," Rin says.

"It might be more comfortable for him."

"I said it's fine. It's easier for everyone if I take most of the weight." Pink colouring rushes into her cheeks. Her shoulders shrug and she steps on Ace's foot. She drops her eyes back down to focus on her feet. "I could be halfway to the library by now if I was doin' this by myself."

"Sure, Ironskin. Don't need any help from us, right?" Niko says.

Rin jerks forward, looking around Ace at Niko. "Excuse me? I have a name."

Eliote stumbles, breaking hold of Niko's hands, and crashes to the ground. Jeff stops just in time so he doesn't squash her.

"*Rin,* this is a team drill." Niko teeters on his toes so he doesn't fall over with Eliote. "Damn it. Now we have to run sprints."

Grunting, Ace holds up most of Marcus's weight as we all

scramble to regain our footing. "Okay, everyone shut up and move together."

Instead of moving together, we stop with Marcus' feet stuck halfway through the door into the arena.

We're not children lining up after free hour in basic ed. We should be able to walk single file without shoving each other.

Brand appears outside the door. Coffee in one hand, free hand on her hip. The entire first-year combat training class turns to look at us. Laughter flows into the room like a wave. Sweat streams down the side of my face. My grip is slipping, and the butt of the rifle jabs my leg. I heave Marcus's shoulder into a better position. Rin yanks him closer to her. Tension fills every muscle of my body. I shake my head at Rin with a glare.

"How's it going?" Brand says, her casual tone makes me itch inside my boiling skin. I want to slam her coffee cup to the ground and torch it.

She takes a sip. The tricky bitch knew this was going to happen.

Ace clears his throat. "I think we need to turn Marcus on his side to get him through the door."

"You doing okay, Marcus?" Brand asks.

"I feel sick," he groans.

"Hang in there, bud, not even halfway there." Brand pats Marcus on the head and leaves us. Marcus groans again.

"Okay, guys, we roll Marcus toward Jeff-Ray on three," Ace says. "One."

"Wait, Ace," I say.

"Two."

"Uh, Ace?" Marcus echoes my concern.

"Three."

They roll Marcus and I spring away before he face-plants into my boobs. Marcus yelps, Rin scrambles to catch him, but instead, knees Marcus in the back.

"Johanna," Ace yells. His sweat-drenched face snaps toward me. "You have to hold on."

"I'm not letting Marcus get a feel, okay," I say, throwing my hands in the air.

Ace hangs his head and a drop of sweat drips onto Marcus' shorts. "Would everyone just hold on and work together?"

"Wait a sec, I need to adjust my pack," Eliote says, holding on to one of Marcus' legs and shifting her pack with her free hand.

"Damn it Eliote, you should have let Rin take that thing." Niko scrunches his nose just short of a snarl.

The cool in my veins has vanished. My blood boils. A switch flips in my brain to let the fire burn again. "You don't want Rin to be in charge of the med-kit," I say. "Even if you're standing right in front of her with your heart outside your chest, the bitch would just let you bleed."

Rin's eyes flash. "Shut up." A breath escapes her as her eye squeeze shut. The muscles in her jaw twitch.

Every time. Every damn time. I can't stay calm with her.

I shut my mouth for the rest of the exercise. After another half hour of sweaty shuffling, we deliver a dizzy Marcus to the library.

"We will be repeating this exercise every day until you can complete the task in under ten minutes," Brand says as we unload our packs and weapons. I groan, peeling my shirt away from my back, preparing myself for the impending sprints.

21

LANCE

Beast slaying.

Basic and essential for all Guardians, but it gets my nerves in a knot. A whole class about intentionally killing living beings—almost the exact reason that got me here in the first place, just without the intention.

Master Lotera has taken us to the outside training grounds for our lesson today. We went through basic drills to get us warm and sweaty, now it's time for the meat—piercing weapon strikes with essence incorporation to break physical and essence-produced beast armours. If I keep it simple, I'll get through the class without an essence surge. If I can keep her out of my head, I'll be okay.

Lotera demonstrates a three-step, armour-breaking process. She grounds herself in her stance as we've seen her do a thousand times before. She sweeps one hand in front of her, gathering a fistful of energy and slaps it onto the sword. A whirlwind starts at her hands and wraps around the blade of her longsword. The wind whips around the metal in slicing discs. She draws her sword back to her side, blade parallel to the ground, and thrusts at an imaginary beast. With a smooth transition, she swings the sword in a full arc to slam it down on the beast at a forty-five-degree angle, and finally she stabs the sword straight down into the ground. The wind slices into the earth, tearing a three-foot trench into the practice ground.

"Pierce the armour, break it open, and then wound the flesh," Lotera says. "Practice the three steps that I showed you with your weapon of choice."

Pierce, break, wound.

I clench and extend my hands a few times as I approach the practice weapons. Touching my thumb to each of my fingertips on each hand, my essence starts to flow. I breathe deep. Taking a longsword, I find an open spot on the training ground a little way from Mycul and Aris. Aris runs through the steps a few times without wind manipulation, but Mycul has fire armour wrapped around the blade of a massive claymore. He thrusts the blade forward and swings it around with a stream of flame trailing from the tip of the blade. The ground trembles as he jams it into the ground with a grunt.

Pierce, break, wound.

I run my thumb over the tips of my fingers one last time and place both hands on the handle. My essence flows in smooth waves through my body. I thrust my sword forward. Essence trembles through my hands. Electricity streams down the blade—a single streak of silver energy. It sparks at the tip. I tighten my grip for control.

"Mycul, did you hear? Some Ironskins broke into a government building last night." Litha's voice raises the hairs at the back of my neck.

The line of electricity shrinks back to my hands with a pulse of light.

"Yeah, it's crazy. Did they find out what they stole?"

"Some documents, I guess."

"Damn, they just want to screw everything up, don't they?"

Rin has been nothing but kind to me. Honest, sweet, curious. She's not looking for trouble. I turn on my heel and march over to them.

"Kind of unnerving to know we have Ironskin Protectors out there that could be in on this," Litha says, leaning on her longsword.

"Uh—"

The sound escapes my mouth, but Litha admires her nails and Mycul spits at the ground. "Damn cutches."

Essence crackles inside me. I clear my throat. "You know I don't think—"

"What's that, Lancy boy?" Mycul's pale-green eyes find mine. His jaw is tense, and he stands tall with his chest puffed out.

Litha's eyes trail him top to bottom.

"I was, well, I was just going to say that . . ."

Mycul's eyebrows raise, for once waiting for me to finish my thought. Heat crawls up my back and spills into my face.

Aris comes trotting over to us. "What's going on, guys?"

A spark jumps between my middle and pointer finger as all three of them stare at me. I clench my fist, swallow, and try to suppress the flow of energy. Mycul is three inches shorter than me. He's broader than me, but with my wingspan he's practically lost in my shadow. My heart pounds against my chest. Why am I scared of him?

"I was thinking we shouldn't talk like that," I say.

"Speak up, Lancy." Mycul tilts his head to me, and shadows fall in his eyes, darkening them to swamp green.

I drop my eyes to the ground. "We should get back to practicing the technique."

The sun glints off Mycul's sword as he heaves it up and rests it on his shoulder. "Let's see you do it then."

"Fine." I turn away from my gawking friends. I draw a long breath. Sweat pours down the side of my face.

In my stance, I press each finger into the handle one by one, stirring my essence into a steady crackle through my body. I exhale and step, thrusting my sword forward, sending the streak of energy across my blade. I swing the blade around. Drawing it above my head, I shove it into the earth. But the earth doesn't tremble like when Mycul did it. The ground doesn't split. The tip of my sword just buries into the ground and the streak of lightning slips back to my hands with a trail of smoke from singed grass.

Mycul laughs behind me and Litha's snicker prickles my skin.

My body goes slack.

"Why are you guys laughing?" Aris asks. "That was really good, Lance."

"He's using first-year essence manipulation techniques, Aris," Mycul says, laughter still in his tone.

I turn back around just enough to see Mycul shake his head.

Aris looks between me and Mycul, running a hand through his dark curls. A smile flashes across his face as he gives me a thumbs up.

"Lance, a word," Lotera says from behind me.

I follow her to the edge of the training grounds, where she sets down her weapon.

"He's right, you know," she says, her taut arms crossing over her chest. "I've been watching you all year. Your techniques are always well executed, but you resort to simple ways of manipulating energy."

My stomach twists. I've been avoiding Master Lotera as much as possible this year. It was just a matter of heading straight to my next class and never getting to class early to stay out of her way. But I knew she'd catch on.

"You're limiting yourself." Lotera pinches the bridge of her nose. "I'm just trying to figure out if it's intentional or not. So, show me how to slay a beast. Because that little spark won't do it." Leaning against the weapons rack, she motions to the open space around us.

I step forward but check over my shoulder. Mycul, Aris, and Litha are turned toward the city wall, practicing the combination. All around the training grounds, energy pulses and burns and flashes, and my heart still pounds. Taking a calming breath, I roll my shoulders back.

"I'd like you to draw a lightning strike from the sky and fuse it to your sword," Lotera says. My mouth opens to protest but she raises an eyebrow. "Do not test my patience."

Just breathe and do it before you lose your nerve.

Feet planted, back straight, I grip the handle with my dominant hand but leave my off hand loose around the leather.

As I fill my lungs with air, my left hand leaves the handle. I reach it to the sky. Dark clouds paint over the blue. They roll into inky black spirals and blanket the school grounds in shadow. My essence flows from head to toe in shooting jolts. I flex my hand. Thunder claps. Tension builds in the voices behind me. I press my lips together. Electricity streaks down from the heavens and hits my hand. Heat spreads over my arm, through the side of my body, and through my toes.

In a wide swoop, I bring the surging ball of energy down and slam it onto the handle. Light bursts from my hands and Khali's face bursts into my mind.

Her bloodshot eyes.

Tears streaked her golden skin. Her chapped lips parted with my name. Her long, wavy, black hair sprawled around her as she fell on her snow-white wings.

Those bloodshot eyes never closed.

My hands tremble and the sparks recede back into my hands. The clouds clear from the sky, letting the sun beat down on my back.

"I can't." I heave a breath and fall to my knees, digging my fists into the grass. The soft green blades are cool against my electrified skin, the ground solid under my shaking arms.

"Take five," Lotera says. Her heavy hand squeezes my shoulder.

I nod, but I can't take my hands away from the ground.

Everything would break if I continued with that ability. Everything would break if I told Mycul off. I don't know where to go from here.

Breath is heavy in my lungs as I stand. I drop my sword and leave the field. My hand finds its way into my pocket, clenching around a pack of cigarettes that have become commonplace in my life again. I roll one between my thumb and pointer. Essence rushing, I bring a spark to the end of the cigarette, just big enough to light it. What's the point in starting over when I always come back?

22

ELIOTE

Academic classes give me a little confidence boost after slugging through combat training each day. Without essence, I'm weaker than all my teammates, which makes sparring with Jeff-Ray—who's half a foot taller and twice my width—all the more exhausting. I rub a black bruise on my bicep as I take it slow on the way to elements class. It's fall, we're halfway through the year, and I'm still picking up bruises. I could use a break.

I walk through the halls, echo-buds in my ears, ignoring the world for a minute. Focusing my eyes on the floor and my ears on the music, I can almost ignore all the auras around me. My breaths are even as they rise in time with the music. But some auras have become more familiar than others. Energy tingles the back of my neck, back and forth like the tide. I turn on my heel and pluck the echo-buds from my ears as my eyes land on Ace a few feet behind me. His head tilts to his history notes. With one long stride, he comes right up to me, just shy of running me over.

He jolts and his aura splashes around me. "Holy Ren. You scared me."

"Sorry." A smile creeps to my lips. I slip my arm around his. "I'm glad I ran into you."

Ace pushes up his glasses. His arm is stiff in mine, like he's trying to straighten his aura. Little does he know, only clear-blue good intentions pour from him, and all his straightening is causing ripples of doubt in the waters. The ripples shiver into me, spreading an ache through my chest. I swallow hard and widen my smile for the both of us.

"I want to run something by you," I say.

"Sure." He looks down at my hands around his bicep and back to my eyes. "What's on your mind?"

"Well," I say, twisting the ends of my hair between my fingers. The waves in Ace's aura subside. I keep my gaze on him to avoid sinking into other auras. "Rin and Johanna had their birthdays this week, and we didn't get to do anything for them."

"Right."

"Since tomorrow is Freeday and we don't have to hit the books right away, we should all go out and celebrate." I shake his arm a little.

"Ah." Ace drops his eyes to the floor. His energy shifts. The calm pool of water deepens to an ominous vortex, spiralling in powerful surges.

"You don't think that's a good idea," I say, leaning into him.

"Well, I don't think it's a *great* idea." He tilts his head away from me.

"Okay . . . why?" The pull of his aura is so strong it makes my mind heavy and want to latch on to things that hurt me in the past, things I've tried to let go of. I don't think his shift was caused by talk of birthday parties.

"Neither of them will like it. I think it would be fun, and it would be good for us, but they won't like it."

"That's what I thought. But—"

"You still want to do it."

"I really, really want to do it. The school year is long, it's not good to work so hard without having some fun."

"They won't want us to make a big deal about it."

I sigh. "Do you know what's up with those two?"

"Trust me, Rin and Johanna's drama is way over my head."

I nod, twiddling my fingers around his arm. A smile brightens his brown skin. I can't coax my lips to smile, though. The indigo tie that always stretches out from Ace's aura, searching for Rin, gets sucked into the vortex. It hides inside the swirling energy. I twist one of the rings in my ear. "Rin's been acting a little weird this week."

"Weird how?" Ace glances at me, eyes pools of concern.

"I don't know, her aura is . . . tight. That's the only way I can describe it."

Shifting his notebook in his hands, his arm tenses again and his lips press together. My breath is tight in my chest until he says, "I think this is the week her parents went to be with the ancestors."

"Oh." My breath gushes out of me, draining my feet of energy, and I stop in the middle of the hall. Ace's arm slips out of my numb hands. "Why doesn't she tell me these things?"

The other students in the hall shuffle around us, their auras crawl over me, wafting over me like perfumes.

"I've asked myself the same question so many times." Ace tilts his head to the side with his smile flickering on his lips. "What does it feel like?" he asks.

"What does what feel like?" I ask, giving my head a shake and refocusing on him.

He shrugs. "Seeing auras all the time."

My heart picks up its cadence. Most people want to know what I see in their aura—if they want to know at all. Getting lost in the indigo swirl around Ace, I sense the doubt again, but it's only a little piece of driftwood in the vast sea.

"It's like having the answers to a test but not the questions," I say. "I have access to everyone's feelings, but I don't know how they got there, and since it's a breach of privacy, no one fills me in."

Ace is still for a moment. "That's not fair," he says.

Even though the air is muddy with colourful spirits and my mind clouds with unconnected thoughts, my soul steadies. The turbulence inside Ace has subsided and his aura regains its gentle flow. His hesitant smile lets light into my eyes.

Ace offers me his arm again. "So, let's just do something really chill for their birthdays, like cake and drinks at a coffee shop. If you think we need it, then we probably do."

I take his arm with both hands. As we walk into the classroom, it's easier to calm my sight without everyone running back and forth through the hall. With less stimulation, I relax, even though I know the calm won't last much longer. I take a breath filled with Ace's scent of lemongrass and hair paste.

We split apart. I take a seat beside Rin, but she's slouched in her chair, staring off into space with her arms crossed, and doesn't look at us.

I glance at Ace as he takes a seat in front of Rin.

"What's she doing?" I ask.

"Thinking," he says.

"I know, but that's what I'm worried about. Her aura's getting darker. Should I do something?"

Ace's lips part to say something but nothing comes out. He turns his attention to his backpack and switches out his history notebook for elements.

I stare at Rin, soaking up a thunderous tremor in the energy around her as a pair of wings spill out of the stream of blue in her aura. The more I look at her, a void inside me opens as if I'm hungry or sick.

Johanna, Niko, and Jeff come into the room and take seats on the other side of the room. Each of their auras produces a different kind of energy—a burn under my scalp, an itch on my side, a grounding sensation in my feet. Our professor comes in seconds later to begin the lecture. He calls for attention and I steel my nerves to focus on his lesson and ignore the bustling galaxies of the other student's auras.

"Welcome, class." He claps his hands together. "Today we will start our new topic with a little discussion.

"From day one of this class, we have progressed from cells to tissues to body systems. This gives us the ability to understand each Illysonian on a basic level. With this knowledge, we can produce medicine and health practices that work for all hédin. But today we begin discussing the unique attributes of each lineage."

I lean forward on my desk and make a heading for my notes.

"So, with any topic in elements, we need to start with the

building blocks. What were the very first abilities that showed up among hédin?"

The professor gives us a moment to think.

Healing and heat manipulation. I peek over at Rin's notes. She's written it down. I raise an eyebrow, trying to urge her to give the answer, but she shakes her head.

Without waiting to be called on, I raise my hand and say, "Healing and heat manipulation."

"That's correct. What are the names of the individuals who first displayed these abilities?" A hush falls over the class. "Oh, come on, I hear you swear by them daily."

Realization sends a murmur and a chuckle through the class.

"Carnity and Dien," someone says.

The professor nods and joins the chuckle. "Now these two, Carnity and Dien, had three children, one of which was the first to display enhancements of a lineage we still observe today. Which is it?"

I wish Rin would answer.

"No one knows?" The professor looks at his class over the rims of his glasses, his chin lowered. "The Ironskin Lineage," he says, folding his hands behind his back. "The Ironskin Lineage is the oldest and longest surviving lineage." The aura that surrounds him is similar to Ace's since he's Nytrue, and as he speaks, it becomes disrupted with waves. "Tell me, class, what is different about Ironskin essence from other hédin?"

"It's demonic," someone yells from the back of the room.

"Unnatural."

"It's fucking freaky, man."

The collective energy of the class becomes hot as the individual auras, with their unique wave frequencies, merge.

Laughter erupts through the room. It's just like being back in my Luminee classes, where everyone called me a freak for not having enhancements. Every hédin these days has essence. Beasts have essence. Even some plants have essence. If anyone is unnatural here, it's not an Ironskin, it's me.

"All right, all right, please, class. Settle down. All essence is natural. Does anyone have a serious answer they would like to share with us?"

Heart pounding, I clear my throat. "It doesn't flow."

"In a sense, yes. Expand, Eliote."

"The other lineages have essence pathways. Ironskin essence resides in the cells, so it doesn't flow through the body."

"Well put, but there is one thing that I would like to correct. Ironskin essence is located in the cell membrane. Just as the cellular membrane is fluid, so is the essence. Therefore, the essence flows, but in smaller spaces than the pathways, thus increasing surface area, and ultimately increasing strength and resilience. This is where we start our lecture—Ironskin cells."

The professor takes a piece of chalk. He marks out a triangle on the board. "You are familiar with the essence affinities: Fire, water, light, animal, body, air, vegetation, earth, weather, and spirit affinities." Glancing over his shoulder, the professor raises an eyebrow. We nod and he goes back to drawing his triangle. "We have these affinities because each lineage has an essence energy alignment that falls somewhere between the three essential energies—jint, fann, and unama."

He writes jint at the top point of the triangle, fann at the right point, and unama at the left. I copy his drawing as he proceeds to write the names of each lineage along the triangle, placing Ironskin right at the top under jint.

"Jint is sustaining energy. This sustaining aspect of the Ironskin essence and its presence in every cell gives rise to the Ironskins' unique physical strength, speed, and impenetrable skin. The purity of the alignment allows for their spirit affinity. Pure jint attracts unama energy and fann, as well as jint. Thus, the jint in their essence pulls at any hédin, giving them life or death depending on the affinity."

My hand makes furious scribbles across my notepad to get everything he says. The professor pauses his lesson to brush the chalk from his hands. I glance around the classroom. The other students scribble notes as well but with furrowed brows.

Ever since being at the academy, auras have been more striking to me. Each one feels more varied than they do in my Luminee community. All my family members and neighbours have similar auras. It must be because they have the same energy alignment.

"The variety of abilities comes from the lifeline code passed from parents to children, of course," the professor says.

Before I start to scribble again, I peek at Rin. She is blank faced and glassy eyed. Her aura is a tight sphere, swirling in lethargic spirals of blue and red around her purple core.

I turn back to my notes with the strange void expanding inside me, right under my sternum. It presses against my heart but it moves lower into my stomach. My mind clouds with the sensation and the other auras in the room aren't as bright, in fact they seem like they're far away, maybe even in another classroom. The void sinks lower and deeper. I press my hands to my face with a slow breath. Everything inside me is dark, filled with a heavy shadow.

Tears prickle my eyes. I can't tell if they're born from my

own emotions, out of exhaustion, or the void I picked up from Rin still deep in my gut. My attention drifts away from the lesson to the window. Outside the trees are turning colours. A leaf falls to the ground. As it drifts, a flash of light pulses around it. The light distorts its surroundings and energy spirals to the blue sky. The same thing happened to the beasts we killed on Moon Hill. The spirit leaving the physical.

I press my sleeve to my eyes to dry my tears. There's energy everywhere, but my body is so dull and tired. *It's not fair.*

23

RIN

"I DON'T LIKE CELEBRATING MY BIRTHDAY, ELIOTE," I say as she tugs at my arm trying to get me off my bed.

"I know that," she says, setting her hands on her hips.

"My birthday isn't something to celebrate."

She rolls her eyes and throws her head back. With one strong yank she gets me to stumble off the bed. That's what this week makes me feel like. I have no control, like I'm being yanked around by the powers that be.

"Don't be like this, Bird Brain." She pushes me to the door, but I brace my hands on both sides of the frame.

She can't make me go. It's the end of the week, midterms are around the corner, and I don't need the stress of people asking me what my favourite birthday memory is.

No, I'm not going.

"Can't we just pretend the day is over?" I say. I've been doing pretty well so far. With training and classes, I've barely thought about what day it is. But now—*Stop looking. He's not there and looking's not going to bring him back from the fucking dead.*

I take a sharp breath.

Eliote struggles to get me to budge by pushing her whole body against me from behind.

"We missed Johanna's birthday too." She grunts and jams her shoulder on my spine. It's kind of nice, like a massage. "Whoa, this is so weird. I'm like in the middle of your aura right now."

I cringe trying to imagine what that must feel like. "Johanna doesn't want me there either."

"You're a pain, you know that? We're a team, we should celebrate our team members."

"What does it matter? I'm sure Niko, Jeff-Ray, and Johanna couldn't care less about me being around."

"That's the point." Her attempts to push me out of our room cease. "We need to do more stuff together. Bond. Now cut the crap and let's go."

I brace myself for a few more seconds. Thinking that she's given up, I drop my arms and turn to her just as she takes a running leap. She rams into me. I lose my balance and we crash to the ground with a clatter of limbs.

She stays on top of me, panting like she has just done sprints. As she lifts her head, a smile beams across her face. Hell, I'm proud of her for taking me down.

"Can you just come?" she whines. "We're going to get cake and coffee and that's it."

"I already had coffee today. I get jittery if I have too much. Would ya get off?" I push her off me.

"Then just cake."

"Fine."

"Is that what you're going to wear?" She raises an eyebrow at me and looks down her nose at my outfit—faded jeans and a loose fitting, navy-blue long sleeve. Comfy.

"It's my birthday. I can wear what I want." I pull the hem of the shirt then let go so it flops back into place.

She shrugs. "Whatever, you look cute."

I snatch my cap off the floor. It had fallen off when Eliote brutally attacked me. I fit it on my head, but Eliote rips it off and turns the brim backward.

"Let's go." Eliote grabs my hand.

I'm sorry children. I can't take this life any longer.

Damn it.

The rest of the team waits for us outside the Kava Guard, a coffee shop popular with academy students. It connects to a string of shops on one side and is shaded by a tree turning yellow on the other. An airship roars overhead, but once it passes, a soft murmur of rustling leaves, chatting shoppers, and the clip-clop of shoes on cobblestone settles over the street.

"There they are," Niko says as we approach. "Finally."

"This one didn't want to come," Eliote says, and pushes me to the centre of the team-circle we've become accustomed to.

I stop myself before colliding with Johanna. She looks right through me, arms crossed, wearing her dad's old Protector jacket. Her eyes shift from seeing what's behind me to contacting my eyes. One second of contact. She doesn't scowl or roll her eyes, just looks at me. For one second the slate is clean. Her face turns into twelve-year-old Johanna—wide, watery, green eyes that see me, not all the beastshit between that day and now. But the second passes. She frowns. Maybe the shit's too strong. She looks away from my offensive presence.

I step away from Johanna.

"Took ya long enough," Niko says. "We're doing this for you, you know?"

"Right." I tuck my hair behind my ear. "Sorry to keep you waiting."

"Well let's go in, team." Niko jumps off his perch on top of a mailbox and swings the door open. "Birthday girls first." He holds the door, ushering us in with a wave of his hand.

The coffee shop is a long, narrow room with the coffee bar on the right and a pastry case filled with decadent desserts—three-tiered chocolate cake, pinichu berry cream cake, tarts of every flavour imaginable, syrup-glazed fruits, biscuits, and cookies. On the left side of the room are tables and booths. Tucked in the back, tech game consoles fill the wall. They flash and make blipping noises, taking away from the comfortable feel of the rest of the shop.

"Berry or chocolate, Rin?" Jeff-Ray asks as we near the till. "I'm buying."

"The chocolate has weckler nuts in it," Johanna mumbles from the other side of Jeff-Ray.

Jeff-Ray turns to her. "Is that a problem?"

"I'm allergic to them," I say.

She remembers? Thought she would die before admitting she remembered a detail about me. I peek around Jeff's massive form. Johanna flicks her eyes to me but crinkles her nose as our eyes lock.

"That's nice of you to remember," Jeff-Ray says. He gives Johanna a surprised but approving nod.

"Ugh, get over it. Order me the chocolate. I'll go grab a booth."

"So, pinichu is okay for you then?" Jeff-Ray turns back to me.

"Yeah, that's fine."

He takes flavour preferences from the rest of the team and the drink orders too. He relays all the orders to the man at the till. Eliote and Ace join Johanna at the booth and the rest of us wait for the food and drinks.

Jeff gives Niko a nudge as we wait.

"What?" Niko says under his breath.

Jeff points his chin at me. "Talk to her," he whispers back.

My stomach flip-flops and my jaw tightens.

"So, like, how enhanced are you, Rin?" Niko asks, his voice tight.

He looks at me out of the corner of his eye, head half dipped, picking at an invisible speck of dirt on his collared t-shirt with colourful vertical stripes. He shifts his feet. I wish I knew what was going on in his head, the intention behind that question. Whatever it is, his nervous mannerisms make my shoulders tense.

"What do you mean?" I say.

"I mean, like, if you can have allergies, then you're not completely enhanced, right?"

The question stabs me in the gut, like he's really asking if I'm actually a normal hédin.

"Well, anything that can get into the blood and nervous system can hurt an Ironskin, no matter how far the impenetrability goes," I say.

Niko nods and so does Jeff-Ray. The server has finished plating the cake, so we each take two and make our way to the booth.

"How far does it go for you?" Jeff-Ray asks.

"I'm pretty sure that every part of me is impenetrable. Skin, bone, muscle, all of it."

I set down my two plates and Jeff and I go back to grab the drinks.

"Is your whole family like that?"

Okay, this conversation is fine. Looks like they're both just curious.

"My older brother's like me, and my younger brother doesn't have enhancements. For my parents, I think it was just the skin and muscle."

Jeff-Ray is silent as he picks up three drinks, and I pick up the rest. Grasping two mugs in one hand and one in the other, I turn, careful not to spill. But Jeff-Ray stays at the counter.

"Was?" he asks, looking down at me.

Heat fills my face, and my armpits start to sweat. "Well, yeah, my parents are dead."

"Oh, I'm sorry to hear that." He looks down at his sturdy fingers wrapped around the porcelain cups. "How'd they die?"

How'd they die? That's what he wants to talk about on my birthday? Well, I don't really want to talk about how my father was tortured for intel until his captors found his weak spot and stabbed him repeatedly. My mother's lifeless body found draped over my father's grave, Ease stubs scattered around her, will be a story for another day.

"Thanks for paying for all this." I turn to the booth, keeping my arms close to my sides so no one can see I've sweat straight through my shirt. "Who ordered this foamy thing?" I ask.

"That would be mine," Ace says with a slight raise of his hand.

"Tea?"

Eliote takes the tea from me, smiling and cupping the mug with both hands.

I slide in beside Niko with my water. Jeff-Ray hands Johanna a black coffee, and Niko some sort of three-layer coffee, fudgy drink, with sprinkles and a cookie stuck in the pile of whipped cream on top. Jeff-Ray sits, leaving plenty of space between us, and adds cream to his coffee, stirring it in with a methodical motion. How lovely. I've managed to offend the one guy who gets along with everyone, even Johanna.

Ace eyes me from across the table. "You okay?" he mouths.

I shrug.

He raises an eyebrow and points his finger to his cheeks.

"Fine," I mouth back and fan myself with my hand. I hope that will satisfy him. It's warm in here but maybe it's just me. I take a sip of water.

The bell above the shop door tinkles as I take my first bite of cake—my first bite in six years. Tangy pinichu berries bite my tongue, the cream soothes it. The sweetness takes me back to the last time my father made a cake for my birthday. He'd put custard in one of the layers and used sorrow blossoms to decorate it. His grey eyes appear behind the flowered cake. *Happy birthday, Rinny.* My heart jumps to my throat. His face is replaced by my mother's pale complexion. *He's not coming back this time, Rinnaya.* I force myself to swallow the bite.

"Hey, would you look at this. The advanced team decided to grace us with their presence."

Two students I recognize from the first day of training, Roth and Jaya, walk up to our booth. Roth smirks at me. Jaya crosses her arms and leans to the side, scanning us with judgy eyes, her short, red hair swishing around her chin.

"Barely see you guys," Roth says.

"What a shame," Johanna says under her breath.

"Come again?" Jaya says. She leans forward, propping her arms on the table.

Johanna just sips her coffee.

"We're all in calculations together," Eliote says in a light, friendly tone. But even her magical smile can't cut the tension.

"Yeah, but that's just class," Roth says. "We don't get to know each other."

Johanna laughs. "No harm done."

"Well, since we're here now, you guys want to have a little competition?" Roth asks.

"What'd you have in mind?" Niko asks, rubbing his hands together.

"You any good at tech games?"

"Pft. Am I any good at—hell yeah, I am." Niko jumps up, banging his knees on the table in the process and shuffles me and Jeff-Ray out of the booth.

"Two against two, who else wants in?" Roth lifts his chin, eyeing us all.

Johanna glances at me. A look of disgust washes over her face.

"Rin, you want in?" Roth asks, a cruel smile spreading his chapped lips.

Johanna forces a laugh. "Please, she's awful at tech games."

"Hey, I kicked your butt in *Soul Captor Revenge*," I say,

gripping my fork.

"And I beat you in every game of *Guardian Duty*, *Cruiser Crush*, *Flight Parade*—"

"Okay, we get it, Johanna, you're amazing," Ace says with a flourish of his fingers. "Just go."

She doesn't budge just yet. "Maybe Rin and I should have a match, hm?"

"Maybe not," I say, and crinkle my nose at her.

She throws her fork down on the table, says, "Move, Ace," and pushes him and Eliote out of the booth.

Jeff-Ray and I shuffle to let Niko go to battle Roth and Jaya. I sit back down and slide my cake and myself into the corner of the booth. My fork slices through the layers of fluffy cake. The cream squishes through my teeth.

"So, Rin. What kind of Protector work does Stephen do?" Eliote asks.

They're hittin' some real good questions today. I'm tempted to go all Senn on them, tell them to mind their own business, storm out, smash a few things on the way. That'd be stupid though.

Is Stephen even thinking of me or is the Revival the only thing on his mind? My thoughts get caught in my last encounter with Stephen, and my tastebuds no longer register the flavours of the cake.

The jingle of the bell announces another group of students entering the shop.

"He's an inter-provincial high-profile guard," I say through a mouth of cream.

Is that a lie? That is what I thought he was doing all this time, but he's not doing it anymore. I can't tell them about that;

the Revival haunts my dreams, so bringing it up in conversation would be a nightmare.

"That's awesome," Jeff-Ray says, a twinkle in his eye. "Does he tell you a lot about his missions?"

"No."

"Oh . . ." The eye twinkle fades. He shakes his head and returns his attention to his coffee.

Everything that comes out of my mouth is crap, so I fill it with another bite of cake.

"Most of his missions are confidential, right, Rin?" Ace says, creating space for me to breathe. I nod.

The bell tinkles again. I peek at the door. My fork drops to my plate. I turn the brim of my hat around so it hides my face, which is probably as red as the berries on my cake by now.

"Why are you being so weird?" Eliote asks, twisting in her seat to see who walked in.

Lance stops at the counter looking at the menu with his hands in his pockets. The light streaming through the windows plays on his skin, accentuating the stiff line of his jaw. He bites his lower lip as he considers his options from the board. His hair is wet like he just showered.

"Oh my gosh. That's the guy. Weapons-training guy," Eliote whispers then squeals.

"What guy?" Jeff-Ray asks.

Ace smirks. "It's Lance."

"Do you want to invite him over here?" Jeff-Ray says.

I shake my head, but Ace raises his hand. "Hey, Lance," he calls.

Lance turns. My hat doesn't hide my face enough and our eyes meet. He stands there staring at me for what feels like minutes but is more likely just a second. A smile fills his face, making my head woozy, like it's going to fall off, land in my cake, and roll across the table. Even though death is imminent, Lance's smile tugs at the corners of my mouth and I smile back.

He tells the waiter his order before coming over to us. Ace kicks me under the table and Eliote giggles. Lance sits, and I get a whiff of whatever he uses in his hair. It smells fresh, like forests and flowers. It mixes with something darker, ashy, like cigarette smoke. It makes me dizzy.

He ignores the others for a second. "Hey, Rin."

"Hey." How stupid is my smile? Why am I blushing? Can he tell how red my face is?

Jeff-Ray introduces himself and Lance is polite, asking him questions about the team, complimenting him on his forearm muscles, which is weird, but I've come to expect some weird from Lance.

"I'm Eliote. Bird Brain's told me a little about your training together."

Oh dear.

Lance glances at me. "Bird Brain?"

I shrug.

"That's cute," he says, and he looks down at his hands.

The server brings him his drink, just an easy-caff coffee, and he adds enough cream to make it almost white.

Eliote strikes up a conversation that occupies his attention. Lance sips his coffee, and his hand shakes a little as he puts down the cup. He runs his hands down his pant legs. What does he have to be nervous about? He's perfect. Every response to a question is filled with an awkward sincerity that takes my breath away, leaving me speechless in the corner.

I'm sorry, children. I can't take this life any longer.

The blips of the tech games and the conversation mesh into one senseless melody. My gaze catches on the grains of the wood table, unwavering. Whatever tethers my mind to my body is cut and I'm left floating above myself. The heat of the room presses on my detached being, hot, but my hands are cold—sweaty, but cold. I press my clammy fingers to my cheeks. The heat of my face neutralizes my cool touch so my fingers disappear into empty space.

Johanna comes up behind Lance. "Who the hell are you?" she says.

Lance jolts and puts his hand over his heart. Now he's the cute one. "Shit," he says under his breath. Johanna stares down at him. "I'm Lance."

"Mm. Eliote, move. I want my cake," Johanna says and pushes her way into the booth.

Ace passes Johanna her plate. "Did you guys win?" he asks.

Niko joins us, a sheepish grin growing across his tan skin. "Well, let's just say we could have done better. We gotta pay for their drinks."

"Wait, who are you again?" Johanna asks Lance as she reaches over both Eliote and Ace to grab her wallet, picking up a smudge of chocolate icing on her sleeve.

"He's the guy I've been training with in the evening," I say.

"I didn't ask you." Johanna's eyes shoot daggers at me. They scream at me—*I hate you, Rin.*

I don't know how long we've been here, but it's been long enough. I nudge Jeff-Ray and make him and Niko scooch out even though they just scooched in.

"Wait, where are you going?" Lance asks.

Oh, please don't ask me to stay, I need to get out of here.

"I'm not feeling well," I say and turn to leave.

"We'll train tomorrow though?" he asks.

I look at him just long enough to get lost in his brown eyes. Kind eyes.

"Yeah, see you tomorrow."

Lance raises his hand as if to touch my arm but waves instead. "Okay. Well, happy late birthday, Rin."

That is the nicest thing anyone's said all day.

I sat on the swing in the school yard like I did every day at lunch. No one bothered me there. Most kids in my class thought they were too old for the swings.

My stomach growled so I pumped my legs, the rain splatting on my head. I swung as high as I could, plummeting down to the ground and swooping back up to meet sky past the towering inner-city buildings. The wind rushed in my ears, rain stung my face, and my heart beat like a happy little drum.

I hugged my legs in, letting the swing slow to a soothing rock.

Something struck my back. I twizzled around to investigate. Johanna ran toward the swing set, jumped, and caught the chains of the swing next to me. I continued to twizzle while she leaned her whole body forward and back to gain momentum, standing on the seat.

We swung in silence, rain soaking our hair, plastering it to our heads.

No matter how much I swung, my stomach did a good job

of reminding me that I hadn't eaten lunch that day. I needed to get my mind off the emptiness in my gut. "So, the other day," I said.

"Yeah, what about it?" She kept her eyes forward, swaying with the swing.

I stared at the ground. I only reacted to my stomach, spoke too soon, and didn't have anything else to say.

"What? That's it?" Johanna scoffed. "Figures." She swooped forward and sprung off the wooden seat. She landed and sent a wave of pebbles at me.

"What's that supposed to mean?" I asked.

"Well, you didn't have much to say that night either."

I stopped twizzling and ground my feet into the pebbles.

What does that have to do with us? she had asked. "That" meaning my parents dying and me being broke. I guess our relationship didn't have anything to do with that.

"Sorry for being a jerk," I muttered.

"There ya go."

She jumped back on her swing, and I watched her for a while. There were bags under her eyes, dark half moons, and her frown was deeper than normal, more permanent.

"Why'd you have to go to the station?" I asked, pumping my legs again.

She licked her lips and lowered herself down so her butt was in the seat of the swing. She kicked a chunk of rocks. "My dad," she said. "He died."

An icy breath caught in my chest. The air froze everything as it went down until my lungs were crystalized. The hinges of my swing screeched, and I drifted to a stop.

Mr. Kingsman? Gone?

Everyone was dying. My dad, my mom, Mr. Kingsman. Who's next? Oron? Liam? Me? Johanna? A jolt sent my heart battering around my rib cage and my breaths swarmed through my frozen lungs.

"Say something," Johanna yelled.

I cringed and the swing teetered.

"I don't know what to say," I yelled back.

I tried to show her my panic through my face, my eyes wide and my teeth clenched. Tears filled Johanna's eyes and the moons below seemed to grow. Her cheeks were crimson from the cold, the tears, everything.

Turning away, I pressed my palms to my eyes.

I have to be strong.

My mother told me not to cry, to be strong.

"Say something, please," Johanna mumbled.

But I was cold, my limbs weak, my mouth non-functional.

"Rin, please," she said.

The world was too big. Too far away and too close and nothing was safe. What was I supposed to do?

"Just say something, anything." The volume of her voice rose, it bounced around my head, clanging against my nerves. "I'm killing myself with my own thoughts here." A sob broke from her mouth.

"Stop yelling at me!" I jumped away from the swing.

Johanna choked on her tears and furiously wiped her face. She stood and faced me.

"Then let's get away from here," she said.

I drew my arms around myself. "What? Leave school?"

"Yeah." The desperation in her eyes stung. I looked away.

We stood there, still as stones, getting soaked in the rain like there was our own personal rain cloud above us. She cried, and I shivered.

"Will you come to the funeral?" she finally asked.

"Uh . . ." I pulled at a chunk of my wet hair. "I uh . . ."

"Come on. I don't want to be the only kid there." She sniffed.

"I probably shouldn't make Liam go to two funerals in a row. Might . . . I don't know, traumatize him or something."

"Leave him home." Johanna squeezed her eyes shut.

"I can't leave him alone."

Johanna grunted. "Then leave him with Oron." She kicked at the swing set. The metal frame quivered, the swings wobbled, their chains clinked together.

"He'll probably have to work." The words escaped before I knew it was another damn excuse.

"Shit, Rin." Johanna's eyes were wide despite swollen eyelids.

"Can you just calm down? I can't think when you get like this." I pressed my hands to my head trying to contain the buzzing, incoherent thoughts.

"When I get like this?" She stomped her foot. "This is me. I'm like this." Her hands shook at her side. She swiped her sleeve over her face. Wet hairs stuck to her cheeks and she swiped again. "Can you just come with me to my dad's fucking funeral?"

Thunder rumbled overhead. Around the playground was a chain-link fence. Raindrops slipped from wire to wire, making their way down to the muddy grass. The wires were grey, the grass was grey, the mud was grey. Suffocating.

Funeral.

Casket.

Dead.

Everyone's dead.

Pressure built in my chest, and I just turned away and started walking back to the school.

"You're walking away? Now?" Her shrill words pierced me like a thousand needles to my weak spot.

I kept walking.

"Come back," she said through broken sobs.

"No," I said, but she grabbed my arm.

"I need you there." Her hands twisted my sleeve. Rainwater seeped from the fabric to drip down my fingers.

My body pushed to the door; my soul pounded fists inside my body. Johanna dug her heels in to the ground as she dragged behind me. There was no escape. I was trapped, not knowing where I wanted to be instead. "You don't understand—"

"I do," she said, yanking me back.

"I can't. Let me go!" I turned around and shoved her hard with both hands. Shock struck her face. She hit the ground, wincing in pain. I had never used my strength against her; I told myself I never would. Cold gripped my neck, ragged breaths grated against my flesh. How could I have done that?

"Fine. Leave!" Her face twisted. Mud coated her hair. She grabbed a rock and chucked it at me. "Don't come to the funeral. See if I care."

The swollen ground squelched beneath my feet. A nasty stirring filled my empty stomach. It swirled around and sank low in my gut, sending waves aching through my middle. It was going to eat me alive. I didn't know if it was because I couldn't speak or because of her yelling, but it made me feel so far away from her. It grew through my legs, anchoring me.

"I'm sorry," was all I could say. *For everything.*

"Sorry? Sorry?" Her voice screeched, making an apology

seem like the most loathsome thing in the world. "I went to your dad's funeral." Slamming her hands into the ground, she pushed herself up with clumps of mud dripping from her clothes.

Casket.

I shuddered and my throat constricted. My parents' dead faces flashed before me. The rain pounded down on me even though it had subsided to a drizzle. My eyes stung, but was it the rain or water from inside me?

"I . . . I can't, I can't." The sickening paralysis in my bones strangled my voice.

Somewhere beyond the schoolyard, an LP siren wailed in eerie warbles.

"Well, if you *can't* then I don't need you. You know I only hung out with you because my dad told me to. He's gone so I don't have to. I'll just hang out with other friends."

A breath parted my lips. "Y-you don't have friends."

"Neither do you."

"Yeah, 'cause I'm Ironskin. You're just an ass." A bitter taste lingered on my tongue because it wasn't true. The last bit of energy I had slipped out, leaving me numb. I was the ass.

"At least I'm not heartless." She raised her arms and motioned to me. Her arms fell to her sides with a slap.

Maybe that's it. That's why my mom killed herself. She couldn't handle me, a heartless daughter. Liam didn't poke me in the chest the night of my father's funeral because my heart was hurting, he poked it because it wasn't there anymore. My chest hurt so much because there was nothing inside; my bones were caving into empty space.

"I hate you, Rin," Johanna screamed. Her words were knives. They pierced something—heart or no heart, something was bleeding inside.

I turned again and clapped my hands over my ears, holding my breath because it hurt less than breathing. I ran back to the school building and shut myself in a bathroom stall for the rest of the day, hands pressed over my ears, trying to lock out the sound of Johanna's voice from the prison of my mind. But her truth was too strong.

I hate you, Rin.

24

JOHANNA

Tʜᴇ ᴘᴜʀᴘᴏsᴇ ᴏꜰ ᴛʜᴇ ᴇxᴇʀᴄɪsᴇ is to use small movements to channel our essence into a steady flow that allows for a controlled state while trying new essence abilities. It's different from just letting my essence flow and blasting out a stream of fire. I twiddle my fingers, clench my fists, roll my wrists as Eliote watches me.

"Have you figured it out yet?" Eliote asks.

I glare at her. "It's not as easy as it looks."

"Yeah, well sitting here watching your aura steam isn't as easy as it looks either."

I suggested we work together so I could try reading her mind with Mind Fire and she can identify changes in my aura. We stand facing each other in the corner of the training room while the rest of the team tries out new abilities throughout the room and the instructors weave through them giving tips.

"Okay, I think I figured out a pattern."

"Show me. I will critique your essence flow." Eliote straightens up and flicks her purple hair behind her shoulders.

Rolling my eyes, I spread my fingers wide on both hands, press the tips together, and start tapping, letting the pads of my fingertips touch and spring apart.

One of Eliote's eyebrows arches and a half smile pulls her cheek into a dimple. My face fills with heat.

"That's it?" she asks.

The repetitive tap sends warm waves through my body, back and forth. I grit my teeth. "Yes, it is, do you have a problem with it?"

Eliote shakes her head, silver hoops waving back and forth from her ears. "No problem, your essence is very active. But you know it would be really good if you—"

"For Zenta's sake, just think about something and let me read your mind."

She claps her hands together and stands poker straight pressing her eyes shut.

I take a long breath through my nose. Essence flows through me with a gentle thrum that is new and relaxes my body. I focus on Eliote's forehead because I don't know where else I should look. Pushing all thought from my mind and blocking out sound from my ears I can almost hear my own essence rushing beyond the beat of my heart. I lock onto Eliote's voice by replaying phrases she's said to become familiar with her tone, her mind.

Your essence is very active.

She peeks with one eye. "Working yet?"

Working yet?

Sarcastic and sweet. A slight darkness but warm and airy.

My fingers tap.

IF SHE WOULD JUST STOP HIDING AND TEACH ME AS AN IRONSKIN, MAYBE I WOULD MAKE PROGRESS.

The thought streams through my mind, like icy breath fogging through my psyche. It's not the right thought. It's Rin's mind, her voice, with its annoying rasp and sucker punch cold, not Eliote's dark warmth. My eyes fly open but they deceive me. I gasp and a gale-force wind washes through my lungs. Everything is dark, I've lost Eliote. Niko, Jeff, Rin, Ace. No one is here. There's nothing. I spin in circles, drawing as much air in my lungs as possible but the air sloshes inside me, heavy. I stamp my feet below me. No sound reaches my ears. Endless darkness stretches beyond me in every direction.

What the fuck?

I did something incredibly wrong.

"Eliote?" All that is with me in this dark is her name from my lips. It lingers in my mind with a taunting bite.

In the distance, which could be anywhere from two paces ahead or two worlds, a light shimmers, pure silver. I shudder as it comes closer. The shudder is more of a wave in the ocean than a jerk of muscle—my body is gone, I am a blush-pink light. I am air and fire and energy.

The figure is before me. A woman.

She is still. The deep void of her eyes draws me in and my mouth fills with the taste of ash. She tilts her head to the side. Wind lifts her silver hair.

"*Caatslaka adasa de seya le retnolada hold eekala.*" Her ethereal hands motion around her with the ancient greeting. One by one, lights appear all around us. My heart beats through the light shining from my own airy form. Each light clarifies into the form of a woman, each clear and unique, tinted by every colour imaginable.

"You are in the Wander Lands." The silver woman's voice is as pure as if it was my own thought.

"Like—" the word cuts into the expanse. It is the fire of the nine hells, but it is gentle. It reminds me of my mother—a soft finger on my cheek and a burning command to the Protector at the funeral. It is my voice, and it thrills through me with unquenchable delight. "Like the spirit world?"

The wraith dips her head. "No, only a path beyond death."

I gasp. "Fuck, I'm dead?" My rosy, pink hands clasp my body.

"You are Soul Tethered," the wraith says.

Whispers erupt in every stretch of darkness around me. "You are Soul Tethered," they say.

Damn it. Not this again.

"What does that mean? How does that get me here?"

"The one you are tethered to has command over life and death. She is your bridge to the Wander Lands. With your Mind Fire you connect with all those who are unable to leave the Wander Lands. This allows you to see us while you are still connected to the Karess."

Rin. Rin must be this Soul Tether because she has command over life and death. My mind swarms with questions and an overwhelming urge to sleep even though energy courses through me.

"Why does Mind Fire connect me to Wander Wraiths? Why does it connect me to spirits?"

The wraith is silent as a silver smile paints her face. All around us, wraiths giggle and whisper to each other. As I listen to them, something clicks. I'm not listening. In the training room I focused on the things in my mind and actively pushed away sounds. I closed my eyes. Now, I don't feel anything. Their whispers are voiceless. They are in my mind.

"You're not spirits," I say.

"The mind creates powerful energy and does not accept death easily." A deep silence washes over my mind.

"Why?" is all I can say.

Laughter floats through the space between my mind and the mind of the silver wraith. "That is the question we all ask." She steps back. "You cannot stay here." She turns her back to me, hair waving in the wind of her own energy.

The lights of the other wraiths slip out of the void. I reach out to the silver wraith. "Wait how do I get out?"

"The same way you got here."

Her voice echoes through me. With a flash she vanishes. All around me is black, my mouth bitter with cinders.

There is nothing to touch, nothing to ground me. No air, no light, no sound. Only me. My energy shudders again, itching for touch.

Shit. How did I get here?

I take a useless breath and bring my fingers together. Pink tip to pink tip, I press them together. I tap. The flow begins, brightening my fingertips and streaming all around me. I keep tapping but nothing happens.

"Let me out," I yell.

I press my fingers together one last time. Calm floods my mind.

Ice.

A touch of cold licks my mind. A far-off whisper sounds inside me, echoing, through me.

I'LL NEVER GET ANYWHERE LIKE THIS.

I capture the voice as it pelts my mind.

Breath fills my lungs. My feet are on solid ground. Sweat pours down my face. Gravity compels my body and I fall to the ground. Eliote rushes over to me.

"Johanna." Her mouth hangs open. Her eyes are wide, shaking as they search all around me.

I plant my hands on the gritty training room floor, revelling in the dirt coating my hands.

"What happened?" Eliote's warm voice comes into the air as a whisper. It hits my ears before my mind, thank Zenta.

"Well," I say in the same dead voice I've heard from my throat all my life. "I didn't read your mind, that's for sure."

The room around me spins, making everyone wobble in my vision. I press a sweaty hand to my forehead. My skin burns. "Would you help me up?" I grunt at Eliote who still gapes at me, clutching her lightstone.

She starts. "Yeah, yeah, sorry." She grabs me by my hand and supports my back as I stand. I have to grip her fingers extra hard to keep them from slipping.

"What did you see in my essence?" I ask her.

Eliote's long eyelashes flutter, and the glitter on her eyelids glints, sending pain through my head.

"Nothing," she says.

"What do you mean?"

With a hard swallow, she says, "I mean nothing. Your essence stopped moving. Y-your aura stopped moving. Your body stopped moving." Her hands clutch her torso. "It was like you didn't need your body. You weren't here."

25

RIN

I STARE AT A BLANK SHEET OF PAPER, my pencil poised, Liam's letter open beside me. My knees bounce under the desk without my command. Liam is doing well, really well. He loves his classes, and he's been hanging out with Ace's little brother Anik. On the back of his letter is a drawing of a garden with every detail accounted for in the flower petals and leaves, moths among the plants, a bird in the centre, and an intricate metal fence surrounding the garden. At the bottom of the picture, he writes: *this is what comes to mind when I think of you.*

It's beautiful, but I don't know what to write back to him. The usual things like training is hard, learned a new technique, and still can't control the affinities are not what I want to write today. Living with Oron has done him so much good. Maybe all he needed was me out of the way.

That boy needs you, Oron once said to me. I'm not convinced.

I drop the pencil and push away from the desk.

"Wanna see if anyone's duelling in the arena?" I ask Eliote.

She's hunched over her notes at her desk. "You studied for less than an hour," she says without looking up.

"Yeah, I just need a little break."

Eliote shakes her head. "I'm in the zone, no distractions." Looking up at me, her eyelids are heavy, her cheeks are rosy without her makeup.

"You look like you could use a break," I say.

"I'm okay. Have some fun for me, Bird Brain." She smiles, just for a second.

"Will do." I head to the door. "Don't work too hard."

I get to the arena, and there're just two guys duelling. I recognize them as Lance's friends, Mycul and Aris. Looks like they're about to start a round so I take a seat in the bleachers and study their movements. Mycul attacks with a quick thrust of his fist, leading into a crisp pattern of punches and kicks—definitely Dawntimdato, no Emberstead would practice anything else. Aris dodges the strikes flowing with Mycul's attacks until he finds an opening. Aris sweeps his leg to Mycul's head. Instead of landing the blow, he stays poised with his foot by Mycul's ear.

They laugh, slapping each other's backs as they grab their water bottles. Mycul guzzles the whole bottle, Aris just takes a swig.

Voices from the other end of the bleachers draw my attention away from the duel. Lance comes from the side stairwell with a massive Fyrra man in a Protector uniform. My heart skips a beat with Lance's presence that has become so familiar. He's got on a hat with the rim turned backward, loose white tank top, jeans, and of course, a book stuck in his back pocket. The Protector shakes Lance's hand with a mighty grip and he sets his other hand on Lance's shoulder. A Medic badge catches my eye. Does Lance have a Monitor? Protectors only monitor people who have killed someone with an uncontrolled essence pulse.

My shoulders tense as the Protector leaves.

Lance leans over the railing to talk to Mycul and Aris. I can't hear what they're saying, but Lance throws back his head and laughs. A smile sets on my lips.

The guys get back to duelling below and Lance leans back in the stands to get lost in his book.

Maybe I should go sit with him. Or maybe I should leave. If that was a Monitor, then Lance might not want to be bothered right now. But what if he does want company? No, he could go down to Mycul and Aris if he did. I twiddle my fingers on my knees.

Lance reads, flipping pages, engrossed in the story. His face morphs with the words—his brows tighten and release, his lips part, smile, his eyes soften. It's as if I absorb the message of his book just by watching him—a story of infinite ups and downs. My eyes drift away from his face, over his wings splayed behind him, down his neck. They trace the smooth line of his toned arms. My stomach flutters and my face flushes. I stand up and make for the door. I'll just go for a walk.

Even though my mind is set on leaving, my feet turn back to Lance.

Walking over to him, I wipe my sweaty hands on my jeans. Lance looks up at me as I sit, leaving one chair in between us.

"Look at that, there *is* life around here," he says, putting his book down and resting his arm on the chair in between us. "I kind of hoped you'd be here." Colour warms his cheeks as he casts his eyes to the side.

Why's he got to be so cute like that?

"This place is dead. Where is everyone?" He looks back at the guys in the arena.

"Studying," I say, crinkling my nose.

"Think you're ready for midterms?"

"As I'll ever be."

"The weapons exam is kind of a killer, just so you know."

"What? You don't think I can handle it?" I press my lips to conceal a smile.

Lance dips his head. "I'm pretty sure you can handle just about anything."

I laugh a little and clutch the edge of the seat, so I don't float away with all the hot air filling my head.

"Mycul and Aris are pretty good," I say, turning back to the arena.

"Yeah. We've been duelling on Freedays since the middle of first year."

I draw a long breath. "Why aren't you down there with them today?" The breath holds in my lungs.

Lance adjusts his cap, clears his throat. "I just had something I had to do today."

I let the breath go. I wouldn't want to tell anyone about a Monitor either.

We watch them for a while. They're evenly matched. Both of them fast and precise. They play off each other, anticipating the other's movements for a counterattack.

"Hey," Lance says. "I have a question."

"Mhm?"

"Well, all the martial arts are named in Slyvic, right? I was wondering if you knew what they mean?"

I nod. With my finger, I draw out the symbols for Telando in the dust on the glass barrier.

"Telando is the style of the Ironskins. This symbol, *te*, means eight, and this one, *lando*, means limbs. It's called eight limbs because the style uses punches and elbows, kicks and knees. You have four limbs but eight ways to strike."

As I draw the symbol for Dawntimdato, Lance scoots into the seat next to me. His arm brushes mine, his skin warm on my skin. My head gets fuzzy, and my finger doesn't know how to make the symbols because my arm is busy deciding whether to move away or lean in.

"Uh, *dawn* means dead or deadly, and *timdato* means discipline. Deadly discipline," I say. I pull my arm into myself, so it's not touching him, but still close.

"Lavarians grow up learning Masstimdato. So that means . . . somethin' . . . discipline?"

"Military discipline, I think. I don't remember the symbols though."

Lance leans back, his arm now hooked on the back of my chair. "It's cool that you know that."

Cool? Most people make fun of me for knowing such an obscure language.

"Hey, Lance," Aris calls, "You guys wanna take us on?"

Lance turns to me, a gleam in his eye. "You want to?" he asks.

Before I answer, he's out of his seat. He hesitates, hand on his head. "We don't have to if you don't want to."

"Well, it's kind of what I came here to do."

"Good." He vaults over the railing, his wings spread wide, and glides down into the arena.

My heart jumps as the three guys look at me, waiting for me to join them. They beckon me down.

I jump over the rail and let myself fall to the ground. I land light on my feet and join the guys in the bright centre of the arena under the skylight.

"So, first team to have both fighters outside the red lines loses," Lance explains, and hands me a vest, helmet, and gloves from a closet along the wall. There's a mechanical aspect to each piece, embedded with a yellow crystal.

"What are these for?" I ask.

"They're so we can go all out," Mycul says, slipping his vest on. "The star crystals absorb the energy of essence strikes to protect us. I could burn Lance's arm, but the crystal would absorb the damage, no harm done."

I try on the vest and the gloves. It lies right over my weak spot.

"So I can strike without breaking bones?" I make a punching motion.

Mycul and Aris share a look.

"You can hit with all you got. No holding back." Lance throws his hat to the side and shakes his hair out. As I stare at Lance a little too long, Aris raises an eyebrow at me. A knowing smile crosses his face and there is kindness in his eyes. That doesn't stop my eyes from hiding from him. I inspect my gloves, making a fist.

"Let's do this," I say.

We line up two against two, but before we start, Mycul and Aris huddle up and Lance gives me a few pointers.

"We've got the element of surprise on our side, since these guys have never sparred with you before. I'll go after Aris since we both can take it to the air."

Tōmas was never shy about putting air manipulation abilities on display, and I know what Lifebloods are capable of so I wouldn't be caught off guard, but this is probably for the best. I can't really do anything if I'm swept up in the air.

"You go after Mycul. He plays dirty, but you can handle it." He winks and my legs turn to jelly. I might collapse here, let Mycul and Aris take the win. I peel my eyes away from Lance's deep-brown eyes, grasping for clarity. "Stay closer to the middle of the court. I'll stay closer to the lines in case you run into trouble. Sound good?"

I nod. We just have to knock them out of the circle and watch each other's back. Simple.

Mycul starts a count down. "Three."

Watching him closely as he takes his stance, I lock eyes with him, making it look like I am going to go right after him.

"Two." He squints his sharp, green eyes.

I crack my knuckles.

"One."

I shoot off to the side and circle around Mycul, keeping him close to the centre, while Lance, with a powerful stroke of his wings, moves back toward the outskirts. Mycul's back is still turned toward me, so I take a chance with a clean roundhouse kick. He's quick to dodge and comes at me with a fist combo. I bob right, left, back, evading his strikes.

With a sweeping crescent kick and stream of flames, his foot slaps me on the side of the head. The flash of flames and the bright pulse of the star crystal bleach my sight, and my eyes fill with spots.

Before he can get another hit on me, I back up to clear my eyes.

"Bad move, Rin," he says, charging toward me.

I'm right at the line.

Mycul jump-kicks. I thrust my arms out to block it. The kick doesn't move me an inch.

His brow furrows, frustration leaving an opening for me to strike. I swing my elbow at his head. My bone collides with the helmet. Streaks of white light stream into the star crystal. The crystal glows, pulses once, then dims.

I strike with my left fist. He deflects but can't block all my strength and back steps. I strike again and again, moving Mycul back through the centre of the ring toward the opposite end.

Aris notices me bullying his teammate closer to the lines and swings his arm, creating a whirlwind that surrounds all of us. I slam my palm into Mycul's chest. He flies back into the whirlwind. It catches him and flings him back into the centre.

Lance executes a spinning kick and sends Aris colliding into Mycul. Once they untangle themselves, Lance engages Aris again—arms swinging and bone snapping between blocks. Aris jumps in the air and uses a gust of wind to keep him hovering above us. Lance flies up to meet him, taking their fight to the air.

I land a punch to Mycul's shoulder. His eyes burn as a bright flash is absorbed into the crystal on his chest.

"What?" I say. "Not enjoying getting your ass kicked?"

"The crystal shouldn't be absorbing so much energy from physical strikes."

My brow furrows. The crystal in my vest hasn't flashed and the one in my helmet has been dark since he slapped me with flames.

Mycul smacks me hard in the face and gets a foot to my diaphragm. It knocks the wind out of me, and I gasp for air. The sensation sends nausea prickling through my stomach. I don't know why the star crystal didn't absorb it. The air just left, nothing would be damaged I guess, but I'm left dizzy. A fist hits me right between the eyes.

"You're Ironskin, aren't you?"

The wrath in Mycul's eyes sends chills streaming down my body. My lungs burn and he strikes me again like he's trying to knock the essence out of me.

With the lack of air to my brain, my body jolts me into motion and my grasp on reality fades away. My eyes flood with blue haze. For a second, everything is blurry. But my vision comes back better than ever.

I lunge forward and jam my knee into Mycul's chest. He stumbles back. I take one, two, three steps and jump. My keen vision lines up Mycul and Aris flawlessly. My foot plummets into Mycul's gut and both he and Aris are knocked into the whirlwind. They sail straight through the storm and slam into the wall.

The wind dies.

Bent over my knees, energy pulsates through me. My breath won't stay, each one is shorter than the last. My stomach aches, my head throbs. My eyes catch every detail of the dirty arena floor, the lights above flair around my field of vision. *Go away. Just go away.* I might as well be Eased.

Lance whoops with victory. "Nice work," he praises, holding out his hand. I slap it, only half aware of what I'm doing. I swallow a wave of nausea and press my eyes closed. The life affinity fades. Eyelids fluttering back open, my breaths are still rapid.

Aris and Mycul untangle themselves from each other, grunting and fussing. Aris doesn't even acknowledge us before storming off to the showers.

Mycul marches toward me, whips off his helmet, and chucks it aside.

"You're a freak," he yells.

"I think the term is Ironskin. Chill," Lance says, stepping in front of Mycul.

"You let us believe she was Beastblood, man. You let us walk into a fight without knowing she's demon spawn?"

"Ironskin. Iron. Skin. It's not that hard to say."

"Ironskin. Freak. It's all the same to me." He wipes sweat from his forehead. "This was supposed to be a friendly match and you made it a war zone." He points his finger at me, teeth bared. "Stay away from me and stay the hell away from Lance, you're no good for him," he snarls. His eyes burn through me.

Stepping around Lance, he reels back and spits at me. Saliva splats all over my face.

I cringe and my insides churn as the spit slides down the bridge of my nose. I will not give him the satisfaction of seeing me cower and wipe my face.

"You stupid cu—"

Lance grabs Mycul by the collar, whirls him around, and decks him in the mouth. The smack echoes through the arena.

"You're way out of line, man. Get out of here." Lance shoves him after Aris.

Mycul slinks away as a glob of saliva oozes down my cheek.

"I can't believe those guys." Lance clenches his fists and the veins in his wrists bulge. Releasing his grip, he reaches out to wipe the spit from my face, but I slap his hand away and do it myself.

"I can't believe you." I want to scream at him, but the words are soft.

I only catch his eyes for a moment—wide and wondering. He holds the hand I slapped to his chest. I tear my helmet off. Hair sprawls into my face and my bottom lip quivers. I bite it hard. Lance shuffles his feet, wings tense.

"He's right," I say. "You should stay away from me." My face burns but my mind goes cold. *It's better that way.* I turn to the exit. "You can't even tell your own friends I'm Ironskin."

"No, Rin, wait. Don't go." He grabs my shoulder with a gentle hand. "Let me explain."

"Explain what? You only defend me when I'm around?"

I shrug off his touch. *Let him talk, I should let him explain.*

Lance touches his forehead. "No. I—"

"Only when it's convenient for you, right?" Energy grips my heart. It runs through my veins, poisoning my words and shaking me at my core. "What happens when I'm not around? You call me those shit names too?"

A breath shudders out of him. He throws his hands up and clasps them behind his head, elbows drawing forward to hide his face. "I didn't mean it to happen like this. I meant to tell them." His voice cracks.

My eyes cloud with light. I slam my palms to my eyes. In the darkness behind my palms, the light fades. But with every breath, my chest tightens. The dark is cold and endless. Spiralling through the void, my hands go numb, spreading cold through my face.

"I'm sorry," Lance says in a hushed voice. His hand finds my shoulder again.

"Don't touch me." I step back with my arms shaking as I lower my hands. "What if Mycul hadn't been wearing the vest? I could have killed him." Any one of my life-affinity outbursts could have killed someone. Liam could be dead. "Stay away from me."

I'm just a heartless cutch.

"I have training with Brand and Hans, in essence control. Doesn't look like it's payin' off," I say and sprint to the doors, leaving behind what I thought was the sweetest, kindest boy I have ever known. But Liam's letter swims in my mind. That's the boy I'm here for. I can't get distracted anymore. I'm here to train.

26

LANCE

I HAVE TO RUN.

There's no debate about who I should run after.

I sprint across the arena. My head rushes with what to say as my hands slam into the door. Steam spills around me, assaulting me with the stench of socks and crotch. Aris sits on a bench, his vest propped beside him, and the helmet stacked on top. He leans over his knees. Mycul is pacing between the lockers, shirtless, a towel slung over his shoulder, venting about what just happened.

Mycul turns to me. "Finally come to your senses and drop the bitch?"

"Yeah," I say.

Mycul crosses his arms as a slick smile smothers his face.

I clench my fists. "You're the bitch."

Aris' head jerks up, his jaw drops.

"Come again?" Mycul's eyes are swamp green again. Sweat glistens off his red hair.

"You don't treat people right." It all rushes out in a breathless burst.

Fire burns deep inside the dark swamp of Mycul's eyes. "You were a pathetic loner before Aris and I took you in. You should be thankful to be in my crowd." The reply is so quick, like he's been wanting to call me pathetic right to my face for a long time.

"I was, I am." My lungs itch for breath. I shrug off his comment. I don't care. "And you want me to stay that way to make you look—"

"So, what are you going to do? Be more pathetic and go hang out with Ironskins instead of your friends?" He jabs his thumb at his chest.

"You're not my friend." I take a step toward him. "You know how I know that? Because you're angry by this instead of hurt. You're angry and talking over me instead of listening."

The temperature rises with every one of Mycul's breaths. A flicker of fire skitters from his fingertips up his arm.

"Come on, Aris, I know you see this too," I say.

Aris raises his hands in front of him. "Lance, please don't bring me into this."

My heart drops to the pit of my stomach. Aris' face is beet red. His hands fall to his lap and his eyes dart between me and Mycul. Maybe he's more scared than I am, or maybe he just doesn't see the problem. I want to tell Aris that he's just as bad as Mycul, sitting and saying nothing while he badmouths other lineages. But Mycul gangs up on Aris more than he does on me sometimes. Aris stood up for me the other day. I know his intentions are good, at least some of them.

"You trying to pit him against me too, Lancy boy?" Mycul shoves me in the shoulder. If I didn't still have my vest on, I'd have a welt on my skin in seconds.

"No," I say, taking a step back.

The hot, smelly room fills with the even more stifling sense of loss. I don't want to do it. I don't want to lose my friends because under all Mycul's shit, I needed his comradery. But maybe I need something else even more. Whatever is holding me to them is holding me back from making better decisions for myself.

"Just get out then." Mycul yanks the towel off his shoulder and turns his back to me.

Through the steam, Aris stares at me, his head lowered like a wounded animal. He leans over his legs again, dropping his head in his hands.

For a moment, my feet don't know what to do. They're used to following. They're used to standing still, doing nothing to fix a problem. They're used to stumbling after vices. My steps are slow as I move to the door. The steam clings to my clothes.

I open the door. The arena doesn't smell much better than the wet-sock smell of the shower room, but at least it's lighter. I take a deep breath and a few more steps. I move faster and rip my vest off. I'm running as fast as I can, just to run. Out of the arena, across the courtyard and I keep running to the cliffs above the shore.

My arms pump at my sides, my feet pound the earth, and I leap off the edge of the cliff. Wind beats my face in icy torrents as I plummet headfirst to the sand below. My wings stretch out and catch the air. My body jolts and the air swims over and under and all around me as I sail to the ground.

My feet hit the sand and my muscles give out. I fall to my knees. A sob crawls out of me from deep inside. It jerks me forward. I catch myself, planting my fists in the sand. Tears flow unhindered, hot and heavy down my face, saturating the sand in dark pools. My sobs shake me to my core like they're trying to rid my body of all the poison I've fed myself throughout the years.

I should have run sooner. I shouldn't have had to run toward them to run away. Way back when I started to get caught in the wrong crowd in basic ed, I should have run away from the people I was hanging around. If I had, then Khali would still be here.

Mycul saw me when I wasn't the loudest drunk in the room. That's why his friendship meant so much to me. I was quiet, self-conscious, inhibited. I just didn't know he wanted me to stay that way.

27

RIN

I BARGE THROUGH THE WEAPONS-TRAINING ROOM DOORS ten minutes late for training with Brand and Hans. Instead of finding two, blank-faced instructors, Adrianne replaces Brand.

Hans huffs, and it sizzles inside me. "Come, we mustn't waste time. We haven't made nearly as much progress with the life affinity as we should have by now."

"Where's Brand?" I ask.

My voice is still laced with a beaten desperation. I expected Brand. I expected her stone-cold mystery that was becoming a comfort. But she's not here and I want to scream. My throat is tight with the urge. Where is she? She's supposed to be here. Every Freeday. She's not here today. Will she be here next week? I swallow hard and squeeze my eyes shut for a moment. I open them and Adrianne's tan face smiles back at me, her emerald eyes glittering with sincerity.

"Miss Highcaller had an errand to run, so she asked Miss McCarthy to join us today."

I nod. *Just go with it.*

I take my fighting stance as I usually do for my warm-up. I focus on the punching bag with the star crystal. Setting my feet in my fighting stance, my fists up at my jaw, I blink.

Brand was supposed to be here.

Blue mists my eyes.

I blink, breath held in my chest, and blink again, fluttering my eyelids until the mist clears.

"All right," Hans begins. "Let's start with a three-strike combination, jab, cross, front kick. Three times through. First, just against the air to feel the movement of your body. Second, slowly, paying attention to every muscle engagement. With the third strike, use your awareness of your body to draw out energy to form wings, like you would a projection." He motions for me to commence.

I bounce on the balls of my feet.

"Breathe in," Hans says.

I inhale.

"And exhale with each strike."

I thrust the jab, letting air escape through pursed lips. My fist draws back with new breath, and I release it with the cross. In again, and I kick. Energy jolts through me, icing over my lungs with a greedy pull of air. My forehead tenses as I fight the energy back. I'm not supposed to release it yet. Shaking out my arms, I blink away the blanket of assertive light.

Adrianne crosses her arms as she watches. She tilts her head to the side. "Hans—"

"Draw strength from your core." Hans paces around me. "Slower."

I re-centre myself in my stance. With a deep breath, I flinch, expecting the blue ghost to infect my skin. It doesn't come, but my breaths quicken, colliding one after another and another. My stance breaks as I press shaky palms to my eyes, my shoulders draw in, and my feet pull together. At any second, I could squat down and curl into a ball. I fight the urge, shaking like a stick in the wind.

"For Carnity's sake—"

"Professor," Adrianne's voice cuts through Hans' reprimand before it burns into the dark spiral behind my hands.

I keep my palms pressed to my eyes for a beat of silence. As I lower them, Hans sighs and rubs the bridge of his nose.

"Hans," Adrianne says. "May I have a word with Rin alone, please?"

Hans clicks his tongue and adjusts his glasses. "Yes, of course."

Professor Griven's shiny black shoes tap a beat on the hardwood floor that cracks through my ears. I cross my arms, but with Adrianne looking right at me, my skin crawls. Tension seizes my muscles. I can't think, I can't breathe. My senses are running at max capacity, threatening to shut down. Another useless breath slices through my throat, this time like fire, and my vision blurs with black spots.

A sound comes out of my mouth, a mix of air and whimper.

Don't cry. Don't cry. Don't cry.

Adrianne's hands are on my shoulders. I've thrown beasts into trees, but her hands are heavier. I crumble under the weight. An icy tingle grips the back of my neck and strangles my body into paralysis, crouched on the ground.

"You're safe, Rin," Adrianne's sweet voice drifts around me. "You're safe, you're okay. It's just a panic attack."

My body tenses even more at the suggestion.

"I need you to just listen to my voice and take slow breaths. Nice and easy, don't force them in or hold them." Her hand rubs my arm, warm, heavy. "Panic attacks are nasty little motherfuckers, but they only seem scary. Show them a little kindness and they melt like butter."

Breath shudders in and out of me. Cinnospice from Adrianne's gum lingers in the air between us. I cling to it. My blood still rushes but smoother now.

"Did something happen today?" Adrianne asks, still crouched in front of me.

I shrug and press my fist to my mouth to hide the quiver in my lips. My body caves in on itself a little further. Heat rushes my cheeks. I can't believe I'm sitting on the ground shuddering like a baby Rover. I'm stronger than this. But my body won't move—it wants the gentle vise of Adrianne's hands holding me down even if everything in me screams to run.

"Rin, what happened?"

"Nothing. It's fine," I whisper.

I open and close my fists a few times, keeping my eyes away from Adrianne. Her hands rest on her knees as she waits for me in soothing quiet. Until it's not. The quiet fills me, her presence so apparent and unwavering, just like when she tested my essence. Her grasp was firm. But eventually she had to let go. Everyone lets go. Even if they don't have to, they do.

I push away from the ground with shaky legs.

"I . . . engaged the life affinity earlier," I say, crossing my arms.

"Did you mean to?"

"No." The word slips from my lips, a quiet, empty stab.

"All right, let's walk through it."

"Walk through it?"

"Yes. Why do you think you engaged the affinity?" Adrianne sets her hands on her hips, challenging my criss-cross arm shield.

The clock on the wall ticks a steady rhythm into the training room. I match my breaths with the clock just to keep them going. Glancing up at Adrianne, we share a second of eye contact. "I don't know," I say and look away.

"What were you feeling before it happened?"

"I was duelling with some guys, I don't know, I felt ready to fight."

"That's not what I mean. Just listen, okay?"

I pace in little circles. "Fine." I sigh and look up at the lights.

"Brand told me that the spirit affinities are linked to strong emotions. So, I want you to think back to the first time you engaged the life affinity. What were you feeling?"

"Wha—I . . ."

I uncross my arms, cross them again, touch my hand to my forehead. My skin is cold and sweaty. I shut my eyes and the firestone rifle is at my back, pressing into my weak spot. The beat of my heart fills my ears.

I was going to die.

The life affinity didn't give me a chance to accept that fate.

I shake the thought from my mind. Eyes open, I search the room, not for something, just to look. It's familiar now with the weapons case on the wall with that big Ironskin sword taunting me. The practice weapons are lined in neat rows. The wood floor is solid under my feet. Adrianne still stands with me, watching me, one hand wandering to scratch under her bra strap.

"You don't have to tell me," she says. Her tone is soft but deep, filling the space between words with warmth. I drop my eyes to my feet. "Just think about what emotions come up before you engage the affinity. For some, the life affinity is triggered by feelings of peace or even sadness. Others describe loneliness, fear."

Without my consent, my head jerks up to her eyes. I cringe and my shoulders pull in.

"The death affinity can be triggered by love or hate, anger. Think about how these emotions feel for you. Do you get a headache, feel sick, chills up your spine, an overwhelming heaviness? You can use the emotional energy to direct the affinities."

That doesn't make any sense. It seems like my emotions steal my ability to control the affinities. The emotion is overwhelming, the life-affinity energy is overwhelming, and I can't control either of them. I thought I would have died the first time, Liam too. I engaged the affinity but ended up hurting Liam. I wanted to protect Johanna but messed up our formation at the beginning of the year. Today, the look in Mycul's eyes shook me, the affinity came out, and everything went wrong.

Adrianne steps away, clearing a path to the door. "You're free to go." She nods to me. "Or we can work on a few things together."

The clock slows, the seconds double. The gap between heartbeats lengthens and my sight narrows on a spot on the wall behind Adrianne's head. Everything was fine before Registration—back when all I had to worry about was Liam. I had control then and he was safe. I did just fine on my own.

Adrianne brings a hand to my shoulder, no longer heavy but light, nonexistent.

"I'm doing just fine on my own." I push past her and leave the room before everything inside me unravels and I can't take it back. If I want to avoid another instance of panic like that, then I'll have to stay away.

The next day, on the journey between classes, my eyes dissect the floor of the academic corridor. Small, square, white tiles checker the floor. Scuffs mar the snowy whiteness. After every few tiles, there's a series of red and blue ones that create a diamond shape. The pattern is simple, but far more fulfilling than lifting my head to the people around me. The floor is a better view than the one in the Senn public-school halls. The buzz around me is the same now. After I left Mycul, Lance, and Aris, my name and my lineage started to spread. They all know who I am now. Even though some students guessed it right off the bat, for the most part, anonymity did me well.

But it's fine. I'll just keep my head down, stick to myself, and focus on my training. It's normal.

I want you to think back to the first time you engaged the affinity. What were you feeling?

The question hangs at the back of my mind.

I was going to die.

The buzz of voices quiets a bit. A shadow spills over my view of tiles and then a pair of feet slips into my space, and then another. An abrasive perfume assaults my nose in a heady whiff. I look up. Jaya and Roth block my way to the calculations classroom.

"Hey, Rin," Roth says.

What could they possibly want?

"Hi," I say. My face is stone and my tone a short jab.

"Didn't expect to see you here." A smile flashes his white teeth, too white, chemically whitened, I bet. His eyes widen with mock innocence. Jaya chuckles at his side.

"Why wouldn't I be here?" My eyes squint. It takes everything in me not to recoil at Jaya's high-pitched laugh that lets out some sort of unidentifiable toxin into the air.

"Just thought you would have up and left like the rest of the Ironskins," Roth says, looking down at his nails with a straight face.

My hand reaches to touch my forehead, a deep sigh escaping me. "What the hell are you talking about?"

"You haven't heard?" Roth's nails click. My stomach roils as a tiny speck of gunk flies across the hall.

"Oh my gosh, she doesn't even know." Jaya nudges Roth in the ribs with her bony elbow.

"Know what?" I drop my hand. Jaya's cruel smile growing as I fidget.

"Ironskins all over Illyson have been dropping out of Guardian duty, Guardian training, regular dead-end jobs. They're disappearing."

He's got to be making this up. Or he's just stupid. We started disappearing a long time ago, the ass. But is that why Brand wasn't here yesterday, did she just leave? It can't be true. I step to the right, but Roth steps with me, crossing his arms over his bulky frame.

"You should too." He leans forward, getting in my face so

his breath spills over me as he says, "Disappear."

I can't disappear. Liam needs me to be strong. He needs me to be here.

His breath is nasty, his eyes violate my skin with a poisonous gaze. He plants a weed in my mind that I've had to pluck over and over again. But it keeps coming back.

"There you are, Rin. Come quiz me on Guardian Basics before calculations." Eliote grabs me by the arm and gives me a tug away from Roth and Jaya. Her starry scent fights for attention in my nose, but Jaya's is stronger.

Feet planted, my eyes meet Roth's. "I'm not leaving," I say to him.

Eliote fastens her other hand around my arm. "Rin, your aura—"

"Forget my aura." I yank my arm away from her.

"Aw, is the demon spawn getting a little testy?" Jaya says, her nose scrunching and eyes murderous.

"Yeah, maybe she is," I say, giving Jaya a shove.

"Rin, just leave it alone."

"No. They've got to get used to my face around here. Move, Roth."

"Make me," he says.

I step forward, ready to grab him by the shoulders and lift him out of the way like I used to do when Liam was being stubborn. But Eliote steps in front of me. Her eyes are wide as they dart all around me, searching through my aura. "Your aura is going crazy," she says. "This will only end badly. It's not worth it."

My body freezes. The urgency in Eliote's gaze cuts into me, squeezing tension into my chest. Her lips are parted, her eyelashes flutter, and a smudge of mascara is just noticeable under her left eye. They think they're better than me, just like Stephen said. They think they own me. And part of me believes it. Does Eliote believe it? Does she refuse to let me defend myself because she thinks they're right? She tells me to stop, not them. She faces me, blocks me, not them. It's my aura that's the problem, not theirs.

Mycul's saliva was like a corrosive chemical that left a brand on my skin. I will never be able to wipe away the sensation of it oozing down my face. It's there right now, licking my cheek.

I grit my teeth as my eyes prickle. Maybe Stephen is right. Things aren't changing. But is the Revival the way to change them? Put lives in jeopardy? No, if Eliote blocks me, then she must have a reason. It's my aura that's the problem. The life and death affinities put everyone at risk.

Jaya sneers at me. "Yeah, little Ironskin. Listen to the iron-lover. Take your crazy and get out of here."

Eliote's face floods with pink. It complements her hair, creating a softness to her even in embarrassment, while I stand here sweating, my insides turning to ice. My vision darkens as an invisible barrier slides between us. I don't try to make it go away. I can't jump and shake my arms or blink to clear my eyes. I back away from Eliote.

"Rin," she says, but my back is turned.

I walk away, down the hall, eyes fixed on the floor. The colours aren't bright. The scuff marks are darker. The red squares are deep maroon, and the blue are the depths of the sea. There must be shades drawn over the hall windows or the lights went out. The middle of the day should not be this dark. Voices around me should not be as dim as memories.

"Rin."

All voices but that one. It draws my eyes up to Lance's handsome face. My vision clears a little, letting in the light of his smile. It's not his usual smile though. He's not trying to tell me something with it; he's going to say it. I don't want to hear it. My heart stirs, sending a rush of blood through me that makes my stomach fold over.

I turn but Roth and Jaya are still at the other end. I turn back and Lance's eyes plead with me. I brush my face.

"C-can I talk to you?" Lance asks.

His voice is the first and the last thing I want to hear right now. My head dips to the ground for safety but I can't get myself to move. If he wants to talk, he can do the talking.

"I'm sorry," he says.

Breath releases from my lungs. It slips through my lips, soundless, and my shoulders drop.

"What happened yesterday was wrong and it was my fault."

I sneak a peek at him through the curtain of my hair, my pulse pounds in my throat. His eyebrows scrunch together, and his mouth turns down in a frown. The black of his wings catches some source of light in this dead hall and reflects a shimmer of blue into my eyes. Lance pushes a slow breath of air through his tight lips as his hands grab the folds of his pants.

"I should have told them about you at the very beginning. I want you to know that I'm not going to be hanging out with them anymore."

"You don't have to do that," I say before I can stop myself.

"Actually, I do."

I don't want to cause him any more trouble, I don't want to cause any more rifts in his friendships by associating with him.

He reaches out to push the hair out of my eyes.

Don't touch me.

I jerk away from the touch and run the other way. Finally, there's an open door to the calculations classroom and I dash inside and grab a seat with Ace and Eliote before anyone gets in my way.

Ace is hunched over his calculations notes, elbows tucked into his belly, reviewing for our midterm tomorrow. His glasses have slid down his nose and every few seconds he takes a bite of a cookie. Eliote glances at me as I sit but busies herself by unravelling echo-buds and sticks them in her ears. Her eyes fall closed.

I clutch the desk with numb hands.

With a sniff Ace looks up. He leans back and stretches his arms over his head. A smile lightens his face, and he reaches into his pocket, brings out another cookie, and hands it to me. "Everything okay?" he asks.

I nod. "Yeah," I say, breathy and unconvincing, and throw on a quick smile. I bite into the cookie as the professor starts the review.

I attend to the review as best I can, copying down practice questions, trying to keep the information straight in my head. At the end of the class the professor puts two questions on the board. He calls Roth to solve one. "Rin would you like to come solve the other?"

I take my time getting to the board sorting through everything we've just reviewed. The professor hands me a piece of chalk and instructs the other students to quietly review on their own. Papers rustle as they begin. Whispers tickle the back of my neck. The hushed voices grate on my nerves.

I think I know the first step to solve the problem, so I start marking out my work. I don't know the next step though. Roth has already finished and throws his piece of chalk down on the rail in front of me, just to rub it in my face.

What an annoying little ass.

I glance at Roth's problem, but his work is a mess, so I have no idea how he got his answer.

"Rin, do you need some help?" the professor asks.

The whispers get louder and force my shoulder muscles into tight knots.

"Roth, why don't you give Rin a hand and show her what you did?"

Chalk coats my fingers with a thin film that tickles my skin. My nails catch on the white stick as Roth comes back to the board. Shivers run down my spine.

"I'm not going easy on you, Rin." Roth sneers like he did that first day of training. He points to the problem and pretends to tell me how to do it.

"I wouldn't dream of it. Get out of here." I shove him away.

I think hard and solve the problem as best I can just as the bell rings. The professor circles my errors. The other students file out of the classroom, but I stay staring at my mistakes. Someone stops behind me. A calm presence, with kind eyes that don't set my senses aflame.

"I can help you with this stuff tonight if you want," Ace says once the room is quiet.

"I just need to study it a bit more." I turn away from the board and head back to my seat to grab my things.

"I don't mind helping you."

"I'll get it, just need to apply myself more. Don't worry about it." I try to pass him, but he stands in the way of the door.

Has everyone forgotten that I can throw their asses through walls? Or do they only think me a mischievous demon, a ghost without solid hands?

"Why do you do this to me?" He crosses his arms and stares me down.

"Do what?

"Why won't you ever let me help you?"

"It's nothing, just forget about it."

Ace stares at me with his familiar, blue eyes, his messy, blue hair stands on end, but space expands between us. If I reached out to him, I wouldn't touch him.

"Rin, come on, why do you freeze me out?"

"I don't know. Move."

"I'm not moving until you tell me."

"I don't want to tell you."

"Rin, I need to know."

"Fine. It's because . . ." My brow furrows as I struggle for words. "Because one day . . . you'll be gone, and I'll be alone again. If I always get your help, what am I going to do when you're not here?" Something inside me pinches. It insists I reach out and touch him, even if my fingers only catch air. "And I do really stupid things when you're not around," I say under my breath.

Aces eyes soften and his arms fall to his sides. "No, Rin, that's not going to happen," he says. "I care about you. I'm not going to leave you."

His words hit my eardrums like a foreign language. My heart starts to pound. I need to move with all this blood coursing through me. I shuffle my feet.

"Why? I've never done anything for you." I look to the side

to hide my face from him. "All I do is cause trouble for people. When I'm around, people get hurt and . . . and they hurt me."

The hallway buzzes behind Ace but he is still. His face flushes red. Running a hand over his face he drops his eyes from me. "It's not about what you do for me," he whispers.

I draw my arms around myself.

"You are extremely impulsive and once you make a decision you commit to it, and I've always liked that about you. But . . ." he shakes his head. "That night—"

"Don't," I say.

"I have to. I have to let it out." With a heavy breath, his eyes fall shut and his posture stiffens. "Your friendship is irreplaceable to me. But I had to watch you commit to leaving. You stopped saying goodbye to me after school. I watched you stop eating, watched you lose so much weight. And then when I carried you to the hospital that night you kept saying 'just leave me' and I couldn't. I watched too much, and I couldn't let you leave."

I can't bring myself to find Ace's eyes but tears stream down his face. He presses a sleeve to his cheek to wipe them, leaving it there as he draws a long breath. My voice is too far in the deep pit inside me to find it and use it. I have no words to describe everything I feel for Ace.

"I had to scream at a nurse just to get her to put an antidote mask on you," he says into his sleeve.

Blood pumps in furious waves through my body, sinking the words further inside me and stuffing a lump into my throat. My hand shakes as I draw it away from myself and clamp it around Ace's arm. Warmth swells from his skin to mine. His muscles are firm in my grasp. From the depths of my mind, I draw the memory of his arms around me that night. Through the haze, the pressure of his arms sunk into my empty shell. Rain streaked my face, Ace's cheek pressed to my forehead. And the melody of the song from the party flows into the present, threatening to bring forth everything from that night crashing back to reality. What were the words to the song? *If only you knew you already had me by the heart strings.*

To speak would never honour the words Ace has given me. I am desperate to hold him. But darkness covers my desperation. I am repulsed by what I have done. The beauty of what he sees in me, why he values me, I can't find it. My grasp on his arm loosens. My hand falls to my side.

Just let me go.

I don't want to think it, but it's the permanent weed in my mind.

Even in sleep, I can't escape.

My feet hover above the ground, over a field of herbs, dried and trampled—cinnospice, scolya, and whisper weed. I move forward through the endless field of grey sprigs, surrounded by suffocating silence. Crouching down, feet still planted on an invisible plane above solid earth, I reach for the herbs. My fingers wrap around a stick of cinnospice; it shatters into dust. Crackling and snapping, every spice, weed, and herb crumbles to piles of dust. Stirred up by a vacant wind, the dust swarms around me—whispering through my toes, sifting through my hair—until it solidifies into a door in front of me.

The door swings open. A creek of the hinges pierces the silence and a sliver of light leaks through. White light slithers from the crack between the door and the line of nothing that separates it from the wasteland around me. Light slips around my feet, sending warmth tingling up my legs. I wiggle my toes in the fresh sensation, a reprieve from the ominous void my body hovers in.

From the light steps a cat. It prowls around in the warmth, licking its paws and stretching its back. It looks up at me. It moves toward me. I step back, but it only comes at me faster. It leaps at me, and I sprint away as fast as I can. My foot slams into a rock that materializes from the excess dust of the shattered herbs. I fall but never hit ground—it rises and smacks its gritty surface to my face. Wind stirs around me, and I raise my head to the swallowing grey sky. A house plummets to the ground and collides with the earth, sending a bone-rattling tremble through me. The house sucks up the plumes of dust.

My mother opens the door. Her hair covers one side of her face and a mask of the first Ironskin, Keena, covers the other. She wears a long, full-skirted, red dress with flowing sleeves and a golden collar. Atop her head is a crown of cinnospice. She motions for me to come in with a hand adorned by gold rings. I scramble to my feet and tremble into the house—my old house, home. The door slams behind me.

My mother hovers through the kitchen, her bare feet dangle below her dress, gold bands encircle her ankles. I sit on the floor and reach my hand to her. She looks down at me. Pushing aside her hair, she exhales, and a tear falls down her face to my fingers. It slides down my arm.

"We will never all be together again," she whispers.

Her dress billows in a wind I can't feel. Dust sheds from the walls, the counters, the brick of the fireplace, and accumulates under her feet. Eyes appear on the walls—grey eyes, everywhere, everything turns to eyes. They blink in unison and my heart pounds. I stand as the floor below me blinks. My foot slips under an eyelid. I yank it free and stand on the dark pupil.

My mother's mask falls. Her face appears, blotchy red from tears. Her body dissipates into a sweet smoke that tingles my skin. I grasp at the smoke. It tangles around my fingers and swarms into my lungs, stealing my air. I clutch my throat.

There's a pounding at the door. Dark shapes outside, screaming and yelling. The window shatters. The eyes blink. The room floods with nauseating blue light. The eyes blink again, and the room falls into total darkness. They open, blinding me with blue light.

"I'll come back before the Festival of Two Moons," they scream without voices.

I scream back at them, but no sound escapes my smoky throat.

A firestone rifle blasts through the commotion and everything goes silent.

The eyes fill with blood. It pools around my ankles, hot, sticky.

The house collapses under the weight of the sky hitting the earth.

Bolting upright, I gasp for air. My body is slick with sweat and my hair clings to my forehead. The blankets twist around my legs. I thrash under their unbearable weight, my body trembling.

Eliote stands above me, the whites of her eyes pierce through the dark. "Hey, it's okay," she says, surrounded by shadows. "It was just a dream." She puts her hand on my shoulder, but the gentle touch is heavy like a brick. I draw my knees to my chest.

Eliote lifts her hand away from me and turns on the light. It washes over the shadowy room, revealing the familiarity. I focus my eyes on Eliote's empty bed, sheets thrown on the floor.

Eliote rubs her arms and hugs herself as she sits down at the edge of my bed. The vessels in her neck pulse. She takes a long breath; it comes out shaky. Did she experience the dream with me?

"You want to talk about it?" she asks.

The eyes blink at me from behind my eyelids. I shake my head as I run my hands down my legs, paying attention to every bump of my skin, every dry patch, every hair, keeping myself grounded to this moment, trying to, at least.

Eliote locks eyes with me. "Are you sure?"

I nod, rubbing my dry eyes.

Pressing her lips together, she tries to straighten my covers. Her hair swishes in stringy strands as she nods and takes a long shuddering breath, prompting me to take one of my own.

Eliote gets up.

My heart drops, pulling the air from my lungs. An icy draft prickles my sweaty skin as she turns her back to me. "Wait," I whisper. "Not yet."

Her feet shift on the carpet. The prickle subsides with her warm-brown eyes facing me again. Eliote gets back on my bed and sits cross-legged across from me. She leans her chin on her hand, I lean mine on my knees.

"What an awful dream," Eliote whispers.

Wind howls, shifting the trees outside our window so they tap against the glass. Moonlight slips through the branches, creating spindly patterns across our floor.

I'm doing just fine on my own.
Liar.

28

ELIOTE

WE ARE SILENT, all except our feet marching through the arena. The med-kit weighs on my back, just as always. I grasp Niko's arms with a steady grip, eyes fixed on the ground a few paces ahead—it's the safest place for me to look. There are no auras in sight, my eyes are clear, my heart rate steady, and Marcus' weight barely registers. Now that we've done it so many times, the exercise is easy, but the next leg of the journey is what I dread.

A few more paces and we'll drop Marcus and go it alone. I draw even breaths. I'm at the front of the group now, but my lane for the next drill is the farthest one along the wall. Three paces. I lock my eyes on my timer. Two paces. I steel my nerves, swallowing hard, and I draw as much breath as I can. One pace. My teammates' energy sparks behind me, but it is not my concern; I have to stay ahead of them, I cannot look behind. If I see their energy, it will just weigh me down. We pass through the training room door. We lower Marcus to the floor.

Fire rips through my thighs, up my torso, and into my arms. I burst into a sprint. Jeff's feet thunder behind me. I push forward, head dipped, arms pumping in mad jolts. My hand slams the timer and I wheel around the stand, urging forward without pausing. *Don't look around.*

My feet move faster and faster, strides long, fluid. I skid to a stop at the end of the training room. I leap, catch the rope hanging from the ceiling, wrapping it around my feet. Hand over hand, my biceps burn, my breaths already searing my lungs. I cling to the rope. My hand wraps are soaked in sweat. The med–kit is a vile weight throwing my balance. I grit my teeth, engaging my whole body to throw myself up the rope.

"That's right, Eliote, use those arms. Better wear a sleeveless dress to formal tomorrow to show 'em off," Adrianne says as she paces below us.

"I thought we were busting our butts to kick ass in battle, not a dress," Johanna grunts.

Adrianne chuckles. "Doesn't hurt to do both."

At the top, I hit the timer, expelling a breath just to go back down hand over burning hand. I drop to the ground, and the kit slams hard on my back.

One teammate is already sprinting back to the other end. I push my legs back into motion. I have to get in front of them. Their aura paints the corner of my vision with bleeding red and blue. Rin. My stomach turns. I push my legs harder, head low, every muscle screams. I keep moving and Rin's aura slips out of sight. I need to get as far as possible in front of her for the next leg of the exercise because she'll beat me no problem.

Muscles on the verge of cramping, I slam my hand on the time tracker. Along the wall are six dummies. I squat low next to the closest one, Rin's light footsteps getting louder. I sling the dummies arm over my shoulder. Balancing the sandbag body on my shoulders, ignoring the weight of my pack, I press away from the floor, thighs trembling and sweat trickling down my face.

"Keep it up, everyone, remember if one of you beats the record today, you'll be allowed to go to the Two Moons Festival," Adrianne yells from the sidelines. "If no one does, then you'll be running the drill next Freeday instead of eating fried keeta at the festival."

I just want to beat my time, but if I don't stay in front, that won't happen.

There's a thud and a shift and Rin's shadow crosses my path. I haven't even straightened my legs yet. I am stuck under the weight of the dummy.

"Come on Eliote, you got this," Ace says, through ragged breaths.

He passes me. Johanna passes me. Jeff and Niko pass me. Their auras run over me, taunting me with vitality.

My eyes ache to cry. Teeth clenched together, I anchor my eyes closed, and lurch forward. One long step. I can do the next challenge no problem. I just have to get through this one. Another step, and my ankle groans under my body, the med-kit, and the dummy. It's just me and my muscle, no other energy courses through me. Momentum is my friend. The dummy tips forward and I move with it. Finally outside, I drop the dummy, but a slit in my nail catches on the canvas. As the dummy falls it rips my nail off. Hot blood pulses through my finger.

I snatch three throwing knives as auras swirl around me and icy air stabs my lungs. I train my eyes on the target. The cool steel of the knives is like coming home. They are the perfect weight. They slip between my fingers. My teammates take multiple tries to hit the targets with all the knives. I heave a breath and fling all three knives. They slice through the air and hit the target with a series of satisfying thunks.

"Nice work, Eliote," Brand says. "Back inside."

My body is like stiff metal chains grinding together, but Brand's praise greases my joints. I bolt back inside for the final leg of the exercise—hand-to-hand combat with whichever instructor calls my name once I enter.

Sweat stings my eyes and the fluorescent lights flair above me.

"Eliote."

Marcus is at the far end of the training room. I sprint toward him. His aura is burgundy shards all around the lines of his muscles. Charging straight for him, I draw my fist back to strike. He evades and his aura flashes up his leg. I block his kick and strike with quick jabs. All I need is one hit to his body. *One hit before the others come in.* My arms are trembling, lead mallets, but Marcus' strikes are hammers of fire.

Footsteps pound the ground behind me.

"Rin," Adrianne says.

The snap of skin and bone cracks through my ears.

"Jeff."

"Johanna."

Breath is nonexistent. I throw my fist, but Marcus spins me into a headlock, and I have the whole training room in front of me. Marcus' arm cinches around my neck. Sweat pools between our skin. I claw at his arm.

"You know how to get out," Marcus says.

My eyes sting. My heart thrums. The room is filled with light, yet my eyes cloud.

Johanna's blush-pink aura bursts with a hit to Brand's side. "Johanna, time."

"I—" I say between gasps. "I can't."

"You can," Marcus says, his grip even tighter.

Adrianne pushes Rin's fight closer to us. With a flash of light and a pulse of energy, Adrianne transforms into her Beastblood form—a majestic, armoured tiger. As the light from her transformation fades, a new light emits from Adrianne's core. Streams of soft yellow string together in a lacey web, flowing from a dark centre of raging orange embers that fill me with pain. My head buzzes and I blink my eyes, stunned by the first sight of Adrianne's aura.

Adrianne leaps forward. Rin screeches a blood-curdling cry and falls to the ground. She cowers under Adrianne's new form.

"Everyone, stop," Brand calls.

But Marcus doesn't let go. My knees give way and my body slips to the floor. Marcus yanks me back up. "If you want to help Rin, you have to get out."

In a split-second, Rin's aura darkens and slows. The swirling tornado of her soul melts to a stagnant grey pool.

A grunt rips out my mouth. I step one lead riddled leg behind Marcus just as Adrianne showed us. I wrench my arm behind his back, my hand wraps chafing my skin. My hand finds Marcus' face. I yank him back, step forward, and slam my fist down on his chest.

Marcus lets me go and I fall to the ground in a heap, sweat pouring off me, blood staining my hand wraps. "D-did I beat my time," I ask, the taste of metal at the back of my throat.

Kneeling beside me, Marcus sets a hand on my shoulder. "No." He pulls me to my feet. "But you got out. Get some water."

My soul is a slug inside me as I wobble over to the others. *I failed.*

"The idiot's afraid of cats, Adrianne," Johanna says as I approach.

"Shit. Sorry, Rin. I didn't mean to." Back in her hédin form, Adrianne barely looks at Rin. Her face is white and she trembles, raising her hands to cover her mouth. "I didn't mean to," she mutters to herself. Dropping her head, she rushes out the side entrance.

Jeff offers Rin a hand. "You okay?" he asks, trying not to laugh at her.

Face red and teeth gritted, she gets up by herself. "I'm not afraid of cats." She swipes dirt off her face with the back of her hand.

"Johanna broke the record time, so we'll call it," Brand says. She picks up her PAT and stops recording our timers. "Take five."

I pass by Rin to grab my water bottle from the benches— straight through the cold, grey pool surrounding her. It wraps around me, slow and tar-like. My skin prickles even though the blood inside me boils.

Clenching my water bottle, I collapse onto the bench along the wall. I drain what's left in the bottle in two gulps. Rin joins me and takes a drink from her own bottle. Her hands shake, spilling a little water down her chin. Her eyelids droop with the almost unnoticeable flex of a smile.

"Take a seat, Bird Brain." I pull a smile onto my face and pat the bench with my bloody, sweaty hand.

As she sits, I say in a soft voice, "There was a cat in your dream last night. It means something to you."

"I'm not afraid—"

"I know."

Rin leans her head back against the concrete wall. Her face returns to its natural pale white. "It was just a dream." She cracks her knuckles with her thumb on one hand and clenches the water bottle with the other. "Adrianne just startled me, that's all. Just a coincidence."

"I don't think so, Rin. I think it means something to you and you need to let it out."

"Eliote, it's nothing."

"But—"

"Just leave it!"

My cheeks flood with heat. I completely failed the exercise. I let everyone's aura overcome me. Their auras mean something. Rin's aura is saying something, but she doesn't want to listen to what I have to say. *Just give me this one thing.*

"Rin," I whisper. "Please—"

"Everyone, outside for essence training," Marcus says.

Rin gets up and her aura retracts back into its whirlwind protection, regaining some of its colour, first the life-affinity blue, then a faint glow of death-affinity red. She follows the others outside, giving me a moment's reprieve from her chill.

I couldn't get out of the headlock fast enough to help her, and I can't even use my natural sight to help her. It's as if my soul is insignificant in this world of bursting colour and renewable energy supplied by essence. My soul is trodden by all the others. It is a thousand years old and no longer knows how to communicate with the rest. My sight is useless.

I push away from the bench. My bones rattle like the bones of an old woman.

29

RIN

My blood rushes in my veins and my brain decides to stir up images of my mother—her two-toned face in the firelight the last time I saw her. A pain stabs me in the gut. Why does Adrianne's transformation have me so shaken? It's not like I didn't know Adrianne's Beastblood form was a tiger. I hope to Carnity that Eliote can't see me shaking.

"Outside, guys," Marcus commands.

I force my feet to follow Marcus, and the rest of my exhausted team lags behind me.

"Come on. Pick up the pace. Move it," he says, ushering us into a sprint.

Outside, the air nips at my panic-induced sweaty skin. Leaves cover the ground behind the arena and make a pleasant crunch under my feet. Moon Hill is covered in orange and low clouds swim around its peak. My breath fogs the air.

I hope it snows soon. In Senn, the lights weren't so abrasive when it snowed. The snow covered some of the smell and quieted the commotion. A calm change would be good right about now.

A series of stone pillars stick up from the ground, constructed by Jeff-Ray before class. The tops of the pillars are flat and about a foot wide. There are six tall ones, at least seven feet tall, and then smaller ones of different heights surrounding them.

Marcus picks up a ball from the ground then hops onto one of the shorter pillars.

"This"—he tosses the ball high into the air—"is an exercise in control." He catches the ball. "Mental control over your body and your essence."

Beside me, Niko groans and throws his head back. "I have no control over my body, every muscle is twitching like it wants to party, but I *do not* want to party."

"That's the point," Brand says from behind him. She slaps a hand on his shoulder, and he winces. "You all can do anything you put your mind to, even when your body feels achy and tired."

From the other side of Brand, Adrianne huffs with her hands braced on her hips and her eyes glued to the ground. Her transformation was unexpected. In an instant, her eyes changed from focused to hungry. With a shake of her head, she fought the desperation from her eyes, but it took hold. Her beast form had taken over. I know what that's like.

Marcus jumps to a higher pillar. He performs a combination of kicks and fist strikes, all the while balancing on one leg and juggling the ball. His movements are controlled. His eyes are focused, his breaths long—in through his nose, out through his mouth.

"Fire is destructive," Marcus says when he's finished his sequence. "But when controlled, it can be useful."

In an instant he has encased the ball in fire armour, so it hovers just above his hand. He hurls the ball toward us. The second it leaves his hand, the glow of fire fades. Adrianne thrusts out her palm. The fire reappears around the ball an inch away from her hand. The ball hovers again, encased in ember plates. Adrianne is still, as if she's holding her breath, all except for the desperate shake in her eyes.

"When we are tired, our control over our essence is weakened. That's why we need to train our bodies and mind to stay in control. On the battlefield, we don't get breaks. Now, everyone up on the tall pillars." Marcus jumps back to the ground, and we drag ourselves over to the pillars.

Ace, Jeff, Niko, and Johanna use their essence in some way to get themselves up. Eliote stares at her stone pole. Taking a moment to flex her fingers, she squats low with a grimace and jumps. She grasps the top of the pole, and her body quivers as she tries to pull herself up. She holds onto the pole for a few seconds but slides back to the ground.

"Need a boost?" I ask, lacing my fingers together to give her a foothold.

For a moment, her eyes narrow and flash with the reflection of sunlight. I know she doesn't like to seem weaker than the rest. Part of me doesn't want to help her. I am small under her gaze, an inconvenience, like I was in the hallway the other day. My fingers drift apart.

I shake my head and stick them back together. She's not weak—she was ahead of me in the last drill almost the entire time, and in my gut, I know she didn't mean to make me feel bad. I match her stare and don't budge.

"I've got your back," I say.

Her glare fades and she fits her foot into my hands. I lift her enough for her to get her feet onto the top of the pillar without having to pull herself up. She gracefully straightens and smiles to me in thanks.

I get onto my own pillar next to Niko and across from Ace with one leap, but I can't seem to find my balance, so I wobble and flail my arms about like an idiot while my teammates stand perfectly still on theirs.

"Get to the point, Marcus. Why are we standing on these stupid stumps?" Johanna asks. She stands on the pillar farthest from me, her arms are wrapped tight around herself, hands rubbing up and down, and her feet step in place. A shiver passes through me.

Marcus paces below, weaving through the stone forest. I still haven't stopped teetering about, so I crouch down to lower my centre of gravity, placing my hands on the rock for support.

"You guys are going to pass this ball to each other, controlling it with your essence as much as possible. I want you to dig deep and use your most advanced skills. When you pass the ball, you attack, when you catch it, you defend yourself. Johanna, I don't want you using your hands at all for this, just Mind Fire."

Johanna nods and takes a breath, closing her eyes to focus.

"Jeff-Ray, I want you to try manipulating gravity today. I've seen you do it, but you need the practice," Marcus says. "Ace, I know you've got tricks up your sleeves that you haven't shown us yet. Eliote, focus on your teammates' essence flow, see how it changes when they are ready to attack so you can be more prepared to catch the ball."

"What about me and Rin, boss?" Niko asks as he cracks his knuckles.

"You just have fun keeping your balance as an enormous bear on that tiny pole. Rin, you're going to try and engage the life affinity."

My heart skips a beat. It's been a few weeks since I engaged the life affinity in the fight with Aris and Mycul. I haven't even tried to engage it intentionally. It may be exhilarating in the moment, but life, like fire, isn't something I want to play with when I don't know how.

I force myself to nod to Marcus. Standing back up, I breathe in and out like he did during his demonstration, and tune into my muscles like I've been practicing with Brand and Hans. With a few breaths, I'm able to get my legs steady.

"Just go in order for now. We'll change it up after a while. Start us off, Johanna."

Marcus tosses the ball to her. As the ball falls in front of her face, it stops, hovering in the air. Johanna's eyes are fixed on the ball. A smirk crosses her lips as she moves it in circles around her and sends it speeding over to Jeff. Jeff thrust his hands out in front of him. He grits his teeth, and the ball slows before it can slap his hands. In a small patch below the ball, the ground trembles. Pebbles and dirt float up to circle around the ball. Jeff wobbles a bit, sweat dripping down his face.

There are four passes yet before it gets to me, but I don't even know where to begin to activate the life affinity. No, that's not true. I glance down at Adrianne, who watches us, processing each of our movements in this exercise. She told me where to start. Emotion.

What am I feeling right now? I'm embarrassed from earlier, I guess. I'm uncomfortable that the instructors are watching from below.

The ball is in Ace's hands now. What has he got up his sleeve? I've known him the longest and I don't even know his tricks.

That sinking feeling hits my stomach. Why does it always come at the weirdest times, like when I'm in my room alone, or in a crowd, or now, when everyone's staring at me? It's overwhelming, like my body is being pulled down by some invisible weight. It detaches me from the rest of the world, so I'm lost, sinking instead of swimming when I shouldn't even be swimming at all; I should be standing still on a pole. Am I going crazy?

I need to focus on Ace's move. He rolls the ball over in his hand. Everyone is silent. My attention on the drill fades. The air picks up an intense chill and crystals of ice sparkle around me. Everything slows; my movements, my teammates' movements, everything except my mind. My mind races to figure out how to process what's going on and engage the affinity before Ace throws the ball. I don't have anything to pull at though. Nothing stirs inside me except for this mysterious plummeting sensation. If anything, I'm numb. Just numb.

Energy shocks my body as the life affinity bleeds through my veins, breaking the slowness. With the affinity heightening my senses, my muscles regain their natural movement. I shift my feet on the pole but each of my teammates is still, the air remains prickled with ice, and the ball is tethered in the space between me and Ace.

"He stopped time," I whisper. Air trickles from my mouth.

It curls in slow, white streams, so slow they might be paint on a canvas and life is just a picture.

My fingers twitch at my sides. Ace stands on his pole, one hand stretched out in control of the icy void of time surrounding our team. With his other hand, he waves.

"Careful," he says, his face breaking into a delighted smile.

His hands drop. The ice fades, freeing the air to move again. The ball snaps back into motion and the energy coursing through my body forces my hands to snatch it just in time. The pulsing energy fades as quickly as it came.

"Nice work, Rin. Throw the ball back to Johanna and go through the exercise again, faster this time," Marcus says.

I throw the ball right at Johanna's smug little face. Her eyes widen. The ball just about smacks her in the nose, but in a split-second, a sphere of embers surrounds the ball. She wobbles and flails her arms.

"Hey," Marcus says. "No fire armour."

I steal Johanna's smirk for my own face, wishing she would fall.

The ball is back in play. Eliote does well, anticipating Jeff's attacks and is even better at knowing when to attack Niko. Although she can't throw it as hard as the rest of us, she catches him off guard. Niko can't keep his gigantic bear paws on his pole, and he topples off.

The instant his paws slip, my body jolts and everything is blue. My feet leave the pole and before I know it, I am on the ground and Niko lands in my arms. He transforms back into his hédin self. My adrenaline fades away.

"Thanks, Rin," Niko says.

My heart pounds in my ears and my breaths come fast. I

squeeze my eyes shut and try to calm myself. I don't want to lose it in front of all my instructors and my team.

Niko kicks his legs. "Can you put me down now?"

"Sorry," I mutter, and set him down.

"Focus and maintain some of that energy, Rin," Brand says, her voice like an iron poker at the back of my head. "You're in control."

I get back to my place, but my legs are like lead, and my arms are stiff. Even though time is back to normal, it's as if I lag behind reality. The life affinity drained everything in me.

I take a long breath and focus on the ball. Ace uses the same technique, but this time, life does not flood through me. The heaviness inside me matches the cold, timeless expanse surrounding me. Lost in Ace's trick, the frost tingles my skin— it's calming like fresh snow, and my mind latches on to the sensation.

The ball hits me in my stomach. I fall, slamming into the ground flat on my back. Pain spreads over my weak spot. Cold lingers on my skin as I pick myself up. Everyone's eyes are on me, but I can't look at them. The ball is heavy in my hands, my body begs me to run. I just want this to be over.

My stomach is empty and aching once we finish the drill. I duck my head, hoping to escape from any discussion about my performance on the pillars. But Brand calls my name. She waits for me by the stand with the throwing knifes we used earlier. Her hair is pulled back in a twist with a clip, and she wears a black turtleneck. The dark circles under her eyes are deeper than normal, but she holds her shoulders back with poise.

"The activation of the life affinity the first time was good. I'd like you to talk me through it so we can build on it in our next session."

The only thing I want to talk to her about is why she wasn't at my last training session. Even that I don't want to talk about. I shouldn't care, and maybe I don't, but it tugs at me.

"Was Adrianne able to talk to you about—"

"Why weren't you there?" I ask. My hands shake at my sides so I bury them in my pockets.

"Let's talk in private," she says, her face unchanging as she focuses on something behind me.

A Protector is talking to Hans in the doorway to the training room.

Brand puts a hand on my shoulder to steer me back to the school. Hans points to us. Brand clears her throat, her hand tightening. A flicker of muscle under the skin of her jaw sends my head reeling for information.

"What's going on?"

"I have an office in the main building, we can talk there."

And we're walking.

"Miss Highcaller, a word." The heavy tread of the Protector's boots spikes my nerves.

Brand sighs. The fall cold sinks deep inside me. She turns back to face the Protector, pushing a stray curl behind her ear. "I am conversing with a student. I will be with you in a moment."

"We have it on good authority that you were in contact with an Ironskin LP who recently dropped out of Guardian duty." A chill spikes the air as the LP takes a step closer. "In fact, on multiple occasions, you have been sighted with Ironskin citizens who have mysteriously disappeared."

Is that why she wasn't at our session? I turn to Brand, her grey eyes grab mine.

"With your Ironskin status and connection to these disappearances, we have reason to believe your activity is connected to an Ironskin revolt and other criminal activity in the past years."

"You have it all wrong, I was networking with my fellow Ironskins to make sure they felt safe. Their disappearance is what I was worried about," Brand says. "Now if you give me a moment with my student, I will answer your questions."

"You'll be questioned at the station, ma'am—"

"Commander," Brand says, her chest rising with breath.

"Commander, until further evidence is found, you are under arrest for treason against Illyson."

Brands arms are bound behind her back with an essence-neutralizing cuff. Students gather around the steps of the school watching as Brand is led to a cruiser. Each moment passes in a silent blur.

I am drawn to the open window of the cruiser, where Brand sits inside, bent forward, hair mussed, and shadows swimming around her face.

"Rin," she says under her breath. "I didn't tell those Ironskins to leave. Stay at the academy, stay safe." Her grey eyes flash, Ironskin eyes, and the cruiser pulls away.

Just as I'm starting to grasp my life affinity, just as I'm getting to know another Ironskin, she's taken away from me. Stephen's barbed wire words. Locked doors and broken handles. Now, handcuffs. I'm always locked out.

The entire floor is filled with an acidic cloud of mingling perfumes and smelly sprays. Eliote went to the bathroom to have another girl help her pin her hair. I shut the door to the excited commotion. Eliote found a dress for me to wear and laid it on my bed. She's provided a short dress since any of her long flowy ones would leave me tripping. The zipper glides open like a blade across ice. I slip on the dress. The blue velvet is soft on my skin and provides weight to keep the skirt down if there's wind. Golden stars are embroidered through the fabric. Eliote said the gold would match my brown sandals well enough.

My reflection in the mirror is a girl of subtle beauty, her figure thin in the elegant blue dress. She's not as thin as she once was, and her hair shines a little in the light. The girl resembles me, and I resemble the girl, but I can't quite connect the two. Some part of me is not in the reflection. I close my eyes to it. If I don't think about Brand or the Revival or the sinking in my gut, maybe I can enjoy the night.

For a final touch of shine and a hope to connect the two foggy images of myself, I open my wooden box on my desk and pull out the gold pendant given to me by my father. It lies cold on my chest. I close the box before my eyes can find the note. I leave my room before my mind can read the words to me.

Ace is in the lobby waiting for the rest of the team. He wears a black suit, a bowtie with red sorrow blossoms on it, and two, shining diamond studs in his ears. He keeps his eyes on the ground while he waits. As I come up to him, he rubs his shoulders and rolls his neck. A grimace taints his face as he massages a point between his shoulder blades.

Looking up, his pained face is eased by a smile. "You look amazing," he says.

"Thanks," I say. "Don't even recognize myself."

Ace shrugs. "Lots has changed."

Such a sweet, confident reply, but my stomach still cinches. "Do you wanna sit while we wait?"

"Ah, you see I've been debating that for a while now and I've come to the conclusion that I should stay standing so my thighs don't cramp up." Ace bobs his head as his hands pat his legs.

"Oh hey, speaking of which, I think I've actually built some muscle too." I lift my arm to flex my bicep. "Look, it bulges now." I poke my muscle.

Ace throws his head back and laughs. If anything, this little bicep shows I've done something right. At the beginning of the year, Hans was on me about not using proper muscle control. I think I've fixed it now.

I don't know how to fix anything else though. Ace expressed so much to me. I should have responded. He should hear me say that I care about him too.

Behind us, a soft shuffle of fabric grabs my attention. I turn to find Eliote, finally curled and dressed. Her hair is done up in a bun with a few curls hanging down to frame her face. A silver chain is strung around the crown of her head with a moon pendant hanging between her eyebrows. Her eye lids are weighed down by makeup, or maybe not. They hang low over her eyes and her mischievous half smile isn't as full as it usually is.

Eliote steps closer and twirls in the centre of the lobby under the glow of the chandelier. Her dress billows around her—a rippling pool of rich, inky violet. I imagine her aura looks about the same.

"You sure clean up nice," she says to Ace as she tweaks his

bowtie. Ace blushes. He wraps his arm around Eliote's waist, drawing her close to whisper in her ear.

Niko and Jeff-Ray join us. Jeff-Ray wears a crisp, white shirt with a satin vest pulled tight by brass buttons, black-leather pants, and polished loafers. He busies himself folding up the cuff of his sleeve. Niko sports an all-black ensemble. He's gelled his hair into controlled spikes and has painted his beast *Vishal* on his forehead.

"Where's Johanna?" Jeff-Ray asks.

"Her roommate was fighting her with a curling iron earlier so it might be a minute," Eliote says. She pops one hip to the side and points behind her.

"For Zenta's sake, I'm here, idiot," Johanna calls from the stairwell. She glides over to us in her five-inch heels and skin-tight red dress. Just a few feet away from us, her heel catches on the carpet and she falls, face first to the ground with a thud.

"You are one classy lady," Jeff teases as he and Niko lift her back to her feet.

Johanna scowls, her face is a perfect match to her red dress. Eliote takes the liberty of resituating Johanna's curls. "Get off, Eliote," she says as Eliote moves one last curl into place.

"Now that everyone's looking sharp," Jeff-Ray says, giving Johanna a slight nod, "we can party."

Johanna and Eliote's heels clip crisp beats as we cross through the icy cold of the courtyard. We enter the arena through an archway of twisted branches and pale-pink frost blooms. The arena, used to practice killing people, has been transformed into a dreamland. Sheer, white fabric drapes overhead, concealing the skylight and the stands. Lightstones are strung through the fabric, and round paper lanterns hang down, casting an amber glow about the room.

There's a long table piled with food, drinks, and desserts for us to eat as we please. Tall tables surround the perimeter of the room, decorated with tiered candlesticks and flowers. The greasy scent of crispy-fried hot peppers wafts over to me. My heart drops. The smell isn't tempting at all.

The music must be a magical spell to wash away pain because Ace starts to move the moment it plays. He bops his head and shuffles his feet. Taking Eliote by the hand, he twirls her around, and they join the other students dancing in the centre of the room. Eliote sways, sweeping her arms through the air with the same elegant precision as when she fights, and Ace just makes up his own moves. Jeff-Ray joins, immediately showing them up with his smooth dance moves. The rest of us who are more suited for the original purpose of the arena stay behind.

"You ladies want some of that pink stuff they have to drink?" Niko asks.

"Sure," I say, glancing at Johanna. She crosses her arms and shrugs her shoulders.

"Three drinks coming up," he says and heads to the buffet.

Johanna and I stand side by side. I shift my feet and run my hands down the front of my dress. Johanna adjusts the elastic band at her waist. The scent of her styling cream wafts over to me but unlike at Registration there is no burnt undertone. I glance at her. Her green eyes are shadowed perfectly. A breath of heat hits my mind. Johanna rubs her temple and sighs like just standing next to me infuriates her.

"I'm gonna find somewhere to sit," she announces and walks away.

She probably wouldn't appreciate it if I followed her, so I

stay where I am and sway to the music a little while I wait for Niko to come back.

Beyond the dancers, Lance stands alone at one of the tables along the wall. He's not eating or drinking and pays no attention to the people around him, just leans against the table reading a book. He wears a suit, and his hair falls messy around his face, but it still looks nice. He seems so calm—confident in his own skin, in his silence.

He lifts his eyes, and mine are glued to him as he scans the arena. Taking in the dance floor, a smile crosses his face. My stomach jumps as his gaze shifts in my direction. I turn away. My heart pounds and the music turns to an annoying thrum in my head, interrupting all my thoughts. Maybe he didn't see me. Did I want him to see me? No, I don't want him to see me. I step back to the wall, my hands clenching my dress, cheeks filling with heat. Keeping my head low, I peek through my hair. He's coming over. Damn it. Why is he coming over here? What if his dumb friends see us?

"Blue is a good colour for you," he says as he pulls up next to me. He doesn't even need a colour to look good. I smile a little but can't get my mouth to respond.

Lance shifts his hands to his pockets and leans one shoulder against the wall so his wings can spread out behind him without getting in the way. The foot of space between us fills with his fresh, smoky scent. "Are you ever going to talk to me again?" he asks. "I miss you."

I scrunch the velvet of my dress between my fingers. He misses me?

His sincerity swims in the gap—our small space of quiet. Even though he didn't tell Mycul and Aris about who I was, the words he's spoken to me have never given me any reason to doubt his sincerity. He's always been honest. There's never been a moment when he wasn't kind to me. But *I'm* not always kind, like there's a monster in me waiting to come out. I don't want him to see that. He wouldn't miss me then.

He steps closer. "Look, I really like you, but if you don't want to be with me, then just say it."

"No, it's not like that," I say.

My palms are slick with sweat, and the music slips in again. I don't know what to do. Tension builds inside me, twisting my nerves into knots. I need to punch something. All I wanted was to become a Guardian. I don't want to have to deal with this.

I just want the words to come out. "It's that—"

"There you are, Rin. We've been looking for you," someone says.

I squeeze my eyes shut for a second, wishing them away, wishing I could get through a sentence, to actually say what I want to say. With a huff, I turn to Aris and Mycul. Aris holds a box in his hands.

"What do you want?" I ask, eyeing the box.

"Well, after that duel we never congratulated you on the win, so we wanted to make it right," Mycul says. His cool tone grinds on my twisted nerves.

"It's a little late, don't you think?" Lance snaps.

Aris steps forward to hand me the box. "Better late than never. So, we got you a little something."

"Thanks, I guess." I take the box. There's some weight to it, and the cardboard is warm on the bottom. I glance at Lance. He looks back at me with a furrowed brow.

Just as I open the box, Mycul says, "We heard you like cats."

My breath catches in my throat, and I recoil as a fluffy grey kitten stretches a paw toward me with a mew.

"Enjoy, cutch," Aris says.

Mycul laughs cruelly.

"What the hell?" Lance says as the two of them take off.

I am frozen. I don't know whether to drop the box or hold it until I can dispose of the kitten somewhere else.

"Sorry it took me so long," Niko says, coming back with his fingers curled around the handles of three crystal cups. "Got to talking with another Beastblood at the bar. What'd I miss?"

I tip the box so he can see inside.

"Oh." The happy expression on his face drops and the drinks spill. "What kind of sick joke is this?"

"Niko, did you put them up to this?" The words spill from my mouth before I can stop them.

"Wha—no. Of course not. Why would you say that?"

"Well, how else would they find out?"

Lance cocks his head to the side, a dumb look on his perfect face. "Are you afraid of cats?"

"I'm not scared of cats, okay? I'm not, I just . . ." Both of them stare at me—a glint of annoyance in Niko's eye, and concern in Lance's. I'm trapped in a glass box that dims the lights around me and stifles all sounds. I take a deep breath, but I can't smell Lance anymore. I can't smell the fried peppers. I want to tell one of them every truth in my heart but not the other. I want to scream but my voice is cold.

What's the use?

"I . . . You know what? It's none of your business." I shove the box into Lance's hands. He reaches inside and strokes the kitten on the head. I turn on my heel and head to the exit.

"Rin," Lance says, coming after me. He puts a hand on my shoulder. "Please stay."

"Stop." I shrug his hand away. "Leave me alone. I didn't want to come to this thing anyway."

Lance looks to the side, holding the box tight as his face flushes. "Right, uh sorry." His eyebrows knit together. "I didn't mean to upset you."

The music pounds through my head. My stomach drops and my heart beats too hard. "No, I . . . I just have to get out of here."

I make it to the door without running, but the moment I step out of the arena I break into a sprint.

I'm halfway to the main building and fluffy white snowflakes drift around me. My feet stop moving as the winter air tingles my skin, sinking into my bones. I breathe in and out, focusing on the cold. Snowflakes catch in my eyelashes. I can't bring myself to blink them away—they bring me calm.

The sound of dress shoes tapping across the cobblestones from the school slips into my consciousness. I lift my head just as they stop. Professor Griven stands a few feet away from me. The last person I want to talk to tonight.

"Good evening, Rin," he says. He always sounds so polished. It adds to my desire to punch something, someone.

"Evening," I mutter.

"I have something for you. It's from Stephen," he says, handing me a white envelope. It flutters in the wind while he waits for me to take it. His dark eyes are patient with me, the corner of his mouth turns up, softening his stonewashed demeanour. Why would Hans be delivering a letter from Stephen? If Stephen had something for me, he should give it to me himself. I snatch the letter.

"Thanks," I say.

"Enjoy your evening." With the eerie kindness of his words tainting the ice in the air with warmth, he nods and continues to the arena.

I rip open the letter. All it says is:

Rin,

Meet me at the Kava Guard at 1:00 a.m.

Stephen

He wasn't supposed to come until next week. My mind buzzes, my limbs shake, the air around me fogs, and the chill seeps into my bones until I am frozen all the way through. My body stops shaking. Maybe instead of staying here, trying and failing to feel like I belong, I should go with Stephen. We'll get Liam, we'll all be together. If I have to do the Revival Ritual, then so be it.

I head to my room. I change out of Eliote's dress and lay it neatly on her bed. I take off my necklace and hide it away again. Slipping into bed, I don't wish for sleep, or for my body to thaw; I just wish my mind would drift away from the memory nagging for attention.

It had been a month since my father's funeral and my mother's death. Each day stretched on longer than the last, not letting me get any further away from the horrific events. Liam and I were still living in our parents' house. Stephen was at the academy, so it was just me taking care of Liam and the house.

I went to school and did my homework like normal, but I also made meals, took out the trash, learned how to pay the rent, bought groceries, and looked for a smaller place to live. I did the dishes and tucked Liam into bed every night. No matter how hard I worked, the house was still a mess, I forgot things, and I couldn't focus in class. I did it all with gritted teeth and funeral flowers floating in my head.

Oron helped when he could, taught me how to go about making payments for rent and such. He was supportive, but all I wanted was to curl up with my father by the fire and have him tell me it was okay. I wanted my mother to kiss me on the forehead, to tell me she loved me.

It was the end of the week. I had just gotten Liam to sleep, and I slipped into bed without changing my clothes, without brushing my teeth, without anything I made Liam do. I drew the covers to my chin. My body sank into the mattress. I waited for the bed to devour me so I could finally sleep. But my eyes were wide. The wooden walls creaked. My body twitched. The wind howled outside, singing to my pounding heart. I forced my eyes closed but they sprung back open.

Liam needs new shoes.

I forgot to buy milk.

Be strong.

Casket.

Every long, drowning second counted. If I slept, I would miss something, something bad would happen, the house would explode.

My eyes stung from staying open for so long. I tried shutting my eyes again and focused on the pitter patter of the rain until sleep began to pull me in. I was almost asleep when a piercing shatter broke the silence. My blood froze. For one second, I was as stiff as a board, the next, a jolt of panic fired through my heart and I jumped out of bed.

I held my breath as I padded across the hall to Liam's room. He was fast asleep. I pulled his door closed behind me. One step at a time, I crept down the stairs, heart pounding in my ears and breath stuck in my throat.

Maybe someone broke in, planning to kill us, the last Ironskins in the city. Maybe some kids threw a rock through the window with a nasty message attached to it.

Whatever it is, I can handle it. I can handle it.

My stomach churned.

Halfway down the stairs, I peered into the kitchen. The side door was wide open, letting a frigid draft swim around my bare feet. Did I forget to lock it?

Water spread over the wood floor around the base of the kitchen counter—pieces of a shattered vase strewn through the puddle, dead flowers among the shards.

Or did someone break in?

I continued down the stairs, head swirling like I was injected with core energy. My feet hit the bottom step and something thin, wet, and hairy squished between my toes. Shock fired through my body, icy hot. I slapped a hand over my mouth, but a squeal still slipped through my fingers. I tripped over the last step and fell to the ground. A second scream started out low and scratchy, then rose to a high-pitched screech. The sound pierced my eardrums, and I hid my face with my arms, cowering on the floor.

The source continued to hiss. I peeked at it through the space between my arms. The moonlight reflected off its eyes. They looked like the eyes of a ghost that could steal my soul and send me to the darkest pit of the ninth hell. Its shadow stretched across the floor and its fur stood on end, making it look huge. I thought it was going to eat me alive the way it growled and bared its teeth.

I scrambled to my knees, and I swung my hand at the cat. It scratched at me, then scurried out the door. The motion made me lose my balance again and my hand landed in the mess of dead flowers on the floor. I stared at my hand in the pool of murky water and flower petals—a razor-sharp shard of glass under my palm. I wished it could tear open my skin, just to feel a pain that would match the one in my heart.

The damp air spilled into the kitchen. It fell heavily on my skin. I heaved a breath and then another. I tried to get enough air into my lungs to make my head stop spinning, but it escaped too soon. My hands went numb.

"Why?" The word slipped out between tormented breaths. "Why, Mom?"

On my knees, I rocked back and forth with my palms pressed to my eyes. "Why did you leave me? I can't do this."

The wind howled and my body shuddered. My mother's face appeared in my mind, as haunting as reflective cat eyes.

"I wasn't enough?"

Heartless was the word Johanna used. Fitting for a girl whose skin doesn't break. If I couldn't bleed, then maybe I didn't need a heart. Girls in my class had begun to mention their monthly cycles. My mother didn't talk to me about those kinds of things—she might have meant to, but I would never know. I didn't know when I would start to bleed.

Sitting, shaking on the floor, something deep in my chest pounded, there was a pulse in my wrist. A heart, blood, vessels. I was flesh and bone. I was hédin with a face, a body, and essence.

Did all hédins feel this cold and numb? Did they ache inside from invisible wounds?

I grasped the piece of glass.

Johanna was wrong.

I had a heart. I just needed to prove it.

My hands faded in the dark, and only the piece of glass was in sight. Muscles and mind at war, my hand drew the shard to my back in a jerky motion. My shirt slipped up. The point of the glass pricked my skin. I pressed it in farther and fire shot through my back. The fiery pain swelled as I dragged the glass from one end of my weak spot to the other in an angry, crooked path.

Air passed through my lips.

Tears made tracks down my cheeks.

My blood ran over my fingers, tepid, smooth like silk.

Heat and ache filled my mind. It was real, it was on my hand, my back—dripping from my heart and I deserved it.

My pain was significant for one terrible moment, but a thump sounded over me. Liam. He would see me. My blood was everywhere. I had no bandages, no wraps, no disinfectant to heal my wound. I planted a sickly weed and couldn't pluck it; it grew too fast.

I yanked myself from the flower sludge, knees knocking as I crossed the kitchen, and grabbed a dish towel. My skin screamed at the rough cloth. I bit my lip.

"Rinnaya?"

Liam stood at the top of the stairs. He clung to the banister with his tiny hands, wide-eyed, his mouth parted by quivering lips. The fear in those eyes matched what was in my heart. It was a monster consuming me and lashing claws out at Liam.

"Go back to your room, Liam," I said.

"What happened?"

"Just please go back to your room. Everything is fine. I'll be up in a minute."

Liam backed away, his face pale.

I had to clean up and go to him so he wouldn't see what I had done. For a moment I bent over the sink, holding the towel, vision blurring in and out, fingers sticky. Heartless. It turned into worthless in mere seconds.

All I wanted to do was scream, but I held my frantic breaths. I swallowed my screams. I let the cold on my skin sink into my bones. The words I wanted my mother to hear crystalized and shattered in the dark.

When the wound stopped bleeding, I threw out the towel and closed the door, locked it, and went upstairs. At Liam's door, I wiped my eyes on my sleeve. I found a neutral position for my face.

I crawled into Liam's bed and wrapped my arms around him. Somewhere in my mind, I found a place that wasn't touched by the terrible events that had composed my life in the last month. It wasn't touched by glass or pain or cold. I sat in that place with Liam warming my arms.

I went back downstairs to check the locks on the doors three times.

30

JOHANNA

"Come on, Johanna. Get on the dance floor, you know you want to," Jeff taunts me from the other side of the buffet. He bobs his head to the music and shuffles his feet.

"Not a chance. This is all I want right now," I say, sliding a second piece of cake onto my plate.

"How about a slow dance, just you and me?" He wags his eyebrows at me.

"I can barely move my legs, let alone dance, Jeff." I turn and march back to the row of empty chairs tucked in the corner of the arena. Leaving Jeff to wiggle his way back to the dance floor, I take a seat, but he follows me with hands in his pockets.

"Can I at least sit with you?"

Thank Zenta, he's stopped dancing. I roll my eyes and shift over so he can get his bulky shoulders in next to me.

Focusing on my cake, I scrape the icing off the top and shove it in my mouth. I lick the fork clean to take a bit of icing-less cake. I watch the crowd and Jeff watches too. I eat my cake and he taps his feet to the beat of the music. The corner is just quiet enough to give contrast to the party in the middle of the arena.

"You know, I really admire you," Jeff says.

A piece of cake falls to my lap as I side glance at him.

"I mean it," he says with a smile. "I had to work really hard to get here. My dad left when I was little. I want to be the best I can be for my brothers and my mom. Takes a lot of work." He leans forward, propping his elbows on his knees. "Nice to see someone take this shit as seriously as I do."

It is nice, but I don't think it's true. Eliote works way harder than me. "You're fucking right, I do," I say with a wad of cake in the pouch of my cheek. I pick at a smudge of icing on my dress.

Jeff nudges me with his shoulder.

"Ew, don't do that." I shift away from him and he laughs.

We both lean back—I cross my legs, Jeff rests his arm on the empty chair next to him. I'm glad he's here.

"Where's Rin?"

Just like that, he ruins the damn moment. "Like I care."

Jeff is quiet. He leans on his knees again, his dreads sliding forward to dangle around his face as he stares at his hands. "I think you do care."

Who in the fucking nine hells does he think he is? "Like hell I care about that bitch." My essence pulses inside me, radiating heat from my head to my toes.

Jeff turns his head to me. "I'm just saying, to hold a grudge this long you've got to really care about the person." He inhales, unlacing his fingers. "Why don't you just talk to her about it?

Whatever *it* is."

I scoff, blow air through my lips, making a buzzing noise, and top my fit off with a snort. Jeff raises his eyebrows at me and a soft smile parts his lips.

"It's not like it's a novel idea," he says.

"Every time I try to talk to Rin she finds a way around my question, or . . ." I sigh. My head buzzes from thinking about Rin too much. "I don't know, she's impossible to talk to."

"You know you're not the easiest person to talk to either, right?"

"Whatever."

The warmth in my body slips away. I clutch my arms, digging my nails into my skin, and it's as if I'm standing in the rain again on the playground.

Just say something, anything. I'm killing myself with my own thoughts here.

Stop yelling at me.

I went to your dad's funeral.

Can you just calm down? I can't think when you get like this.

She walked away, like I was nothing better than shit on a stick.

"No, I'm not talking to her."

You've got to care about someone to hold a grudge, huh? All the times I've tried mind reading, or didn't try mind reading, it was always Rin's voice I heard. After talking to the wraith, I'm almost sure Rin is my Soul Tether. That is, if Soul Tethers and Wander Wraiths are even real, not just figments of my imagination.

"Jeff?"

Jeff shifts to face me.

"Have you ever heard of a Soul Tether?"

He turns even more. His knee touches mine. I can't pull away because his eyes fix me in place. "Yes," he says. "My aunt is Soul Tethered."

I grip my plate. "What do you know?"

Running his hands down his legs, his gaze drifts to the crowd. He is quiet for a while. My heart pounds in my throat.

"She says it's special. That it's just as it sounds," Jeff says. "Your soul is connected to something else. Never says what she's tethered to. Tethering only happens to hédin with really powerful essence. It limits their power in some ways but amplifies it in others."

Icing coats my teeth and my tongue. I try to swallow, but there's a lump in my throat. The tether limits power. My tether limits me to reading Rin's mind?

"One thing she always says is that you choose your Soul Tether, but they might not be tethered back to you."

Pressure builds behind my eyes.

"You think you might be Soul Tethered to Rin?" Jeff's voice dips low.

"What? No, that'd be stupid. I don't think . . ." I swipe a finger under my eye before a tear can break my eye liner.

"If you are Soul Tethered, then one more try with Rin could be the best thing for you." Jeff sets a hand on my shoulder. I let it rest there without protest. After a few moments, Jeff stands. "I'll let you be now," he says, and starts to jive to the music again.

He shuffles back into the crowd and rejoins Eliote and Ace.

Jeff's soothing tone is stuck in my head, telling me over and over to talk to Rin. The thought makes me want to torch the place. I get up and strut over to the buffet to grab another piece of cake. I reclaim my seat, but a group of gossiping girls sits down next to me.

Dear Zenta, no. Jeff, come back.

I don't want to know who hooked up with who or what the latest fashion trends are. My whole wardrobe is out of date. Except for my shoes. My shoes are always on point.

I toss the last bit of cake in the trash and take my leave.

Back in my room, I put away my heels and exchange my dress for something more comfortable. As I start to go through my evening exercise routine, my echo flashes. I grab the echo from my nightstand, plop myself in the middle of the floor, and click the stone into place.

"What?"

"Hi, princess."

My aching muscles go rigid with the shrill voice from the other end. I left the formal to get a moment of solitude, but now I have to deal with her.

"Hello, are you there?"

"Yes, Mom, I'm here." I force the words out with a sigh.

"Oh, I thought you might have hung up on me."

"No, I'm here. What do you want?"

"Can't a mother call her daughter?"

Sure, but she never does. Why start now at the end of the school year? I'll see her in like three weeks.

"Why are you calling so late?" I ask.

"It's the winter formal today, isn't it? I thought I might catch you if I called you later in the evening. You didn't stay very long, did you?"

I roll my eyes.

"Don't roll your eyes young lady, it's not very attractive." She always knows. "Did you go with anyone to the dance?"

"I just went with my team, Mom," I say, scooting over to prop myself up against my bed.

"Is there anyone you have your eye on to take you next year?"

Leaning my head back, I can imagine the schoolgirl smile on her lips. I grit my teeth. "No, Mom. I'm here to become a Warrior, not find a man."

"What about Rin? How is she doing? Did she go with anyone?"

"What does it matter? I don't care."

"Don't yell at me."

"I'm not yelling." I huff and jab my fist into the carpet.

"Have you been eating enough?"

"Yes, I've been eating plenty. I had three pieces of cake tonight."

"Johanna, that is unacceptable. You need protein. Final exams are coming up and you need to be eating healthy. Zenta, what is wrong with you?"

"What is wrong with me? What's wrong with you? You don't call me all year and when you do you just nag me the whole time."

"Please, it goes both ways, princess. Oron tells me Rin sends him and Liam a letter every month. What do I get from you? Nothing. You have a way to call me, but still I get nothing. You don't pull your weight, Johanna."

"And you just compare me to Rin. Why can't you let me be myself?" My voice cracks with the rising lump in my throat. I swallow hard, but it comes back up.

I'm always too much for her or not enough. My hair is too orange, too big, too curly. I train too much. I don't train enough. Eat this, don't eat that. You're getting chunky, Johanna, do more cardio, less weights. When will she just look at me as her daughter and leave it at that?

"I just think that Rin's good for you. You used to do things together when you were young. I don't see why you stopped."

"Do you even hear yourself?"

"Johanna—"

"She's the one who pulled away."

I don't want to think about Rin. I just want my mom to think about me and what I want for once. I want to become a Warrior, get into the real world, make a difference, see things change. Can't she be proud of me for that? Dad was always proud of me. He made me feel like I could do anything. "You don't know what you're talking about, Mom . . . you . . . you don't get what happened. She . . . you never asked . . ."

I take in a long breath of the piercing silence from her end. It burns my lungs.

I jump as the door opens. Sasha comes in with a boy. Her mouth drops, and she whispers "sorry," ushering herself and the boy out with her long, colourful dress swishing.

With the click of the door, I rest my head on my knees, still clutching the echo, not willing to hang up or mess with the silence.

"Joey." The name slips into my ear, innocent. It breaks through my hateful thoughts. I can't remember the last time she called me that.

"Joey . . . I know we never talked much about your father,

or Cassy and Peter. I always felt like there was nothing I could ever say that would make any of it better. Life was just . . .”

I hug my knees closer, press my lips together.

“Rough,” she says finally. “And we had to make it through, just you and me. But I wanted you to have . . . someone else you could count on. I lost my husband. Cassy was my best friend and I lost her too.” She sniffs and everything inside me aches as tears stream down my face. “On Registration Day, I said I didn’t see Rin standing there. But it wasn’t that. I noticed her, I”—a pained laugh escapes through her sniffs—“I thought Rin was Cassy for a second. The outfit Rin wore looked like something Cassy was wearing when we first met. What I had with Rin’s mom was priceless, and I lost her.”

Her honesty weighs on me. It swims inside me with my stomachache. Maybe if I was easier to talk to, she would have told me sooner.

“Is it snowing there, princess?”

I lift my head from my shaking knees. Moonlight streams through the window, illuminating the flurries twisting in the wind.

“Yeah,” I whisper.

“It’s snowing here too,” she whispers back. “Goodnight.”

The echo goes silent and the glow by my ear fades.

Another wave of tears spills from my eyes. I grit my teeth. What does she want me to do? Forget everything? I chuck my echo across the room. It smashes against the wall and the case cracks. How could she? Making it all about her with that story. This is all so fucked up.

I crawl into bed and bury my face in my pillow.

31

ELIOTE

The energy in the room flows through me. Each of my peer's auras radiates delight in their own way—some like starlight, others with streams of periwinkle, or blush-coloured clouds. I sway through the dreamy kaleidoscope of auras, feet slowing down as the minutes pass. If I could see my aura, if I have one, there would be no energy, no blush.

"You're tired," Ace says close to my ear.

I twirl around to face him. The dancing crowd reflects in his glasses. There are no colours swirling around the dancers though, only the ones from the dresses, silk ties, and traditional clothes—it's a little calmer, a little more bearable in his eyes.

I nod.

"Let's go then." He tilts his head to the door.

We shuffle through the crowd and back through the

archway of delicate flowers. The cobblestones outside are dusted with a new layer of snow. Ace draws me close, shielding me from the cold. He walks me all the way to my dormitory. As we near my room, Rin's aura latches on to me, infusing her storm into my heart.

Ace lingers, holding my hand in the quiet hall. He gives my fingers a squeeze then says, "I know you want her to let you in." He pauses, avoiding my eyes. "She will when she's ready."

I lean against the wall, my hand still in his, and wait for him to continue his thought. Ace's sapphire essence ripples around us. The comfort of his hand helps lighten the load of Rin's aura.

"More than anything, she just needs to know you care."

"I know," I say. "But my sight has been so overwhelming lately. Every time I look at her, all I feel is pain. I just wish I knew why."

Ace hangs his head. "I know."

His words bring a tsunami of his own pain washing over me. My entire body cringes under the weight. I slap my hands over my face as a fat tear slips from my eye and rolls down my cheek. "I see so much energy around me, and so much pain, that I can barely hear my own heart. What am I supposed to do with that?"

My eyelids fall heavily, sending a wave of hot tears down my face and off my chin. In the dark, I am thankful for Ace's warm hand finding my other hand hanging lonely by my side.

"I don't think a sight like yours is supposed to take any of that away," he says.

"What do you mean?" Opening my eyes, my sight is smeared by salt water and Ace's aura.

"It's not your job to fix other people's problems."

"What if it is? What if that's all I'm good for? I almost pass out every training session, how am I going to keep up if I can't get a hang of my sight?"

"Eliote, sit." He tugs my hands.

"What?"

"Sit with me. I've got to sit." Ace winces, his legs tremble as he sits down cross-legged in the centre of the hall, still holding both my hands. I plop down in front of him, my dress floofing all around me. "I think you're punishing yourself for not having essence," he says.

I try to let go of his hand to wipe the tears streaming down my face, but Ace refuses to let go. So, I bring his hand with mine and wipe my cheek with the back of my wrist.

"You don't have to prove anything. It's your sight. It's meant to protect you. Try telling me what you see in my aura, not just aspects of it, but what you like in it?"

For the last few months, every aura has been a danger zone filled with puzzles to solve, but Ace's is never like that. Squeezing his fingers is life giving, sitting in his aura is a reprieve from feeling and solving and running.

"Your aura is calm," I say as the tears quell. I tilt my head, a smile returning to my lips as I search his face instead of his aura. "But you always use ice, which is more rigid and cutting than fluid water abilities. It's stronger. It's kind of like how you're able to do such amazing manipulation with low essence pressure. You know a little goes a long way and staying calm is an asset. It makes me feel safe."

A blush spreads over his warm, brown skin. His eyes are steady on me as I speak. A smile twitches his lips. "And by knowing that, you keep yourself safe. If anything in my aura were to change, you would know how to react. If someone's aura was hostile, you'd know to get away."

"Yeah," I say, though my voice cracks. I nod and sniff a loud, obnoxious sniff that fills the hallway. I nod again. "Yeah."

"Maybe you just need to get to know your sight again. Just because you feel pain doesn't mean you have to fix it. The emotions you pick up from others aren't you."

The gentle reminder seeps in to find my heart, soothing every place of hurt. My hurt.

Quiet settles on us, with warmth so deep there must be fire in my bones. Ace's lips caress mine. I sink into the gentle touch. My hand wanders up his sleeve to his neck, exploring every inch of his skin my fingertips can find. Breath is sweeter so close to him.

His lips leave me, not a moment too soon, and don't linger long to make me want more than I can have. The kiss is a gift, one that will be savoured.

Ace helps me off the floor. No more words enter our calm. His eyes are tender, saying everything that needs to be said, and he leaves me for the night.

In our room, the lights are off, and Rin is in bed. Her aura is too active for her to be asleep, but I try my best to close the door without making a sound. She lays with her back to the door, blanket pulled up under her chin. Her sheets hang crooked off the side of the bed. A pile of clothes takes up space on her desk, the closet door is ajar, and on the other side of her bed, textbooks lie open, strewn all over the floor. The one thing in place is the little box set on the corner of her desk.

I change out of my dress and unpin my hair. My head is heavy and so is my heart as I hang my dresses. I stay on my side of the room to avoid stepping into Rin's aura. Even as I get into bed, close my eyes, and bury my face, her swirling energy stirs in my chest. How am I supposed to sleep with a galactic storm in the next bed?

I nod in and out of sleep, but a sudden spike in energy and the light shift of Rin's covers falling to the floor, brings me fully conscious. I peek open one eye. Rin sits on the edge of her bed. She finds her boots and puts them on. Standing, she pulls a sweater from the pile on her desk. For a moment, she presses her hands to her face. She opens the door and leaves—all without making a sound.

Where are you going, chicky?

I can't solve her problems, but I can make sure she's all right. Wherever she's going in the dead of night, I'm going too.

I grab socks, my runners, and a sweatshirt. Slipping on a pair of mittens, I wait to follow her until she's farther down the hall. As I sense her stormy spirit turn the corner to the staircase, I step into the hall.

Though quiet, the hall is full of life. Under the cover of darkness, the red carpet is now a dance floor for the spirits of sleeping girls behind closed doors. The dim amber light spilling in from the stairwell slips through their ethereal forms. I tiptoe past a spirit dancing a Lifeblood traditional dance. The peach of her aura spills around her as she spins in a circle, clapping her hands overhead to a beat only she can hear.

To the spirits in the hall, I am nothing, not even a ghost. They dance, they run, they work on invisible projects, and fight treacherous battles against the phantoms of their souls. But none of these dreams terrify me like the dreams Rin has. I saw everything she saw in her nightmare the other night, not just her sleepy spirit. The eyes that appeared from the glowing blue streams of her aura still haunt me in my own sleep. I saw the cat, her herbs, her house. Why didn't she go through the door?

But there was one dream where Rin danced. She danced by herself in an abandoned Ironskin palace. Rin was dressed in silk robes of blood red and electric blue, gold jewellery around her ankles. She danced in the queen's chambers where no one could see—arms stretched out, hair down and flowing around her shoulders as she stepped gracefully from foot to foot. She had the most beautiful, energetic wings and two strong horns crowning her head. I wondered if Rin was dreaming of someone else, but her storm was unmistakable.

That dream was back at the beginning of the year. Since then, I haven't seen the queen appear in my room.

My chicky queen is at the bottom of the stairs now and turns right, heading out the main entrance, leaving a gust of icy wind to snake through the lobby. I follow her, keeping my distance, hoping she can't hear my feet crunching through the snow. She takes us all the way to the Kava Guard. Outside, a figure waits for her. A single stream of crimson red spirals around him. The beginning and end of the stream are pointed like spears, the spiral is like a whip with red energy oozing off it, dripping into pool at his feet to re-enter the stream. It's almost as crazy as Rin's.

I squat down beside a planter where light from the lampposts doesn't touch the sidewalk.

"I didn't know if you would come," the man of dripping aura says. The whites of his eyes pierce the night, grey pupils staring at Rin.

Rin shivers. Her aura shudders too—it's drawn to his but is also repelled by it. The longer I observe, the more my gut twists and tears prickle my eyes.

"You're early. Why did you want to meet now?" Rin asks.

"Things have changed. New information. We need you to come with us now."

"Does the new information involve Brand?"

"Highcaller? No. She's been in our way for a while now, and if all goes well, she'll stay out of our way. And what about you? Are you going to help us?"

Rin is quiet. Her fingers clench in and out of the sweater. It's a purple sweater—my sweater.

Both their auras are disturbed by the other's presence. They near each other and quake as if stabbed by shards of glass. Maybe they were a couple, and the pain is from a breakup. No, that's not it. I ball the ends of my sleeves over my mittens and dab my eyes. That doesn't sound like Rin, it just sounds like my romantic imagination running away from me. I try to get a better look at the guy. He's wide in the shoulders, tall and lean. The features of his face are familiar with sharp angularity. His jaw is long and his nose slender. It's like looking at a masculine version of Rin. He must be her brother, Stephen. But what does he need her help with?

"I need more information first," Rin says, curls of breath rising over her head.

Stephen's eyes narrow and the muscles in his jaw tense. "He's here."

"What?"

"Geret is here. He wants to speak with you."

My heart races. What is happening? Who is Geret? Why did

Rin bring up Brand? And why on the beautiful green Karess is Rin involved in any of this?

Static bristles between them. Rin's aura quiets. Her storm rumbles to a standstill. The blue and red energies hug her, but the bird wings do not flutter around her soul. She's reserving her energy.

Worry squirms through my veins as Stephen opens the Kava Guard door. The bell clings like a siren squealing through the night. I expect a sinister aura to be inside, something that matches Stephen's unrelenting drip. The door lets out stray tendrils of aura that must belong to Geret. They are rose gold, slick. Floating over to me, they touch my soul like warm breath. If I could smell the aura, it would be the scent of fresh bread. It would be strong with deep notes and lingering sweetness. A cologne my father wears is like that. But in this aura and my father's cologne, there is something not quite right. The bread is burnt.

The cold sweeps around me, and I press my mittens over my chilled face. I shuffle into an alleyway and slink down into a crouch along the wall. I have no reference point with Rin. There are so many layers of hurts and mysteries that getting involved seems like the farthest option for me now. Something is not right about this, and yet maybe it is right. I can't tell.

I shiver in the dark, shaking cold tears from my eyes. Ace's voice sounds through my head, urging me to reintroduce myself to my sight, to understand auras in terms of myself. What do I like about Rin's aura? Through the shadows of the street, through the door of the Kava Guard, shining through the other auras, is her soul. It is bright, pure. It is innocent. Or at least it was, a long time ago. Despite Rin's undeniable power, I am always drawn to her, her soul is a comfort, and I shouldn't be so afraid when her power stirs.

Leaning my head back and wrapping my mittens around my lightstone to draw strength I can't harness, I wait.

I'm here for you, chicky. I'll stay here until you come back out.

32

RIN

T HE TECH GAMES ARE QUIET. A few wall sconces supply light, but otherwise the coffee shop is dark, the pastry case empty, and the air is no warmer than the blustery night. A woman leans on the counter. She is wide in the middle and broad in the shoulders. Her midnight hair covers one side of her face, but a scar seeps out from the curtain to paint her light skin with peachy red. She nods me to a booth.

A man sits in the booth. Geret. His back is to me. Stephen puts a hand on my back, urging me forward as my feet forget how to walk. Geret stirs a cup of tea with a shaking white hand. My footsteps are heavy as I round the table and slide into the booth across from him. I dig my fingers into the seat covers.

"I'm happy you came, Rinnaya." His voice is an unexpected, gentle murmur, his face young, defying the old man shake in his hand.

"It–it's Rin."

A smile curves his lips as he hums a note of acknowledgement. His blond hair is combed back and styled. His face is shaved but for stubble along his jaw and upper lip. He takes a sip of tea, lowers the cup back to the table, and raises his eyes to me—clear ocean water, green and glassy. "My name is Geret Aronson."

Aronson. The name has a ring to it. It echoes through my mind, trying to trigger a memory.

"Stephen and Adia are my most trusted members of the Revival." Geret tilts his head to the side. Stephen and Adia step toward the booth. Stephen watches me with a wild wariness in his eyes. Geret opens his mouth to say something but the tension building inside me has no interest in waiting.

"What is the new information you have?" I ask.

"Yes, of course. I've intruded your sleep so I shouldn't chat. Our people have gathered missing pieces of the Revival Ritual, specifics that you have not been given since Stephen contacted you."

Geret's voice rises and falls in waves. He holds his eyes on me but shifts his gaze now and then. Bracing his hands together on the table, he leans forward.

"The Ritual is ineffective without the blood of an Ironskin with spirit sight. We have an idea of who that might be. The final piece to our puzzle is the time. We must perform the ritual when the two moons are in the sky so that there is enough jint, fann, and unama energy in the atmosphere."

Blood. Someone else's blood and mine are needed for this to work. My insides crawl. I shut my eyes tight, my thoughts racing. I pluck one out and say, "I haven't engaged the death affinity."

"You haven't?" Geret looks at Stephen raising an eyebrow.

"That's why you need to come with us, you're not learning anything at the school," Stephen says, crossing his arms and shaking his head.

"Patience, Stephen. We will teach you to engage your gifts, Rinnaya. I can teach you mastery over the death affinity just as I taught Stephen, and Adia can teach you more about the life affinity."

I hold up my hands to Geret. They shake and I slip them back into my sleeves. "And what is your goal for the Revival?"

"To bring us together, of course. I want you, Stephen, and Liam to be a family again. Not only will the Revival bring back those who died in the war, but also who died since. My own family."

Deep inside my numb chest, my heart thrums. "What happened to them?"

"The Fourth Great War brought all the lineage leaders together with the Nine Lineage Summit for Union. They worked for the betterment of all hédin. But some resisted. There were many who believed that there would not be true peace until all Ironskins were eliminated. I fell prey to them."

The simplicity of his statement is filled in by his posture. His shoulders are drawn down, his elbows pull tight to his sides, his eyes find something new to look at.

"An Emberstead manipulated me, using Mind Fire, to kill my wife and child with Demon Palm. I was only able to free myself from him once he had already stripped the two most important things from my life."

Geret swallows hard. He rubs his neck and takes a sip of tea, the liquid quivering in the tiny cup.

"The reality is this," Geret continues. "That man is not an outlier. Adia took their wrath just as I and so many others did. Your mother, in fact. I want to reunite us all with what we have lost."

"One day you'll go through the fire," I say under my breath. *Fenlach calaikah.*

"Ah, I see you've come across a hédin of that mindset as well."

All that grounds me to reality is the ache in my heart. The losses we have endured are too great to count. Adia's hand drifts to her scar, Stephen is rigid, his face unreadable.

"Won't it start another war?" My voice is strangled by the weight of the words.

"The war never ended. It has merely been quiet for fifty years, my dear Rinnaya. Hate has not lost its grip on the world."

I set my eyes on a poster for the Two Moons Festival on the wall. It's only a week away. "How will you keep us safe?"

"Being together, united as an Ironskin nation, is the safest place to be."

Silence swells among us. My breaths come in shallow bursts. Though his face is still turned away from me, Geret eyes me, a shadow swallowing one side of his face. "Why do you wear that Luminee sweater?"

I wrap my arms around myself, crumpling into the soft, purple fabric with silver stars and planets embroidered over the front. The Luminee will suffer from the fighting. Ace's sweet family will be put in danger. Lance, Johanna, Niko, and Jeff. We will all be hurt if war breaks out. And I will be the one to cause it. But my people do deserve to live. There is no easy answer.

"Rin, all I want is for you to be with us," Geret says.

But if he truly wants to be united, I should have been brought under his wing long ago. Stephen should have made sure of it. I should not have been separated from him. Liam should not be growing up without his brother. Stephen doesn't care about us. And if Geret is as influential as he seems to be, gathering Ironskins left and right to leave their jobs and join his cause, then the words about unity must be empty. They should have rubbed off on Stephen by now, but Stephen does not open his mouth to confirm it. His silver-eyed gaze is empty, he doesn't see me, he sees my affinities.

"That's all I want," Geret says.

I shake my head. "No, it's not."

Stephen always tells me such sweet lies. He said he would make it home for my birthday, that never happened. He promised to come to Registration. On the echo call, he started with easy conversation before bringing up his true intention and then blamed me for thinking of myself. Does Geret sell such false hope?

My body is stiff as I get up from the table.

"Rin," Stephen says, grabbing my arm.

My eyes do not search for his. I yank my arm out of his grasp and open the door. As the cold air bites my face Stephen says quietly behind me, "The dual moons will not be wasted this year."

The door clicks behind me. I stand in pale moonlight with frozen limbs. Snow drifts around me. The faint sound of crunching snow pricks my ears, but I don't search for the source. I lift my head to the sky. The green stars shine over Akinnera with eerie closeness while every snowflake, every cobblestone, every planter is lifetimes away.

The Revivalists do not follow me as I make my way back to the academy. How could they follow me when my hand does not touch a heart as I press it to my chest? I am nothing but shadow in the night and I should be left alone.

You are not the demon. It is a beast, a powerful beast, but you are its master. You are not the angel; the angel is a manifestation of the goodness inside you. These affinities are gifts, not curses.

The affinities are gifts—beautiful, elusive gifts—and I am the curse. I don't want to curse anyone else.

As I get back to my room and into bed, the memory from the year before I came to the academy that I buried in the darkest hole in my mind sinks its roots deeper and sprouts a leaf.

A knock at the door rattled me. My calculations textbook lay open, none of the questions were done. My eyes flit around my apartment. The angles of the kitchen appliances were dull, flat. The light was dimmer than normal, everything was fuzzy. It was dark outside—I was sure it was light only seconds ago when I sat down to do homework. Somehow it was 6:00, and I had been sitting there almost an hour.

A knock sounded again.

I pushed away from the table and rubbed my eyes. What was I thinking about that got me so off track? Was I thinking? Was I even there? Where did I go?

It was as if that hour of time had vanished from reality.

"Rin, we're going out," Ace said as I opened the door.

"What?"

He pushed past me and took in my apartment. There were dirty dishes scattered around the room, schoolbooks and shoes sprawled by the door, clothes draped over the back of the couch, and I just let him look, didn't try to hide anything. I didn't care that it was a mess. I hadn't cared for months.

"Get some pants on, let's go." He clapped his hands together.

"I'm wearing pants."

"No, like *pants* pants, not sweatpants."

"I'm doing homework."

Ace wandered over to the table. He picked up the pencil lying on my blank notebook, he twirled it between his fingers and tapped it back down as he eyed my lack of work. "Doesn't really look like it, so let's get out of here. Tomorrow is Freeday"

Rubbing my eyes, I asked, "What are we going to do?"

"Ralin's having a party tonight. I thought we could go."

"I don't even know Ralin."

"We have just over two months before we leave for the academy."

"Yeah, and only a few days before final exams."

"Exams will be fine. Come on, last Senn party before we go."

"More like first Senn party."

"Exactly. Where's Liam?"

"With Oron."

"Well," Ace clicked his tongue, "looks like you're out of excuses."

"I don't need an excuse. I don't want to go."

"I hear Ralin always has good food and good music at his parties. You like music. You like food. So, let's go. We don't even have to talk to anyone, just chill and eat crunchies."

I stared at him for a while. Food sounded good. Something I didn't have to cook was the only convincing thing at that moment. The last time I had eaten escaped me.

"Fine. He better have fire-pepper crunchies."

"Oh. Wait, that's it? That's all I had to say to get you to go? I had so many other things in mind. You can even wear your sweatpants if you want."

"No, I'll change," I said.

From the centre of the apartment to my dresser, to the streets of Senn, and to the party, I can't remember a thing, except for the clothes I chose to wear—thick socks with a red stripe, ripped jeans, and my black sweater. I wanted the sweater because it was knitted, had ridges I could trace. It had the hole in the sleeve I could play with. The jeans had strings hanging from the rips I could wrap around my pinky finger when I sat.

Besides the clothes, there was no evidence that I walked out the door to that party. It was a dream, or at least that's what the last few months had felt like.

And then I found myself with Ace at a table filled with food. Nothing healthy. Crunchies, cake, and other sweets. Ace handed me a napkin filled with fire-pepper crunchies and insisted I eat them. Music played from amplimonitors all over the house. An Ease Beetles song played, and I stuffed my face with crunchies until spicy salts covered my hands and maybe my face—I didn't check.

Little did I know you had me by the heartstrings already, the song sang on repeat. The electro beat pounded in my head with the same dreamlike quality of walking over and not knowing it. I had to say something with my own voice to push back the dreaminess.

"So just two months now, hey?" I said to Ace.

"What?" he said mid head bop, mid crunchie binge.

"I said, just two months now until we go to the academy." My words had my tone, but it was as if they were borrowed from someone else's throat.

"Oh, yeah. It's getting me pretty nervous." His voice drifted through the stuffy air and fought over the music to get to my ears. Once the words got there, my brain didn't know what to do with them.

Ace took a step toward me and hunched over just a little, blocking some of the noise. He put his hand on my shoulder and repeated, "You ready?"

"I guess," I said right away, so I wouldn't lose my thoughts again. "What are you nervous about?"

Ace shrugged and I pushed my thumb through my sleeve-hole, then plucked it right out again. As long as my fingers were moving, there was blood flowing through them.

"It's going to be hard leaving family and getting used to training. And well . . ." He paused to adjust his glasses. "Just want to be sure this is the right thing for me."

"I'm sure it is. I think it's a good sign if you're concerned about it."

"What do you mean?"

"If you're concerned about it now, then you'll be concerned about it later, you know? You'll work hard because the stakes are high."

What was I even saying? For the past month, I ignored thoughts about the academy. It was far away and all the present moments I had lived were even further. I couldn't find the concern I described in my own heart. It wouldn't matter if I stayed in Senn or went to Akinnera. That was the only thing I was sure of.

Ace squinted his sapphire eyes. "I've never really thought about that." He took a sip from his cup, then motioned to the crowd. "Wanna dance or something?"

I wanted to move, run, fight, but in the centre of the mob was a face I didn't want to be near. The smile on Tōmas' face fell as he caught me staring at him. His brows furrowed, demonic angel eyes glinting with disdain for me.

"No," I said to Ace.

Tōmas' hands slithering over my body would never leave me.

"Fine by me. Hold this for a sec? I'm going to find a bathroom." He handed me his cup.

Ace headed to the bathroom, and I spotted a free space on the couch.

I manoeuvred through my dancing peers on ghost feet. Across the room, Ace got caught by a classmate. As they talked, their gestures became animated—hands flying, eyes widening— and they burst into laughter.

Would I laugh if I was a part of that?

It didn't look like their conversation would end anytime soon, so I settled into the couch and took a sip from Ace's cup. It was spiked with something that warmed my throat. I took another sip.

Everyone around me got further and further away, as if I was sinking under water. The music drowned out the voices, the voices drowned out the music. The lights twinkled around my vision as close as stars.

I pressed my fingers together, but the touch was blunted,

like gloves on paper, almost nonexistent. I pressed again, trying to identify any sensation—the creases of my palms, my nails, the texture of my skin. Nothing triggered my nerves. With each press my heart pounded, but it might as well have been the heart of a girl across the room. Everything was out of reach. My deadened fingers couldn't feel, my eyes couldn't make sense of what they saw, my heart was pumping, but not for me. Everything was nothing. And it was terrifying.

The clock in my head that always kept me from wasting time had stopped, but time kept going on around me. People kept living, laughing, loving. I wasn't living, not even surviving. Being wouldn't even describe it at its best. I was gone, so why shouldn't my body be gone too?

Someone was sitting next to me, either before or after I sat down. He blew plumes of Ease into the already intoxicating air. He leaned his head back, biting his lip as he smiled. Somehow, through his fog, he noticed me staring at him.

"Ever tried it?" he asked.

My heart beat faster, a war drum miles away.

"No," I said.

His smile grew, and he moved the joint toward me. "Try it, if you want."

I shouldn't.

"It makes everything feel good. Like you've never felt before."

My fingers wrapped around the joint and the guy lit up another. The slightest bit of warmth seeped through the rough paper.

Ironskins take up Ease too fast. It will end everything for you. Remember that, Rinnaya.

My mother told me that. My mother who was gone. The same woman who told me not to, smoked Ease and killed herself.

She's gone. My father's gone. My brother wants nothing to do with me. I broke any connection I had with Johanna. I'm gone. Liam needs someone who's here.

The kid needs an adult, not a screwed-up teenager taking care of him.

Crying's not going to bring him back, Rinnaya.

Bitch.

Cutch.

Ghost girl.

My eyes targeted the glow at the end of the cigarette. The warm, red light was captivating. I drew the little rod to my lips. A trickle of smoke filled my mouth, spreading fire through my lungs. I exhaled and sweetness lingered on my tongue. A chill crept over my skin.

My heart came alive again as it slowed.

I took another breath of Ease. It burned and chilled everything inside me. I relaxed into the couch that was now a cloud. Another breath dimmed the lights to glowbugs flitting around my vision, the music to a lullaby.

A few more breaths and the rod was nothing but a stub. I leaned my head back and there was nothing but a swirling mess of lights and tingles that seemed to last a lifetime and no more than a moment. The sweetness on my tongue and madness in my mind pulled me into the dark.

Fogless air and a glimpse of harsh light brought me back. It was quiet—no sounds fighting for the forefront of my consciousness.

I blinked and my sight landed on a small crack in the ceiling above me.

Breath went into my lungs. Every muscle tightened.

I wasn't supposed to be there. If only I could've been pulled into the infinite darkness of that little crack.

I tried to sit up, but my vision blackened. As it cleared, my head throbbed. After struggling in my sheets, I propped myself up on one elbow. Across the sterile room, Ace and Oron slept in two uncomfortable-looking wooden chairs.

Oron woke first. The grey of his eyes pierced through me. I set my jaw as he stood, and I drew a long breath, trying to keep the tears from falling. Oron rubbed his hand over his face and jostled Ace. He woke with a start.

"Is . . . is she okay? Is she awake?" His frantic eyes darted around the room.

"Yes, she's awake." Oron's voice was gravelly from sleep, and it grated on me like my nerves were exposed.

Ace got up and pushed a hand through his hair so it stood on end. He came over to the side of my bed. "How are you feeling?"

Awful. Awful is what I should have said, but I couldn't speak. I blamed it on my thirst. "Ca-can I have some water?"

"Yeah. Of course." Ace turned to the stand next to the bed and filled a cup.

I took it with a shaking hand, my heart shaking in my chest. Ace's eyes were bloodshot, and after he handed me the water, he drew his arms around himself and pressed his lips tight. I dropped my eyes to my trembling hands.

"Ace, why don't you go home and get some rest. We'll give you a call later."

Out of the corner of my eye, I could see Ace nod, but he

didn't leave. He kept his arms crossed and continued to nod every few seconds.

"Yeah," he said. His voice choked, making my own throat constrict. "I guess I'll go."

He stayed put.

In agonizing silence, I waited for him to leave because with him there, staring down at me, pain bleeding from his eyes, mixing with the pity written across his mouth, I didn't know if I could take much more. My heart crushed under the weight of his silence—I wished I was dead even more.

"Why did you do it, Rin?" Ace whispered. "Why?" He put one hand to his face and kept the other wrapped around his middle, crumpling into himself. "I don't understand."

I sucked in a shaky breath and swallowed hard. I opened my mouth to speak words that were nonexistent. My mouth closed before I could sob.

Ace shook his head. "I'm just glad you're okay. Call me, please?" He put his hand on my leg and squeezed before turning to leave.

"I'm sorry," I whispered just as he went out the door. He sniffed, continuing down the hall.

The silence returned. My hands gripped the cup harder. The water inside quivered. I tried to take a sip.

"Ease, Rin?" Oron said.

My hand jerked and water sloshed over the side of the cup. It trickled down my arm. Oron grabbed the cup from me and set it down on the bedside table. The tap of glass hitting wood bit my ears.

"What were you thinking?" he shouted.

Little did he know, it's hard to think when you can't feel,

and the only thoughts that come are the ones that hurt the most.

"I don't know what to say," Oron said.

"Then don't say anything," I said.

A heavy sigh escaped Oron's lips, and he started to pace. He paced, and I focused on the throbbing in my head. I deserved the pain.

"Where is Liam?"

"When Ace called me, I left him with the Dalaans." His face twisted. "And what about Liam?" The words split the air so I couldn't breathe. "That boy needs you." His voice rose. He paced straight toward me and gripped the railing of my hospital bed. "You can't leave him like your mother did." The bed shook under his grasp. "Do you hear me?"

The image of my mother's solemn face, pale in the firelight the night of my father's funeral, drifted into my mind and a tear streamed down my cheek. My hand shot up to brush it away before it hit my chin. I bit the inside of my cheek.

That boy needs you.

Those words stung straight through the emptiness, burning through my flesh, branding my heart.

My fingers started to tingle. Tiny pricks at the tips. I touched my pointer finger to my thumb—a breath of pressure.

"Rin, do you hear me?" he shouted.

I nodded, avoiding his eyes. "Maybe I shouldn't go to a Guardian Academy. I'll go to an Essence Academy. It's closer and less time away."

Oron sighed and ran his hand over his face. He started to pace again. Shaking his head, he said, "Taking care of someone doesn't mean you can never do anything for yourself. You've always wanted to be a Guardian."

"Fine. I'll go."

Anything he said after that didn't reach me.

You can't leave him like your mother.

Guilt spilled into my blood, infecting every part of me.

In the morning, my room is chilly, the windowpanes frosted over, obscuring the morning light. I'm not sure how much I slept. My eyelids are heavy and there's a faint pressure around my eyes. I wish I hadn't woken up.

I pull the blanket back over my head.

Beyond my warm cave of darkness, the door opens and closes. I draw my knees in close. The crackle of paper sifts through the blanket, a thud. A tap as something is placed on the nightstand. The bed dips as Eliote sits down right on my feet and pulls the covers off my face.

"Mm." I wiggle my feet out from under her.

"For you," Eliote says, holding out a steaming cup of coffee to me. A box wrapped in purple paper that matches her purple hair sits on the bed next to her.

Sitting up, I wrap my fingers around the warm ceramic mug. Eliote resituates herself cross-legged with her own cup of coffee as I take in a long breath of the rich black liquid and sprinkle of cinnospice.

I stay tucked in bed, and Eliote cradles her coffee as if it were life itself. She rubs the bridge of her nose like I saw her father do on orientation day. Her hair is tied in a messy bun on the very top of her head and tilts to one side. There are dark circles under her eyes and her long lashes hang low. Still, she smiles at me.

"How are you feeling today, Bird Brain?"

Keeping my eyes fixed on the floating cinnospice, I tap my nails on my mug. "Okay."

Eliote nudges me with her foot, so I look up. She frowns and raises an eyebrow. I should know not to hide anything from her. But I don't know what to say, the words just aren't there.

"Drink up, sleepy."

I take a sip. "What's with the box?"

She slides it across the disaster of sheets on my bed. "Don't worry, it's not alive," she says, shaking her head.

I stare at it and savour the thought of a present. There's no special occasion and I don't deserve it. Eliote slides the box closer to me.

I un-tape the sides, slip the box out of the paper, and take the top off. Inside is a pair of running shoes. I almost forgot about Jeff-Ray's comment to buy me new shoes that first day as a team—didn't think it would ever happen. Tears threaten to spill from my eyes. I take a long breath, heart thumping, and blink the tears away.

"Are these from all of you?" I ask, tracing the laces with my finger.

"No, just me."

They're flexible and light, good quality. The fabric is grey, silver in some places, with blue Tether logos on the sides. I would never be able to afford them.

"I should have bought them for you sooner."

I shake my head. A smile tugs at my mouth, lightening my heart. "Thank you, Eliote."

"It's nothing. You needed shoes, that's all," she says quietly, taking another sip of her coffee.

It's not nothing. She remembered the cinnospice. She remembered the shoes. She tries to make sure I'm ok. I haven't felt this much gratitude for a person in so long. It is a warm hush, quieting the mess inside me. I take Eliote's hand. She squeezes back.

33

JOHANNA

IN THE MIDDLE OF THE NIGHT, I woke up with an excruciating headache that hasn't subsided one bit since. Every muscle in my body is raw, like they've been gnawed by beasts throughout the night. Stomach aching from too much cake, I drag myself out of bed.

I throw on a loose, black top and shorts. Out of habit, I look in the mirror. Staring into my green eyes, I suck in a long breath, assessing every inch of crazy. Dark smudges of makeup adorn my eyelids from last night. A matching set of bags hangs underneath. Only a few patches of tamed curls remain, the rest are frizzy and out of control. One chunk in particular takes the liberty of sticking straight up from my head.

I grab a handful of hair, a brush, and a tie. "Just stay down," I mutter as I brush one side, then the other, stuff the hair through the tie, twist, and snap. The hair tie springs out of my hand.

"Fuck it." I throw my hands up, letting the brush clatter to the vanity. My hair poofs back out.

I leave my room, slamming the door behind me.

Just focus on training. You came to this academy to get away from all the shit back home and make a difference in the world. Focus.

In the training room, Eliote and Rin are already stretching as usual.

"Sleep much, Rin? You look like hell," I say as I walk in.

"Someone hit you with a sack of lemons?" she says, and mutters, "'Cause you're sour." She cringes and turns away, her cheeks flushing. It sure wasn't her best sting.

I roll my eyes, which sends a shooting pain through my eye sockets. Bending down to touch my toes, hamstrings about to snap, I peek at Rin. There is something different about her. She wears pretty much the same thing she's worn every day this year. But her shoes are bright and shiny new.

"You steal those kicks off an old lady, Rin? Or did you win them in one of your underground fight clubs?"

Rin's eyes widen, warning me not to say another word about Dawnranfet. "Shut up, Johanna," she says through gritted teeth.

JUST LEAVE ME ALONE.

A breath of heat washes around my head, mixing with the throb, but my skin goes cold. Rin's thoughts are so clear now. My mind is quick to pick them up.

"Johanna?" Eliote comes over to me and puts her hand on my shoulder. "You look a little pale, are you okay?"

"I'm fine. Mind your own business."

Scrunching her nose, Rin stares at me as if I've grown a tail. Her grey eyes make me want to scream. Why does she have to look down her stupid little nose like that? I turn away and continue stretching.

The guys saunter in one at a time, yawning and rubbing sleep from their eyes. Jeff tries to talk to me, but I ignore him—he's already in my head.

Adrianne calls us to attention. Hands planted on her hips, she says, "I know you're supposed to be working with Brand today." The room goes quiet. "Brand has been arrested, and that's all the information I have."

Jaws drop and lips twitch for words, but no one seems to have them. Rin braces her hands on top of her head. Her eyes press closed as she lets out a slow breath. My mind ices over, but I'm not going in there. I bring my eyes back to Adrianne.

"So, today we're gonna go over the same things as last time, blocking and avoiding attacks to warm up, then go on to counter attacks later on. I'm going to pair you off, and I want you to switch up who's attacking and who's defending every few minutes. I want Jeff-Ray and Eliote together, Ace and Niko, and Johanna and Rin."

Shit.

"Choose who's going to start attacking. We'll switch after five minutes." Adrianne claps her hands to get us moving.

I ball my fists. Huffing, I trudge over to Rin, eyes on the floor. Her runners come into view. Nice new runners from her nice new friend.

Rin and I square off. Without giving her a chance to choose offence or defence, I throw my fist at her face. My veins bulge in my wrists, my muscles are tense and shaking. She dodges back.

I swing a jab, a cross. Our bones smack together as she blocks, and I punch.

Adrianne circles around us.

"Johanna, tone it back a bit, keep it controlled," she says as she passes and moves over to watch Eliote and Jeff.

Rin's cold, steely eyes drill into me.

You think I'm a monster. I know you do. But what about you, huh?

Heat swishes through my head.

Rin steps back, hesitating and lowering her guard. "What?" she says.

"Too fast for ya? Or do you want some more?" I tilt my head to the side and let a cruel smile invade my face.

"This isn't a contest, cool it," Rin says under her breath.

"Stop avoiding and hit me, Rin." *Is a fight the only thing that gets your attention?*

I swing my leg high at her head, and she blocks with both arms.

"What are you talking about? I'm supposed to be avoiding you." She throws her hands in the air, halting our spar.

"We've been at this for years. Aren't you tired of it?" I say, and jab my finger at her sternum. The poke ignites sparks in her eyes, and she slaps my hand away.

"You're bringin' this up now, of all places?"

"Don't run away from it," I say through clenched teeth.

"Back off," she says. There it is. The Senn slips off her tongue.

She turns away.

First-year basic ed. Rin was in the back of the class at a table by herself. I just came back from the principal's office after a discussion about my cursing. The second I walked through the door, Rin sprang out of her seat, ran over to me with a glue stick and a piece of paper in her hands and threw her arms around me. She squeezed me so hard I lost my breath and when she let go, she swiped some glue on the lopsided paper star and slapped it on my forehead. *A star because you're the fucking best,* she said. Our teacher dragged her out of the room to the principal's office. I had a bruise on my head for a week.

Soul Tether or not, that's the day that sticks with me. Not because I was the fucking best, but because I wasn't, and she stood by me. But everything went to shit, and she stopped running to me and started walking away. I didn't—don't—have anyone to run to but her.

Today, I'm not toning it back. I'm not calming down.

I grab Rin by the shirt and throw my fist at her face.

34

RIN

I CATCH JOHANNA'S FIST. Her fingers writhe within my grasp. Every muscle in her arm is tense, shaking with energy, infusing me with her poison. Her other hand is wrapped around my shirt collar, getting tighter every second. Behind me, the snap of skin and bone connecting as our teammates spar slips away from existence.

My head buzzes. I'm tired of taking Johanna's crap and the awful remarks from the kids in the school. I'm tired of holding the secret that Stephen has plagued me with. Damn it. I'm so tired.

I shift my right arm up and out, slapping away her hand caught in my shirt and shove her back. Johanna's eyes flash. Hundreds of tiny flames burst into the air. They stream around her and solidify into a full suit of fire armour.

"You know everything about me," Johanna says. I swing my fist at her. It collides with fire and heat swallows my arm. My muscles go lax with the searing fire in her eyes. "You know everything. You never judged me, but then you just turned your back on me."

I punch again. Sparks explode from her block, and she skids backward, giving me space to gain momentum and land a kick. Spinning once, I aim my leg at her side, but she deflects and fire blasts me. I fly backward and catch myself on all fours.

She launches forward. I get up, but not fast enough, and her foot digs into my stomach with a blazing inferno. I slam against the wall. Pushing off just as fast, I run back at her. At the last second, I duck down and slide, taking her clean off her feet. She topples forward into a roll and ends up on her feet again.

"Damn it, Rin. Why'd you turn your back on me?"

My breaths come faster as my gut twists like it's fighting its own battle, and I still can't get the words out. I couldn't express it then, and I can't express it now. My tongue is trapped.

"Rin. Johanna," Adrianne yells. She marches over to us. "What the hells are you doing?"

"Tell her, Rin. What are we doing?" Johanna says.

"Nothing," I say. "I'm not getting into this right now, not in front of everyone."

The muscles in Johanna's neck bulge. She runs her tongue over her teeth, shakes her head, and scoffs. "Of course." Her hands fly up and slap back down to her thighs. "Of course you don't want to talk. So, fight me." Red curls quiver around her face as her challenge jolts out of her mouth.

I press my lips together, drawing a long breath through my nose, but it does nothing for me. The breath takes up space, putting pressure on whatever sludge is in my brain.

Adrianne steps between us. "No," she says. Two projections of fire form at her hands and she uses them to push us away from each other.

Johanna smirks. She turns around and sprints away. I sidestep away from Adrianne's shield, spin behind her, and chase after Johanna.

"You little shits," Adrianne mutters behind me.

I throw a jab at Johanna's face, then a right cross. I slam my elbow into her jaw, crushing her armour into splinters of flames. The flames turn to smoke and her head snaps to the side. She loses her balance and hits the ground.

Johanna spits, splattering the ground with blood. She gasps for air and furiously wipes the blood from her swollen mouth. She grunts, lifting herself off the floor and slaps me across the face with the back of her hand. The hit stuns me and before I know it, she hammers down on me with her fists.

I block a hit, jab to create space, and land a front kick. She stumbles back. I jump and punch her in the face while I'm still in the air. She smacks against the wall. As I draw my arm back, aiming at her face again, she slips out of the way. My fist plows through the concrete with a thundering crash. It crumbles and cold air spills into the training room through the gaping hole.

"Don't you dare hold back on me." The reflection of her flames flickers in her glassy eyes and a black, makeup-filled tear streams down her face.

Dashing away the tear, Johanna circles around me with her fists up.

I grunt and slam my fist into her gut. Her fire armour sizzles, burning brighter, anchoring her in place.

"Pathetic." A cruel laugh oozes out of her. "Show me how you really feel. Outside. Now."

Something breaks in me like glass. The shards slide through my veins, ripping and tearing, digging up every stinging hurt. The cavernous hole in my chest throbs as it fills with blood.

Johanna jumps through the hole. I dive after her and the wall closes with fire, locking us outside.

With my feet planted on the snow packed over sturdy stone, the electric blue spikes at the edge of my vision. A thrill of terror lashes through me. I grab it, sink my teeth into it. The energy swells. It ensnares every muscle. I draw clean breaths and take my stance. As the snow falls between us, the life affinity locks its greedy fingers in my eyes.

Johanna slams her fists together. A burst of flame spreads over her body, suturing her armour back together. Her full set of armour burns bright in elegant spikes on her shoulders, it cinches in at her waist, and accentuates every limb with long, glowing lines. She is magnificent, like Zenta herself. Giant swords of flame burst into the air and circle around her.

Johanna thrusts her armoured fist forward and the blades speed toward me. I fling my arms out, slamming down the blades as they assault me. Each one flies off to the side to decimate the ground. The fire and snow spread mist all around us. The veil is thick, but no match for my sight. Johanna sprints to one of the fire blades. She jumps, grabs hold of it, and uses it to swing her body at me. Her feet hammer toward me. I spring back. Johanna spins a full circle around the blade. Boots of fire hit the ground and she yanks the blade free.

My hands find one of the discarded blades. I heave it over my head and slam it down on Johanna. Sparks explode between the two ember-plated weapons. From the tips of my fingers to my toes, to my head, static spreads through my nerves. My body shudders.

YOU GAVE UP ON ME SO EASILY.

Johanna's mouth is still, her eyes steady, her hands vices on her blade, and her voice vicious in my head.

YOU BLOCKED ME OUT WHEN I NEEDED YOU.

Regret wells up in me and claws at my insides, pumping my blood in agonizing waves. Every pulse knocks at my heart, telling me she's right. My face burns and a lump forms in my throat.

The energy inside me digs in deep. It infuses my bones with venom. With one swipe of my hand, I disarm Johanna of her blade. Taking both blades, I slam them over my knee. They splinter into tongues of fire and dissipate into steam among the snowflakes.

I open my mouth to speak, but my lips quiver. Johanna's ireful link to my mind burns just enough to melt one thought.

You always want me to jump to your level, Johanna. The thought is a shrill scream through my mind—*But I'm never ready*—a terror in my veins.

The only way I can shake it is to move. I sprint at Johanna. Leaping straight at her, I wrap my legs around her neck and use my momentum to bring her crashing to the ground. I roll to the side.

Johanna scrambles to her feet. "Didn't you care that my

father died?" She swipes a wad of slush from her arm.

"Of course I cared. But who the fuck knows what to say about death?"

Johanna jump-kicks, her curls flying behind her, but I grab her by her foot. Twisting her body upside down, I fling her over my head. She flies across the courtyard and crashes into the side of the arena. Her lavish armour crumbles to flickers of light.

Just like that, the life affinity is gone, stealing all my energy. My dull vision returns and my feet stumble.

Johanna's body hits the ground with a thud, and she lies there, crumpled into herself. She drags her arms out from under her—pieces of cement grinding under her skin—and pushes up from the ground. One foot after the other, she drags herself off the ground. Her hair hangs in kinky strands around her face. Dust billows around her, rubble at her feet.

"I needed you." She gasps for air.

Johanna stretches her hand out. Heat engulfs me as streams of fire tangle around my arms, bind my legs, cinch around my waist. A warm pressure fills my head. My feet leave the ground. Johanna clenches her fist, yanking me through the air, and smashes her fist into my jaw. "You could have just stayed with me."

I shriek, but she hits me again. My head snaps to the side. "I-I couldn't."

"Why?" She drops her fists, stamping her foot in the slush.

"It was too much." My body teeters away from Johanna, over to one of her flaming blades stuck in the ground. Water leaks from my eyes, a sob bursts out of me as I brace myself on the blade. "Everything was crashing down on me. My dad died—"

"My dad died too, Rin. You should have known how I felt. We should have got through it together like we always did."

"Shut up." My voice is the embodiment of a winter gale. "You wanted me to talk, so I'm talking. My dad died. My mother killed herself. She killed herself and I didn't know what to do." Words spill out of me in torrents of ice. Breath collides with thought and blood inside me. I cling to the flames sizzling under my grip. "You punished me. You said you hated me and yelled at me for not being able to deal with your pain right away. And you've punished me every day since."

"So the blame's on me then," she says. I lift my head as she comes over to me clutching a bloody scrape on her elbow. "Fine. I'll take it. But that's only half of it. Come on, Rin, why'd you leave me?" Pushing me away from the flaming stake in the ground, she puts up her fists again.

I try to keep up, but she strikes so fast, too fast. I can't think. With one last blow to my chin, I stop thinking and just scream, "I was scared!"

I throw my arms in front of my face. Johanna's chest heaves with every breath, but I can barely breathe, let alone comprehend my own thoughts. My body shakes and words just spill from my mouth. "I didn't want to be left again, so I left first."

"Look what happened." Her every word hits my ears like a rifle shot. "Look where *we* are." My stomach churns. Johanna's face scrunches and a new wave of tears streaks her cheeks. "And you made new friends. Ace. Eliote."

"I know, I know, and I hate myself for it. I hate myself for everything."

It's not enough for her. Her lips are bloody, her hair soaked with sweat. For a moment, her eyes lock with mine—emerald washed in bloodshot pain, pleading for the truth.

"I didn't want to make it through."

There. I said it. Finally, the ugly weed is out in the open.

Johanna snaps her eyes shut, spilling more tears. She brings her fists to her eyes to fight off the leak but throws them to the side with a grunt. She aims her punches back at me. I block her blazing fists with my arms braced in front of my face, but sparks fly to my eyes, and I snap them shut. With one wrong step, my back is turned.

Johanna's foot slams into my weak spot. Searing pain radiates from my lower back to my toes, to the top of my head. With a jolting spasm, the striking pain centres at my weak spot, digging deeper and more crippling each second. I fall to the ground. Now I'm the one knocked down in the schoolyard.

As spots fill my vision, Johanna sinks to her knees in front of me. Her hand, bruised and trembling, reaches to my face. The tremor stills just enough to tuck my hair out of my face, displaying strength I have never had in her warm touch. Shoulders collapsing around her, she hides her face. Her sobs lull me into darkness.

35

ELIOTE

The silence that falls over the courtyard as Johanna collapses to her knees is deep enough for the snowflakes to hit the ground like pebbles. I clutch my fingers around my lightstone, my knees shaking. A shiver terrorizes my skin.

Adrianne is a statue with her hand poised over her mouth, watching Johanna sob. The hand falls to her heart. A sigh escapes her, and she shakes her head. "We need to get Rin to the infirmary."

"She won't want to wake up there." Ace hangs his head, hand on his hips. "Not again," he says under his breath.

"The kid got knocked out cold. She needs medical attention," Adrianne says. She turns to Ace, her brows creasing.

Ace runs a hand over his face, and says, "If you heard any bit of what those two just said, you have to know Rin won't want to wake up anywhere but her own bed. What are the nurses going to do for a weak spot that you couldn't do?"

Adrianne swallows hard. Her eyes are glassy. "You're right." The burning orange of her soul infuses the tangled web of her aura as it shrinks into a tight knot. "I'll monitor her until she wakes up, and I'll get high-grade curestones."

We follow Adrianne over to Rin and Johanna. Adrianne checks Rin's pulse. She starts to lift her off the snow, but Ace stops her.

"I'll take her," he says.

A dull ache swells inside me as Ace pulls Rin off the snow. Her hair drapes over her face and her white shirt is marked with bloody fist prints. My heart pounds so fast, so loud, it might as well be outside of my chest.

"Thank you, Ace. I'm cancelling training for the rest of the morning. Eliote, Niko, Jeff, and Ace, please attend classes this afternoon. I'll go talk to Headmaster Evelyn about the incident." Adrianne gives the order with caring attention and nods before she leaves us.

"What were you thinking, Johanna?" Niko says once she's gone. He casts a shadow over Johanna, still crumpled into herself on the ground. "You can't just beat up your own teammates."

"Niko, calm down," Jeff says.

"You're telling me to calm down? Look what she just did."

"Come on—"

"She's the one who should have calmed down. Look what she did to Rin."

"Damn it, Niko, shut the hell up. You spent the whole year treating Rin like crap and now you defend her? Get your head right, man." Jeff grabs Niko and pulls him away.

Johanna brings a grubby palm to her face. She swipes away a stream of tears but ends up smearing blood from her lip over her cheek and dirt in her eye. She furiously wipes her face on her sleeve before more tears take hold. She gasps for breath. They just keep coming.

"Hey, it's okay," I say, crouching in front of her. I put both hands on her sweaty shoulders.

Muscle twitches under my hands. The smell of slush and smoke and sweat fill my nose. My body shivers. Johanna is in front of me, beaten and bruised. The space around her is clear. There is no cloudy pink of her aura or shine of her soul, or flow of her essence. All that's in front of me is her physical form.

I take a breath, blink, and my sight shifts. The pink cloud appears around her, bit by bit it shifts into brittle, fragile crystals. I blink again and ground myself in a deep breath of the battlefield. Her aura fades.

"Let's get you out of here," I say as I wrap my arms around her.

From the fragility of her aura, I know that anything I say may break her, which is why I need the tells of her physical hédin form in my arms, the things I can care for right now. I pull the curls out of her face, and she lets me lead her to her room.

Once I've settled her, I get her ice, some warm water, and some cloths to wipe her face and the cuts on her knuckles. Johanna sits on her bed, and I kneel in front of her. I slowly take one of her hands, expecting her to pull away. But her hand is limp, cold, and clammy. I dab the warm cloth to a cut. Johanna winces, biting her lip just as tears tremble from her eyes.

I clean both her hands, wiping away dirt and blood, hoping to warm them a bit. As I finish, the skin is red and purple at the knuckles. Taking a new cloth, I run it under her eyes, picking up remnants of tears and last night's makeup.

"I knew she had it harder than me. I'm not an idiot," she says, her gaze cast beside me.

"You don't have to explain," I say.

Johanna shakes her head. I'm tempted to peek into her aura and search for any emotional tidbits I can draw from. Instead, I focus on the smudges on her face, paying special attention so I don't aggravate the cut on her lip.

"I . . . I'm sorry," Johanna whispers, digging her nails into her knees. "I just lost it."

"Yeah."

Johanna looks straight at me for the first time today. Her irises quiver under swollen eyelids, the whites of her eyes are pink.

"I think we all would," I say. A small smile creeps to my lips. "Maybe not in the same way, but we would."

Despite how broken Johanna is, how much pain was poured out in the courtyard between her and Rin, my heart is light. I get up to find Johanna a change of clothes and my muscles are strong even though they're stiff. As I prepare to leave, Johanna's face is pale, her lips parted, her eyes dry of tears, and my heart beats a heavy rhythm for her.

Hand on the doorknob, I say, "I'm your friend too, you know?"

A long quiet moment passes.

"Thank you," she whispers.

I shut the door behind me. Tears spring from my eyes and an ache fills my chest. Pain swells in bitter waves inside me, purely my own. I hurt because I care for her, but my shoulders aren't weighed down by pain that is not mine to carry.

36

JOHANNA

Today, the calm is just as violent as the fight.

Running my fingers over my clammy knees, Eliote's statement burrows into my gut. It's hard to believe those words after the way I've acted.

My heartrate lowers to a steady rhythm, only noticeable as it pulses through the cut on my lip. A draft sweeps through the room, sending chills up my spine. All the cruel words I've spoken to Rin throughout the years turn on me, berate me—the insults I spit at her, the looks, the laughs, all of it. I ended up hurting myself, warding her off like that, and now I hate myself. The things I said today, I needed to say. If only I'd said them years before. Maybe we could have worked it out and maybe she would have wanted to make it through.

Silence again. I sit on the edge of my bed, bent over my knees with my face in my hands. My body aches and so does my heart. Throughout the day, Sasha comes in and out. I ignore her. Lying down, I replay the scenes of my life, trying to magically change them with my mind so none of this would have happened. Sasha brings me something to eat around lunch, but I don't touch it.

The hours of the day pass me by. As I pull my feet back to the floor, it's dark outside and Sasha is in bed.

If I am Soul Tethered to Rin, it seems like I did it to myself, and the tether is unbearably one sided. The connection interferes with my ability to read minds that aren't in that thick skull of hers. When I tried to read Eliote's mind, I only heard Rin's thoughts. Since my control was not centred on Rin, my Soul Tether connection and mental state took a path of their own. I guess my mental abilities worked with her death affinity to connect with the Wander Wraiths. If I am so connected to Rin, what happens if I try to enter my own mind?

I draw my legs back up onto the bed to sit cross-legged. My shoulder blades grind around knotted muscles as I push them back. I bring my fingers together—they tap on their own from the shake in every exhausted muscle. My eyes fall closed. When I did this with Eliote, I had her voice to focus on. So, I think back to the fight with Rin to isolate a memory of my voice.

So the blame's on me then.

It's the voice of a bully who's finally figured out that she's the idiot. It's like biting into the bitter end of a whisper weed and getting punched in the face with my own fist. A weaponized vocalization.

I hold the quality of my voice in my mind, then dig up the voice I heard spill from the mental projection of myself in the Wander Lands—fire and gentleness.

My fingers tap. My essence runs in stinging waves through my aching body. With each tap, the two ends of my own vocal spectrum collide, and all sensory perception washes away—the twinge of strained muscle, the musty air, the sour, ashen smell of my body, all gone, replaced by fiery rose quartz hands and an energetic body.

I am alone in a great expanse, no Wander Wraiths in sight to laugh at me. There is a path glowing pale blue under my feet. I move forward along the path, energy pulsing through my feet as I step. I follow for a while, but I find a new path that writhes and nips at my ankles, drawing me in to follow it. It pulls me with gold light, and I find myself on a grassy hill.

The hill responds to my rosy toes as they glide through a swath of grass. Flowers spring around me, violets and lilies and energy suckles. Mist swirls through my legs. At the top of the hill is a twisting tree trunk of obsidian bark as abrasive as a thousand needles. The branches stretch out over the hill. Leaves of pure firelight radiate heat over me. I reach out and pluck one.

The leaf shrivels with a flame-like crackle. Its light pulses then sinks into my hand, imprinting its veins into my pink palm.

Darkness shrouds me. A searing dagger of pain slices through my mind. It burns and pounds. It dizzies me. And now I am home.

I am in the living room and it is two months before I leave for the academy. My mom cradles my head on her lap, she strokes my hair. She puts the vision tech on so I can listen to a show and be distracted from the pain, but I don't know what is playing. All I know is crushing pain in my head.

The original blue path my feet first landed on as I entered my mind bursts around me, yanking me from the memory. The path of ghostly blue light wraps around me and pulls me through darkness. Tendrils of ethereal light deposit me in a new mind. Everything is dull, and too bright. There are people all around me. Something is in my hand. I smell salt and music swells. In a moment I am on a couch, in another I am handed Ease, the next my entire being is euphoric and I never want it to end. But the longest moment is one where I wish not to go on. I want the darkness and absence of desire, absence of pain, absence of self. A voice enters the absence—*Rin, stay with me.*

This is not me. This is Rin—her memory.

She was dying.

Was I dying with her? Or maybe my tether was breaking.

Be careful. You are Soul Tethered.

Clarity takes my mind in an unrelenting grip. Clarity leads me back to my hill with my tree of memories. I am Soul Tethered. And if Rin dies, I die. It all makes sense now. When she makes a decision to go to Akinnera, I make a decision to go to Akinnera. When I get too far away from Rin, I get sick. When her soul is fading, her body breaking down under the influence of Ease, my own body feels that agony.

But clarity is a heavy-handed bitch, and she is flighty. I don't know what this could mean for the rest of our lives.

My stench comes back to me, my ache returns to wreak havoc in my limbs, and my body plummets back to my bed. Tears swell in my eyes. I grit my teeth to suppress a sob. I had no idea I could have really lost her, the one person I have ever really felt to be my home.

37

RIN

My eyes open to darkness that swims around my head and collides with the stabbing pain inside. The darkness presses on me—dense, ominous, familiar. I squeeze my eyes shut, wishing it away along with all sensations in my body. But my stomach protests like there's a hundred moon beetles with razor-sharp wings inside.

I lie in bed stone still, avoiding any movement that would induce pain. After a few minutes, I peel myself off the mattress. My head spins and my stomach clenches, the contents lurching up my throat. I slap my hand over my mouth and brace myself until the wave of nausea passes.

Swinging my legs over the side of the bed, I gasp as the searing ache spreads through my body. I should wake Eliote. No, I'll barf all over her. I just need to get to the bathroom.

Holding my breath and clutching my stomach, I cross the treacherous path to the door and into the hall. My legs shake and my back strains to keep myself up, so I slump against the wall for support. Just a little further. *Oh, Carnity, help me.*

With another stabbing pain swelling through my body, my vision blurs. I collapse, gagging back vomit, and crawl the last few feet of the hall on my hands and knees. I shove the bathroom door open. My fingertips graze the floor, and I heave the minimal contents of my stomach onto the white tile. I lie there beside the vomit as my throbbing head is soothed by the cold floor, my breaths heavy.

After a few more waves of nausea, I have just enough strength to pull myself up. I brace my shaking arms against the sink and stare at my reflection, taking a good long look at myself.

"You," I say. "You disgust me."

Silence slithers around me.

"Why are you here, Rin?" I whisper at my face. "What are you good for?"

I draw a breath. My soul is hot inside me, and black as coal. The soot seeps through my being, making my skin crawl. Dirty Ironskin.

A hot tear slips from my eye.

I let down the one person who's always been there. She needed me, and I ignored her. I left my little brother alone in a horrible, corrupt town. I left him in a crumbling apartment with barely enough money and drug dealers in the apartment below. I pushed away the one guy that I have ever had feelings for, and I made Ace bear his pain on his own.

"You're worthless, worthless. You deserve to be spit on. You're not strong. You deserve this pain." Each word slips from my mouth, so quiet, like the dripping faucet in front of me. They hit my ears with a corrosive sting. My heart pounds and my face twists itself into an ugly contortion.

"How can you be a Protector if all you do is hurt people?" I scream at my reflection. "You want to call yourself a Guardian? Would your father be proud?" My throat stings. I didn't know I could yell myself hoarse. I don't know anything. "Who are you?"

The white walls close in on me, blending into my pale face, white shirt, and mousy hair until there's no resemblance of a person in the mirror.

I hurl my fist at the glass. It shatters into innumerable pieces and the wall behind caves in. A scream escapes my mouth, tearing at my vocal cords, as the impact breaks open the skin of my fist. I fall to my knees, clutching my hand. My breath catches in my throat. A bright red drop of blood trickles from my busted knuckles down my arm.

My weak spot. The damage must be bad enough to throw off my essence regeneration. *Everything is a mess.* Tears break free from my eyes, stream down my cheeks, drop from my chin, and trickle after the blood.

Everything inside me falls—my mind, my heart. It all sinks deep and crashes in a heap, heavy at the bottom of my stomach, more sickening than ever. Sitting here with the life slipping out of my eyes and my fists, my body aching, I wish more than ever that the Ease would have worked. If only that sweet cloud had taken me away so I could be free of my memories, of mistakes and pain. If I had just slipped away into that warm, sleepy darkness and had never come back, I wouldn't have caused any more pain.

A glint of glass on the floor catches my eye. I could do it right now. End it. No more pain or confusion. I wouldn't have to mess things up for anyone. I wouldn't be a disappointment to Stephen. I wouldn't have to feel so far away from everything and everyone, even though I'm surrounded by people.

The glass scrapes along the tile. It is in my trembling hand, reflecting my hollow eyes.

No. Damn it, what am I thinking? I should have never gone so far, trying Ease, because now it haunts me. That one taste of darkness left a stain on me. I can't get rid of it.

I double over, too overwhelmed to even hold my body upright. I cry and the blood from my hand seeps through my shirt where I clutch my stomach, creating a bloody, sticky mess.

Through my weeping, a pair of bare feet poking out from one of the bathroom stalls comes into focus.

The stall door opens. I hide my face. The feet pat toward me, bringing a pair of knees to join me on the floor. Whoever the knees are attached to, doesn't say anything. They don't move, just sit there in front of me.

RIN, LOOK AT ME.

The words sift through my thoughts, warm, not threatening or commanding. But they should be.

"Why are you in my head?" I ask, my voice pinched in my hoarse throat.

I lift my head and Johanna lifts her hand to wipe her eyes. She sniffs, shaking her head. "It just happens."

Johanna shifts to sit cross-legged. Her eyes are fixed on the floor in front of her. Her shoulders drop, like the same weight in my stomach is on top of them. She sucks in a long breath and with a palm pressed to her forehead she says, "I don't hate you."

Her hand drops. "In that moment I did, but it was a pretty short moment."

I pull the collar of my shirt to wipe my face.

Johanna's hands lay limp in her lap. They're red and scraped, just like my own. She's always told the truth, the ugly truth. No sugar-sweet lies for me. She cuts to the core. My rotten core.

"I know. And I . . ." My eyes prickle again, but I'm not going to stop the tears or hide the shake in my voice. "I am sorry for turning my back on you when we were both going through the same thing. It was selfish. I am so sorry." The words are almost unintelligible as I weep into my hands.

"No, I'm the one who should be sorry." She swallows and tries to wipe the tears from her eyes. "It was me, all me. I was hurt. But I could have been better. I shouldn't have come after you like that."

"Stop." I push away from her. My back screams in pain, sending fiery spasms twisting through my spine and I slump against the wall. "Stop apologizing."

I'm the problem. I'm worthless. I don't deserve to live.

"Don't." Johanna crawls over to me and grabs my shoulders in earnest. "Don't talk to yourself like that." Her grip pinches my skin. "That kind of thinking is what got us into this fucked up mess. You think you're so deep in shit that you can't get out, but that's not true."

You may hear my thoughts now, but you don't know everything. You don't know the years of violent thoughts in my head.

The muscles in my neck give way. My head falls heavy. But Johanna grabs my chin, forcing me to look at her. I shudder at the gash on the corner of her mouth, burgundy blood clotted hard and a grizzly purple bruise infesting her skin. I snap my eyes shut.

"But I know you don't deserve the pain they caused. And I should have seen how badly you were suffering." She hesitates with quivering lips, her eyes losing focus on me. "I should have . . . so you wouldn't have gone as far as you did."

Somehow, she knows. I don't know how her Mind Fire got so powerful, but she knows about memories that I tried to forget about. She sits beside me, back to the wall, knees pulled to her chest. With her beside me, a pile of vomit three feet away, and a trickling toilet in the corner, the sinking inside me stops. She knows everything about me too.

"Look," she says. "I know I'm a jackass, but can we just start over?"

The thought seems so simple, so simple it might be impossible. I guess I owe it to her. She may be a jackass, but so am I. She leaned on me years ago and I let her down. We've fought so long and now she's finally beat the stubbornness right out of me. I could have leaned on her all along too.

I let my head fall to her shoulder. Despite the headbutt-like gesture, she leans hers on mine.

"Yes," I whisper. "I'll try."

The door to the bathroom opens. My body jolts with the intense awareness of the destruction I have caused in this bathroom. Glass everywhere, a hole in the wall, and vomit creeping between the tiles. Heat floods my face as I lift my head off Johanna's shoulder. Adrianne appears in the doorway, and I lay my head back down on my knees. My hair falls around me to hide my shame.

"Hey," Adrianne says, kneeling down with us.

Johanna and I are quiet. It must be contagious because Adrianne doesn't say anything. A few minutes pass. My butt is cold from the tile. I dread any movement that might send my back into spasm.

Adrianne takes a long breath. "I should disinfect that cut, Johanna."

"It's fine," she says, in a thin rasp.

"I should really do something for it, or it will scar."

As slowly as possible, I lift my head. Johanna looks down at her knuckles and licks the corner of her mouth, but winces as her tongue touches the cut. "Let it," she says and pushes away from the wall. "I'm going to bed."

She leaves the room.

As the door clicks behind Johanna, Adrianne shifts to sit cross-legged, and she opens her med-kit.

I run my hands up my legs to rest them on my knees.

"Johanna hit your weak spot, didn't she?" Adrianne asks.

I bite my bottom lip with a slow nod.

"Seemed like she knew where it was."

I nod again.

"Bitch."

A smile stretches the chapped, crack skin of my lips. Another part of my skin that has never broken before.

"Do you mind if I take a look?"

I don't want to show her all the damage that's back there, but she's the only Medic I trust enough to look. A shuddering breath escapes my lips as I press my hands to the floor to turn as much as I can without blacking out. With my back to Adrianne, my face stretches into a full, ugly grimace.

Adrianne lifts my shirt. She taps her finger from the top

of my weak spot to the bottom. My skin smarts after her cool touch. Silence descends over us. My skin knows the exact shape of the scar, its jagged edges, its discolouration, yet my eyes have never been curious enough to look at it. Now it burns under Adrianne's gaze. Her fingers don't trail my scar, and she doesn't say anything about it.

"She really did some damage on ya, girly. You're in a lot of pain, hey?"

My shoulders slump lower and I take a sharp breath.

"I'm going to use a high-grade curestone on it if that's okay. It should take away the bruising and make sure there's no nerve damage."

"'Kay," I whisper.

Adrianne takes a curestone the size of her hand out of a cloth wrapping. The creamy-white stone is buffed smooth in a rectangular form and sparkles in the light.

"All right, I need you to take a deep breath for me. I'm going to put the curestone to your weak spot. Okay?"

I nod. The skin of my lower back stretches as I take a laboured breath. Adrianne holds the curestone up to the wound Johanna plagued me with—or was this one self-inflicted too? The instant it touches me, a mist escapes the stone to cool my skin. A white glow spills out behind me, and my pain is ripped from my skin into the space between me and the stone. I gasp. My body shudders like poison is being sucked from me, and tears fall freely from my eyes.

"Shh. Breathe." Adrianne runs her free hand through my tangled hair as I cry. Her nails scrape my scalp, they catch in tangles, but it is soothing, making the process bearable, and I never want her to stop. "I'm going to hold it here for thirty seconds."

The fire that fills my weak spot retracts. My muscles twinge as they are repaired, my spine clicks.

"Ten more seconds," Adrianne says.

But a sharp crack sounds, and I jump.

"What happened?" I ask, looking over my shoulder at her. The movement is smooth again. My skin doesn't pull and my muscles don't scream.

Adrianne inspects the curestone that is now split in two. The edges crumble at the touch of her finger and it no longer glows. "Well . . ." She purses her lips. "It died."

The pieces of the curestone have inky black swirls throughout the white. I let my eyes drift away from them, back to my busted knuckles in my lap. My eyelids fall closed and sweet rest washes through me. Only for a moment, though, since there is still stiffness in my physical body, twinges of pain here and there. The curestone couldn't take all my pain. An inky black tendril slinks through my mind.

I open my mouth to speak, my heart pounding, but nothing comes out. I swallow to clear my throat. "Adrianne?"

"Mm?"

"I don't know if I can do it."

Adrianne places the two halves of the curestone back in her pack and swivels around to face me.

"Johanna wants to start over." I brush my hair out of my face. "But how do I start over when . . . I don't feel like I can go on." Hand still poised by my ear, fingers tangled in hair, my breaths deepen. They move my whole upper body as I sit with this one storming thought.

"I know what you mean."

I almost don't hear her say it. I wouldn't have heard the words if they weren't so earnest, if they didn't sink right into my heart, right where the weed grows.

Adrianne clears her throat. Her fingers find a clump of her hair to glide along. "I want to tell you why I'm here."

Though swollen and dry, my eyes are eager to meet Adrianne's. A crease forms between her eyebrows as she leans her head back against the wall.

"I don't talk about this a lot. I mean ever. The only people at the academy I've talked to about this are Evelyn and Marcus." She twiddles her thumbs around and around. "Fuck, this is hard to say."

A nervous laugh escapes her. She stops spinning her thumbs and grabs her hair again, then clasps her fingers tight together with a shake of her head.

My eyes are glued to each of her fidgets. They sing a song I know.

"When I came to the academy," she says, but stops to clear her throat once more. "I was really self-conscious. I constantly worried what others thought of me. I struggled with identity and tried to find it in all the wrong places. I saw myself through the eyes of the people around me, or the way I thought they saw me. Too fat, too skinny, my weight and my emotions were all over the place. I tried to find myself in my lineage but was I more Beastblood or Emberstead? I was really lost, you know? I didn't think I could go on either. I attempted sui—"

Her eyes become vacant and glassy, stuck on the wall behind me. I wonder if she sees faces? Maybe she hears angry voices, pained voices, someone else's or her own, washing through her mind. My skin crawls as I take in the words she's dug up for me to hear.

"I attempted suicide." Her head dips with the weight of the words.

A sweetness fills my mouth, smoke in my lungs, a warm tingle in the tips of my fingers.

"Sometimes I look back on it and it seems . . . silly, or my reason was too small," she says. "But when you don't feel alive in your own skin, when you can't hear your own thoughts or find your own way, it doesn't feel small. Nothing feels small. It's all totally overwhelming."

Her eyes turn away from the images in her head and find me. Everything inside me is raw under her strong gaze. I sniff and look away, but her hand is on my knee, and I flinch. Warmth swells through me.

"Since then, I've learned to look for myself in myself and accept what I find. I had to redo first year, but I didn't have all that pressure on myself to do it right. It's not like everything got better after that. Every day is still a battle against depression, self doubt, and anxiety is a mother fucking asshole, but I started making choices for myself."

"Choosing to be a Medic was the first choice I made without thinking about what other people wanted from me. I still don't know what I really want in life, but I know that choices define us more than our desires. The choice to keep going after already going through so much is the hardest."

Adrianne, with her honey hair, perfect skin, badass fighting skills, and foul-mouthed honesty, has lived through my hell. But here she is, emanating strength that I can only hope to grasp, and the deepest kindness. Still her story leaves me with questions that have been buried inside me for years.

Tears flow from the floodgates Johanna destroyed. Every tear holds a dreadful thought that I have never voiced. Adrianne moves closer to me and runs a hand over my back in soothing circles. The gentle touch only makes the tears heavier.

I draw in a deep breath to get enough air to speak. I put my head in my hands, holding back a sob long enough to ask my question. "But how did you move on?" The words come out as a whisper. "From your attempt?"

I'm finally able to lift my head and look up at her. She smiles her sweet smile, and her eyes are soft. My head buzzes with anticipation, my heart shakes with rapid beats.

Adrianne swallows hard. "You never really get over something like that, it stays with you forever."

Wiping my face with my sleeve, I stare at the fabric soaked with tears. Mother wiped the tears from my eyes with her own sleeve before she left. Adrianne takes my wet hand and holds it, idly stroking my thumb.

"I still struggle with the same thoughts and feelings I had back then. I still take my days five seconds at a time." Adrianne's careful eyes watch me consider what she's just said. Her words are sincere and her tone calm. "But at one point I just had to forgive myself for it."

A wave of heat spreads from my puffy eyes, moving down my cheeks, down my neck. "Just forgive?" I say.

Adrianne hums a note of acknowledgement.

"How do I forgive her for leaving us?" I choke on the words as another wave of tears spills forth. Saying it out loud makes it so much more real than it has been in a long time.

"How do I forgive her? How do I forgive myself? How do I forgive myself?" I clench my fists and unclench them. I dig my fingernails into my knees and release. "Didn't she want to be with us anymore? D-didn't she care what would happen to us?" My shoulders tense and my stomach clenches into a bigger knot than ever before. "And I almost did the same thing to my brothers—I was this close!"

A horrible sob leaves me, and I double over, holding my arms tight around my aching body.

Damn it. I was this close to leaving just the way she did.

Adrianne shifts me so I'm leaning on her lap instead of myself. She continues to make the circles around my spine.

"My mom didn't want to be with me," I mutter into Adrianne's lap. "Stephen doesn't want to be with me . . . I don't want to be with me. I can't imagine why Johanna would want to be my friend."

My body is heavy and weightless at the same time. Despite my weight, Adrianne lifts me from her knees and looks me in the eye. She has caught each of my agonizing words and woven them with her own into an accepting smile. Her golden skin is marred by tears that spill from pools of grief in her eyes.

"Forgiveness isn't saying it was okay that something shitty happened," Adrianne says, her voice choked. "It wasn't okay that your mom left you. But I can tell you this, she didn't want to leave you. She was in pain. You'll always feel that pain when you think of her. You've been carrying her pain and your own for years, girly. Don't be hard on yourself for wanting out. Forgiveness is giving yourself permission to step away from the bad and into something new."

I stare down at my lap, my face still soaked even though I just cleared away a wave of tears. My head is throbbing, and my eyes are itchy. Even so, Adrianne tilts my head up, trying to keep my gaze.

"You are not your mother," she whispers.

She pulls me into a hug so tight that I can't speak or even breathe. I lean into her embrace, letting her support me, breathless in her arms. It's the most wonderful feeling in the world because as she lets go, it's like I'm breathing for the first time.

"All right," Adrianne says with a nod. She smiles and helps me off the ground.

The ache in my back has dulled enough for me to stand straight again, but moving is still a struggle. Adrianne puts her arm around me and walks me back to my room.

"Get some sleep, and in the morning no coffee, just scolya root tea. And have a cup before bed too. It will help you regenerate your essence throughout your body," she says.

Reluctant to let her go, I nod and hope my face shows some gratitude before she walks away. I don't know how much I can forgive yet—not myself at least, not yet. But I do want to.

LANCE

The rush of my essence over my muscles is a little too fast to allow me to sleep, so I wander the academy halls. The moonlight shines through the tall windows, casting shadows that transform the academy into something different than it is in the day. My thoughts are louder, more jumbled, as they all want to come out at once in the quiet. I can't keep friends, I still have trouble controlling my essence, and I got shot down by the girl I like—again. I'm a joke.

I find myself in the dining hall. At the end of the empty buffet line is the coffee and tea station, always stocked for sleepless occasions such as this. I take a package of scolya root tea and set the water to boil. I cross my arms, waiting, listening to the kettle whistle. Even though I'm restless, there's something about being awake in the middle of the night that makes all the sad aspects of wandering the dark deserted halls not so pathetic. In the comfort of sock feet, hooded sweater, and pyjama shorts, watching the snow fall on the academy grounds under the moonlight settles something inside me.

Everyone is asleep, but I am awake. Like at the party at the beginning of the year, the Emberstead girl that I now know as Johanna danced in the middle of the crowd with an unopened ale. Everyone was drunk but she was awake. I wanted that feeling, that freedom, to be strong in my own skin—skin that doesn't crawl.

In this moment, I am awake with crashing thoughts, no one pushing me around.

"Hey."

With a start, I fumble my tea bag into my empty mug. I turn and find Rin behind me.

"Sorry," she says and fiddles with the hem of her baggy green t-shirt.

My breath catches in my throat. I haven't seen her since the formal four days ago.

"No, it's okay. I just didn't see you, uh, I mean hear you. I didn't hear you come up." The back of my neck gets hot as I babble.

Rin gives me a half smile that makes my heart melt, but behind that smile I hear the words she said to me at the formal— *Leave me alone*—and my chest tightens. I drop my eyes to my mug with the packaged tea bag. I pick up the mug and tap my fingernails on the sides.

Rin selects a mug from the stand. She cups both hands around it. "Didn't think anyone was gonna be up."

"Yeah, I couldn't sleep."

"Mm, I haven't been able to sleep well either these days."

"Yeah? What's up?"

I look to the side just as she looks at me. She lets out a shy laugh and scratches the back of her head. "I got beat up."

"Wait, what?"

"It's fine. My essence is just all out of whack now."

"Who beat you up?"

"Johanna. I had it coming." She shrugs. "She hit my weak spot. When that happens, all the essence in my body is channelled to heal it. The hit was so hard that my entire body was weakened. Super unfortunate timing too. I got my monthly cycle the day after and it felt like a Rover was clawing a hole inside me." With a cringe, she shakes her head. "I don't know why I just told you that."

Even if the comment makes her feel uncomfortable, it lightens my heart. It's like the first day we met. She said what came to mind—she just talked to me.

"Well, you should have scolya root tea," I say. "It helps with essence stuff like that."

Relief plays in Rin's eyes. "That's what Adrianne said too."

"Then, here." I pluck the tea bag out of my cup and hand it to her.

She chuckles and takes the bag, opens it, and plops it into her own mug. Keeping her eyes on the array of tea in front of her, she falls silent. I want to know what she's thinking. Is she happy to see me, or does she want me to get away?

I grab a new tea bag and flap it between my fingers. After a few seconds of fiddling, I clutch the bag tight. *Ancestors help me. How annoying can I be?*

The water rolls to a boil. I take the kettle off the stand,

gesture with the pot to Rin, and she presents her cup.

"Thanks," she says as I pour the water, slow and steady, careful not to spill on her. Her left hand has a bandage over the knuckles. I don't say anything about it, I just lock away the fact that she may be tough, but even iron can break. Something to remember.

Adding a teaspoon of sugar and a sprinkle of cinnospice, Rin says, "I hope you can get to sleep soon."

Pouring my own tea, I keep my eyes on the trickle of water, although all I want to do is look at her. "You too." My voice cracks and I press my lips together, hoping it wasn't noticeable.

Rin's bare feet tap on the tiles as she walks away. I fight the urge to call after her, ask her to sit and drink with me. We don't have to talk; I just want to be with her. But she asked for space. I should let her have it.

But the tap of her feet stops. "Lance?"

I turn around way too fast, spilling tea all over my hand. "Yeah?" I say, ignoring the searing hot water pricking my skin.

Eyes fixed on the floor, Rin shifts from foot to foot. A crease forms between her dark eyebrows. Her lips part, but whatever she has to say doesn't come out. My heart pounds.

Please just talk to me.

With a sigh she says, "Lance, I'm sorry."

Each beat of my heart brings it closer to jumping out of my chest. I hate the way her face flushes, how uncomfortable she looks standing there biting the edge of her lip. I want to run over to her and tell her not to worry, not to be sorry. But my feet are locked in place, my mouth frozen.

"I'm sorry for the way I've treated you." She taps her nails on her mug. "I keep running off without any explanation, without

. . . well I keep pushing you away, and I don't want to do that."

As she lifts her head, a stray hair slips from her ponytail. She tucks it behind her ear and meets my stare. Even in the dim light, her silver eyes sparkle and pull me in. I can't look away.

"So . . ." She closes her eyes, shutting me out for one unbearable second, then opens them again, squaring her feet. "Can you forgive me?"

I almost want her to say it again, maybe I heard it wrong. When was the last time I heard someone apologize with sincerity? When was the last time *I* asked for forgiveness instead of justifying my actions? Or accepted the forgiveness I asked for? But no, she doesn't have to say it again. I heard her. "Yes. Yes, of course I forgive you."

All the tension in her face melts—dropping her eyebrows back into place, clearing out the flush in her cheeks, sinking her shoulders down. "Thank you," she says.

A smile spreads her pink lips, and she plays with the stray hairs again. Her smile is so kind and real that my own mouth jumps to match hers. My stomach flutters.

"Okay good." She turns to leave but pivots right back around to face me. "We are going to the Festival of Two Moons, my team and I, that is, on Freeday. Would you like to come? I'd like it if you'd come with us."

Oh, good Carnity. I can barely contain myself with my heart and my stomach dancing for joy. "I'd love to go with you . . . with you guys . . . with you."

Rin's face turns the colour of pinichu berries but attempts to hide it and looks back down at her tea. "Great. Goodnight, Lance."

"Goodnight, Rin."

The first time I went to Sii for the Festival of Two Moons, I was six and went with my parents. I received a little glass charm for Carnity's blessings and marvelled as a storyteller told all the children how, just for a week, the jint energy in our planet pulls a second moon into the sky, and how the shift in energy empowered the essence of our ancestors Carnity and Dien. When the magical twin moons appeared in the sky and fireworks exploded, adding a mortal flare to the display, I was filled with wonder, so alive.

I check my watch. Rin told me we would meet at the side entrance at 3:00 p.m. I've been waiting for ten minutes, and I even got here late. I had to deal with the cigarettes that keep making it into my pockets and the ones stashed in my cruiser. Starting over for the hundredth time. Hands jittering and anxious as hell, I'd rather this than not being able to trust myself.

Buttoning up my wool-lined jean jacket, I jump as the side door opens. Eliote comes out wearing a purple jacket that matches her hair and tall furry boots. She sees me, props her hands on her hips and says, "Look, he's here already and he's annoyed. We kept him waiting."

"He's fine, it's not that cold out here. Rin needed better shoes," Johanna says as she slips on a wool winter hat. The hat squishes her curls around her face. She fusses with the mass of hair for a while but gives up and lets it stick out however it pleases.

"Did we have to make her try on every pair of Johanna's shoes until we found a pair that matched her outfit perfectly?" Ace asks as he and the rest of the squad files through the door.

"Yes we did," Niko says. "Johanna's style is so different from Rin's, it just wasn't working for me."

"Nah, man, any pair would have been fine," Jeff chimes in.

He breathes a puff of air on his hands and zips up his long, felt jacket all the way to his chin.

"Why do you have so many boots, anyway?" Eliote asks Johanna.

Johanna gives Eliot a cold stare. "I like shoes, okay? Get over it."

"Can we just go already? My feet are warm, and they thank you," Rin says, nudging her teammates away from the door.

Niko takes the lead. Jeff and Johanna come up around him and start to joke and laugh, or Niko and Jeff laugh. Johanna just supplies the witty banter. Eliote and Ace are close behind. Eliote takes Ace's hand, and Ace leans over to kiss her on the cheek. Rin hangs back.

I don't want to get sucked along with the crowd anymore, where people can't hear me over their own chatter. I just want to be with her. We fall into step a few metres behind the rest.

She seems different today. Almost like she has new eyes to see the world—they're clearer, a lighter grey than usual. Like the other night, they sparkle. Even though a small smile sits on her lips, she fidgets with the bandage on her hand. I get the feeling that she doesn't feel like herself. Maybe it's the boots, it's never comfortable to wear someone else's shoes. She looks pretty though, in her red jacket with her hair tied back.

"Are you feeling better?" I ask.

I don't know if I should ask about it because I don't know exactly what's been going on with her, but I want to know how she's doing.

"A little," she says. My breath catches, waiting, hoping for more information. "Slowly getting back to normal. I guess when Ironskins go down, we go down hard."

"I'm glad—"

A burst of laughter from the others stifles my words. I stick my hands in my pockets, the familiar urge to just shut up and fade to the back, not make trouble, wells in my chest. Rin touches my sleeve.

"What were you saying?" she asks. Her stormy eyes capture me, focused.

My heart aches, like a weight has been lifted and it's still sore from being confined, but it can finally beat freely. I love her unsmiling face, watching for me, waiting for me.

I breathe a laugh. "I'm just glad you're okay."

"Me too," she says in a small voice.

She keeps her eyes on me. I un-pocket my hands. Shaking out the tension, I say, "I just quit smoking."

The words pop out so easily. I've been hiding so much, and she's been running away. Being close like this with all that behind us makes every word effortless.

The most genuine smile I've seen yet barely turns the corners of her mouth. "That's amazing," she says and moves closer to me.

As we walk, the snow absorbs the sounds around us, keeping our walk quiet even as we get to busier streets. The snow piles up in soft mounds against the whitewashed buildings and flutters around frosted iron light posts. The trees with their scraggly branches covered in white look like lightning—powerful even without their leaves for cover.

The airbus station buzzes with excitement. Festival goers bundled up in colourful winter coats, hats, and scarves file onto the buses. Some people wear traditional clothes. An Earthkin woman at the entrance wears a long, emerald-green cape with black satin trimming, and gold markings on her dark skin indicate her as an Ancestral Seer. She hands out charms for Carnity's blessing and says, "Strength of the ancestors." My companions thank her with bowed heads.

The Seer's dark-brown eyes latch onto me through the gleaming, beaded tassels of her head covering. She holds up her hand. The wide sleeve of her dress drops to her elbow, revealing a two-headed night snake coiled around her slender arm, basking in the vibration of her essence. My breath catches as the golden rings around her irises glow bright like sunlight. She shoos the heads of the snake away from her wrist and unhooks a charm from a bracelet.

"Seena walks in your shadow now," the Seer says. "You should be proud."

Taking my hands, she places Seena's ancestral charm in my palm and closes my fingers around it. Her touch is strong, and for one moment, it links me to the infinite flow of energy through the Karess. Her grip drops. The glow of her eyes fades, and she turns her smile to the other hédin travelling to Sii.

My group has moved on to buy tickets all except Rin. She counts out small pieces of saphrite in her palm. Looking up, a patient smile lights her face. "You ready?"

I roll the glass charm between my fingers. My essence runs wild inside me, and I do not wish to quiet it. My skin doesn't itch. But my mind is thrown by the mystery the Karess gave me through the Seer.

"Yeah." I look back at the Seer whose eyes have found me once more, and she nods to me.

I've always looked for someone else's pride, so I'm not sure I even knew I could be proud of myself.

39

RIN

Looking over the crystal waters reflecting the sunlight, I grip the side of the airbus. My knees are uneasy from being so high. Akinnera fades from sight as we sail through the clouds with the frigid air blowing through my hair. The academy stays in view a little longer. Loria, the first Protector, stares at me from the stain glass windows. She asks me her question again. Do you deserve my badge?

No. But I will.

My shoulders relax as I take a deep breath of sea-salt air.

The island of Sii drifts into view. Icicles dangle from the rocky bottom. Core energy emanates through cracks in the earth. The specks flow toward the sky—like snow falling in reverse. Long-stemmed purple snow blossoms cluster around the airbus station. Their velvety petals emit a soft, violet glow.

A rush of excitement washes over me as the airbus touches down. The other passengers crammed into the bus shuffle off and disperse into the crowd. Booths line the streets selling all sorts of trinkets, from stuffed animals, to candles, to jewellery. Larger tents sell full meals with a place to sit down and eat. Colourful streamers bridge the gaps between booths and lightstone lanterns set the streets aglow. A singer's voice floats over the crowd. Children rush past us, weaving through legs and around booths, headed for a candy cart. I wish Liam was one of those little boys right now, licking lollipops and laughing at his friends with sugar sprinkles adorning their faces.

"Meet back here at six o'clock and we'll watch the fireworks together," Niko says, clapping his hands.

Before I know it, Ace and Eliote have bounded off together, hand in hand, toward a ride. Niko, Johanna, and Jeff are already heading toward the food booths.

"Guess it's just you and me," Lance says. He stretches his hand out to me. "Would it be okay if I held your hand?"

A tingle spreads through me, down to my feet, enticing me to turn away. But he waits, patient, looking into my eyes. My hand twitches and I reach out. Wrapping my fingers around his hand sends warmth creeping across my skin. Lance's smile widens as he squeezes my hand tight. We move into the crowd, and he never loosens his grip, not even for a second.

I let Lance lead me through the festivities, taking deep breaths of his forest scent and smile knowing why that undeniable smoky undertone has faded a little. He lets me stop and look at whatever I like. When the crowd gets tight, I hold his arm with my free hand, pulling him closer to me. But his pace quickens as he spots something down the way, and a childlike gleam invades his eyes.

We weave through the people around us over to a booth with golden tapestries and tables set up with glittering paints.

"What's this?"

"It's a Lavarian tradition," Lance says, and sits us down at one of the tables. "We choose symbols to paint on each other's foreheads. We choose something that we think is the person's most admirable quality." He pushes a booklet of Lavarian symbols over to me.

"That's kinda nice." I flip open the book. "I think I'll give you—"

"No, no, we can't tell each other."

"Why?"

"Don't want it to go to our heads, do we? Lavarians are very big on humility."

"But how do I know you're not going to just write shit-stick on my head?"

"Well, because you're not a shit-stick. Now hold still, I have one for you."

He doesn't look through the pamphlet, just moves a pot of silver paint into the centre of the table and picks up a paintbrush. He dips the brush in the paint, taps the excess off on the side of the jar, and takes my chin in his hand. His touch is gentle but firm, with the smallest scrape of a calloused finger, steadying my face so he can work. Heat floods my cheeks, but I try my best to stay still as his paintbrush slips in clean strokes over my skin.

As he finishes and the paint dries, he bows his head to me and says, "May this strengthen your soul." He sets down the paintbrush. "Okay, your turn." He leans forward, grinning.

"Hold on, I haven't picked one yet."

"What, you're not fluent in Lavees?"

"No." I pick up the book and situate it right in front of his face so he can't see which one I pick.

All the options are so intricate with their swirling script, all fashioned to fit in a small space. Right away, I find one that fits Lance. *Tama ni orohan: The caring soul—one who is kind, helpful, and forgiving.*

"Okay, I've got one." I choose a sparkly black paint so that it will stand out for everyone to see.

I take his chin the way he took mine, resisting the urge to let my fingers wander across his chiselled jawline. He leans closer and I prepare to make the first mark—checking the booklet again, adjusting my grip on the brush, biting my lip. Just before I make the first mark, Lance laughs.

"Stop laughing at me. I've never done this before."

"I'm not laughing at you."

"Yes you are."

"Okay, I won't laugh." He presses his lips together and shuts his eyes.

I make the first mark. The paint shimmers on his golden skin. I try to connect my strokes with as much grace as possible, but the symbols don't come out as precise as the guide.

"Done," I say, wiping a stray drop of paint off my wrist.

"You didn't say it. Doesn't work if you don't say the prayer," Lance says with a wink.

"Oh, sorry." I bow my head. "May this strengthen your soul."

"Thank you. Now we're done."

"Do we have to pay?"

"Just a donation. What ever you can give. It all goes to the hospital."

I fish a copper saphrite from my pocket and plop it into the donation box at the entrance. I step out of the booth. As the chill sets in again in the open air, I turn back to Lance. He glances around to make sure no one is looking and slips twenty-five saphrite into the box. *Tama ni orohan.* He takes my hand.

We continue our aimless walk through the festival grounds, but don't get very far before someone calls to Lance. We turn as Lance's family runs up to greet him with hugs and laughter. His mother and sister have long black hair, sparkling brown eyes, and delicate black wings that look as if they were sewn out of satin. His father stands taller than the rest of the crowd and shares Lance's enchanting smile.

"I thought you guys weren't going to make it to the festival this year," Lance says.

"I begged them to come home early," his sister says. Her wings flutter as she talks, and her feet leave the ground for an instant. She looks about Liam's age.

"Things were pretty much wrapped up at the conference anyway, so here we are," Lance's dad says. His wings wrap around his wife and daughter, and he looks at Lance with kind eyes. It warms my heart as the family loves on each other.

Lance turns to me. "This is Rin. We go to the academy together." He smiles and waits for me to say something.

My heart stops mid beat and I've forgotten how to speak.

"Hi," I say, but it comes out like a question. I clear my throat. "Hello."

The next thing I want to do is introduce myself, but Lance already stole that bit of conversation material from me. So, bridging the gap of awkwardness I've created, I stretch my hand out and offer an Ironskin handshake to Lance's father.

"An Ironskin girl. What a pleasure. *Caatslaka Adasa,*" he says smoothly as he takes my hand. The Slyvic greeting slips into the cold air with a cloud of breath, a sweet sound to my ears.

"*Heerenada. Caatslaka Adasa,*" I say, thanking him and returning the greeting.

"My name is Levi, this is my wife, Ella, and my daughter, Chiara."

"Nice to meet you all," I say. Not a question this time.

"What year are you in, Rin?" Ella asks, giving me a light touch on the arm.

"First," I say.

"But she's on an advanced team so she'll be graduating early," Lance adds. "She's really talented." He captures me with a soft, brown-eyed gaze and I'm honoured to be complimented by him in front of his parents.

"That's very impressive. It's a tough school. Are you enjoying it?" Ella asks. The interest in her dark eyes relaxes me.

"It's been tough, that's for sure. And people don't like me much . . ."

Ella looks at me with gentle eyes. "From where I'm standing, I don't see anything not to like."

Her sweet comment seeps into my bones, but if she really knew me, she wouldn't be so quick to say that. My hand wanders to my forehead, tapping at the silky paint, face growing hot. "Lance told me you're an engineer."

Ella nods to confirm but before she can elaborate with details of her job, Chiara says, "Look at that. He actually thinks about us when he's away." She smiles cheekily at Lance.

"Of course I do," he says and tweaks her on the head with

his finger.

Rubbing the spot where he hit her, she says, "You guys did *tama hantoro*." She claps her hands together and looks straight at me, eyes gleaming.

"We did what?" I ask.

"Soul painting. Aw, it's so cute." Chiara scampers over to me, grabs my hands and whispers, "I can tell you what he wrote on you."

"Nope, okay, we're leaving now." Lance's face turns bright red.

"We'll let you two go then," Levi says through a laugh. "Don't get into too much trouble."

Lance grins, rubbing the back of his neck. Levi smiles back at his son and starts to usher the rest of his family away. But Ella pulls Lance aside.

"I am so glad that you are able to move on after Khalie," Ella says, putting her hand to Lance's face. "It took a bit of life out of you. It's back again."

Lance kisses his mother on the cheek and we wave goodbye. I can't get what Ella just said out of my head.

"Khalie, she—"

"Was my girlfriend," Lance says. "She's part of a dark time in my past."

His eyebrows draw together, crinkling my not-so-beautiful script on his forehead. Pain slips into his eyes, stealing his smile. He shifts his gaze away from me to set it on something off in the distance.

"I got messed up with a bad crowd a few years back." He breathes a laugh. "Drugs, parties, alcohol." He pauses and wrings his hands. He shifts his weight and lets out a breath. The air fogs around him.

"You don't have too—"

"I want to. I want to tell you." His words are soft, so distinct from the clamour around us. "Usually, Lavarian enhancements show up around age twelve, but I was already sixteen and still didn't have them. I tried to engage them so many times, so I thought I was unenhanced. I was high when they showed up. I was so out of it. I couldn't control them. The sky filled with clouds. It was so dark. Electricity surged around me . . . Khalie couldn't get away." His eyes drop to the ground, and he runs his hand over his face. "She died."

My heart aches. That amazing smile of his hides a lot, and I finally understand what he said to me the first day I met him, that he hates to see anyone get hurt.

"I could barely get out of bed for months," he continues. "When I did, I hated myself and took it out on my family. I ignored my sister, yelled at my mom, and disrespected my dad. But even though I treated them like trash, Chiara would still give me a hug every night and my mom still said she loved me. My dad patiently encouraged me to go to the academy. He said that even though I took one life, I could save a lot more."

Still not looking at me, Lance starts to walk again. I walk with him in his quiet for a moment. The sun has gone down and the pale green of the stars shines through the clouds.

"So that's why you have a Monitor?"

Lance nods. "I can control my enhancements now, but my essence is still overreactive, some sort of trauma response to the accident." He kicks up the snow like he's mentally kicking himself.

"You know what the worst thing is?" He stops short in the

centre of the cobblestone street, causing the group behind us to split apart and go around. "I really cared about her. And I'll never know how she felt about me, you know?"

Being the one left behind is something I know well. An ache so deep spreads through me. Even if Adrianne is right and my mother didn't want to leave me, it is still raw, it still hurts. I'll always wonder if she really loved me. "Yeah, I know."

Slipping his hand out of his pocket, I put it back with mine. I tug him along through the festival again. The smell of iidai leads me to a quiet area of town. I buy us two bowls and sit us down by a trickling stream running through an open square.

"Thanks for telling me," I say.

I want to tell you things, too, Lance. I really do. I want to know you and I want you to know me.

The deepest part of my heart wants that. It's going to take a while before my heart thaws and I'm able to access that part.

For now, I'm just going to have to sit with you.

Still focused on my noodles, I take his free hand to give it a gentle squeeze. He squeezes back.

"What happened to Mycul and Aris' cat?" I ask.

The smile I love warms his face. "He's living in my closet. I named him Ravi."

Tama ni orohan.

40

ELIOTE

Ace puts up with me all afternoon, patiently waiting in lines and insisting on paying for trinkets and games. But something is calling me away from the fun. A sick feeling in my gut keeps prompting me to look for Rin in this mess of people. I'm so familiar with her essence that I can spot it even though she's all the way across town. But each time I find her, her aura is peaceful for once, swirling in swift easy spirals around her shining soul.

"Want something to eat?" Ace asks, bringing me back to his sweet face.

"Yes, whatever is making that amazing spicy smell, I want to eat it."

Ace smiles. "Then we'll find it."

He takes my hand, and we follow the spicy scent that has

been driving me crazy ever since we stepped off the airbus. We find a small booth selling the vegetables and my mouth waters. An old Emberstead woman hunches over a cutting board chopping ruby-red fire peppers. Her long, red hair, salted with white streaks, is piled on her head and she sports a wrinkled smile as she chops and hums. She sweeps the peppers into a sizzling mixture of vegetables and gets to chopping weckler nuts for the final touch.

She fries the mixture to perfection and Ace exchanges ten saphrite for two plates. He hands one to me and the spice of the steaming vegetables stings my eyes. I take a bite.

It hits my tongue like the fire of the nine hells have been released in my mouth. "Oh . . ." I say through the mouthful of flaming veggies.

Ace has a mouthful, his lips are together, but he does not chew. His bottom lip pouts. "Mm . . ."

The heat spreads to my cheeks.

"Eliote," Ace mumbles through his mouthful. "Eliote, it's so hot."

I push what I have in my mouth down my throat. "Holy Zenta," I say.

Ace still hasn't swallowed, or even chewed his first bite. Tears stream from his eyes. "So hot," he says with a whimper.

I shovel in another bite. I chew and suck in cold air at the same time. Swallowing again, my insides twist. I stamp my feet in the snow like I have to pee and fan my mouth with my hand. All the while, the old woman cackles behind us. "That's why we call it Dien's Garden," she says.

With a grimace, Ace swallows his first bite, neck muscles straining. "Well," he says, his voice a whisper. "That was an experience. You don't have to eat that if you don't want to."

"I have to." My cheeks bulge with veggies. The skin inside my mouth is numb, or melted off, I can't tell. "You bought it for me."

Ace stares at me with wide-eyed intensity as I power through the last bites. The back of my neck is slick with sweat, my jaw munches and munches. Acid reflux in full force, and the skin of my digestive tract as raw as road rash, I drop the plate into a trash bin. I unzip my jacket to fan my armpits. "I did it, Ace. I did it."

"Yes, you did. You deserve a reward." Ace puts a hand on my shoulder to steer me away from the trash. "How about a plate of syrup-glazed fruit?"

"Yeah." I clutch my throat. "That sounds nice."

We shuffle into a line for fruit. As we inch closer to the front, a force builds around the city. It accumulates like it is regaining consciousness after a deep sleep. It is a groan in my soul, ancient, pulled out from the mire of death. I search through the crowd, but only smiles pass over faces, only laughter sails over the festival din.

I find the fruit in my hands, so I take a bite, trying to push the feeling away. As the sweet tangy flavours burst in my mouth, the ominous sensation clouds my mind like the void left behind after we slayed those beasts at the beginning of the year. Lost energy. Stale energy.

It is above the city, in the clouds, searching the city. A wisp of it wraps around my ankle. A brittle-bone crackle shunts through my soul. The stale, fleeting energy takes on the glow of a demon's eye. All of it streams in one direction. It centres on one starry soul protected by bird wings.

Tossing my fruit, I grab Ace. "We need to get to Rin." I

run, following her aura across town, keeping an eye out for the others as we go.

"Eliote, what's wrong?" Ace asks as we push through the crowd.

"Rin's in danger," I say. "Move," I yell at a group of drunk guys in front of us and they scatter, stumbling over each other.

The other night, Stephen used phrases like "things have changed" and "we need you to come with us now." Whatever he was talking about, I think it's happening. The energy that surrounds the city is burnt.

My heart pounds hard and the energy gets darker. With its uncanny glow, the emerald night sky is lost to me.

"What kind of danger?" Ace's aura spikes with a wave of navy-blue and catches up to me before his feet.

"I have no idea. We just have to get to her."

We find Rin and Lance in an area that doesn't have many booths, so it's a little less crowded. Thank the good light of Vin, the energy hasn't reached her yet. I need to talk to her alone, ask her about her secret meeting with her brother, get her out of the open. There, a dress shop. That will work.

"Rin," I call, trying to stay calm. "I want to show you a dress I saw in this shop. I think it would look great on you for graduation." I pull her away from the bench.

"I have to wear a dress to graduation too?" she asks through a mouthful of noodles. "I'm not even graduating,"

"Yes, Bird Brain." I drag her toward the store.

"Usually we just wear our uniforms to graduation," Lance says.

Ignoring him, I push open the shop door. A little bell jingles above as we walk in—it's like a gong crashing in my ears.

There's no one in the store except the employees. They're engaged in a conversation and don't pay attention to us. I pretend to browse through the dresses. My hands fumble through fabric. The force in the city chokes me, but I force the words out.

"Something's not right," I say.

Rin crinkles her nose as I hold up a dress to her. "Besides that dress and the fact that you pulled me away from a really cute guy?" She blushes.

She's got a point, but I play it out and continue to pretend to find the perfect dress.

"I'm serious. I think it has something to do with what Stephen was talking to you about."

"How do you know about that? *What* do you know about that?"

"Nothing, that's what worries me. I don't know what's happening, but you're at the centre of it." I clench a pink-satin dress in my fists. "It's happening now."

Rin's eyes widen. She puts her hands over her face and paces through the aisle. "Now?" she mutters. "It can't be happening now."

The aura shakes inside me. "There's something out there."

Stopping short, she stares out the window, frozen.

I move over to her and take her by the shoulders. With a jolt I say, "It's getting closer, Rin. You have to tell me what's going on."

"I don't know," she says, her tone a quick snap. "They can't be doing it already, they need me. But maybe . . ." She presses a palm to her forehead. "He said the moons wouldn't be wasted this year. Maybe they're doing something else. What do you see, Eliote? What do you feel?"

The aura around the city consumes me. It rips a scream from my throat. My body trembles into Rin. The shop keeper rushes behind me, the door opens, Lance and Ace surround me. Rin holds me with strong arms.

"Eliote, what's happening?" Rin asks.

"I–I feel death. A soul, it's broken. And it wants you. It needs you to do something."

For a moment, the force of darkness becomes me. All I am is rancour. All I desire is death. *No, I don't want it. This is not me.*

"It's going to be okay, I won't let it hurt you." Rin's voice flows through me.

I clasp my hands around her, shut my eyes, and take a deep breath. Coffee and cinnospice and iidai. I latch onto my trust in Rin and the sensations of myself.

My eyes burst open as I separate myself from the aura. It rips away from me but not far. "Rin, it's here." My sight bridges the gap between the aura and my body. "There. In that alleyway."

Rin's eyes grow wide, they are piercing, grey starlight, as the cloud of decaying aura smoulders behind her. She turns to look out the window, across the plaza, and to the accumulation of aura that only I can see.

"Rin, we have to get out of—"

"No," she says. "I can't leave." Looking back at me, her eyes fill with light, illuminating the silver paint on her forehead. The stream of light-blue aura that usually wraps so tight around her core breaks free and charges her being with seraphic energy.

41

RIN

Light swarms my eyes. It soothes darkness out of every corner. Every dark fabric is shining, every line is cutting, it paints Eliote's brown eyes amber. The life affinity presents itself to me and I grab it. It grants me energy willingly. Its claws are not greedy, it is open handed and freeing.

In the alley, a pair of gold eyes glow in the shadows. Disembodied pupils slink along the alley and peek into the square. The light reveals a hideous hédin figure, not much more than a skeleton wrapped in ghostly grey skin. The monster lifts a clawed hand and a red tongue parts his greasy lips. He takes a step forward, his back hunched, his steps lethargic, eyes fixed on a boy in the middle of the square. The boy is no older than four. He trails behind his mother and stops to inspect something in the snow.

My bones chill as the glowing threat takes another step forward. My heart buzzes with the urge to protect the boy, but it drops to my gut, filling me with nausea for all the times I didn't protect people—all the times I hurt people. Emotions flow through me, and I take control of their energy. I suppress the urge to push them aside. I let them bring me to life.

With a burst of speed, the monster leaves behind its lethargic steps and races toward the boy.

My heart pounds with a surge of energy that spreads through my body, prickling every inch of my skin. The energy inside me is responsive, making my movements exact. I let go of Eliote and burst through the doors of the shop and sprint across the square. I swoop over to the boy, wrapping him in my arms as I skid across the snow. I rush the boy over to his startled mother.

As I turn back to the monster, its eyes are trained on me. My spine tingles. It doesn't pay any attention to the boy, his mother, or anyone else in the square.

It charges at me with an eerie, wobbling gait.

I slam my fist under its crooked jaw, sending it high into the air. Jumping to meet the monster, I hammer my leg down on its back. It plummets to the ground, scatters the snow in a splashing wave, and craters into the cobblestone underneath.

I leave the demon in a disoriented heap and turn my attention back to my friends. To my horror, a monster just like the one I destroyed barrels down the street. A woman stands in its way. It wrenches its arm back and plunges its claws through her chest, digging it out again, dripping with blood. The thud of the woman's body hitting the ground churns my stomach as her essence coils to the sky. The monster leaps at Eliote. She yanks two daggers from her boots.

"Eliote," I scream.

The monster plummets onto her but she stabs her daggers into the demon, and they hit the ground. A savage grunt bursts from Eliote as she heaves herself off the ground, the monster clambering away. Ace encases himself in a glowing sheet of ice armour and hurls ice daggers at the monster.

"Rin, behind you," Lance yells.

I whirl around and the same monster I just packed into a cobblestone grave slashes a bony fist at me. It hits me in the stomach. I land hard against Lance, but he wraps his arm around me, and with a powerful swipe of his wings, lifts us both up into the air.

The chaos is quiet against the rush of blood in my ears and the wind beating against my face. Lance grips me tight. I am safe despite the screams below. The terrified festival goers are frantic ants scurrying for shelter. For a moment, up here, removed from danger, it's not my fault. I can see the Local Protectors join the fight; they should be able to handle this. But the innocent people falling dead in the street beckon me back down and the moment is over. The whole city is plagued with these horrific beings that are coming for *me* from all directions and cutting down anyone who gets in their way. One of them stops and points a knobby hand at me and Lance hovering over the square. It lets out a shriek.

"Hold on to me," Lance says.

The sky darkens and I wrap my arms around his chest just as he lets go of me. He flexes his fingers and a streak of lightning sparks his hand. Body tense within my grasp, he hurls the electricity at the monster.

Thunder claps.

A thrill pulses through me.

The bullet of energy spears the monster in the throat with an explosion of sparks. The monster crumples to the ground, seizing.

Lance swoops us down, and I hit the ground running back into my reality.

I swing my fists at my demons. Lance takes on another with a pool of electricity surging all around him.

Stephen's visit plays in my head. I roll to the left to avoid a strike. *The dual moons will not be wasted this year.* I dodge right. Is this why? Did Geret use the energy of the moons to create these things? To take me by force for not joining him? How could Stephen let this happen? And how are we going to fight these things off if they don't die? A monster swipes at me with a claw, sliming my face with some grey substance. I grunt and smash my leg into a demon, and he crashes into a lamppost.

The monster crawls back to its feet. Ace's ice shards don't do any damage, Eliote's daggers don't even break their skin, nothing breaks their skin.

Ironskin. And they all look the same. Clones?

Everything around me slows as I take the image before me and paste it next to a grotesque sketch in an ancient text that made its way into my apartment. Stephen has been involved in this for years. Years of secrets and planning all for this.

I spring away from the chaos.

The clones are moving but they can't be fully alive with their grey skin, glazed eyes, and the way they walk; they're caught in limbo, some hell between life and death. Geret and Stephen are playing a sick game, but if I'm right, and they are clones of the same dead Ironskin, then I just need to find one weak spot.

Two monsters come at me, clawing, punching, kicking, and snarling. I hit one monster in the gut, the other on the legs, the arms, and the back. Nothing. I smash one in the face. Nothing.

The life affinity hasn't faded for a second since I engaged it. Now, it blurs. My eyes clear and narrow in on one of the demons. Its neck burns red.

Of course. Lance's lightning bolt hit that first monster in the neck.

I lunge forward, reach out with both hands, and grasp its head. I twist it hard and cringe as the crack reverberates through my hands. The body goes limp, falling in a heap on the ground. It doesn't move again.

Another one charges for me, and I smash a fist into his jugular, taking him down.

"The neck is the weak spot," I yell to my comrades.

"Got it," Ace says, and freezes a monster's neck. It claws at the ice, squeals slipping out of its constricted throat. Ace swings his icy fist at its neck. The ice splinters. The head topples off the body and crashes to the ground.

As we clear the stream of horrors, Johanna, Niko, and Jeff-Ray come running up to us red faced and panting.

"What is going on?" Johanna grunts between heaving breaths. "Those things. What the hell are they?"

They all look at me with wide eyes, their confusion weighing on me. How do I tell them that these clones are here to drag me away so I can revive an entire nation to destroy their homes and families? Or are they to scare me, scare the world?

"We're not done yet, guys. Look." Lance points to the sky.

Johanna gasps. Jeff stands his ground with shaking hands. Eliote clasps her hand over her mouth to muffle a cry. The corners of Ace's mouth are drawn down in disgust.

"You've got to be kidding me," Niko exclaims, throwing his hands in the air.

On the other side of town, a clone towers over the buildings. It arches its back and roars to the sky. The ground trembles and reverberates through the soles of my shoes, creeps through my bones, and jolts my heart up to my throat. The wails of the people in the city set my teeth chattering and my head buzzes. All I can do is stare at it. This is a monster, a physical threat, but it feels like my life—ominous and terrifying, something I haven't handled so well in the past. I've failed before and I'm scared of failing again. But I'm not going to back down. I just have to keep going—face it head on.

With the roar blasting my eardrums, I take a step. That's all I have to do. One step, then another and another until I am running at full speed. My friends follow me. I don't trail behind them, they are behind me, supporting me. I set the pace and lead them across town.

Halfway through the city, we are ambushed by another pack of the man-sized clones.

"Keep going, Rin. You're the only one who can stop that monster." Lance pants, electricity coursing around his fingertips. "Johanna and Ace, stay with her. We'll take care of these ones."

I look back. Jeff anchors a demon to the earth with gravity manipulation and Eliote slashes her knife at its throat. Grey goop splatters her face. She furiously wipes it off.

"Go," she screams.

I can't waste time.

I keep running, quickening my pace. Down every alley, in every square, there are Protectors battling to keep the people safe. Johanna shoots out in front of me to protect me from a predator with a tornado of flames. Ace guards my side with an icy shield.

As we approach the ghastly giant, Johanna shouts, "You have to get to higher ground."

There are no stairs to the roofs in sight, so I am going to have to jump. I take a few steps back and ready myself. A rush of energy floods my body. I channel all my strength to my legs and jump, sending a shock wave over the cobblestone. Over the clones, the booths, up to the roofs. I land hard, kicking up the tiles, and let my adrenaline carry me back into a sprint across the roofs. Leaping from rooftop to rooftop, my legs don't slow.

I lock my eyes on the monster as he crashes through the city. Above, the moon that orbits the planet year-round glows silver against the blanket of dark-green sky. The second moon looms in front of the first with warm honey radiance. They shine over the Ironskin, sharpening the bones protruding from its slick skin. The Ironskin takes a thundering step and a swarm of moon beetles erupts from their hiding place. The buzz of their wings fills my ears as they circle the Ironskin, flashing bits of moonlight in every direction.

I leap over the gap between two buildings. The monster raises his fist and slams it down on the watchtower, scattering the beetles. I land my jump as the tower crumbles and shakes the ground, and the house beneath me trembles. My feet slip on the quivering tiles, and I tumble down the roof. I brace myself for the fall, but I slam into a sheet of ice. Beside me, Ace boosts himself with a pillar of ice. He grabs my hand and pulls me back up.

"You good?" Ace asks.

I nod.

Johanna launches herself up to the roof with a burst of flames.

"Move your asses," she yells and kicks the clone that followed her off the roof.

We sprint across the last rooftop and with one final explosion of strength from my legs, I propel myself at the giant and Ace shoots ice at its arms to try to keep it from knocking me off course. I fly straight toward it and grasp the skin, digging my nails into his shoulder. An acrid stench fills my nose as he thrashes and roars, and I hold on with all my might. Its muscles tense beneath me, flexing, relaxing, stretching, writhing.

Johanna hurls fireballs at the giant and the LPs below try to immobilize its feet in any way they can. I furiously throw punches at its neck, channelling every bit of energy I have into my strikes. But they still aren't strong enough and my feet slip across the decaying skin. The moment I have enough grip to get a good hit, a scream from below pierces my ears and the giant's enormous hand swats me off. Flying backward, flailing my arms trying to grab the monster again, I can't get a hold of him and plummet to the ground.

Frigid air whips my face, it stings my eyes, and tears spring forth as I resign myself to falling. A furious force wraps around me. It yanks me back up. For just a second, I catch Johanna's eyes. She stands strong on the tallest building, hands stretched out to me, holding me with invisible flame. She grimaces and with my body tethered to her through Mind Fire her voice swarms in my head.

GET IT TOGETHER AND LAND A HIT, IDIOT.

Johanna anchors my feet to the monster with her mind. I draw my arm back to strike at his massive neck. Something so exhilarating and so horrifying leaks out from the very depths of my soul. Something that I am not familiar with but know what it is right away as it clouds my mind with a hot grip. I've seen it in Stephen as if it was seeping out of his veins. I've seen it in Johanna, and it poisoned her.

I can't imagine how hard your heart would have to be to send these beasts into a town filled with people, filled with children. All this destruction is because I refused to help bring back Ironskins from the dead. But bringing them back to overthrow the Emberstead will only lead to more separation and hate. I might lose my friends because of it. I've already lost Stephen because of it.

I grind my teeth as anger overcomes me and I can no longer control the life affinity. My mind burns and my vision blurs to red. I lose control of myself. My eyes itch. My consciousness floats away as if I am watching myself slam my open palm into the giant neck. A sheet of electric red energy pulses over the entire body of the monstrous Ironskin.

My energy surges around him, tethering his spirit to mine. I scream as the being's soul is ripped from its body and channelled into my own. The Ironskin cries to me in inaudible, incomprehensible tones, filling me with its desires and pain. All his regrets spill through me like even his massive body beneath me couldn't contain them.

The pulsing stops and the monster ceases thrashing. His life force rattles through me, then tears away from my soul. All my energy slips away with it.

I held the black sweater in my hands. The pain in my head dulled to an annoying twinge that hit every time I looked at the fluorescent hospital lights. I would have preferred it to stay constant. I played with the hole in the sleeve, rolling the broken wool fibres between my fingers. My mother wore that sweater—a lot. I would come home from school, tired or upset about something, and she would hug me. She always smelled too clean, like detergents. She'd lean her head over mine, blond hair cascading over my face and tickling my ears.

My hands started to shake, hidden in the black sweater. The stinging, citric scent of hospital cleaning supplies assaulted my nose. She was still all around me, inside me. Face wet, body trembling, I shoved the sweater in the trash. Holding my breath, I pulled on the green sweater and a pair of sweats Oron brought for me.

Once dressed, I peered into the trash at the dark crumple of sweater. I left it there.

"Ready to go?" Oron asked as I came out of the bathroom. He held his hands together in front of him. The lines of his face were deeper than normal, but his anger had subsided to a simmer in his eyes.

"What time do you need to be at work?" I asked, clutching my sleeve, and lowered my eyes to the vinyl floor.

"I have some time."

"But what time?"

Oron's stiff sigh cut the air. But his next words were soft. "Four o'clock."

"What time is it now?"

"It's two thirty." Gentleness grew in each of Oron's answers.

I started down the hall. "And what time will Mrs. Dalaan bring Liam home?"

"She said she could get him home by five."

"I'll have to figure out something for supper. I should have some meat. I can thaw it before then."

"She's going to bring you something for supper—"

"No, I can cook—"

"She's bringing you food." Oron's massive hand rested on my shoulder before I could exit. He turned me around and held my coat open for me. I slipped my arms through the sleeves, wondering how it ended up with him. Did he have to go to Ralin's house to pick it up? Did Ace grab it when we left? There was a shoe print on the front and it smelled of Ease. I squeezed my thumb to keep from barfing. "Now, let's get you home, sweet girl."

My eyes stayed glued on the ground as he ushered me into a pay-cruiser, into our building, and my apartment. Oron gave me his echo so I could call him at work if I needed to, and to call Ace when I was ready. He made me drink a cup of water, sat with me until I had finished it, and turned on my space heater.

He left.

I turned each bolt on the door as his footsteps faded down the stairwell. With the last click, I was locked in. But not safe, not with me inside.

I shouldn't have done it. I'm so stupid. Idiot.

My feet began to pace. They patted over the wood floor in a consistent rhythm. The heater hummed in the corner. Before long, it was stuffy, and my head was filled with thoughts I hated.

I shouldn't be here. This world doesn't need me. Liam needs someone who is stronger, good. But me, Oron, we're all he has. I can't leave him like Mother.

I shut off the heater, opened the window, and let the damp, frigid air sting my face. The room cooled and so did my thoughts. Warmth and thought and feeling left my body in exchange for a cold void that was much more manageable. But that longing for nothing was what got me into this mess. I slammed the window shut, grimacing as tears threatened to be my undoing.

Hands pressed to my eyes, I took long breaths, focusing on the rush inside me and nothing else.

I dropped my hands to find Oron's echo flashing from the dining table. It flashed and flashed like a candle next to my parents' graves, taunting me—they're gone, flicker, flicker, and you're still here, flicker, flicker. I stood poker straight in the centre of the room, staring at the flashing echo.

I don't fucking deserve to be here.

The echo stopped flashing and a voice message played.

"Hey, Rin, it's Ace." There was a long pause, and a few of his breaths washed through the speaker. "I just wanted to make sure you got home okay. I-I'm sorry for what happened. I'm always here for you . . . Please eat something, okay?"

Silence swelled. I rubbed my arms.

A knock at the door sent my blood gushing through my veins. My eyes clouded with spots, my neck prickled, my heart pounded. *Liam.* I was paralyzed between the overwhelming need to wrap my arms around him and the need to protect him from what I had done.

The need to hold him won. I stepped to the door, almost tripping over my feet, fingers fumbling over the locks.

Liam got to me first. He latched on tight. "What happened,

Rinnaya?"

I ran my fingers through his hair. "Just got a little sick last night."

Mrs. Dalaan smiled at me, holding up a pot of soup. I shuffled to the side so she could come in, Liam still stuck to me, head on my stomach. I couldn't tell if Mrs. Dalaan knew I wasn't telling Liam the whole truth. I thanked her for the meal, and she said it was her pleasure. Her smile never faded. She squeezed my shoulder with an unfamiliar strength before she left.

I dished out two bowls of soup. The room was warm now that Liam was home. I didn't need the heater. The soup spilled soothing tones of spices and salt all around us. We sat on my bed, in the light of my flower lamp, and ate. I made sure to eat every last drop of that soup, for Ace. He was the only reason I was sitting there with Liam.

Liam slurped the last of his soup straight from his bowl. Wiping his mouth with the back of his hand, he took a slow breath, eyes on the green patchwork flowers. "You do a good job. I love you very much, Rinnaya."

For a moment, I thought I was going to cry. My eyes prickled, no, they itched. Heat filled my face. He always knows what to say.

As Liam snuggled into me, I wrapped my arm around him and leaned my head on his. My arm rose and fell with his breaths. The void inside me was filled. Even though it was fleeting, I clung to the moment, to Liam. My head stopped reeling. I rubbed Liam's arm, allowing whatever filled me to pour onto him.

I blinked and the flowers of my quilt were red.

I blinked and the flowers of my quilt were green.

Just some lingering Ease in my head.

The affinities were so out of reach. They seemed so powerful, so ominous, that I never thought they could show themselves with such gentleness, especially not an affinity likened to a demon.

There was movement at the window. It wasn't raining, so it wasn't just water running over the window, and it wasn't snowing.

Liam sat up. "Hey, what's that?"

We both crawled over to the window. On the other side of the glass was a little beetle crawling along the sill. Its wings twitched, casting off a flicker of light. Purple and green swirls covered its body. It crawled closer and closer to me.

"It likes you." Liam laughed and snuggled back into me.

Heavy curtains drape around me as I lay in a bed of clean linens. Am I back in my little apartment and Liam is on the other side of the curtain? The air bites my nose with the scent of cleaning products. No, I'm not back home with Liam—that smells like coffee and spice and old wood. After a few blurry glances around the room, the Akinnera crest becomes apparent on one of the curtains.

My mind plays through my memories. Lance's warm hand holding mine, his family. The little boy and his mother's horror. The screams, the monsters, the thrill of energy. The death affinity stripping the colossal Ironskin of its soul.

My body tenses as if the Ironskin's life force is still coursing through me. The air in my lungs stops moving and my head swims in the Ironskin's cries.

I gasp, concentrating on the rise and fall of my chest and the air slipping through me. I grip the bar on the side of my bed until the memory dims.

The curtains are pushed aside, and Johanna pokes her head around the fabric.

"Hey," she says in her usual flat tone. "I thought I heard you shifting around in here."

She comes over to sit by me. She pours me a cup of water from the pitcher on the stand next to me. I drain the cup, still clenching the bar.

"So, what happened?" I ask.

Johanna's face stays in its neutral position between apathy and annoyance. "Well, after you got your shit together, you took that thing down with one hit. I don't know, with Demon Palm, I guess."

"Yeah, I got that much."

"Shut up, I'm talking." She glares at me. "It took everything out of you, and well, I was kind of beat, so I let you fall. Thankfully, Lance made it in time to catch you." She winks at me but keeps talking. "When you took the big one out, all the little shits went out too. The Local Protectors took us back to the academy personally—they send their thanks. Headmaster Evelyn wants to talk to you about what happened. She sent me to come get you." She waves a hand. "But take your time."

Johanna leans back in her chair, arms folded across her chest, feet up on the bed. "You were amazing, by the way."

I can't believe she got those words to come out of her mouth. "Yeah?" I say with a chuckle. "How amazing?"

She throws her head back. "Ugh, can't you just take the compliment?"

"Fine. Thank you. And thank you for having my back. I wouldn't have been able to do it without you."

A subtle flinch shakes her curls. My comment draws out a pause. Eyes itching to turn away, I keep them focused on Johanna, on everything about her that I had forgotten.

"You bet your ass you wouldn't." She drums her fingers on the arms of her chair.

Leaning my head back on the pillow, I close my eyes. A smile sits on my lips and my face is relaxed. Even though yesterday was terrifying, and the Revival looms over me, I am okay in this moment.

"Rin," Johanna says.

I open my eyes. "Yeah?"

Johanna stares off into space. "That rumour about you and Tōmas."

My chest tightens. "What about it?"

"I never believed any of the rumours. But I never asked for your side either. So . . ." She turns to me. "Was it true?"

I curl my fingers around the blanket, running my thumbs along the threads. "Sort of. We didn't do it, like everyone was saying. He just tried to take things further and when I told him to stop, he kept pushing."

Johanna sighs and her brows tighten.

"I kept resisting, and he said some really . . . some really shitty things. He made up that rumour himself." I shake my head. "It wasn't even at a party. It was at Dawnranfet."

"What an ass."

With the heat in my face and the pounding of my heart comes pressure to my lips, a cage around my head. But just letting Johanna know the truth, sharing what I went through in simple terms, one of Tōmas' demon hands is pried away. And she didn't believe the rumour. She had my back even when I didn't know it.

The calm inside me is twisted in a knot as I enter Headmaster Evelyn's office. Evelyn smiles, graceful as always in a burgundy pantsuit and her hair bouncing in ringlets around her face. Gold bangles clink together on her arm as she ushers me into the warmth of her presence. But there is cold behind her. Brand stands in the corner of the room, looking out the frosted window. The chill of familiarity is always with her. She turns to me as Evelyn tells me to sit.

"You're here," I say, clutching my chest.

Brand crosses her arms, the leather of her jacket scrunching. "Yes," she says, looking down at the ground. "The case they had against me was not strong."

"I have so many questions. I was worried that I would never see you again."

Evelyn clears her throat. "There is a lot that needs to be explained, Rin. Take a seat, please."

I plop into one of the leather armchairs, my eyes fixed on Brand's perfect, tan face with the little cluster of freckles beneath her eye. The fireplace crackles behind me.

Evelyn sits at her desk across from me. "The first thing I think we should discuss is—"

"You're Ironskin," I say. Brand's grey eyes find mine. "Why didn't you just say so. I mean, I knew it the first time I saw you. Others might not make the connection but—"

Evelyn glares at me with one eyebrow raised. She steeples

her fingers. "As I was saying, the first thing we need to discuss is your connection to the Revival."

Brand turns herself back to the window. She props one hand on a firestone rifle in a holster on her hip. The knot inside me twists tighter, a million questions at the tip of my tongue.

"Brand was at your Registration as a Guardian representative, so she knew about your affinities from the beginning. She knew Geret was on the lookout for an Ironskin with dual affinities, so she kept track of your application. One of the reasons we put your team together was so we could keep a closer eye on you and be sure of your whereabouts. We'd hoped that we would be able to protect you here, but we failed. Last we heard, they were still figuring out aspects of the ritual."

My gaze shifts between Evelyn's calm at her desk to Brand's straight back. "Did you know about Stephen's visits?" I ask.

Brand's head twitches to look over her shoulder. "We knew he contacted you at the beginning of the year. But were there other visits?"

"The night of the formal," I say, looking down at my hands. "Stephen met me at the Kava Guard with Geret and another woman, Adia."

The two women exchange a look. Evelyn leans back in her chair with one hand propped under her chin. The only sounds in the room are the fire crackling and the bubble of a fish tank behind Evelyn. Maybe they'll punish me for meeting someone after curfew.

"This isn't the way I wanted things to happen," Brand says. She turns to me, but her face looks away. "I was going to tell you everything. Before Ironskins started disappearing, I thought establishing a team for you here would help if Geret contacted you. I hoped you would feel supported enough—"

"I was going to leave." I dig my nails into my knees. "Why wouldn't I want to be connected to my people?"

Barbed wire, locked doors, and handcuffs. It's like Brand puts those handcuffs on herself and locks a door between us. She grips the firestone rifle; does she want to use it against me, or is it just a security measure she's used to? There are no lines on her face to tell her feelings, not a frown or a furrow.

"Rin." Evelyn's voice is lowered, softer, and it makes my stomach turn. "The city of Sii is indebted to you for your act of bravery in defeating the clones. Your heroism is acknowledged. But if Geret is willing to destroy a city, then being where Geret can get to you puts you and others in danger."

A silver fish swishes behind Evelyn's head. Every thought from the past year slips into my mind, filling my head with a deafening buzz. I pop my fingers on one hand, the other remains a fist. "I-I can't leave."

I have to become a Guardian. For Liam. He needs me to succeed.

A crease forms between Evelyn's eyebrows. Her brown eyes are full of understanding, but it does not spill into her words. "I have requested a pass of absence for you. Brand works for an organization that will protect you. She's going to take you where you can be safe."

"No, I can't leave."

"Cloning is a taxing process." Evelyn slips on gold-rimmed spectacles and selects a book from the shelf behind her. "The process was mere speculation until now. Scholars believed it would take the combination of life affinity abilities and Mind Fire."

Flipping through the book, she comes to a page about

cloning. Evelyn taps her finger over the text. "The most likely scenario is that The Revival has an Ironskin-Emberstead halfie working with them. They would have had to sacrifice one of his people to be cloned. Which means they needed a good reason to do so."

"The Revival Ritual," Brand says to me. "It needs someone who has control over the life and death affinities. But before yesterday, you hadn't engaged it. We think Geret wanted to force you to engage the death affinity so that you can start to control it. And as someone with the death affinity, he knows you will have to learn or it will destroy you. I will help you control it, in a safe place."

My heart pounds as Evelyn slides a pass of absence card across the desk. A tear slides down my cheek. I dash it away and snatch the card. "We need to get Liam."

"By law you cannot be with your brother until you have completed your first year of essence training."

"Fuck that." The tears are too many to wipe away. "I'm not going anywhere without my brother."

"We'll get him," Brand says. Evelyn casts a disapproving look at her. The line of Brand's jaw tightens, her eyes meet mine, and she holds my gaze. "We will make sure he is safe, I promise."

"Fine, where are we going?" I ask.

"That's classified information. I'll inform you more when we get there."

A deep groan escapes me, and I hide my face in my hands.

"We will tell your team the important details today. Brand and Hans will escort you to Senn to pick up your brother tomorrow."

I open my mouth to protest.

"Our decision is final," Evelyn says, and I am dismissed for class.

My breaths are short and ragged as I leave.

The door eases shut behind me, but Evelyn's voice still makes it through. "You need to tell her, Brandy. More than ever, you both need your family."

Turning back, my hand reaches for the doorknob, but it freezes. *Tell me what?*

42

JOHANNA

I WAIT IN THE LOBBY, trying to ignore the regular morning chatter through the halls and footsteps down the stairwells. I press my hands to my ears. Rin should be down here soon, the team too, and we'll all say goodbye. It will be over quick, and we can get back to training.

As I let go of a breath, my knees bounce. What's taking them so long? Rin's supposed to leave in five minutes. My hands shake for no apparent reason, and I clench the arms of my chair.

From the boy's dormitory, Lance comes into the lobby. Evelyn said we would start class late so the team could say goodbye, but Lance should be headed to class. He has his hands in his pockets and keeps his distance. He paces with twitchy wings. Every time he comes close, he ducks his eyes even though I stare right at him.

"Sucks, huh?" I say when he gets close again.

Finally looking at me, he stops pacing. It takes a moment for him to register what I'm talking about but then he sighs. "Yeah," he says and comes to sit in the chair next to me.

We sit, quietly waiting for Rin. Lance shifts a few times as I watch him out of the corner of my eye. He chews on his thumbnail. All the students have dispersed to classes now, letting the quiet settle in. Lance's brows draw together like his thoughts are pulling at them.

"She's got to come back," he says.

I'm not sure if this comment is for me or for himself, but his determination spurs me to reply.

"She's *going* to come back. I don't care what anyone says, we'll make sure she does."

We exchange a glance. Lance nods, then leans forward, propping his elbows on his knees. I think I like this guy. He knows what he wants. Of all things, he wants an emotionally stunted, stubborn, boney, Ironskin girl. Good for him.

I pity him though. She's a pain in the ass.

Brand and Hans come in and sit by the window on the opposite side of the lobby, but Rin still doesn't show up. My hands twitch on the arms of my chair—what the hell is wrong with me? It's like my essence is flowing too fast, even though I know it's not. I can't seem to settle down so I channel the extra energy to bounce my foot.

Five past ten.

I push myself off the couch, leaving Lance and the instructors in the lobby, storm up the stairs and down the hall to Rin's room.

I stop in her wide-open doorway, my feet unwilling to step inside. Rin stands by her bed folding a shirt. Her eyes are glassy, her hair hangs limp around her face. Words get stuck in my throat. I've seen this look on her face too many times now. Lifeless, washed away by too many bad things to think about.

Eliote is bustling around the room, packing the rest of Rin's things for her. She looks up for a second and drops a pair of boots in the suitcase before grabbing my arm and pulling me out the door without Rin noticing.

"This is really eating her up," Eliote says once we're out. Her voice is as level as always, but her eyes are red.

"Yeah, well . . ." I cross my arms in an attempt to convince Eliote I don't care that Rin is leaving.

Eliote stares right at me, waiting for something.

"What?" I snap. "What are you staring at?"

"You can't be okay with this. Not after everything that's happened," she says, and closes the door.

Eliote focuses her glittering eyes right at my chest like she's checking out my breasts, not searching my aura. I feel ugly under her gaze, standing next to her annoyingly silky hair and perfect, sandy skin. I hate that she knows what's going on inside me.

"I know you're scared, Johanna," she says, taking my hand.

With a roll of my eyes, a tear tumbles down my cheek and I give her hand a squeeze. "I didn't want her here in the first place, and now I don't want her to leave." My lip quivers as I try to laugh it off. "Life is such a bitch," I whisper, and another tear slips from my eye.

Eliote flings her spider arms around me. "Yeah, she is," she says. "But you're not losing Rin, and you're not here alone. Okay?"

I try to nod and swallow my tears, but her grip on me is so tight that all I can do is hug her back. Loosening her python grip on me, she wipes her own tears with the back of her hand.

I can't tell her how much that hug meant to me, but I know she knows, and I think I'm okay with that.

"Make sure the guys are down there to say goodbye. I'll get Rin," I say.

With a final, teary look, Eliote smiles and heads down the hall to get the guys.

It takes a few more wipes than I would like to clear my face of my tears. With a deep breath I open the door.

Eyes on the floor, careful not to look at Rin's eyes, I tie my hair back and say, "Why aren't you packed?"

"I'm almost done," Rin says. The energy in the room shifts as she chucks a book into her bag.

"Come on, you're dragging this out. You're being stupid."

"Ah, so you've come to give me a pep talk."

I look up just high enough to see a smile slip onto her lips.

"Well, is it working?"

"Oh yeah, you're super encouraging."

For once her sarcasm warms me, giving me something normal. It calms the jitters inside me, allowing my hands to take a break from shaking. I move over to help Rin fold the last of her clothes. Even as we finish, I haven't found the words to express what I'm feeling.

"Lance is waiting downstairs. You'd better get your ass down there and say goodbye."

"I have to pack my pictures." She motions behind her.

"I'll get them." I clear the lump rising in my throat. "Don't worry."

Rin taps her fingers on the edge of the suitcase, eyes fixed on something—I don't know what but it's not me.

"Okay," she whispers.

She stalks to the door in her dusty, old boots and over-sized green flannel. Turning back to look at me, her eyes aren't so cold. I nod to her, and she heads down the hall.

Gritting my teeth to fight the tears, I handle the pictures of her family with the utmost care. The picture of her parents is from their wedding day. Peter smiles at Cassy in her red, lacy wedding dress. He holds her close at the waist, and she leans her head on his shoulder, her eyes closed, a soft smile touching her lips.

Mom has a similar picture of her and Dad by her bed. It always made me happy to see the two of them together, to remember them as a "them" and not just my mom nagging me about repelling my father's spirit.

I tuck the pictures away in the suitcase and snap it shut. I sprint down the hall to my room to grab my memory-tech. We'll need something to hold onto while Rin is gone.

43

RIN

If Geret and Stephen continue their attempts to bring me to their side, then anywhere I go, I'll put people in danger. The thought screams at me as I make my way down my hall for the last time. Morning classes have started leaving the halls quiet, but it just makes my head so much louder. My fingertips are numb, and my heart might as well be on fire. Reaching the staircase, the clamour of thoughts and uncomfortable sensations in my body fade, replaced by a kind, sweet voice behind me.

"You leavin'?"

Adrianne leans against her doorframe, still in her pyjamas, hair hanging in tangled strands all around her.

Her comfortable presence draws me in and I take a few steps toward her, but I pull up short and cross my arms in front of me.

"Hey," she says, "Don't freeze me out like that." Her

eyebrows furrow and her bottom lip pouts a bit. Her glittering green eyes pierce my armour. My arms drop to my side and I take a step closer.

I know Adrianne is someone I can talk to, someone I can be completely honest with. She's taught me so much this year and all I do is repay her with silence. Pathetic.

"Sorry I won't be at your graduation," I mumble.

Adrianne's pout turns up into a smile and she chuckles. "Nothin' you can do about that."

I want to smile but it takes too much energy. I'm not sure if I can get through the rest of my goodbyes if I use any now. Adrianne's face contorts into a frown with my failed effort.

"This is a really tough situation. There's nothing fair about it," she says.

She could say that a million times and it still wouldn't express how much I hate this. My heart pounds in my chest, burning again, I wish I could cut it out and leave it with her.

"I should probably—"

"Oh shit, I almost forgot," Adrianne says, and runs back into her room.

She rummages through a pile of papers and textbooks on her desk, then finds what she's looking for under her med-kit. She comes back over to me and dangles a little, gold chain in front of my nose. On the chain is a delicate triangle filled with a milky white stone.

"I want you to have this." Adrianne unclasps the chain and drapes it around my neck. "This is one of my favourite necklaces, and I thought it would look nice on you."

"Adrianne, I can't take this," I say.

"You can, and you will. Because part of it is yours."

"What do you mean?"

"The stone is a piece of the curestone I used on you."

My fingers gravitate to the little triangle. The stone is cool on my fingertips. In the centre, the grains of the stone swirl a little darker than its surroundings.

"I know it's kind of weird to literally carry your pain around your neck." Adrianne scratches her head, leaving a few strands of hair sticking up. "But I think it's good to remember that you can beat your pain, hey?"

I nod, my eyes prickling with tears. "I think so too."

Adrianne shrugs. "Just a little something to remember me by," she says and gives me one of her death-grip hugs. "Now get out of here before we both start blubbering." She gives me a gentle nudge toward the stairs and waves me off while wiping her eyes.

"Thank you, Adrianne," I say and try to swallow the lump growing in my throat.

In the lobby, I ignore my instructors and head straight to Lance, who's dressed for combat class.

"So, I guess this is goodbye." I keep my face neutral to prevent it from revealing my tears. "They're sending me away before I could hate the arena," I say, but the joke hits my ears like a rock.

"We'll see each other again soon, don't worry," he says.

"I'm not so sure."

"Hey, don't talk like that."

"No, don't you get it? If I'm a target, then everyone I know is a target. I don't want you to get hurt." My face did so well hiding it, but my mouth ran off on me. "I couldn't live with myself if you got hurt. I can't come back."

Lance takes my hands and pulls me close. He slips his arms around me and holds me. I can't put my arms around him because I don't want to know what that would feel like in case I never see him again. It would be another thing to miss about him. So, I lean my head on his chest, listening to his heartbeat, breathing in his smoky forest scent.

"Just stay safe then." Lance's chest rises with a long breath. "I want you to come back. Only when it's safe." He pushes away to look at me.

Tears spring from my eyes and I clasp my hand over my mouth to keep from sobbing. I'm so scared of leaving and I'm so scared to stay. My mind is such a mess that his words are hard to take. I hide my face in my hands, but Lance pulls them away and kisses me on the forehead. His kiss sends warmth through me, locking my joints into place unwilling to move. "Rin, it's okay to cry," he whispers.

Dropping my hands back to my sides, Lance holds me again, and his sweater soaks up my tears. I let them leak all over him, but footsteps pierce my foggy mind from across the lobby. As my team approaches, I wipe my face with my sleeves and rub the itch in my eyes.

"Shouldn't you guys be heading to class?" I say.

With my palms still pressed to my eyeballs, Niko comes over, nearly knocking me off my feet as he engulfs me in a hug. "You kidding me? And let you leave without saying goodbye. I don't think so."

Aw man. I was just starting to get to know this guy. At the beginning of the year I never thought he would be on my side.

Niko lets go and Jeff gives me a bigger, gentler hug.

Eliote embraces me, crying enough for the both of us. "How am I supposed to sleep without your stormy spirit on the other side of the room?"

I don't know how I'm going to sleep without her in the same room either. I think she might be the only reason I slept at all.

Ace wraps his arm around me, "Stay safe, 'kay?" he says, his voice choked.

Once we've said all our goodbyes, Brand comes over to break up the huddle.

"We really should be going, Rin," she says.

The sight of her brings a sickening red to the corners of my vision. I snap my eyes shut to make it disappear. As I open them again, they fall straight on Lance. He takes my hand and gives it a final squeeze.

I memorize his face and stick the memory in the locked box of my heart. I hide the key away in the dark expanse of my mind, only to be dug up again when the time is right.

"Wait," Johanna says as I turn to leave. "Let's take a memory."

"I didn't take you as the sentimental type," Niko says with a chuckle.

Johanna pushes us all into a cluster. "Get over it, Niko," she says. "Just the team."

I nod.

Johanna hands her memory-tech to Lance. Ace and Eliote pull me into the middle and wrap their arms around me. Niko and Johanna slide in close beside them and Jeff drapes his arms around all of us from the back, poking his head between me and Ace. A laugh bubbles through me, taking the burn of my heart away.

The memory-tech clicks.

Johanna grabs the tech back from Lance and taps in a command. The tech beeps, spitting out six copies of the memory. She hands one to each member of the team. Coming to me, she hangs on to the last copy. She grips it between her fingers, staring at it, crinkling the edges.

My heart thuds in my chest. I'm not small next to her anymore. I don't have to defend myself against her.

She hands me the picture.

I reach for it.

This image, not the physical one clenched between Johanna's fingers and mine, but all of it—my hand, her hand, connected by this team—will be seared into my memory forever.

On the way to Senn, Brand and Hans take turns pacing the corridor of the train. I hate the thought of explaining all this to Oron and Liam, so I focus on seeing their faces again. Liam's dimpled smile comes to mind. And then his voice.

I love you very much, Rinnaya.

Registration's gonna be ok, Rinnaya. I'll be with you.

He always knows what to say.

A tingle crawls up the back of my neck.

When Liam was six, he said something strange to me, strange and beautiful. *You have flowers inside you, Rinnaya.*

In one of his letters, he drew a garden, said it's what comes to mind when he thinks of me. There was a bird in the garden.

My mind puts Eliote and Liam side by side. *Bird Brain.* The two faces squint their eyes and tilt their heads to the side.

Spirit sight. Liam has spirit sight.

The Ritual is ineffective without the blood of an Ironskin with spirit sight, Geret said.

Brand eyes me. She leans forward, leather jacket scrunching. "What's wrong?"

My lower lip shakes. "We need to get to Liam."

It's dark as we pull into the station. The gritty scent of wet pavement fills my nose the second the doors open. Sour garbage and the intoxicating aroma of Ease swirl around me as Brand hails a pay-cruiser. We pile in and I clutch my head in my hands, nauseous from the lurching ride through centre city and the memory of the last time I rode in one of these.

"Something's wrong," I say, getting out of the cruiser.

Brand stops and scans the area. Her curls are heavy with rainwater and stick to her face.

A streetlamp flickers above us. With a pop, the lightstone bursts, raining down bits of stone. Not unusual, but paired with the deathly silence, it makes the eerie streets even more haunted.

"I'll take a look around the corner. Brand, you take the rear. Rin, stay put," Hans says.

Hans manoeuvres around the corner and Brand takes a ready stance. Core-energy hubs hum, the rain picks up, my heart pounds.

Dim light slips into the night from my apartment window, a person passes by, blocking the light—too big to be Liam too small to be Oron. A freezing drop of water slips down my neck past my collar, chilling my chest. My body tenses.

A hooded figure drops from the shadows of a balcony. He lunges toward us.

Brand turns, spraying water from her curls, and sprints at

him, moving like an electric shock. Her feet move faster than anyone I have ever seen. Ironskin fast.

She leaps, flipping in the air, and crashes her leg down on the man's shoulder.

More phantoms emerge from the shadows, surrounding us. One grabs my shoulder. I spin around to slam my elbow to his temple, but the strike doesn't faze him. He grabs me again. I rip myself away from him. I throw punch after punch, my fists numb from the cold, but he takes every hit. He must be Ironskin. The Revival is here for me and my brother.

I need to get to Liam.

A scream tears through the night.

"Liam?" I whirl around. Two Revivalists drag Liam out of the building. I lunge forward with all my strength, but someone's fist slams into my gut and I tumble backward.

"Rin, don't do it. Don't go with them," Liam cries. He kicks and thrashes his arms, but his efforts are in vain, and they drag him out of sight.

"No!" My heart rips inside me, drawn with Liam into the dark.

I spring to my feet, but the Revivalist that knocked me down is still in my way. I clench my fists, grit my teeth, and engage the life affinity. A burst of energy waves through the alley, and the light from my eyes pierces the shadows.

I raise my fist and slam it into the Revivalist's face. He flies back, flipping head over heels, and slams into the windshield of a beat-up cruiser. Just as the glass shatters, he pulls himself up out of the wreckage and launches himself into the air above me. I roll out of the way in time to block a lightning-fast kick. I grab his cloak. Pulling him toward me, I knee him in the stomach and throw him into a lamppost.

Someone comes behind me and I kick my leg back. Another is at my side. I seize her by the throat and throw her into the one behind me.

I have to get to Liam.

Someone hits me from the side, and I land face down in an icy puddle. I grunt and energy rips through my body, forming my wings. They crash into the Revivalists as they swarm around me. I knock them back, but a small, spherical object lands at my feet. It cracks open, letting knockout gas spill into the alley. My assailants drop to their knees, coughing and wheezing.

I heave a ragged breath. The gas burns as it fills my lungs and my wings dissipate, jolting my body with the return of energy. The shadows leak back into the alley.

My knees give way and my body crumbles to the ground as the gas rages through my lungs. "Liam," I whisper, choking on the bitter smoke.

Heavy boots slosh through the puddle I lie in. Rain pelts my body. A man wearing a gas mask kneels beside me.

He lifts my chin.

Through the visor of the mask, familiar eyes stare at me— grey, soulful eyes, sunken and kind. My father's eyes. But how could that be? He's dead, Stephen is against me, and Liam has been taken from me. Nothing good could be caught up in this mess.

As I stare into the face of a dead man, the night, the cold, the gas, takes me. But it does not take my clarity. Nothing will stop me from getting to Liam. Not this. Not now. Not ever. I gave up on him once. I won't do it again.

GLOSSARY

SLYVIC PHRASES

BEASTS

Noltwyn Alzuke – Black-winged Alzuke
Nodaha downfōst – Horned death beast

MARTIAL ARTS

Dawntimdato – Deadly Discipline (the Emberstead discipline)
Feeltens – Wind Palm (the Lifeblood discipline)
Fōsttimdato – Beastly Discipline (the Beastblood discipline)
Masstimdato – Military Discipline (the Lavarian discipline)
Noladakatz – Flowing Hits (the Nytrue discipline)
Oalande – All Leg (the Earthkin discipline)
Selhet – Calm Hand (the Fyrra discipline)
Shodahet – Shadow Hand (the Luminee discipline)
Telando – Eight Limbs (the Ironskin discipline)

Seya le kaset lon Illyson – Way of the Illyson long sword
Set fassoa – Stance

MISCELLANEOUS WORDS AND PHRASES

Caatslaka adasa – A heartfelt hello
Caatslaka adasa de seya le retnolada hold eekala – Welcome to the way of the frozen mind
Deshna ownoloda tens – Demon Palm
Deshna ownolada tens dentreyna ee – Demon Palm steals life.

Dawnranfet – Death Brawl

Heerenada – My gratitude (thank you)

Heerenada, Rin. Yet tuyonna shietz – Thank you, Rin. Now a power strike.

Hédin – The enhanced nine lineages

Otan sho com tuyo com slyv, otan kin tuyonne, otan caat tuyonne tiho – Our skin as strong as iron, our blood stronger, our hearts stronger still.

Ee comtuyo en down comtuyo – Life affinity and death affinity

Eeshna ownolada tens – Angel Palm

Eeshna ownolada tens treyda ee tor pam keh odadown – Angel Palm sacrifices life for a person who is dead.

LAVEESE PHRASES

Tama hantoro – Soul painting

Tama ni orohan – The caring soul—one who is kind, helpful, and forgiving.

FIRTŌN PHRASES

Fenlach calaikah – Iron wretch

Nima – Grandmother

Nipan – Grandfather

OTHER

Vishal – A marking specifying a Beastblood's beast form

ACKNOWLEDGMENTS

When I started writing *Moon Beetles*, I never expected it to look so different in the end. By that I mean with this beautiful cover, elegant formatting, and a story that still makes me cry. Without the help of so many talented and loving people, this book would not have been possible.

I want to start by thanking my best friend in the world. My brother. You were the first to see this book and the only stamp of approval I needed. Thank you for always listening to me babble about beetles, beasts, and essence affinities. Mom, you helped me keep going on the days when I thought my head was going to explode and my heart was going to crack down the middle. Thank you for catching my tears. Dad, thank you for all the nights you prayed for me and kept me strong and for believing in me every step of the way. Also, thank you for encouraging me to take breaks. I needed that.

To my critique partners, Dani Abernathy and Sorche, thank you for taking the time to wade through early drafts with me. Working with both of you was where I really felt myself grow as a writer for the first time. To my friends who were willing to read my words and answer all my questions, I hope you know how much that means to me.

To those of you who took a chance on me to beta read or ARC read, thank you a million times over. Taking time out of your day to read a stranger's work and then give meaningful feedback gives me hope for humanity. I'm also thankful that it was an opportunity to reconnect with people in my past. You are always in my heart.

Elle Fort, thank you for your meticulous comments, attention to detail, and encouragement. All those long messages back and forth, helping me sort through my ideas and plot, enabled me to be more confident in my storytelling. I am continually amazed by your willingness to help in any capacity.

Julia Scott, you helped me before I even hired you, answering my questions about indie publishing and laughing over writing memes. I am so glad you took on the task of formatting my words to look so beautiful because I would not have hair if I had done it myself.

Finally, thank you to my cover designer, Franziska. Life got in the way, and we had ups and downs, but I am so grateful that you stuck with me and worked so hard. The cover is beautiful. You are a one-of-a-kind talent.

ABOUT THE AUTHOR

B. Joyce moved around a lot growing up. The movement made it into her blood, and she has never lived in the same house for more than four years. For now, she lives in the woods, by a lake, with her parents, her brother, and their cats. B has taken her time to get to know her path in life, first with a quick jaunt through the scientific realm of psychology and biology, but went quickly back to artistic endeavours. Alongside her writing, she takes care of her mom, who suffers from a rare autoimmune disorder. Between writing and caretaking, she can be found playing videogames, drawing, and taking long walks.

www.ingramcontent.com/pod-product-compliance
Lightning Source LLC
Chambersburg PA
CBHW072034190726
48294CB00005B/1262